OUTSIDER

OUTSIDER

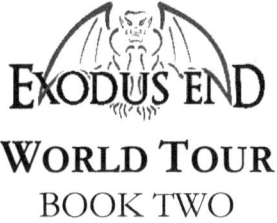

EXODUS END
WORLD TOUR
BOOK TWO

OLIVIA CUNNING

ISBN-10: 1-939276-24-1
ISBN-13: 978-1-939276-24-7

CHAPTER 1

ETHAN STOOD in the wings, his attention riveted to the man putting every ounce of his soul into the guitar strings beneath his fingertips. He'd never tire of watching Trey play live. He was, however, already tired of watching him lean up against Brian Sinclair's back as they played one of their dueling solos. Ethan knew the intimate solos were part of their act. He knew seeing the two guitarists touch familiarly made the women go wild. He also knew that Trey had once been in love with Brian. What Ethan didn't know was whether he'd ever completely take Brian's place in Trey's heart.

Ethan didn't take a breath until the solo ended and the two guitarists pushed off each other's backs to separate to opposite sides of the stage.

"Sometimes I wish I was Brian," Reagan said with a pronounced sigh.

Ethan knew that feeling all too well.

"I love playing for Max," she said. "For a rhythm guitarist, he does some intricate fret work. But there's something about Brian's sound that works itself under your skin, you know?"

Brian had definitely worked his way under Ethan's skin, but not in a good way. It wasn't that Ethan didn't like the guy; he actually understood why Trey had been hung up on him for so many years. But Brian had had Trey first—heart, body, and soul. And he still held part of Trey. He'd likely always have part of Trey. While Ethan had no problem sharing Trey with Reagan, sharing him with Brian Sinclair was another matter entirely.

"And to have that kind of connection with another guitarist?" Reagan continued. "It's magic."

"Maybe you and Trey should start your own band," Ethan said, crossing his arms over his chest and drumming his fingertips against one tense biceps.

Reagan laughed. "Like Trey would leave Sinners for me. Yeah, right."

"He might if you asked."

Reagan gnawed on her lip as she watched the man in question perform on stage. "I'd never ask it of him. He's exactly where he belongs."

"And what about where you belong?"

Reagan shrugged. "I'm doing okay with Exodus End for now."

But he knew she didn't feel like she truly belonged with the group. In her mind, no matter how much the band showed her she'd been accepted into their fold, she was an outsider. She'd likely always see herself that way, even if they decided to keep her indefinitely.

"What comes after Exodus End?" Ethan asked.

She shrugged. "I'm assuming something less spectacular than what I have already, so I'm not in any rush to move on."

Perhaps not, but he was sure she wanted a band to call her own.

"What's next for you, Ethan?" she asked, brushing briefly against his arm. She insisted that they couldn't publicly flaunt their relationship. Not when the public knew she was dating Trey. If they thought she was a cheater, she'd be raked across the coals, but if they ever found out that she was in a polyamorous relationship with two men, they'd destroy her. Ethan would never allow that happen. So as much as he longed to let the world know she was his, he gave her plenty of space when they were before prying eyes.

"Wherever you are, that's where I want to be," he said.

She glanced up and met his eyes, a dopey look of affection on her lovely face. He resisted the urge to kiss her. He'd save it for later.

After the encore, Trey jogged offstage and traded his guitar for a small towel to wipe the sweat off his face. Ethan longed to push him up against the nearest wall and take everything he currently wanted from him, but that would be far worse than someone catching him with Reagan. So Ethan offered Trey a curt nod and shoved his balled fists into the pockets of his slacks. While Reagan brought out a protective, caring side of Ethan, Trey unleashed his inner beast. The combination was heady. Exciting. Erotic. And in Ethan's mind, perfect. The only negative clouding his sunshine was the secrecy. Though if he was honest with himself, he wasn't sure how he'd deal with the inevitable questions from his family. They were a conservative bunch. He didn't doubt that they loved him and they adored Reagan—his mother already thought of her as a daughter. He had no idea how they'd react if they ever found out about Trey, so Ethan supposed keeping their secret was beneficial to him as well. It was just so damned hard to keep his hands to himself when he'd much rather be putting them on Trey and Reagan.

"I'd better get into position," Reagan said.

Trey grinned at her. "That's what she said."

She slapped at Trey playfully and kissed his cheek. Ethan's stomach clenched—not with jealousy, but with longing. She paused long enough to offer Ethan a heated glance, but there was no kiss for him. He doubted she'd ever publicly show how she felt about him. Not as long as Trey was in the picture. And as far as Ethan was concerned, Trey would always be in the picture.

Reagan joined her band on the floor beside the stage. After having her guitar hooked to the sound system, she disappeared beneath the stage in preparation of the band's grand entrance.

"Do you want to stay and watch Exodus End's performance tonight?" Trey asked. It was an innocent enough question, but Ethan didn't miss the undercurrent of *or do you want to take me back to Reagan's dressing room and fuck me?*

Typically an intermission fell between bands at concerts, but the current stage setup allowed Exodus End to go on immediately after Sinners. In fact, the unmistakable flurry of drumbeats produced by Exodus End's legendary drummer, Steve Aimes, was already filling the stadium. The crowd cheered. Reagan would rise out of the stage any moment.

Ethan leaned close to Trey's ear and said, "The entire time you were onstage, all I could think about was stroking your exquisite cock while I fucked you from behind."

Trey's sexy growl of appreciation grabbed Ethan by the balls and had him reconsidering his next words. But sneaking off with Trey to turn his fantasies into reality wouldn't be fair to Reagan. He knew she didn't like to be left out of their sexual encounters.

"But then I decided I'd rather stuff your cock into Reagan's hot pussy instead. So you'll have to wait."

"It's not nice to get my dick hard with your promises and then make me wait," Trey whispered harshly over the building music.

Ethan leaned away and lifted an eyebrow at him. "When did I

ever claim to be nice?"

Trey grinned, retrieved a red sucker from his pocket, unwrapped it, and stuck it into his luscious mouth. He did things to that cherry treat that Ethan very much wanted him to do to the head of his cock. Fuck, the man gave good head. And Ethan didn't have to assume so based on the wicked things Trey did to his sucker. Ethan knew from experience.

"I guess if I have to wait, you have to wait too," Trey said. He swirled his tongue around his sweet before sucking it into his mouth.

Ethan adjusted his fly, glad it was relatively dark in the wings, and turned his attention to Reagan, who was doing things to her guitar that he very much wanted *her* to be doing to his cock. Fuck. These two would be the death of him.

CHAPTER 2

AS FAR AS REAGAN WAS CONCERNED, there was only one experience better than being kissed awake by the man she loved, and that was being kissed awake by both of them. She didn't even have to open her eyes to know that Ethan's mouth was against hers, his good-morning greeting strong and demanding as he claimed the first kiss of the day. His powerful hand grasped her bare breast, thumb and forefinger tugging at her nipple until she moaned against his lips. Ethan always took what he wanted without apology, and she willingly gave him whatever he desired. Reagan also knew the mouth teasing her *other* lips—the ones between her splayed legs—belonged to Trey. His soft kisses were methodical, practiced, and oh so delightful. The rhythm between them reached far deeper than mere sexual compatibility—she felt Trey in her soul. And that wonderful tongue piercing of his? She felt *that* against her clit. Trey always gave every piece of himself without hesitation, and she eagerly took whatever he offered. At that precise moment, he was giving her one hell of an orgasm.

Ethan tore his mouth from Reagan's as she cried out, her body quaking in bliss.

"You never make her wait," Ethan said.

The repetitive flicking of the metal ball in Trey's tongue ceased as he traced her throbbing clit with rhythmic circles and latched on with a gentle suction. Reagan grabbed for something to steady herself, taking hold of Ethan's bulging biceps with one hand and a tangle of bedsheet with the other.

"Is he wearing his piercing?" Ethan asked with a crooked grin.

Reagan tried to shout *yes, God, yes!* but could only release a shaky moan.

"Cheater," Ethan said. "I guess I'm going to have get my cock pierced so she'll crave something other than your tongue."

She wanted far more than Trey's tongue at the moment. The emptiness inside her was driving her mad. "Oh please," she gasped, too delirious to demand what she wanted. "Please."

Trey released his suction and kissed his way up her belly. His breath tickled her sweat-dampened flesh. "You keep promising," he said to Ethan, "but I haven't seen or felt evidence of a cock piercing yet." He flicked the metal ball in his tongue against Reagan's nipple, and she shuddered, releasing her hold on Ethan's arm and the bedclothes so she could clutch at Trey's silky hair. His mouth moved higher: against her throat, her jaw, and finally her lips. "Good morning, beautiful," he murmured. "I called dibs on your first orgasm while you were asleep. I hope you don't mind."

Mind? How could she possibly mind? She opened her eyes to stare into Trey's sultry green-eyed gaze. The man always looked like he needed to be fucked. Who was she to deny him his needs? Gaze locked with hers, Trey smiled and shifted to rest his hips between her thighs. When he claimed her, her eyes drifted shut with bliss.

"Look at me, baby," he whispered. "I need to see you."

The man had changed so much in the few months they'd been together. She remembered when he'd fought to keep the sex between them impersonal, how he'd refused to meet her eyes when they'd come together. But now, so long as their position allowed it, he demanded that she stare into his eyes the entire time they were intertwined.

Reagan's hands moved from his hair to cup his face, the face so precious to her. One she wanted to see every morning, no matter where they happened to be. And her other love—Ethan—where had he disappeared to? Near her feet, the bed shifted beneath his weight. A pair of strong hands gripped her thighs and urged her legs to wrap around Trey's slim hips. Reagan lifted her head to try to figure out what Ethan was doing, but she could only make out the top of his head briefly before he disappeared between Trey's spread thighs.

Trey jerked unexpectedly, his slow, churning thrusts drawing to a halt. His eyelids fluttered, and his mouth dropped open.

"What is he doing?" Reagan whispered in Trey's ear. When he

didn't do anything but release a passionate groan, she bit his earlobe. Ethan's resounding smack on Trey's ass reminded him to thrust. Whatever Ethan was doing to Trey suddenly had him grinding into Reagan as if he couldn't get deep enough.

"Jesus, E," Trey panted. "You're going to make me cum if you don't stop that."

Never had Reagan wanted a ceiling mirror as much as she wanted one right then. She'd heard that Exodus End's head of security, Butch, could get her bandmates anything they wanted in their hotel rooms. She wondered if she was enough of a fixture in the band to ask for favors from the guy, because she definitely needed that mirror.

"Tell me what he's doing," Reagan urged. "I want some too."

"He can't do this for you," Trey said with a soft chuckle. "Unless your proverbial balls have materialized into reality."

Whatever Ethan was doing to Trey's nuts must have felt fan-fucking-tastic. Trey couldn't stop groaning, and the churning of his hips was grinding his pelvis into Reagan's clit so perfectly that she didn't care that he'd stopped thrusting again.

"Did you forget how to move properly?" Ethan asked.

Trey murmured something unintelligible against Reagan's throat. She smiled and held him close as Ethan positioned himself over Trey's back. Ethan's eyes met Reagan's, and they exchanged a look of understanding.

"You stopped," Trey complained. "Why did you stop?"

"It seems you need a bit of guidance."

Trey lifted his head from Reagan's shoulder, his eyelids fluttering as Ethan eased forward. Reagan was certain Ethan had claimed Trey's ass, but neither man was moving.

"Deeper," Trey demanded.

"If you want it deeper, take it," Ethan said.

Trey pulled out of Reagan several inches, groaning in bliss as the motion of his hips drove Ethan deeper into his ass. Ethan held still as Trey found a motion that allowed him to fuck and be fucked simultaneously. Every dozen strokes or so, Ethan would drive Trey deeper into Reagan with a powerful thrust before pulling completely out, making Trey whimper with excitement and angle his hips to ease Ethan's possession. Trey was not shy about taking all the pleasure he deserved, but he was being uncharacteristically selfish and not paying any mind to Reagan's enjoyment. Still, she was so turned on by his obvious delight that every stroke of his hips made her pussy clench with excitement. Wanting to increase his rapture, she tightened around his rigid cock each time he withdrew.

"Now," Ethan said, "imagine what this would feel like if my cock was pierced."

Trey shuddered violently and pulled out of Reagan, rising up on his knees between her thighs. Still thrusting into Trey's ass, Ethan reached around Trey's body and grabbed his cock in his fist, stroking until Trey found release with a strangled cry. Reagan couldn't keep her hand from between her legs as she rubbed herself to orgasm while watching Trey's cum spurt from between Ethan's fingers and splatter over her belly, her thighs, her mound. Dear God, where was it all coming from? Ethan's thrusting stilled when he buried his face against Trey's shoulder and found release of his own. A few moment later, Ethan eased out of Trey's body and carefully stretched him out beside Reagan.

"You okay?" Ethan asked, leaning over to kiss Trey's jaw. "Too rough? I got a little carried away."

"Perfect," Trey said, his voice hoarse. He rubbed his face against Reagan's arm. "Sorry. I kind of neglected you."

"Don't apologize for being the sexiest man alive," Reagan said with a soft snort.

"Hey," Ethan protested.

"The sexiest *guitarist* alive," she amended.

"You're the sexiest guitarist alive," Trey said.

"Let's just say we're all sexy and leave it at that."

Ethan chuckled and collapsed onto the bed beside Reagan. He tugged her close, one hand cupping her breast. "Next time I get first dibs on the pussy."

"We have all day," Trey murmured drowsily. "I do love these days off between tour stops."

"I have a date with Toni this morning," Reagan said, kicking herself for insisting she would take the woman shopping for some decent clothes in New Orleans. It had sounded like a good idea when she made the offer.

"I guess you'll have to settle for ass then, E," Trey said, his hand searching blindly for a piece of Ethan. He ended up gripping his waist.

"You call that settling?" Ethan chuckled. "That's a mighty good piece of ass you've got there, Mr. Mills."

"You two aren't going to spend all day screwing in my bed, are you?" Reagan asked. Perhaps if she made them feel guilty, they'd save it up for her later that night.

"Just because you have other plans doesn't mean we do," Trey said. He kissed her shoulder and tugged her across the bed and away from Ethan. When he'd made sufficient room, he took her forcibly vacated spot and curled into Ethan's hard-muscled body.

She crossed her arms over her chest. "Ethan gets all the cuddles too?"

"Yep," Trey said, snuggling closer.

"Go have fun with Toni," Ethan said. "I promise I'll keep him out of trouble."

Reagan snorted on a laugh. "Yeah, right. You two should make yourselves useful and install a mirror on the ceiling while I'm gone. I would very much like to watch you lick Trey's balls while he fucks me."

"Such a pervert," Trey murmured. "And for the record, he was doing more sucking than licking."

Reagan forced herself into the shower. She probably needed to invest in a couple of cock cages and carry the keys with her at all times so she could keep those two from going at it without her. She wasn't jealous of their relationship, not exactly. Well, maybe she was a little jealous. She liked that her two lovers got along so well and that their affection for each other grew by the hour. She was just starting to worry that they'd decide they weren't really bisexual, that they were actually gay, and then they'd thank her for introducing them and bid her a fond farewell.

"Don't be ridiculous," she said to herself as she washed the traces of Trey's cum from her belly. She felt confident that both men loved her as much as she loved both of them. It was actually best if the two men had a solid relationship with each other, wasn't it? Yeah, she was sure it was for the best.

Once clean and dressed, she returned to find both men fast asleep—Ethan sprawled on his back, Trey curled up against his side, using Ethan's arm as a pillow. What was she worried about? She was the luckiest woman in the world. She had the job of her dreams, an amazing sex life, the love and devotion of two perfect men, and she was even making new friends while on tour. Still, she couldn't help but worry that her luck would eventually run out. But until that time, she was going to live it up.

Reagan leaned over the bed and kissed Ethan's lips. He opened sleepy brown eyes and squinted at her.

"If you need anything," she said, "call or text. I'll have my phone with me." She followed Ethan's gaze to the industrial-size tub of lube on the nightstand.

"Trey will probably run me out of lube by tonight. Better pick up another gallon or two."

Trey slapped him half-heartedly on the arm. "You're the one that goes through so much of the stuff."

"You should be thanking me."

"My ass thanks you," Trey said. "My dick doesn't get to use it often enough, however."

"I let you fuck me," Ethan protested.

Trey rolled his eyes, looking irresistible enough to lick. "Rarely."

"Are you complaining about being in the middle? You weren't complaining an hour ago."

Trey worried his tongue piercing with his teeth for a long moment.

"Reagan?" he said finally, squirming his ass against Ethan's hip. "Would you mind picking up another gallon or two of lube? I think E's going to need it."

Reagan chuckled and stretched across Ethan to kiss Trey's temple. "I'm sure I'm the only woman in the world who has to listen to arguments about her boyfriends' use of lube."

"Aren't you lucky?" Ethan asked, doing something to Trey under the covers that made him gasp with excitement.

"Hey, don't wear him out," Reagan said. "I get to be in the middle tonight."

When she begrudgingly left the suite, Trey and Ethan were laughing over some joke that Sinners' drummer, Eric Sticks, had told Trey the night before. Why had she suggested a girls' day on the town—why, *why*? Frowning slightly, she took the hotel's elevator down to the ground floor.

She spotted Toni waiting in the lobby. Oh yeah, that was why Reagan had suggested a shopping excursion.

Toni's long brown hair was fashioned into a braid. Her thick-rimmed glasses would have been hipster if she had a defined style. Her entire wardrobe seemed to have been purchased in a 1990's thrift store. Today she wore an ankle-length beige pencil skirt, never-seen-her-without-them brown riding boots, and a white button-down blouse with a ruffle down the center. She was one hundred percent too cute to dress the way she did. Reagan wasn't sure why Logan was so fixated on the woman. Reagan supposed it was because he'd seen Toni naked. Toni had the kind of figure most women would have to purchase.

When Toni spotted Reagan, she waved excitedly. "Logan wants to know if he can come with us," Toni said.

"Nope. He's going to have to let you out of his sight for a few hours. He'll probably die or something."

Toni giggled and slapped at her. "Oh, please. He'll probably forget I exist by the time we return."

Not a chance.

"You can't come," Toni called to Logan, who was sitting on a lobby sofa hiding his face behind an upside-down copy of a *Good Housekeeping* magazine.

"Or follow us," Reagan added.

"But what if someone tries to touch her?" Logan protested, slapping his magazine down on the end table beside him.

"I'm sure she can take care of herself for one afternoon," Reagan said.

"In New Orleans? This place changes people."

"I'll be fine," Toni said. "Reagan knows karate."

"She does?" Logan looked at Reagan hopefully.

She didn't, but that didn't stop her from lying. "Oh yeah. I'm a black belt and three-time world champion. If any man so much as glances Toni's way, I'll pulverize him into dust. Hi-yah!" She made a chopping motion with one hand. Was he buying it? Would he ever let the poor woman out of his sight?

"Don't you trust me?" Toni asked, looking up at Logan in a way that visibly turned him into a pile of mush. Reagan ducked her head so he wouldn't see her laughing at his expense. Man, the guy had it bad.

"I do trust you," he said, touching Toni's cheek. "It's all the douchebags walking around this city that I don't trust."

"I don't think you have much to worry about with her dressed like that," Reagan said.

Toni ran her hands over her blouse. The woman was in her midtwenties and wearing a bona fide *blouse*. Didn't she have friends or a decent female relative to help her see the mistake that was her wardrobe?

"Is it really that bad?" Toni asked.

"With the exception of Logan, who seems to have built up an immunity to its harmful side effects, this get-up you're wearing here?" Reagan traced the outlines of Toni's clothes in the air. "I'm afraid it's cock-withering attire, little one."

"That's a good thing," Logan insisted with his trademark sunny smile.

"Where's the rest of the crew?" Reagan searched the lobby for signs of the wives and girlfriends of Sinners' band members. In recent weeks, the ladies had become some of her closest friends, and she was sure she'd need their help to get Toni to discard her schoolmarm wardrobe. Especially since Logan seemed so keen on her keeping it.

When the elevator doors opened, Reagan heard several familiar voices.

Myrna Sinclair was the first off the elevator. She always wore professional suits with tight, midthigh-length skirts—today's was a dove gray. It was what she wore under them that brought her husband to his knees. And those three-inch heels she wore probably didn't hurt. Nor had her Ph.D. in sex. What man wouldn't fall for a woman like her?

Sed Lionheart's fiancée, Jessica, emerged from the elevator behind Myrna, looking like she'd just stepped out of the pages of *Cosmo*. Strawberry blond and blue eyed, she had heads turning as she passed. Those same heads swiveled back to the elevator when Aggie stepped forward.

The buxom woman rocked a pair of black leather pants and matching jacket—she'd probably been out riding with Jace on his motorcycle—but though she was gorgeous with her flawless alabaster skin, bright blue eyes, and long, straight black hair that moved like a length of silk when she walked, it was her self-confidence that couldn't be ignored. She owned the space around her and knew it. She offered no apologies. What Reagan wouldn't give to possess that much poise.

Bringing up the rear was Rebekah—adorable and petite, with an infectious smile and lime-green streaks in her platinum hair. Beautiful, colorful designs decorated Rebekah's exposed arms from wrist to shoulder. Reagan swore the woman had a new tattoo every time she saw her.

"Ah, here they come. Are you ready to go, Toni?"

Logan squeezed Toni's hand and leaned in close to whisper into her ear. She smiled broadly, her cheeks going pink. "I love you too," she whispered.

Too?

Reagan grinned at the opportunity to torment her band's

bassist. "What's that, Logan?" Reagan said loudly. "Did you just tell Toni that you *love* her?"

Toni stiffened, her eyes wide as she looked up at him. Perhaps she was expecting him to deny it.

"Yeah, I love her. What's it to ya?"

Toni beamed at his declaration while the other women teased him about his newly expressed feelings.

"Don't mess her up," Logan called after them as the six chattering women made their way to the exit. "I like her just the way she is."

"We won't mess her up," Aggie said, her ruby-red lips curling into a twisted smile. "Much."

Reagan sniggered at the horrified look on Logan's face. They all knew Aggie had a dark streak; she'd used it frequently in her former trade as a professional dominatrix. If anyone was going to twist Toni into an unrecognizable form, it would be Aggie Martin.

"You and Aggie have a lot in common," Myrna said as she wrapped an arm around Toni's back and ushered her out onto the sidewalk. "You both have an inexplicable attraction to bass players."

"Oh, you're Jace Seymour's girlfriend?" Toni asked, scrambling to catch up with Aggie. "Is it true that you used to be a prostitute?"

Aggie stopped walking—well, prowling, the woman never actually walked—and turned an icy blue-eyed glare on Toni. "*Excuse me?*"

Toni cringed. "I'm sorry. I read that somewhere. Was my source incorrect?"

Perhaps inviting the journalist along for a girls' day out had been a mistake. Toni did tend to stick her nose where it didn't belong.

"I was never a prostitute," Aggie said, her voice so cool, Reagan expected it to frost the sultry New Orleans air.

"She just charges men to be her slaves," Myrna said. "Isn't that right, Aggie?"

Toni tilted her head to one side and then shook it after she'd had a moment to internalize Myrna's claim. "The very definition of slavery is when one human is bought and owned by another, so why would anyone *pay* to be a slave?"

Reagan snorted. "So, so sheltered," she said. "Let me explain it to you."

She didn't have to explain much. As the group of women walked down the street together, men literally tripped over their own feet when they spotted Aggie. Sure, there were those who were more likely to gawk at Jessica's model-perfect beauty, but Aggie exuded sexuality that not many men could ignore. One guy walked directly into a light post as he watched her pass. Though no men noticed Reagan when she was with this group of ladies, she was content in the knowledge that she had two perfect men waiting for her back in her hotel room.

She pictured them as she had left them, naked, luscious, and entwined. Damn, she really shouldn't have planned an outing on a rare day off.

"So men pay you to hit them?" Toni asked Aggie.

"Some do. Or *did*, rather," Aggie said. "I'm finding new hobbies now that I'm with Jace. Let's go in here."

Aggie strutted into a sex shop, and the rest of the women followed. Toni's feet seemed to have rooted themselves to the sidewalk, so Reagan had to pull her inside. She left her near the entrance, gawking at a leather hood and collar displayed on a mannequin. Reagan could practically see the questions churning through Toni's thoughts. She was glad when Myrna took it upon herself to provide explanations. Nothing embarrassed the woman, not with that doctorate in human sexuality and her experiences teaching at a university. Reagan was sure that Toni could use a course or two in the subject. Though she was from Arkansas, Reagan had never in her life met a woman as sheltered as Toni. She had to wonder if Toni knew how to use the Internet, because, well, *porn*.

Reagan ventured farther into the store. She had a pair of cock cages to buy, and she mustn't forget the gallon of lube her lovers had requested.

"Are you trying to keep those men of yours in line?" Aggie asked as she sidled up next to Reagan at a display counter. A clerk was demonstrating how to fit a cock cage around a flaccid penis and balls.

"Trying to keep them from fucking each other when I'm not around," Reagan said.

Aggie smirked. "Why would you want to do that?"

She shrugged. "I don't know. I guess I'm afraid they'll find enough satisfaction in each other and leave me hanging."

"Are you really concerned about that?"

She stared down at the counter, her heart thudding. Well, she was buying cock cages, wasn't she?

Aggie brushed the hair out of Reagan's eye and urged her to

look up. "Kitten, you have nothing to worry about. When you aren't around, do you know what they talk about?"

"Lube?" she guessed.

Aggie laughed. "Maybe a little. They talk about you, hon. They're both completely in love with you."

"And with each other."

"That too." Aggie nodded. "Didn't you want them to fall in love with each other?"

Reagan cringed. "Yeah. I was glad when they decided they have feelings for each other. It's my issue, really. I still don't feel like I'm enough for either of them."

"I thought that was the whole point of this arrangement," Aggie said.

"It is." But Reagan didn't like the way that arrangement made her feel. When all three of them were together, she felt content. Loved. But when she was alone with either of them or the two men were alone together, she felt somehow betrayed or that she was betraying one or both of them. It didn't make a lick of sense to her. "I'll get it sorted out," she said. But in the meantime she was going to try out a pair of cock cages.

"I don't mean to interrupt," Toni said from behind them. Aggie turned to glare at the poor woman who was only a year or two younger than they were but seemed much less mature.

Toni licked her lush lips and pushed her glasses up her nose with the back of her wrist. "Um, Aggie, I'm really sorry I asked you if you were a prostitute. I feel terrible about it."

"And how do you think your assumption made me feel?"

Toni sucked her trembling lower lip into her mouth. Oh no, she was going to start crying again.

Reagan wrapped an arm around Toni's shoulder. "Never cry in a sex shop," she advised. "It draws creeps."

Reagan glanced around the store and discovered a waifish ghost of a man, dressed in all black, watching them closely. Reagan had no idea if he was interested in Toni—not likely when the lush sexpot that was Agatha Martin was standing with them—but she nodded toward the guy, and Toni's eyes went dry and her lip stopped trembling.

"I am sorry," Toni said to Aggie. "How can I make you forgive me?"

"Let's see . . ." Aggie said, tapping her lush lower lip with one red-tipped finger. "Usually when one of my slaves displeases me, I make him lick his cum off the floor."

Reagan couldn't help but laugh at Toni's wide-eyed, slack-faced expression.

"Actually, that's not entirely true." Aggie shook her head, sending long, silky black hair dancing about her shoulders. "I make them lick it up when I'm pleased with them as well."

Toni resembled a gasping goldfish as she struggled to wrap her head around Aggie's claim.

"Where did you find this one?" Aggie asked Reagan.

"She's writing a book about Exodus End."

"Yeah, I know that, but has she been living under a rock?"

Toni nodded. "Pretty much."

"There you are," Myrna said as she walked up behind them. She nodded toward Toni. "She wandered off when I was telling her the best way to make a man beg for his butt plug."

Toni flushed. "Um, I appreciate the gesture, but Logan teaches me all he wants me to know about that kind of thing."

"So he's training you to be his perfect lover?" Aggie asked.

Toni nodded.

"And you're okay with that?"

Toni smiled. "I'm grateful to him. I love him so much, I'd do anything for him."

Aggie glanced at Myrna. "Doormat much?"

"Uh," Myrna said. "It depends." She turned to Toni. "Do you have any hard limits?"

When Toni merely stared at her, Myrna asked, "Is there anything you won't let him do to you or refuse to do for him?"

Toni's face lit up. "Oh, of course." She shook her head. "No anal."

"You won't give anal or receive it?" Myrna asked.

"Give?" Toni's face blanched as she apparently caught on to what Myrna was suggesting. "Neither!"

"You are missing out," Reagan said. She was lucky in that Trey always made it feel good. She rarely let Ethan take her ass. He was too rough for her tender back door, but dear lord, the man could pound a pussy just right, and Trey craved rough fucking, so the sex always seemed to work out right between the three of them. It was the emotional entanglements that she was starting to worry about.

"Isn't it gross?" Toni asked. "I mean won't you get poop on his wiener?" she whispered out of the corner of her mouth.

Aggie chuckled. "Did you really just call it a wiener?"

"It's less dirty than you'd imagine," Myrna said in her professorial voice, "but if that bothers you or him, you can prepare for penetration in advance. Clean yourself out, so to speak." Myrna wrapped an arm around Toni's shoulders and led her toward a section of enemas, lubes, and anal-sex toys.

Reagan wondered if Myrna missed teaching. She seemed to like instructing Toni in her no-nonsense way, and it was obvious that clueless Toni needed all the instruction she could tolerate. Toni stared at Myrna—partially horrified, partially fascinated—as Myrna explained the ins and outs of enema use, complete with hand demonstrations.

"It's hard to believe someone so innocent still exists in this day and age. Is she super religious or something?" Aggie asked.

Reagan shrugged. "I don't think so. She has a little sister with Down Syndrome, who she's been raising since she was a teenager. I don't think she's had time to explore her sexuality."

"Holy shit!" bellowed the sheltered woman in question as she gaped at a life-size replica of a human fist made of black silicon attached to a wooden handle. "That cannot fit up in there. Cannot. Nope. I don't believe it."

"She's totally adorable," Aggie decided, sharing a throaty chuckle.

"And harmless."

They discovered Jessica and Rebekah in one corner of the store discussing the benefits of Kegel exercises for men.

"So Sed can stop his orgasm completely?" Rebekah looked awestruck.

"He comes, but doesn't let himself ejaculate," Jessica said. "So he can keep going for a really long time."

"Shut the fuck up, Jess. No way!"

"I'm serious."

Rebekah noticed that the rest of the women had joined them. "Can any of your men do that? Come without ejaculating?"

"Only when wearing a cock ring," Aggie said.

"I've tried those with Eric," Rebekah said. "He just spurts right through them. I swear the guy is a cum factory."

"Brian's good at holding back," Myrna said. "Well, he's powerless against the finger"—she wiggled her index finger at them—"but on his own he lasts longer than any man I've ever been with."

"What do you do with your finger?" Toni asked.

"Prostate massage. If you want me to show you how to do it—"

"I've done it with Logan," she interrupted, "but I used one of those things." She pointed at a prostate vibrator sitting on a nearby shelf.

Reagan laughed at how casual Toni was about it. "I guess we have nothing to worry about. Logan seems to be doing a pretty good job teaching you what you need to know."

"He's the absolute best," Toni gushed. "And he never makes me feel stupid for not knowing things about sex."

"Well, if you ever need advice, you can ask any of us," Reagan said. "We all have lots of experience."

Rebekah crinkled her brows at her. "Thanks, Reagan. You make us sound like sluts."

"Well, then, I'll speak only for myself," Reagan said. "*I* have lots of experience." And she didn't care who knew it.

"I've been meaning to ask another woman one thing," Toni said. "Should you swallow?"

The entire group burst into laughter. Even Toni joined in after an awkward pause.

"Only if you love him," Myrna said, patting her on the back. "Are we ready to get this young lady some decent clothes?"

Reagan eyed the cock cages she'd been planning to purchase and set them on a random shelf. If Trey and Ethan wanted to fuck each other when she wasn't around, that should be their right. She did buy a huge tub of lube, though, and asked if the clerk could deliver it to the hotel. She'd likely throw out her back if she tried lugging it around all day while they shopped. She also bought cherry-flavored lube just for Trey. She knew how much he liked the stuff.

"Do you really use that much lube?" Toni asked as they exited the store.

Reagan forced her lungs to draw air as she instantly wilted in the southern Louisiana humidity.

"Ethan and Trey use a lot," she said, fanning her face with one hand. The slight breeze her fingers produced didn't help in the least. She'd become accustomed to LA's scorching summers, but this heavy, sticky air was plain miserable.

"On you or each other?"

"Both," she said. Now that they were out of the sex shop, she didn't much feel like divulging the intimate details of her sexual relationships.

Jessica trotted ahead to a fashion boutique and peered into the glass storefront. "I think we have a winner!"

While Jessica and Myrna thought Toni was best suited for professional attire, Reagan and Rebekah insisted she'd be better off wearing T-shirts and jeans. She'd fit in with the road crew in casual clothes and wouldn't stand out as odd while she was touring with the band. But they soon discovered a problem with trying to fit Toni into a T-shirt: she was so chesty that the cotton threatened to split over her breasts and the hems of the tops didn't come close to reaching the waistband of her jeans. So the jeans worked fine, but the T-shirts were a no-go.

"I think she'd look cute in a sweater set," Jessica said. Well, of course she thought that. The woman owned sweater sets in every color imaginable. But sweater sets on Toni created a different problem: Toni's boobs stretched the neck down until she had so much cleavage, everyone in the store was ogling her breasts.

"I hate clothes shopping," Toni moaned, trying to yank the sweater up over her exposed cleavage.

The button-down shirt Myrna had her try on gaped several inches between Toni's breasts. She couldn't get the third fastener closed at all.

"A bigger size perhaps," the clerk suggested. She probably feared someone would lose an eye if a button happened to pop.

All her life Reagan had envied women with large breasts, but now that she saw the struggle Toni had in finding clothes that fit, she was grateful for her small chest.

"You have the perfect figure for a corset," Aggie said, eyeing Toni's body appreciatively.

Toni's eyes bulged. "A corset?" The word came out as a squeak.

"I'll make you one," Aggie offered. She instructed the clerk to take Toni's measurements and write them down for her.

"Why are you being so nice to me when I said that awful thing to you earlier?" Toni asked.

Aggie shrugged. "I've been mistaken for worse, and I can tell you didn't mean to hurt my feelings." Aggie stroked a loose lock of mousy brown hair behind Toni's ear. "Don't let it bother you, honey."

"I really am sorry."

"I know. I forgive you."

Wow. Reagan wasn't sure how Toni had so quickly gotten on Aggie's good side, but she had to admit it was really hard to stay mad at someone as genuinely nice as Toni always was.

"Where did you get your current wardrobe?" Myrna asked. "This store obviously isn't working for us. Do they have special stores for women with your, uh . . ." Her gaze flicked to Toni's chest. ". . . attributes?"

"I've had all my clothes for a really long time. Over ten years. I've been really chesty since I was in junior high and haven't changed shape much since. We bought shirts several sizes too big and took in the waist, shoulders and arms so they'd fit me right. Well, I didn't. I'm terrible at sewing."

"We?" Myrna asked.

"Me and my dad." Toni flushed and glanced down at her boobs spilling over the cups of her black bra. "He did all the sewing."

"Your father sewed clothes for you?" Jessica said, her eyes brimming with tears. Reagan searched her pocket for a tissue, but came up empty-handed. Rebekah came to the rescue with one from her purse.

"You're not actually going to cry over that, are you?" Reagan asked.

"It's just so sweet," Jessica said, dabbing at her eyes with the tissue. "None of my stepfathers would have done anything like that for me."

Toni's cheeks had gone pink. "I think maybe he was trying to keep the boys away by selecting clothes that were um . . . outdated. *Ugly.*"

"Conservative," Myrna said, holding up Toni's discarded blouse by the shoulders.

"Conservative," Toni agreed.

Reagan winked and said, "It's a good thing Logan got you out of those clothes so quickly. Once he saw what was underneath, he was a complete goner."

Toni laughed. "I wasn't about to turn down the opportunity to finally lose my virginity."

The revelation wasn't news to Reagan—Toni had told her that Logan had claimed her virginity within an hour of meeting her—but the other women in their group were outraged.

From Aggie's "I'll tie his dick in a knot" to Myrna's "It's the rockstar thing, isn't it?" to Rebekah's "Did he take advantage of you?" and Jessica's "Men can be such pigs," Toni defended Logan.

"He didn't take advantage of me," Toni said. "I wanted it to happen, and he felt so bad about it afterward because he wasn't aware that I was that inexperienced. He's really good to me."

The women went off again, talking over one another. Reagan stepped back to watch.

Aggie said, "He'd better be good to you, or he'll answer to me."

Myrna tapped her lip, her gaze shifting toward the ceiling, and asked, "So you would have succumbed that easily to any man you found attractive? Or *was* it the rockstar thing?"

"He seems like such a nice guy once you get to know him," Rebekah said.

Jessica delivered her criticism with waving arms. "Can't you see that he *did* take advantage of you? He's a pig, I tell you."

Toni's lips drew into a harsher and harsher line as she struggled to find her voice.

"Does it matter how they got together?" Reagan asked, giving Toni a playful shove. "The man is obsessively in love with her now."

Toni's face relaxed, and she beamed with happiness. If the others had further criticisms or concerns, they kept their comments and prying questions to themselves. Toni was obviously as happy with Logan as he was with her. So what if they'd gone through the normal get-to-know-each-other, forge-a-relationship, and have-copious-amounts-of-lust-fueled-sex progression entirely backwards?

Toni purchased a couple of pairs of jeans and a pair of the gaudiest tube socks Reagan had ever seen, but she didn't buy any tops, because not a single one fit her. The group stopped at several other stores with the same results. No wonder the poor woman had such an unflattering wardrobe. Everything she tried on either clung, gaped, hung completely wrong, or made her look like she was trying to get a job at Hooters.

"It's hopeless," she said after taking off the third sweater she'd stretched out of proportion at an exclusive boutique.

"I'm not quite as chesty as you are," Aggie said, laying a comforting hand on the small of Toni's back, "but I get it. Clothes never fit me quite right either. Let's try a plus-size store. I'm pretty good with a needle. If we need to make alterations, I'll help you out."

"You will?" Toni blinked back tears and instantly found herself enveloped in a hug from the badass dominatrix who made grown men tremble.

"Aggie's such a softie," Jessica said, as she dabbed at her eyes with her soggy tissue. "She was the same with me when I started stripping at Paradise Found."

"I heard that, kitten," Aggie said sternly.

"She's soft with Jace too," Rebekah said, with a crooked grin. "When she isn't lashing him with a whip."

Toni went white and tugged away from Aggie to meet her eyes. "You don't really hit him, do you?"

Aggie pushed open the door of another shop. "Only if he begs nicely," she said over her shoulder.

Toni had better luck covering her boobs at the plus-size store, but everything hung loosely on her arms and billowed around her waist like shapeless tents.

"We'll fix it," Aggie promised, standing behind Toni and tugging the back of a blue flowing top tight against Toni's slender waist.

"Maybe a belt will help for now," Myrna said, cocking her head.

"Please, no," Aggie said. "We're not trying to make her look like a time traveler from 1985."

"Ah, the good ol' days," Myrna said with a sigh.

While Aggie and Toni decided which tops would be best for altering, Reagan parked her butt on a bench and dug out her phone. She sent a group text to Trey and Ethan. It was more likely that Trey would answer—of the two he was much more dependent on his phone—but she didn't want Ethan to feel like an afterthought.

I think we finally found a solution to Toni's wardrobe situation. What are you guys up to?

When neither man responded right away, she checked her email. A bunch of forwarded fan mail made her smile. Exodus End's manager had ordered his assistant to go through all the email on Reagan's professional account and forward only complimentary messages to her personal account. It probably gave her a skewed perception about how many of Exodus End's fans liked what she was doing. She couldn't help but wonder how much hate mail she received but never got to read.

Her phone dinged as a text came in from Trey. It simply said *3.*

3 what? she texted back.

3 orgasms each since you left. Thanks for the lube. The cherry was yummy.

She snorted and sent another text. *Save some for me.*

Too late. We used it all.

All? Surely he was joking. She should have stayed in bed that morning. Or sent Toni out with Aggie. The pair were doing fine without her assistance. But Toni barely knew the other women, so it wouldn't have been right to dump her. Ah well, no matter what Trey claimed, Reagan knew both men would be willing to please her when she saw them later.

I'll stop by the store and get some more. This time don't use it all before I get home.

I'm just messing with you. We haven't had sex since you left. We're hanging out with the guys in Sed's room. Why does the lead singer always get the best room?

When she returned to the hotel, Reagan would have to check to see if Max got superior accommodations. She had no idea if his room was better than hers.

She grinned as she thumbed in her next message. *They need extra space for their enormous egos.*

LOL! Good call. You'd better get back to pretending you're a real girl now.

She laughed softly. He knew her too well. Shopping so wasn't her thing. She'd much rather be hanging with the guys.

You know I'm a real girl, she texted. *You've seen the proof.*

Tasted it too.

Reagan glanced up when several sets of feet stopped in front of her. Her party had collected themselves back into a group and was ready to leave.

Love you both. <3 Back to girling.

She shoved her phone into her pocket and followed the others out of the store.

She wasn't terrible at girling. She chatted while they all got their nails done. And had a diet Coke instead of a beer with her lunch. She drew the line at salad, however. She refused to join that trend. When it was her turn, she ordered steak.

"I changed my mind," Rebekah said. "I'll have steak too."

"Oh God, that sounds delicious," Myrna said, her eyes rolling back as if she hadn't eaten anything but plain celery sticks for a month. "Change my salad to a ribeye. With a loaded baked potato. And throw a veggie on there so I don't feel so guilty."

"I thought you were trying to keep Brian from noticing all the hot young women throwing themselves at him," Jessica said.

Myrna snapped her menu closed. "A little splurge won't hurt."

"I really want mac and cheese," Jessica said. "Smothered in mayo."

Reagan screwed up her face in disgust and tried not to hurl. "You're not really going to make us watch you eat that, are you?"

"When you get pregnant, you'll see what it's like to have these bizarre cravings," Jessica said.

"Guess I'll never know what it's like, because there will be no kids in my future," Reagan said.

"Mine either," Rebekah said glumly.

"I thought you were going to adopt," Myrna said, reaching over to squeeze Rebekah's hand.

"Eventually," she said, "but I don't think I'll crave mayonnaise on everything while Eric and I are signing the paperwork."

Jessica sighed. "I don't want to make my friends uncomfortable," she said to their server.

"Too late!" Reagan said.

"So just give me a turkey club with extra extra mayo, a side of macaroni and cheese, and an order of fries with—"

"Mayo!" Reagan finished with her.

Jessica slapped Reagan with her folded menu and shifted her gaze to the server, who had to be more confused by the minute. Reagan saw a large tip in the overworked waitress's future.

"Mayo and ketchup," Jessica whispered to the server, who smiled in understanding.

"I'll add a steak to my order as well," Aggie said. "Rare. Salad on the side."

"Are you changing your order too, miss?" the server asked Toni.

Toni glanced from one of them to the next. When they'd all ordered the salad, she'd had no problem following everyone else's lead, but now that everyone had gone with heartier fare, she didn't seem to know how to respond. Reagan got the feeling that she'd never been out with a group of female friends before and so was trying desperately to fit in. Reagan wasn't cruel enough to comment, but she made a mental note to get the woman out with the girls more often. Even on the bus, Toni was reclusive. She spent a lot of time with Logan, but not much time with anyone else. But maybe that was because she and Logan were having so much sex. Reagan thanked God that unlike the Sinners back bedroom, the lounge at the back of the Exodus End bus was soundproof. If she tried, she could convince herself that Toni and Logan were doing aerobics back there and that was what was making them both appear so hot and sweaty whenever they ventured out into the main cabin of the bus.

Toni pushed her glasses up her nose with the back of her wrist. "Uh, I'll have soup with my salad, if that's okay."

"What kind?" the server asked.

After listening to the list of available soups, Toni settled on chicken noodle.

"When's the baby due?" Toni asked Jessica once the server collected their menus and left the table.

"Not until February." Jessica's face went pink. "And I'm already showing." She ran a hand over her perfectly flat belly.

"You are not," Reagan said, shaking her head.

"My pants are getting tight."

"That's all the mayo you've been eating," Reagan said.

Jessica stuck her tongue out.

"And the Rocky Road ice cream," Myrna added.

Jessica turned to direct her stuck-out tongue in Myrna's direction before focusing her attention on Toni, seated on her left. "Are you coming to the wedding with Logan?"

Toni's eyes widened behind her thick-rimmed glasses. "Wedding?"

"Sed and I are getting married in a couple of weeks. Didn't Logan mention it?" When Toni shook her head, Jessica rolled her eyes. "He probably forgot. You're invited to accompany him if you want to come."

Toni smiled brightly and touched Jessica's arm with trembling fingertips. "Thanks."

"So are you and Logan getting serious?" Myrna asked, cutting a slice of hot bread from the basket the server just dropped off and spreading butter over it.

"We went tandem skydiving yesterday," Toni said, her face flushed with pleasure.

"Is that what kids do these days when they're serious about each other?" Myrna asked.

Kids? Logan was only a few years younger than Myrna. Of course, he acted like he was still in his teens most of the time.

"As we plummeted toward the ground, he told me he loved me for the first time," Toni said, her lips curved into a smile as she stared at the table in front of her. "It was a magical moment."

"Aww, how romantic," Jessica said as her eyes overflowed with tears. "Sorry." She sniffled and, abandoning her disintegrating tissue, she dabbed at her eyes with a cloth napkin. "I don't know why I'm crying again. Sheesh!"

Reagan didn't know either. Jessica wasn't the type of woman who cried easily, but she'd been on the verge of tears most of the morning.

"It's just the hormones," Myrna said, passing the loaf of bread to Rebekah.

Aggie rubbed Jessica's back soothingly. "Don't cry, kitten."

"Sorry," Jessica said. "It's just . . . I miss Sed."

"You left him just a couple of hours ago," Reagan said, though she understood. She'd started missing Trey and Ethan as soon as they were out of sight.

"Go call him," Aggie said. "It'll do you good to hear his voice."

Jessica nodded. "Planning this wedding has been making me crazy." She slid her chair back and grabbed her purse. "That's why I'm so emotional."

"Hormones," Myrna interjected as Jessica headed to a quiet location to call her fiancé. "And it's going to get worse before it gets better."

"Poor Sed," Rebekah said with a laugh, passing the loaf of bread—minus another slice—to Reagan.

"Things will settle down a bit after their wedding," Aggie said.

"For a week maybe," Myrna said. "Then we're heading to Europe. That's sure to be chaos."

"Good chaos," Reagan said. She'd never been to Europe. She couldn't wait to see the world and share the experience with Trey and Ethan.

"I envy you all," Toni said.

"You're not going to Europe with us?" Reagan asked.

Toni shook her head. "I should have enough material for the book in a few days. I just need to capture more footage from the crew's point of view in Albuquerque and get a few more candid shots of the band on stage."

This interactive book Toni was working on—the entire reason she was following the band around on the American leg of their world tour—was going to be so cool when it was finished. Reagan couldn't wait to see how Toni worked all her plans for the book together into a cohesive whole.

"Does Logan know you aren't joining us in Europe?"

Toni shrugged. "I assumed it was obvious to him."

"Never assume anything is obvious to a man," Myrna said. "The key to a lasting relationship is communication. So, basically, you tell him what to do."

Having just communicated with her own man, Jessica returned to the table all smiles and tranquility. "All the guys are hanging out in his room watching golf."

"Golf?" Reagan asked.

Jessica shrugged. "I guess they're bored. Though babysitting Malcolm seems to be keeping them all on their toes." She smiled at Myrna, who was probably missing her baby boy even more than the rest of them were missing their men. Malcolm was a cutie.

"Maybe we should head back to the hotel after lunch," Rebekah said, tracing the edge of the table with one finger.

"Aww, does someone miss her darling Eric?" Reagan teased.

"If he doesn't get his afternoon blow job, he's cranky until bedtime."

Toni, glass at her lips, sprayed Coke all over the table. She dove for her napkin and began wiping up the mess.

"I'm not joking," Rebekah said, her eyes wide with sincerity.

"We know you're not," Reagan said. "We've lived with the guy, but Toni's never been on Sinners' bus. She doesn't know what the guys are like behind closed doors."

"I'd like to, though," Toni said.

"Sorry, honey, but Eric's already taken," Rebekah said, visibly bristling.

Toni's face turned the color of the red napkin she was using to dab up stray drops of Diet Coke. "Uh, I didn't mean . . . I would never . . . I just—"

Reagan patted Toni's hand, hoping to calm her. To Rebekah, she said, "I think she meant she would like to write an interactive biography about them. Like the one she's doing for Exodus End."

Toni nodded. "That's what I meant."

Rebekah relaxed into her chair. "Well," she said, "that might be sort of fun."

The food arrived moments later, and they were all too busy stuffing their faces to talk much. Even though she was ready to return to her men, Reagan was glad she'd suggested this girls' day out in New Orleans. She missed all her friends back in Los Angeles, and even though she'd always been a tomboy, she still enjoyed hanging around with other women. She liked every one of Sinners' ladies and was already quite fond of Toni as well. She hadn't expected to like Toni—mostly because she considered Toni a journalist and didn't like people to stick their noses into her business—but Reagan already considered her a friend. And she knew how much Toni needed female friends her own age. But it wasn't pity that had made her ask Toni on this excursion—though she had considered burning the woman's entire wardrobe so she'd have no choice but to buy new clothes. It was genuine trust and affection. Toni was the only journalist that Reagan trusted with the knowledge of her relationship with two men. Reagan knew the reclusive sweetheart would never do anything to hurt someone she cared about.

"Are you coming to the after-party tonight?" Reagan asked Toni, who paused with her soup spoon halfway to her mouth.

"Me?"

"Yeah, you."

"I already got enough footage of the after-parties," she said.

"Good. Then I can get you slobbering drunk without feeling guilty. Aggie, do you think you can have a corset ready for her to wear by then?"

Aggie shrugged. "Probably." She popped another bite of bloody steak into her mouth.

Toni's eyes widened, and she shook her head at Reagan. "I couldn't possibly wear a corset in public."

Reagan laughed. "We'll have to see about that."

CHAPTER 3

TREY BURIED his face in the sleeping baby's neck and inhaled deeply. He wasn't sure what it was about the scent of baby powder that made him feel so at peace with the world, but he could lie there on the bed with little Malcolm sleeping on his chest for hours. He pressed a kiss to the soft fluffy black hair of the perfect human Brian had created with his loving wife and rubbed the baby's back while Malcolm slumbered, completely unaware of how cruel the world could be. It didn't bother Trey that the reason he was babysitting his godson was so Brian could fuck Myrna senseless. Well, didn't bother him much. He supposed new parents needed alone time more than anyone.

Ethan came out of the bathroom rubbing a towel over his short black hair. Steam from his shower billowed through the open door behind him. He stopped when his gaze landed on Trey.

"Now isn't this homey?" he said with a twisted smile, before scanning the room. "Didn't I hear Reagan come in?"

"She took one look at this precious baby and ran off to help that nerdy chick find something to wear after the concert."

At the sound of Trey's voice, Malcolm stirred, shoving a tiny fist into his mouth and sucking. Within seconds, he went still again, relaxing against Trey's chest.

"You'd like one of those of your own, wouldn't you?" Ethan asked, nodding toward Malcolm.

"Hell no," he said, but his swelling heart didn't agree. "This is enough baby time for me."

Ethan sat on the edge of the bed next to Trey and gently stroked the soft fluff covering the baby's head. Malcolm's hair always stood on end no matter how much any of them tried to flatten it.

"He sure is cute," Ethan said.

"He looks like his father." Trey grinned down at Malcolm's adorable sleeping face, which resembled Brian's a little more every day.

Ethan's hand went still on Malcolm's head and he stood, going to an open suitcase for a shirt.

"Reagan doesn't want kids," Ethan said.

The hard edge to his voice made Trey squint at his broad back. Had he said something to offend him?

"I know," Trey said quietly so he wouldn't disturb his sleeping godson. "We don't have any business bringing a child into the world. Not when we're involved in such a complicated relationship."

"I'm not stepping aside so you and Reagan can play house." Ethan's motions as he jerked his shirt on over his head made Trey think he was angry. Or upset. But getting Ethan to talk about his feelings was damned near impossible.

"No one asked you to step aside. I'm one hundred percent committed to both of you. Aren't you happy?"

"Yeah," Ethan said gruffly as he strode across the room, disappearing into the suite's living room.

"I think something's bothering him," Trey said to Malcolm, who gave the fist in his mouth a few sucks before going still again. "Can I lay you in your basinet while I try to get him to talk to me?" Trey inched toward the edge of the bed and slowly rose to a sitting position. Malcolm's face twisted in displeasure, and he released a loud cry of protest. Trey sighed in resignation and reclined back into the nest of pillows, patting Malcolm's diaper to get him to settle again.

"Ethan," Trey called. "Can you come here for a sec?"

After a moment, the tall dark hunk appeared in the doorframe. "What?"

"I think we need to talk—"

Ethan's strong jaw hardened. "Later. I have somewhere I need to be right now."

"Where?"

Ethan's gaze flicked down to the baby cradled against Trey's chest. "Somewhere." He turned away.

When the suite's door banged shut a moment later, Trey took a deep breath and released it in a frustrated huff. He slapped around the side table trying to get a hand on his cellphone without disturbing Malcolm. Finding it, he did his best to send a call with one hand. He could use some advice, and there was only one person he trusted to shoot completely straight with him.

"What do you want?" Dare answered, trying to sound annoyed, but Trey could hear the smile in his big brother's voice.

"I'm babysitting."

"Congratulations."

"Everyone's deserted me. Come keep me company."

Dare chuckled softly. "You never could stand to be alone."

"I'm not alone," Trey said, still patting Malcolm's bottom with his free hand. He just felt alone. "Malcolm doesn't talk much, though. Not yet anyway."

"Quit your moping. I'm on my way."

The call ended in his ear.

Trey scooted off the bed so he could let Dare into the room when he arrived. Malcolm didn't appreciate the shift in position. Startled, his tiny hands flew open, and again he wailed a protest. Trey lifted him so his head was nestled against his neck and bounced slightly. The weird thing was, Trey didn't like babies with the exception of *this* baby. This baby was precious to him. He still thought Brian and Myrna were dumb for picking him as Malcolm's godfather and trusting him to care for their little one, but it warmed his heart to have a tiny perfect person completely dependent on him. That didn't mean he wanted a kid of his own.

The moment Dare arrived, he claimed Malcolm for himself, scooping the baby out of Trey's arms and holding him in the crook of one arm. "Is he hungry? Wet? Does he need to burp?"

"I didn't call you to take over babysitting duties," Trey said. "The two of us are doing just fine."

Dare's green-eyed gaze settled on Trey's eyes. "Well, something is bothering you. You only call me when something's not right."

"That's not true."

Dare snorted on a laugh. "Yeah it is. So what is it this time?"

Trey considered arguing—maybe he just wanted to chill with his brother for a little while—but it was no use. Dare was right. Something *was* bothering him, and he had called his big brother to help him sort through his troubles.

"Ethan."

"Ah, Mr. Tall Dark and Broody. Is he acting all jealous of Brian again?"

"I don't know. We were talking about having babies."

Dare chuckled and stroked Malcolm's ruddy cheek. "Well, that should defy all laws of biology."

"We were actually talking about *not* having babies. With Reagan, obviously. I don't have the right equipment to carry one. And then he got pissed for no reason and left."

"You had to have said or done something to set him off."

"All I said was Malcolm looks like his father, and then he said Reagan doesn't want kids and that he's not stepping aside so we can play house—whatever that means—then he said he had somewhere to be and left."

"He seems to be feeling left out."

"I don't know why. We all try to stay on equal footing."

"Maybe that's where your trouble lies. Maybe he doesn't feel special to you. Maybe he feels like an accessory to Reagan, like the only reason you care about him is because Reagan allows him—and only him—to be included in your relationship. Maybe he feels you're just using him for sex."

"It's not like that at all," Trey insisted.

"I'm no expert on polyamorous relationships."

"Me neither." Trey raked his hands through his hair and flopped down on the sofa while Dare paced from sofa to windows humming softly to Malcolm.

"Honestly," Dare said after a moment. "I think he's simply jealous of Brian. He probably thinks you want what Brian has—wife and son. Or maybe he thinks that you want to be Brian's wife."

Trey lifted a pillow from the sofa, prepared to launch it at his brother, but thought better of it when he remembered Dare was holding Malcolm. He clutched the pillow between his hands and pulled it against his belly. "I don't want a regular wife-and-kids lifestyle. Not ever. I've told him and Reagan I don't want that. I'm so content and happy in this relationship. I don't know how to make them feel the way I do. They both seem to be struggling."

"Reagan too?"

Trey nodded. "At least I know what her issues are. She talks to me. Ethan? Ethan never wants to discuss anything emotional."

"That's because he's a guy."

"I'm a guy," Trey pointed out.

"A weird one."

Trey threatened to flatten him with the pillow.

"Hey," Dare said, lifting his infant shield. "Drop your weapon. Baby on board."

"I'm not weird."

"You love three people with all your heart."

"Two," Trey corrected.

Dare leveled him with a challenging stare. "Three."

Trey hugged the pillow against his chest again. "I don't love Brian anymore."

"Right. But I don't doubt you could simultaneously love five people with all your heart. Or ten. And that's weird, Trey."

"Everyone knows I'm a man whore. Sed was one before Jessica, but no one gives him grief about it."

"This is entirely different from having multiple sex partners, Trey. You are in love—deeply in love—with several people. Most of us don't—can't—function that way. That's why you're weird. It's second nature to you. You don't struggle with it or even question it. It's just part of who you are."

Trey hauled himself off the couch and reached for Malcolm. Dare had doted on the baby enough. It was Trey's turn to cuddle with the little guy.

"I called you over here to make me feel better, not worse," Trey said as he shifted Malcolm out of Dare's arms and into his own.

Dare laid a hand on Trey's head just as he had a thousand times in the past when Trey had come to him seeking advice or approval or just to be around someone he knew would be in his corner no matter what.

"Your open heart is a gift, Trey. It killed me watching you struggle to keep it shut all those years while you waited for Brian to come around. You're finally discovering what you needed all along, and I'm glad for you."

Trey's heart swelled up into his throat. That was what he needed to hear from Dare. Why he'd called him here. He could always count on Dare to say exactly the right thing and make him feel like he could rise above anything trying to pull him down.

"But it's still weird," Dare added with a laugh and slapped him in the side of the head.

"Gee, thanks."

"Not that you should change. Just realize not everyone can function the way you do. Maybe it's okay for Reagan and Ethan to struggle with this relationship. It means they're willing to fight for it, right, even if it's not easy for them. They want it."

Trey had a lot to think on. He didn't know if Dare was right, but his opinions made sense to Trey. Maybe he could somehow help Reagan and Ethan. He wanted them both to be happy. He loved them both so much. He didn't know if he would survive letting someone else he loved go the way he'd let Brian go. That was Trey's struggle. Not loving more than one person—that was easy for him. Letting go? That was damned near impossible.

"Feel better?" Dare asked.

Trey shrugged. "I guess."

"I should have become a shrink," he said. "If I charged you every time you came looking for advice, I'd be a millionaire."

"You *are* a millionaire," Trey said with a grin.

"Oh yeah. You got anything to drink around here?"

Trey was glad Dare was sticking around to keep him company. He really didn't like to be alone.

"Check the fridge. Just don't drink any of the milk. It's Myrna's."

"You sure Malcolm won't share?"

Dare turned and laughed when he saw what must've been a look of disgust on Trey's face. Just thinking about consuming Myrna's breast milk made him want to hurl.

When Malcolm's parents came to collect him about an hour later, he'd been changed, fed, burped, bathed, and redressed after a spit-up incident, and thoroughly spoiled by both Mills brothers.

"You two should adopt," Myrna declared as she took her son in her arms and snuggled him close, kissing his neck until he giggled.

"Babies are easy," Dare said. "When Malcolm's two, Trey will have to watch him on his own. I don't deal with tantrums."

"You deal with Trey's tantrums all the time," Myrna said, elbowing Trey to show she was teasing.

"I can only handle one toddler at a time," Dare said.

Letting Dare's barb pass, Trey turned to Brian. "Did you finally get her out of your system?" Brian had been complaining about his limited sex life for days and had jumped on the idea of Trey babysitting for a few hours.

"She'll never be out of my system," Brian said. "But I do feel loads better. What do I owe you?"

In the past, Trey would have teased him about owing him sexual favors, but they'd moved beyond that. Trey had let him go. Mostly. He refused to flirt with Brian, no matter how natural it felt to do so.

"You don't owe me anything," Trey said. "Malcolm's a good baby. I don't mind watching him."

"I figured Reagan would help you babysit," Myrna said.

"Last I heard, she's with Toni, trying to convince her to wear a corset to an after-party."

Dare laughed. "Logan will shit a brick if any of her considerable cleavage is showing. I guess I'll have to make his life miserable tonight by flirting with her."

"You're deliciously evil," Myrna said, her face flushed as she looked Dare over from head to foot. So even women recently fucked by Brian "Master" Sinclair were not impervious to his big brother's charm.

"It's a gift." Dare slapped Trey on the shoulder in farewell. "See you backstage later?"

"I'll be around."

The suite emptied of visitors all at once, and Trey found himself alone. He settled on the sofa in front of the TV with a beer and lasted all of five minutes before he retrieved his phone and called Ethan.

"They baby's gone," he said when Ethan answered. "It's safe to come home now."

"Is Reagan back?"

"Not yet."

"I'll be there in a while. I still have a few things I need to take care of."

"Are you avoiding me?" Trey asked, trying not to feel hurt. Failing at that.

"Of course not."

"It feels like you're avoiding me."

"I'm not. I just need to think things through, and when I'm with you, I can't keep my head on straight."

"My brother said I need to try to understand why you're struggling with our relationship. Make me understand, Ethan."

"You talked to your brother about us?"

Trey shrugged even though Ethan couldn't see the gesture. "Yeah. Why wouldn't I?" Ethan was quiet for so long, Trey started to think the call had disconnected. "Ethan?"

"I'll see you later."

The call ended, and Trey dropped his phone on the sofa cushion beside him. He tilted his head back and rubbed his face with both hands to scrub the hurt from his expression. Maybe Reagan could get through to Ethan. She'd known him a lot longer than Trey had. He wondered if she'd be pissed if he interrupted her good time with her gal pals. He supposed he could let the situation rest, but he didn't want miscommunication to tear them apart. And if any one of them was unhappy in the relationship, none of them could be happy in the relationship.

"Are you still babysitting?" Reagan asked when she answered his call.

"I figured that's why you left again as soon as you got back from shopping. Malcolm is perfect. How could you not want to hold him?"

"It's not Malcolm, it's me. I've never been around a baby before. I don't understand how you figure out what they want. All they do is cry."

"The best way to figure out what they want is to be around a baby. You just go down their comfort checklist, fixing potential problems until they stop crying. It's not that hard. It's just troubleshooting."

"It's not a skill I need or want to learn," Reagan said.

Trey sighed. He was sure Reagan would love Malcolm as much as he did if she'd just stick around when he was in the room. "His parents came to pick him up a few minutes ago."

"In that case, I hope both you and Ethan are hard and ready. I've been thinking about being the saucy meat in your manwich all afternoon."

Lust stirred low in Trey's belly. He'd very much like to be a part of that manwich, but without Ethan, he and Reagan would be an open-faced sandwich at best.

"Ethan isn't here. He left right after his shower. I called him, but I can't convince him to return. Does he have something against babies too?"

"He loves babies," Reagan said.

"Maybe you can talk to him. Find out what's eating at him and let me know so I can fix it."

"Ethan gets that way sometimes," she said, not sounding the least bit concerned. "He needs alone time to sort things out."

Trey had a hard time wrapping his head around that tendency. He supposed not every guy had an older brother as caring and understanding as Dare, but without someone to talk to, how in the hell did you get out of your own head long enough to see the real issue? Wouldn't that drive a person crazy?

"Does that work for him?" Trey asked.

Reagan chuckled. "No, not really, but that's just the way he is. You might as well accept it."

Perhaps Trey had to accept that quality in his lover, but he wouldn't accept the possibility of losing Ethan because he kept whatever was bothering him locked inside.

"Maybe he'll come home if *you* call him," Trey said.

"I'll try, but you might be making me fly solo, so you'd better put in your tongue stud."

At least he had one partner who told him exactly what she wanted.

"I'm on it," he said.

"Love you," she said.

"Love you too."

"And Ethan loves you."

Trey would rather hear it from the man himself, but her assertion made him feel a little better. "I'll try to remember that."

Ten minutes later, Trey was lounging naked in bed and using his teeth to play with the stud in his tongue—he loved the way bar felt inside his piercing when he tugged at it. The suite door crashed open, and he heard sounds that made his cock throb with excitement—desperate kissing, ragged breathing, the rustle of clothing being shed, a thud against a wall, a gasp of surprise, Reagan's moan of pleasure, Ethan's answering groan, and the rhythmic pounding of flesh in flesh. What the fuck?

Trey leaped from the bed and stopped in the doorway to stare. He wasn't sure if watching the pair fuck like animals against the foyer wall should turn him on, but the feelings suddenly churning through his chest and gut had little to do with arousal. Shock? Betrayal? Jealousy? He wasn't sure what he was experiencing.

Reagan's eyes flicked open, and her gaze met his. "Trey," she said breathlessly.

"Does he want some of this too?" Ethan said, his voice harsh.

Well, he *had*, but now he wasn't so sure.

"Oh, right there, Ethan," Reagan moaned. "Fuck me harder." Her fingernails dug into his shoulders and her back arched, banging her head against the wall. She cried out as she came, her eyes rolled back and her face contorted in a familiar expression of bliss. Ethan kissed her harshly and then pulled out, letting her slide down the wall to kneel at his feet. He fisted his hand in her hair, and she lifted her head, still breathing hard.

"Suck it."

Her motions were desperate as her hand circled his cock and she directed the head between her parted lips. She drew him deep, sucking hard, her gaze cast upward as if she were asking for Ethan's approval.

Trey's own cock was now so hard, it began to throb. He did want that. Wanted to be coerced. Fucked. Completely dominated. He loved a strong man at his back, holding him down, taking what he wanted.

Ethan turned his head and pinned Trey with a heated stare. Trey's feet rooted to the floor as Ethan pulled free of Reagan's mouth and stepped back. Ethan never took his eyes off Trey as he kicked off his shoes and removed his jeans. The predatory look on Ethan's face made Trey's pulse race. Something inside Trey wanted to run, but the rest of him wanted to be caught and devoured. As Ethan stalked him, coming ever closer, Trey's heart thudded faster and faster, his ass ached, wanting to be filled, and his soul cried out for the man who made him feel this way.

"Ethan," he whispered just as Ethan's hand tangled in his hair and jerked his head back.

The hungry, punishing kiss seared Trey's lips and stole his breath. He wanted to wrap his arms around Ethan, tug his hard body against his own, but his muscles wouldn't cooperate. Trey was being taken, and he had no power to resist. He could feel himself moving backward toward the bed, but it was as if he were a puppet whose strings were controlled by another.

"You're mine," Ethan said against his lips.

"Yes." Usually Trey would protest and remind Ethan that he was both his and Reagan's, but at that moment he'd have been a liar. He was Ethan's, only Ethan's. Just as moments before, while she'd been fucked against the wall, Reagan had been only Ethan's. Perhaps this was the dynamic Ethan needed to feel complete. As Ethan's hard cock brushed against Trey's, all Trey's thoughts evaporated. All but one.

"Take me," he groaned against Ethan's lips.

Ethan turned him abruptly and planted a hand between Trey's shoulders, pressing down to bend him over the bed. Trey was vaguely aware of Ethan dipping his fingers into the open tub of lube on the nightstand, and then with one hard thrust, he was filled from behind. Trey pushed his hands against the mattress so he didn't collapse face first into the bed. He groaned at the pleasure and the beauty of Ethan's perfect domination. And then he gasped when Ethan's strong hand wrapped around his throat, palm pressing firmly against his windpipe, fingers digging into the artery on his neck.

"Do you still think of him when I fuck you?" Ethan asked, his deep voice a harsh growl.

Already light-headed, Trey had no idea who he was talking about. "What?" he croaked, struggling to draw air.

Ethan's thrusts were harsh and rapid. Trey's eyes rolled back as pre-cum dripped freely from his cock. He shuddered when a warm tongue licked at his tip. He glanced down to find Reagan had crawled up on the bed and settled onto her back. The contrast of Reagan's gentleness and Ethan's cruelty had him out of his head with excitement.

"Do you still think of Brian when I *fuck* you?" Ethan asked.

Who the hell was Brian?

"No. Only you. Ethan."

Ethan's hold on his throat loosened, and Trey took a deep breath. Though he was still dizzy, his vision cleared and the beautiful sight of Reagan's pussy came into focus. She'd positioned herself for a little sixty-nine action, and who was he to deny her? Bending over her, he drew the stud in his tongue over her swollen clit. She moaned, her breath hot against the wet tip of his cock. His licks became more fervent as Ethan's pounding cock and Reagan's gentle sucking drew him closer and closer to orgasm. His groans must have tipped off Ethan to his impending release, because Ethan reached between Trey's legs and cupped his balls, giving them a cruel but oddly delightful squeeze.

"Don't let go," Ethan demanded. "Not until I fill your ass with my cum."

Trey swallowed a protest and tightened his ass to squeeze the cock thrusting into him.

"My, aren't you bossy this evening?" Reagan said. Her arm shifted, and Ethan suddenly went still. His breath hitched, and he let go of Trey's balls. His other hand slid lightly down Trey's back until it gently grasped his hip. Ethan's harsh thrusts slowed, becoming the deep, churning penetrations that made it impossible for Trey to hold back his orgasm. He exploded, cum erupting from him in vigorous pulses, splattering over Reagan's chest. But he hadn't disobeyed Ethan's demand by much. Ethan's cock popped free, and Trey shuddered at the feel of Ethan's cum bathing his asshole before Ethan pushed inside again and filled him as he'd promised.

Concerned that Reagan hadn't gotten her fair share, Trey slid two fingers into her soaked pussy and flicked her clit with the stud in his tongue. Within seconds she was screaming, her slick passage rhythmically squeezing his fingers as she found release.

Trey crawled up on the bed and collapsed next to Reagan, his face squashed into the mattress. He smiled weakly when Ethan dropped beside him and pulled him solidly against him, back to belly, and warmed Trey's cheek with gasping breaths.

"I'm sorry I was so rough with you," Ethan whispered after his breathing had calmed and his heart was no longer trying to thud itself through his breastbone. "It's just . . . I don't know."

"I like it," Trey admitted, "when you're rough with me. It makes me feel utterly desired."

"You are. I'm not sure I show my feelings to you the right way. You're so good at it and I . . . I don't think you understand how much you mean to me."

Trey relaxed against him, all the hurt and confusion from earlier flowing free of his body.

"I love you, Ethan," Trey said. "Don't ever doubt it."

"And me?" Reagan said from somewhere near Trey's feet. He chuckled softly. She was always so afraid they'd forget about her. As if that was possible.

"Come here." Trey held his arms out, and she crawled up the bed to settle in his embrace. "I love you as well." He kissed the back of her head.

They lay that way, wrapped in a cocoon of love and physical exhaustion until Sed came pounding on their door an hour later.

"It's time to go to the arena, Trey," he yelled through the door. "Get your ass downstairs."

"I hear you," Trey shouted, but he didn't move from his comfortable spot between the loves of his life.

"We should go," Ethan said, pressing his face and several kisses into the back of Trey's neck.

"Yep," Reagan agreed, drawing Trey's arms more securely around her waist.

"In a minute," Trey murmured, his eyelids heavy as he fought sleep. It took Sed trying to rattle the hinges off the door to get Trey out of bed.

He jerked open the door to Sed's angry face. Sed blinked—

squeezing his lids tightly shut—when he took in Trey's state of undress.

"Can I help you?" Trey asked.

Sed stared at the wall beside the open suite door. "We're going to be late. Get dressed and meet us downstairs."

"I'll be down in a minute. I need to shower. I have cum dripping out of my ass."

Trey chuckled when Sed grimaced and shuddered.

"Next time I'll send Brian after him," Sed said under his breath as he turned and walked away.

CHAPTER 4

THAT NIGHT, ETHAN WAS ONCE AGAIN DEEPLY ABSORBED in watching Trey perform onstage—mostly trying to figure out why it bothered him so fucking much that Trey just *had* to touch Brian every time he came within reach—when Reagan nudged him with her elbow to gain his attention.

"Are you feeling better now?" she yelled over the blaring music, a flash of red lighting up her face before switching to blue and then brilliant white.

He knew why she was asking—she'd found him staring into a nearly empty glass of whiskey in the hotel bar before she'd coaxed him upstairs for some sexual healing—but he played dumb and shrugged. "Not sure why you thought I was feeling poorly."

"Because I know you. We've been together either as friends or lovers or roommates for years. I can tell when something's bothering you."

The tail of her shouted words sounded extra loud because Sinners' song ended abruptly. Appreciative cheers from the audience filled the short gap of silence.

"I'm not bothered."

"Maybe you should be," she said.

She gave him far more grief than Trey ever did. Maybe because they had known each other for so much longer and she wasn't afraid to tell him off.

"Trey called me, worried that he'd done something wrong. He didn't do anything, did he?" It was more an accusation than an inquiry.

Ethan watched the man in question lean close and whisper to Brian. The pair laughed together, Brian smacking Trey in the chest. Some inside joke probably. He looked down at Reagan to squelch the jealousy burning up his throat.

"Not that I know of," Ethan answered Reagan's question. "What was he like with Brian before he became interested in me?"

Reagan gazed out at the stage where the two guitarists were jamming together while Sed prowled the front of the stage and Jace hung toward the back. "Pretty much the same as he is now. I hear the guys joking about how Trey used to try to steal kisses from Brian, though I've never seen him do it. You can tell they're still close."

Really close. Ethan's eyes narrowed as Trey resting against Brian's back as they performed a dueling solo.

"But they're just friends. Relax." Reagan slapped Ethan in the center of his chest. "I've seen how he is with you. He loves you with all his heart, Ethan. Don't let your unnecessary jealousy compromise what you have with him."

"What *we* have with him," Ethan said.

"Right."

"Uh, sorry to interrupt," said a chesty young woman in unflattering glasses. Ethan knew she was writing some sort of biography on Exodus End, but he couldn't recall her name.

"Toni," Reagan said, her tone chastising. "Where's your corset?"

"I'm working," Toni said. "I need to hook up your head camera before you get onstage."

She held up a black headband with an attached lens.

"You promised you'd wear that corset. Aggie went to all that trouble to get it ready in time."

Toni looked behind her—not once but twice—before she opened the ugly sweater she had buttoned up to her throat. She gave Reagan—as well as Ethan—a peek at acres of cleavage spilling from the top of a fitted black leather corset.

"I am wearing it as promised. But I had to cover up," she whispered harshly, "because all the guys were too busy staring at my chest to follow instructions."

She jerked the sweater closed and buttoned it again. Ethan blinked to clear his muddled thoughts. While Toni helped Reagan put the camera on her head—she looked absolutely fucking ridiculous in the get-up—Toni watched Ethan out of the corner of her eye.

"Do you watch both Trey and Reagan perform every night?" she asked Ethan.

Reagan had informed him that Toni knew about their unusual relationship, but he wasn't prepared to answer any questions about it. He didn't like the idea that a writer knew about them. It would be so easy for her to leak their secret to the world. But Reagan trusted her, so Ethan supposed he had no choice but to trust her as well. That didn't mean he'd willingly share information about his personal life, however. He didn't care who the woman was.

"Mostly," he said, shifting his body away from her, hoping she'd take a hint.

Ignoring his body language, Toni asked, "So do you also play guitar? I mean since both of your lovers do, it would seem only natural."

"It's none of your business."

She bit her lip, and her friendly smile faded. "Oh. I'm sorry. I didn't mean—"

"Jeez, Ethan, chillax," Reagan said. "She's just asking a simple question." She turned to Toni and clasped her hands in hers. "He doesn't play. I tried to teach him once. Thought it would be sexy to slide up behind his big, strong body and show him a few chords. But he's all thumbs."

They laughed together at his expense, and Ethan was pretty sure he was glowering. Even though Reagan's claim was generous— Ethan was worse than all thumbs, he was more like all hams—he didn't appreciate her sharing information about him with this, this . . . *reporter*. Was that what the women had been up to while they'd been together shopping and whatnot that morning, whispering secrets back and forth like schoolgirls?

The pair weren't much better at the after-party. Reagan seemed determined to get her new bestie drunk off her ass, and while Trey was allowed to play, Ethan was forced to sit and watch. There were too many prying eyes around for him to truly enjoy the company of either Reagan or Trey, so once again he was the odd man out. He tossed back his whiskey and stared at the wet ring on the table in front of him.

He was surprised when Trey's brother dropped into the seat beside him.

"You look like I feel," Dare said in greeting.

Ethan leaned back in his chair and contemplated at Exodus

End's lead guitarist. "How so?"

"I get the impression you'd rather be anywhere but here."

Not exactly true. At least here he could keep an eye on both Reagan—he'd completely failed her when that asshole had nearly strangled her to death, so his protective instincts were more honed than ever—and Trey, who seemed more interested in Reagan than Brian tonight. Likely because Brian had already retired for the evening to spend time with his little family. But Dare was right. He wasn't particularly fond of these loud and obnoxious rockstar after-parties.

"I'd rather be here than dropped into a live volcano." Ethan was surprised when Dare chuckled at his idea of a joke.

"I'd have to flip a coin on that one," Dare said.

Ethan grinned and lifted his glass to dump a whiskey-flavored ice cube into his mouth. He crushed the mostly melted slivers between his teeth with a satisfying crunch.

"Trey said he asked you for some advice today," Ethan said.

Dare leaned back in his chair and crossed his legs at the ankle, resting his dwindling drink between his hands and against his flat belly.

"He does that a lot," Dare said. "He's always been too complicated and conflicted to sort himself out. But I get him."

That made one of them.

Ethan rubbed the pad of his thumb up and down the side of his glass.

"Did he tell you what he wanted advice about?" Dare asked after a long moment of silence stretched between them.

"I'm guessing it was me."

Dare nodded, but didn't comment. Ethan was a big brother, so he knew what it must feel like to be talking to someone who'd hurt his little brother—no matter that the pain he'd caused was unintentional.

"I didn't mean to upset him. It's just . . ." Just what? Even he didn't know what the problem was. He knew that if he wanted to keep Reagan and Trey in his life he had to make sacrifices, such as keeping his distance from them while in the public eye. He knew Trey had a past with Brian Sinclair and no amount of wishing would ever change that. What he didn't know was how he was supposed to come to terms with such realities.

"He'll always love Brian," Dare said. "Always."

Ethan's breath caught in his throat as his worst nightmare

reared its ugly head. "I suppose you think I should step aside."

"Fuck no. What I'd really like is for you to embed yourself so far under Trey's skin that he forgets Brian ever existed."

Ethan gaped at him, and Dare smiled before releasing a short laugh. "I'm not sure it's possible. Their friendship is important to both of them. I don't know how Trey can let him go when he sees him every day. Hell, it's hard to let go of someone you've loved for ten years even when they're dead." Dare frowned into his glass and tossed back the remainder of the amber liquid in one gulp.

Ethan blinked at him. "You're not suggesting I kill Brian, are you?" He wasn't quite that jealous. At the moment, anyway.

Dare's head turned. "What? No. I was talking about someone else."

Himself, Ethan decided.

"So what should I do?"

Dare's gaze followed his brother as he twirled a giggling Reagan across the dance floor. "Love him like no one is watching."

"I wish that were possible," Ethan said, Dare's advice making his body tense with dread. Hell, he couldn't even love Trey freely in front of his own family, much less the world. "Did you have this conversation with Reagan?"

"She doesn't need to be told," he said, nodding toward the laughing pair as they added a deep dip to their drunken dance. Trey dropped her on the floor and instead of helping her up, decided it was more fun to join her. "She does it naturally."

"But she's not the third wheel in this relationship," Ethan said.

"And neither are you."

Hell, what did Dare know? Nothing. That's what.

Seeming to realize he'd overstayed his welcome, Dare scraped himself out of his chair and gave Ethan's shoulder a squeeze. "Your first session is free." He walked away chuckling to himself, though Ethan had no idea what he found so humorous.

A few minutes later Trey dumped a very tipsy Reagan into Dare's recently vacated seat. "Did you miss me?" she asked, first leaning against his arm and then sliding down his body until her head was in his lap. His first instinct was to stroke her hair and let her rest there for a while, but he went with his second instinct and helped her sit upright beside him.

"I think you've had a few too many," Ethan said.

"I'm just dizzy because Trey . . ." She blinked her eyes and tried to focus them. "Where did he go?"

"I'm right behind you."

Her head fell back, and she smiled when Trey leaned over her to gaze down into her flushed face.

"That's where I like you best." She burst into an incontrollable fit of giggles.

"I think it's time we head back to our room," Ethan said. At least there he'd be able to touch her—and Trey—without everyone staring. Questioning. Judging.

"But I want to dance with you," Reagan said, grabbing Ethan's hand and tugging.

"We can't. Not here. You know that," he said.

Trey gave him a sad little smile and gazed at him through his black bangs. Ethan's heart twisted with longing. *Love him like no one's watching.* Dare's words echoed in Ethan's mind. If only it were that simple.

"Did you have a nice chat with my brother?" Trey asked, flopping into the vacant seat beside Ethan.

"You're lucky to have a brother like him," Ethan said. One who accepted him exactly as he was. Ethan knew his six half brothers weren't so open-minded.

"I know that better than anyone," Trey said. "I wish you'd stop sulking in the corner and have some fun with us."

Ethan glanced at Reagan, who was slumped back in her chair with her eyes closed. She'd definitely had too much to drink.

"Do you really wish that?" Ethan asked quietly. People would be able to tell that there was more between the three of them than friendship. Maybe Trey would be able to deal with the backlash, but Ethan wasn't sure if he was prepared, and he knew excessive negativity would completely diminish Reagan's natural spark.

"More than anything," Trey said.

Ethan turned his head to seek the sincerity in Trey's eyes—such a remarkable man, how could Ethan not love him—and inexplicably found his lips against Trey's. For the briefest instant Ethan forgot they were in public. He not only accepted Trey's kiss, he deepened it. Then reality crashed into Ethan's skull and he pulled away, checking to see if anyone had noticed. His gaze met Dare's, and the man smiled slightly, offering a nod of approval. As far as Ethan could tell, no one else had seen him kiss Trey. But how could they miss the adoration on his face when he looked at the man? Ethan could explain that look away when it was applied to Reagan; everyone knew they'd once been intimate, even if they didn't know they'd become entangled once more. So when he stared at her with love and longing, outsiders would think he was pining away for her as she pursued Trey. But Ethan had no way of explaining away his feelings for Trey. And Trey wasn't very good at hiding their mutual attraction. Hell, he seemed to enjoy playing with fire.

"Do you really love me?" Trey whispered.

"Of course I do," Ethan said. "Why would you ask me that?"

"You keep turning away from me."

"Just in public. Out of necessity."

Trey dropped his head forward and stared at his clasped hands resting in his lap. After a moment, he shook his head. "I don't feel it only when we're in public." He lifted his chin, raw pain in his eyes. "I feel it when we're alone together too. The only time I don't feel like you're erecting walls between us is when we're fucking."

"It isn't you, Trey," Reagan said, her voice slightly slurred. "It's him. He's always been like that."

"Yeah," Ethan said, adding several layers of bricks to his so-called wall. "I'm a cold-hearted son of a bitch. If you don't like it, file a complaint."

He shoved his chair back and shot to his feet.

"Where are you going?" Reagan asked, reaching for his hand, but missing when he stepped backward.

"What does it matter?" he said as he turned and strode away.

"Ethan," Trey called after him, but he didn't stop. He didn't want to discuss his closed emotional state here. Not anywhere for that matter.

Ethan met Dare's gaze as he slammed both palms into the exit door and sent it flying open. Dare pressed his lips together and shook his head. Ethan glared at him. He didn't need outside opinions. Apparently he didn't need *inside* opinions either.

No one seemed to care that he'd left. He was acutely aware that neither Trey nor Reagan hurried after him when he stormed off hurt and confused. And they thought *he* was callous.

CHAPTER 5

TREY KNOCKED on the bathroom door of the dressing room in Albuquerque. Another night. Another city. Another chance to give Brian a hard time. "Are you done puking? We have to get onstage."

"I'm not puking," Brian called. "Just working on my breathing."

The world-renowned guitarist had played before millions of people in his lifetime and he still got stage fright. Once Master Sinclair was onstage, he was fine. It was the hour or so before each show that he struggled to keep his head together. Trey shrugged at Sed, who was the one who'd insisted he harass Brian in the first place.

"You can breathe later," Sed called. "Get a move on."

The door opened, and a pale, waxy-skinned version of their lead guitarist emerged.

"You'd probably feel better if you just puked," Trey said.

"I'm fine," Brian assured them.

"Get a guitar in his hands," Eric said from where he waited near their shared dressing room's door. "He'll forget all about the twenty thousand people here to witness his every mistake."

"You aren't helping," Brian grumbled at him as he passed.

"I wasn't trying to help." Still chattering away, Eric fell into step behind them as they exited into a cool corridor. "You know, even if you fucked up every note you played, broke forty guitar strings, fell flat on your ass *and* on your face, they'd still cheer for you. You're fucking Master Sinclair."

"Still not helping." Brian tugged at the wrist of one fingerless glove as he flexed his hand repeatedly.

"Eric's right," Trey said with a chuckle. "You can do no wrong."

Several paces ahead of them, Sed reached into his pocket to silence his ringing phone. "Forgot to turn it off," he said.

"Why don't you just leave it on the bus?" Eric asked. "I'm sure Jessica can live without hearing your voice for more than five minutes."

Sed scowled down at his phone's screen. "I need to take this," he said. "Kylie?" he said into his phone. "Is something wrong?"

Sed's face went white, and he swayed, stumbling as his feet stopped before the rest of his body decided to join them. If Eric hadn't grabbed him and directed him to the wall, he probably would have fallen over.

"How is that possible?" Sed said, massaging his forehead with one hand. "I saw him a few weeks ago. He was perfectly healthy."

Trey exchanged a concerned look with Brian. It took a lot to rattle their overconfident leader, but Sed was obviously struggling to keep himself together.

"I have to perform right now, but I'll be on my way home as soon as I finish here." He paused, listening. "No, no, don't worry about it. I'm glad you didn't wait to call. How's Mom holding up?"

Trey stepped forward and clasped Sed's shoulder. Trey knew Sed would never go home midtour except for an emergency. What was going on?

"I'll take care of everything, sis," he said. "Just hang tight for a few hours. I'll be there." He listened for a moment. "I love you too." He hung up and took a deep ragged breath before shoving his phone into his pocket.

He shrugged off Trey's hand and pushed off the wall, walking stiffly toward the backstage area.

"Sed?" Trey called, hurrying to catch up with him. "What happened? Why do you need to go home?"

"My father," he said, his voice tight. He shook his head and closed his eyes, stopping to lean against the wall again.

"Is he hurt? Sick? If you need to leave right away—"

Sed shook his head. "I'll go after . . ." He swallowed hard and a tear leaked from beneath his mirrored sunglasses. "After . . ."

"You can't perform when you're all freaked out," Trey said. He knew a thing or two about trying to perform when you couldn't. "Go be with your dad. You'll feel better if you see him."

"I won't." Sed shook his head vigorously. His fingers disappeared behind his sunglasses as he pressed them into his eyes, and he struggled to suck air into his lungs. "It's too late to see him. Too late to say goodbye. He's . . ."

Trey's lips went numb as he stared at Sed in disbelief. The word he'd left unspoken. It wasn't . . .

"You should go home," Brian said. "Your family needs you."

"I can't just leave." Sed pushed off the wall and started walking again. "We have a show."

Jace dashed in front of him, forcing Sed to stop once again. Beneath his dark beard stubble, Jace was as pale as the platinum tips of his spiked hair. He shook his head, his brown-eyed gaze searching Sed's face, and then he wrapped both arms around Sed, latching his hands together behind Sed's broad back as he hugged him. Trey stumbled against Sed's left side as he added the support of his own embrace. The big guy probably would have been able to keep his emotions locked inside himself if Brian and Eric hadn't joined their huddle of misery.

Sed's trembling intensified until his entire body was quaking. Trey squeezed tighter, hoping to lend him strength and peace, but he doubted anything he could do would make Sed feel better.

After several minutes, Sed's trembling stilled, and he squirmed out of their group hug. "Let's go," he said, his voice steady. He took a step forward, his legs also steady.

Jace and Eric hurried after him, but Brian grabbed Trey's arm before he could follow.

"We can't let him perform in the state he's in," Brian said.

"Maybe it will help," Trey said. "Make him feel like everything's normal for that hour he's on stage."

"I don't know how anything can feel normal for him right now," Brian said. "He has to be in shock. I'm in shock, and I didn't even know Phil very well." Brian stared at Sed's retreating back and scratched his jaw. "Someone should call Jessica and let her know what's going on."

Trey pulled out his phone. "I'll do it."

She didn't answer, so he sent her a quick text. *Can you come to the backstage area ASAP? Sed just got some bad news. His dad passed away.*

That was a terrible thing to break to someone through a text message, Trey thought as he put his phone away and followed his bandmates into the darkened area behind the stage. As soon as he lifted his guitar strap over his head and settled the familiar weight of its body against his pelvis, a peaceful calm settled over him. He hoped Brian was wrong. He hoped performing *would* put Sed at ease. At least for the hour they were onstage.

"You okay?" Trey asked Sed as he stood with his microphone between his hands, his head lowered.

Sed swallowed and nodded.

"You don't have to do this," Trey said around the lump in his throat.

"I can't disappoint the fans."

A blue glow lit the stage floor. Trey bit his lip at their cue to find their places and looked again at Sed. He seemed okay, wearing the same amped-up expression he always wore just before a performance. Trey couldn't tell if Sed was hiding his turmoil behind those mirrored sunglasses of his or if he wasn't processing the reality of his father's unexpected death or if he really was okay.

Trey figured it was just a matter of time before reality fucked Sed over.

CHAPTER
6

REAGAN USUALLY WATCHED Trey perform, but tonight she'd sent Ethan to keep an eye on him while she hung out with her own band backstage. She'd broken routine partially because Dare had advised her that it was the best way to feel included and partially because she wanted to view the video footage Toni had recorded a few nights ago. Each member of Exodus End, Reagan included, had worn a camera strapped to their head because Toni had wanted scenes from their points of view in her interactive biography. Goofy as they'd all looked wearing those headcams that night, Reagan was eager to see what the cameras had captured.

Toni started with Logan's recording—she *was* obsessed with the guy—and they all got a laugh when they realized that the nicely rounded, shiny black object onscreen was Max's ass clad in his tight leather pants. Logan insisted his camera had been crooked and he hadn't been staring obsessively at their lead singer's hind end, but they had to torment him for it. Logan was always good for a laugh—often at his own expense. Steve's footage was a blur of flailing arms and drumsticks. He was moving his head—and therefore, the camera—so much that Reagan's stomach churned. If she had to watch a moment more of that, she was going to be sick. Toni was switching over to Reagan's video when their head of security entered the room. Butch's lips were drawn into a tight line as his gaze flitted from one person to the next and when that gaze landed on Toni, his eyes narrowed into slits.

"Hey, guys," he said. "Sorry to interrupt."

Reagan considered chiding him about calling them all guys when there were two women in the room, but something in the stiff way he held his large body made her think that now was not the time for jokes. The rest of the band stopped goofing off to focus on Butch. He ran their schedules like clockwork. Maybe the reason he looked so out of sorts was because they'd missed an engagement or something.

"Can I see you on the bus for a minute?" he said, dragging his focus from Toni to the gazes of the band members.

"All of us?" Dare asked.

"Uh." Butch's gaze shifted to Toni again, and a muscle in his jaw twitched. "Just the band." When they rose from their spots on the furniture, he added. "And not Logan."

Logan stopped midmotion and scrunched his brows at Butch.

"Not Logan?" Max asked.

Why not Logan? Reagan would have understood if she'd been left out of a band meeting or important discussion, but Logan was a founding member of the band. Why would he be excluded?

"It'll just take a few moments," Butch said before he backed out of the room.

The guys—except Logan—followed Butch out into the corridor, Reagan bringing up the rear. She caught Dare's arm as they made their way out to the tour bus, and he slowed his stride to fall into step with her.

"What's going on?" she asked.

"I have no idea."

That seemed to be the group consensus. "Why are we going to the bus?" Steve asked. "We have to be onstage in less than an hour. Can't this whimsy of yours wait?"

"I wish it was a whimsy," Butch said. "But no, it can't wait. We have to figure out what to do about *her*."

"Who, me?" Reagan said, her heart producing an unpleasant thud. Was she about to be fired? Her mind raced through all the mistakes she'd made while she'd been touring with the band. She'd made plenty. Were any of them bad enough to cut her loose, though? She had signed a contract. Could she fight this decision? Would she want to fight it if the band didn't want her on tour with them? She didn't want to be a burden.

"Not you, Reagan. Toni," Butch said.

"Toni?" Reagan sputtered. That made even less sense than the band firing their temporary guitarist.

Butch didn't elaborate. He practically ran to the tour bus. Reagan glanced up in surprise when Dare's hands covered her ears. He gave her a sad little smile that made her heart twist. Why was he covering her ears? Then she noticed a small crowd of the usual groupie-types pressed up against the barriers near the bus. Whatever they were shouting—and they seemed to be shouting with great agitation—she couldn't make out clearly, thanks to big-brother-to-all and his large hands. But the way they were glaring and stabbing angry fingers at her made her glad she couldn't hear what they were saying.

Once she and Dare had climbed the bus steps, the door swung shut behind them and Dare released his hold on her head.

"Sorry," Butch said. "I didn't think it would spread so fast. I figured we'd have more privacy on the bus."

"What's going on?" Reagan asked.

"You didn't hear what they were calling you?" Steve asked.

"Dare covered my ears."

God, what were they calling her and why?

Butch pulled a stack of newspapers out from under his arm and separated the pages, giving one or two to each band member. He gave seven to Reagan. Expecting to see a bad review or something equally unimportant, Reagan's world tilted as she scanned the tabloid headlines.

"Exodus End's Newest Member Prefers Taking Members in Twos"

". . . often seen with both men . . ."

Oh shit!

"How Does a Mediocre Guitarist Get a Gig with a Mega Band?"

". . . blatant seduction. How else could such a mediocre guitarist grace Exodus End's stage . . ."

Mediocre?

"Reagan Elliot Rocks Her Bandmates All Night and Every Day"

". . . her involvement in orgies . . . "

Orgies?

Reagan was scarcely aware of the guys around her. She could hear what they were saying, but wasn't processing their words.

"It was bound to come out sooner or later," Max said, folding the paper he'd been reading and handing it to Dare.

Dare released a pained sigh and shook his head. "It didn't have to come out at all."

"What a fucking bitch!" Steve yelled. "I can't believe she'd do this to us."

Reagan turned to her third page and read "Bodyguard or Bootie Call? Reagan Elliot's Biggest Secret."

"It appears that having one sexy stud in her bed isn't enough for Exodus End's new guitarist. When she isn't partying with her supposed boyfriend, Trey Mills, she's taking her hunky bodyguard to her bed and . . . "

Fucky McFuckerson!

Reagan read only the first few lines before the paper tumbled from her suddenly numb fingers. "How did they find out? We were so careful."

"How did they find out *any* of this?" Steve said, shaking his section of the paper at her. "Only one fucker knows all this information. A person we thought we could trust."

Reagan was upset that she was labeled a slut and that her guitar playing had been unfairly criticized, but to think that someone she trusted, a woman she'd considered her friend was capable of publishing their secrets in a tabloid was far harder to take.

Dare picked up the paper Reagan had dropped and began reading. Her face went hot, and she snatched it out of his hands. She didn't want Dare to read the articles. They contained personal information that was painted in a derogatory light. And then she realized that *anyone* could read the articles, not only Dare but perfect strangers, her friends in Los Angeles, her past loves, and worst of all, her father.

Suddenly light-headed, she dropped onto the nearest stable location, which happened to be the floor.

"Shit," she said. "People are going to read that and they're going to think—" She choked on a sob. "Going to think it's all true."

"It is all true," Steve said. "It's just slanted in a way that shows us all in the worst possible light."

"I didn't sleep with you guys to win my spot on the tour!" she yelled. That was obviously a lie.

"It doesn't say you did," Dare said. "It says your playing is so mediocre that you must have had to sleep with every member of the band to win your spot. It doesn't say you actually did."

Tears of hurt and anger collided in her eyes and began to drip down her hot cheeks. "You think my playing is mediocre?"

Dare squatted in front of her and scooped her off the floor so he could hug her and pat her back. Like she was four years old and his comforting embrace would make a fucking difference.

"Of course I don't think that, but these people tear celebrities apart for a living, and they know how to make opinions sound like facts while never claiming lies as truths because they'd get sued for slander."

She was too upset to accept the wisdom of his words. "I'll fucking sue them all. But first I'm going to beat the shit out of that lying, back-stabbing bitch."

She struggled out of Dare's loose grasp and pulled the lever that opened the bus door. Now that Dare wasn't protecting her ears from the obscenities the groupies were throwing at her, Reagan could hear their cruel taunts.

"You slut. How could you cheat on Trey Mills? He's an angel."

"Did you just finish blowing all your bandmates so they'll keep you on tour?"

"You suck! You don't deserve to be on tour with them."

"Whore!"

Unable to take the abuse, she smashed her hands over her ears and dashed toward the backstage entrance as if she could run faster than the speed of sound. Her bandmates had enough mercy to allow her to get into the building before they pulled her aside.

"You can't beat her up," Dare said.

"Watch me!" Reagan yelled, throwing off his hand and rushing down the corridor.

"You can't beat her up," Butch yelled after her, "but we can fire her and kick her off the bus."

Reagan rushed into the dressing room, where they'd left the traitorous cunt and her clueless boyfriend only moments before. The room was empty. Reagan grabbed Toni's laptop off the coffee table and lifted it over her head, but just before she could hurl it at the nearest wall, someone grabbed it out of her hands.

"Calm down, Reagan," Max said. "Don't give her the satisfaction of knowing she's hurt you."

"I'm going to give her the satisfaction of my boot in her ass," she bellowed.

"Do you want me to find Ethan?" Dare asked.

"Yeah," Reagan shouted. "His feet are bigger than mine. See how she likes *his* boot in her ass."

"Can you get Ethan?" Dare said to Steve. "He's probably in the wings watching Sinners perform."

"Do I look like a fucking Labrador retriever?" Steve asked.

"Yeah," Dare said without pause as he pressed Reagan down into the sofa. He sat on the coffee table in front of her and took her hands. "Breathe," he said to her.

She tried to still her gasping strangled breaths into something a bit less traumatizing to her lungs, but it was no use. Oh God, her life was so fucked up, she'd never be able to get herself back on track.

Dare squeezed her hands. "Look at me."

She tilted her head, eventually settling her gaze on his piercing green eyes. They reminded her so much of Trey's that her heart twisted, and she squeezed her own eyes shut. Would they be forced to break up over this? She loved him so much. How would she survive without him?

"Reagan, look at me," Dare said, his soothing voice the calm in the churning waters trying to drown her.

Reagan forced her eyes open, and this time she was able to hold his gaze.

"Breathe," he insisted, taking deep breaths with her to remind her how to do what he asked.

After a moment of taking deep breaths in and releasing them slowly, she stopped shaking.

"Better?" Dare asked.

"No," she said truthfully. She could take a million deep and calming breaths, but she doubted she'd ever be able to think rationally again.

Ethan burst into the room, his dark eyes scanning the space quickly, and after spotting her, rushed to her side. "What's going on?" he asked as he pulled her off the sofa and into his arms.

"She's ruined me," Reagan said. "I trusted her, and she destroyed my credibility, my relationship, my career."

"Who?" Ethan said, his body stiff with anger, his arms tightening around her. She clung to him. He was exactly what she needed. He never questioned her reasoning, just supported her through every horrible pile of shit life threw her way. He was always there for her. Always.

"Reagan," Steve said as he crossed the room from the door he'd just entered. He laid a hand on her shoulder, but she shied away from it, pushing herself even closer to Ethan. "I know it seems bad now, but this will pass. Your life isn't over. People forget scandals quickly. You just have to wait it out until the next celebrity does something worse than whatever it is you're accused of doing."

"How the fuck would you know?" Reagan said.

Dare snorted. "Oh, he knows. He was completely trashed by the tabloids during his divorce."

"And at the time, I thought my life was over," Steve said. "The slurs against my character just kept piling up and piling on. At one point I was assured I was the worst man who ever lived. And now it's old news. No one cares."

"You're not helping," Ethan said to Steve. "Reagan obviously cares. And when I find out who did this—"

"You'll what?" Steve said, getting into Ethan's face. "Kick her ass?"

Reagan was used to being sandwiched between two men, but having Steve so close behind her made her uncomfortable enough to drop her arms from Ethan's body and try to get away. Ethan wouldn't have it, however.

"I might," Ethan said.

"If anyone gets to kick her ass, it's me," Reagan said. She was usually a good judge of character, but she'd been completely wrong about Toni Nichols.

"You'll just make things worse," Steve said. "Don't make a scene. Stay quiet, keep your head down, and lick your wounds quietly. If you ignore the shitstorm, it'll blow over quickly."

"That's your advice?" She turned to glare at him, unable to fathom that someone who'd also been smeared by the tabloids would suggest she meekly take this fucking bullshit without a fight.

"It's good advice, Reagan," Max said, crossing his arms across his chest. "I know reading negativity about yourself is infuriating and your first instinct is to fight back, but you can't win against the media. They'll crush you into the dirt if you try. I know you think it's bad now, but it can always become a lot worse."

"Whose side are you all on?" she asked, tears flooding her eyes.

"Yours," Steve said. "Logan's little lamb will never work in this industry again. We'll make sure of it."

Steve's promise was little consolation. Everything Reagan held dear had been destroyed by the traitorous bitch and she got fired for it? Big whoop.

The dressing room door opened, and Toni stepped inside. Her pleased little smile sent rage boiling through Reagan's veins. She dashed across the room and slammed both palms into Toni's chest, sending her stumbling backward into the wall.

Reagan clenched her hands into fists, not sure if it was to keep her from strangling the life out of Toni or to use them to punch the startled look off Toni's face.

"How could you?" Reagan screamed at her. "I trusted you. I stood up for you. How could you do this to me?"

Toni's eyes widened—a clear sign of her guilt. *Yes, bitch, you've been caught.*

"What?" Toni said, her gaze shifting from one person to another. "I don't understand what's going on."

Reagan snatched a copy of the *American Inquirer* from beneath Butch's arm and shoved it in Toni's face. "You sold our secrets to the tabloids."

Toni actually seemed to be reading the headlines. Was she *that* proud of her accomplishment? With a growl of rage, Reagan crumpled the paper and shouted, "What do you have to say for yourself?"

Toni's gentle brown eyes appeared enormous behind her thick glasses as she lifted her face to Reagan's. Her skin had gone ashen. Even her lips were pale. If she was worried that Reagan was about to rip her arms off and beat her with them, it was a legitimate concern.

"Those are terrible," the traitor said. "Awful. But I didn't . . ."

Reagan's jaw ached as she clenched her teeth. Toni didn't even have the guts to own up to what she'd done?

Toni's lips trembled as she whispered, "I wouldn't . . ."

Bull-fucking-shit!

"Don't you dare fucking lie about it!" Reagan shouted. "Don't you fucking lie!" Someone—probably Ethan—squeezed her arm. But it wasn't the strong hand holding her back that gave her pause. It was the tears in Toni's eyes. Her features crumpled, and she inhaled a ragged breath. It was as if Reagan were seeing someone who felt the way she felt—like her dreams were shattered, her life was over, and she'd never be happy again. There was one difference, though. Toni deserved to feel that way.

"Get your shit off the bus and get out of here," Steve said. "We never want to see you again."

"Butch," Max said, his tone authoritative and laced with finality.

Butch stepped forward and bodily removed Toni from the room.

Reagan could hear her protests out in the corridor. "Butch, you have to listen to me. I didn't *sell* any information to the tabloids. I swear."

Oh? Had she handed over the band's secrets for free? That was even worse.

Reagan turned and found herself crushed into Ethan's broad chest. The only thing that could have been better than Ethan's devoted support would have been having Trey there as well. And she knew if Trey hadn't been onstage when this all had gone down, he'd have been in her corner too, just as she wanted to be there for them whenever she was needed.

"So . . . Who wants to tell Logan?" Steve asked. "Not it!"

Reagan cringed. As much as she despised Toni, she cared about Logan's feelings. She knew how much he loved Toni. In the short weeks he'd known her, he'd completely entwined his life and his heart with hers. Reagan didn't volunteer to deliver the news.

"Where is he anyway?" Dare asked.

Ethan pressed a kiss to Reagan's hair and lifted his head. "He's onstage with Sinners."

Reagan frowned and tipped her head back to see his face. "What? Did something happen to Jace?"

Ethan shook his head. "He's not playing bass. He's singing."

"Singing?" That made absolutely no sense.

"Sed got news that his father died just as they were going on stage," Ethan said. "He was so choked up, he couldn't sing, so Logan sent him home and started some karaoke with Sinners to entertain the fans."

Steve laughed. "Anything to get himself in the spotlight."

"I think it's sweet of him," Reagan said.

Ethan extended a hand toward Max. "I was on my way here to ask Max if he'd like to participate and sing a few Sinners songs when Steve grabbed me in the corridor to deal with Reagan."

"*Deal* with me?" Reagan arched an eyebrow at him.

"His words, not mine," Ethan said.

"Of course I'll help out," Max said, crossing the room in several long strides.

"Is Sed okay?" Reagan asked Ethan as they followed Max and the others toward the stage.

"He's really torn up," Ethan said.

"And Trey?"

"You know how he looks up to Sed. The whole band does."

Trey would be beyond upset if Sed was hurting. Sed had helped him through a very difficult period in his life. She didn't want to pile on to Trey's troubles by telling him about the mess they were in—that *she* was in. The article hadn't said anything bad about Trey, just that he was clueless about his whore of a girlfriend's affair with her bodyguard. But she didn't want Trey to find out about the news secondhand either. She'd find a way to tell him. Gently. She wanted him to hear the story in conjunction with the ready support of someone who loved him and not in the harsh, soul-crushing manner she'd been informed.

"What did the tabloid say about you?" Ethan asked. "Was it really that bad?"

Reagan bit her lip, the limited words she'd read echoing through her head. "It wasn't good."

Ethan tugged her against his side and pressed a kiss to her temple. "We'll get through it."

"You really *are* cheating on Trey?" Some woman Reagan didn't recognize sputtered at her from a few yards down the corridor. "Are you stupid? Don't you know there are hundreds of women who would jump at the opportunity to call him theirs?"

"Only hundreds?" Reagan smirked. "Try *thousands*. And it's none of your business, but I'm not cheating on him." It's not cheating if he knows about it and encourages it and *participates*, she wanted to scream at the clueless woman. But she knew that would only make the mess worse. Maybe Steve and the other guys really had been offering sound advice.

"I just saw him kiss you." The woman pointed at Ethan.

"I've had a very trying day," Reagan said, "and he's being supportive."

"Why don't you see your way out of here before I'm forced to remove you from the premises?" Ethan said, his voice hard as steel.

"By what authority?"

"By *my* authority," Butch said, nodding at Ethan. "Not that he needs it."

The woman scowled at Butch and trounced off. "Should I know her?" Reagan asked.

"Local event coordinator. So, no, not really. She's always a pain in the ass," Butch said. "Every time we come through Albuquerque she's mouthing off to someone. Where's Logan? I figure it's time I tell him about Toni."

Reagan gaped at him. "You're volunteering?"

One corner of Butch's mouth twitched beneath his mustache. "It's in my job description."

"Telling the band's bass player that his girlfriend is a backstabbing cunt is in your job description?" Reagan had thought her contract with the band was ridiculous, but Butch definitely had it worse than she did.

"Delivering bad news," Butch said. He lifted his eyebrows in a hopeful expression. "Maybe this doesn't count."

"It's definitely bad news," Reagan said.

Butch's shoulders sagged forward. "That's what I was afraid of."

The lead singer of opening band Twisted Element was currently onstage with Sinners, singing an interesting version of their hit song "Twisted"—fitting, she supposed—and Logan had seemingly vanished. Trey kept glancing toward Reagan and Ethan standing in the wings and watching the unusual performance. She couldn't tell if he knew about the tabloid yet, or if he was looking to them for support over the ordeal his band was going through. Reagan would definitely call the butchery of the hit song's signature battle cries an ordeal. And the band would be lost without their front man. Sed was far more than a lead singer to them all. He was a friend and their leader.

When the song ended and Max headed onto the stage to rescue Sed's microphone from Twisted Element's lead singer, the crowd went wild.

"Thank you, Tobias, for that inspired cover of 'Twisted!'" Max's voice came through the speakers. He approached Trey, tilted his microphone away, and whispered into his ear. The smile Trey always sported onstage dropped from his face, and his eyes met Reagan's. He nodded curtly and headed toward the wings. Reagan groaned inwardly. So much for gently telling Trey about the tabloids. Brian caught his arm as he passed and asked him something, but Trey pulled free and kept walking.

When he reached the side of the stage, he took Reagan's face between his hands and stared into her eyes. "Are you okay?"

"I'm trying to be," she said, her heart thudding with a mix of anxiety over the shitstorm she was currently caught up in and gratitude that she had not one but two supportive men who loved her. True, many of her problems were caused by having two men, but she'd rather weather the storm with them both than be without either.

"How are you holding up?" she asked, reaching for Trey's hand and giving it a squeeze.

"Don't worry about me. This shit doesn't bother me in the least."

Well that made one of them.

Trey pulled free of Reagan's grip and patted Ethan's arm. Reagan could see Trey struggle with his urge to be more affectionate, more passionate. He must continually battle to keep those tendencies—as they pertained to Ethan—locked inside. Reagan wondered if it would make their situation better or worse if they just came out and told everyone that they were all invested in each other. Worse, she decided immediately, her heart heavy and her eyes aching.

"I need to finish our set," Trey said. "Take a few minutes to pull yourself together before you go on."

Reagan's stomach lurched. They wouldn't expect her to perform tonight, would they? She realized at once that they would.

How would she face a crowd that thought she had to fuck her way into the band? A crowd that thought she was capable of cheating on the wonder that was Trey Mills? She nodded and accepted Trey's kiss. She wasn't going to let what that tabloid said about her rattle her confidence—shaky as it had been before this fiasco had been unleashed. No, she was going to hold her head high and show the world that her personal life might be a bit unorthodox, but no one could refute that she was a talented musician. She poured her soul into those six strings. And her music was all that was—or should be—important to the public. Trey's gaze met Ethan's, and they exchanged one of those telepathic kisses they'd been forced to perfect over the past few weeks.

Forced to accept because Reagan had insisted upon it.

It was her fault they couldn't show affection in public. Or maybe it was the public's fault for being close-minded. Or her fault for believing that the public would never accept their relationship. Did it even matter whose fault it was? When Trey turned to dash across the stage to his position, Reagan felt like her heart was being torn in two. Half was affixed firmly to Trey as he hurried away, the other half to Ethan standing beside her. But what choice did it have when the two of them were forced to be apart? Even if their separation was needed to maintain a ruse, it had to tear at them as much as it did her.

"Have you seen Toni?" Logan asked. "She was here a few minutes ago."

So he still didn't know that the woman he loved was a back-stabbing traitor.

"She's gone for good," Reagan said, crossing her arms over her chest. "We fired her."

Logan blinked at her, his eyebrows scrunching together. "What are you talking about?"

"Let Butch explain it to you," Reagan said. "If I so much as hear that woman's name again, I'm going to hurt someone."

"I don't under—"

"Find Butch," Ethan said. He wrapped an arm around Reagan's back and tugged her to his side. Logan scowled at Ethan's harshness, but turned and asked someone if they'd seen Butch.

Reagan tried to concentrate on Max singing Sinners' well-loved ballad "Goodbye is Not Forever"—though his voice wasn't as deep as Sed's sultry baritone, Max sounded amazing—but her gaze seemed determined to affix itself to Trey. He was playing his guitar as he was supposed to, but his attention was focused inward and his expression was tight and grim. He wasn't playing from his heart the way he usually did. Not even Brian could draw a smile from him. Reagan couldn't stand to see him like that.

"Are you going to get ready for the show?" Ethan asked.

She'd forgotten she still had to perform as soon as Sinners' impromptu karaoke set was over. "I don't think I can do it." She cringed when she realized she'd voiced her fear.

Ethan's arm slid up her back and pressed her more securely to his side. "I know you can do it. I'm sorry I got us into this mess."

"You?" Reagan caught his troubled gaze and shook her head at him.

"If I hadn't suggested I could fulfill Trey . . ." He was speaking quietly, but still he checked to see if anyone was listening.

"If anyone is at fault, it's me," she said. "I allowed it so I wouldn't lose him." She pressed her hands into her eyes so she wouldn't cry. She was glad things had turned out as they had and that they'd forged a committed relationship between the three of them. Using Ethan for sex, which had been their original plan, wouldn't have been fair to him and her heart wouldn't have allowed it. He meant too much to her. He always had. The time they'd spent as only friends and roommates hadn't changed how she'd felt about him. She'd never stopped loving him. She understood that now.

By the time Sinners' set was over, Ethan had lent her enough strength to perform. She wasn't strong enough to change into her usual sexed-up stage costume and have her hair and makeup done.

Tonight the fans would be seeing the rawest version of Reagan, the version she preferred. She didn't think she was capable of being fake both onstage and in the public version of her romantic relationship, so if she had to be seen as a slut to protect Ethan and Trey from being outed, she sure as hell wasn't going to pretend she was a rock diva tonight. Worn blue jeans, combat boots, a black T-shirt that read Fuck Authority, no makeup and bed hair. Yep, that was the look she was embracing this evening.

"You're going on like that?" Butch asked when she showed up near the entrance that led to their start positions under the stage.

"You got a problem with that?" she asked.

Butch stepped back and raised both hands in surrender. "Nope."

"I can't believe she'd do something like that," Logan said to Steve as they hooked up Logan's bass guitar.

"She had us all fooled," Steve said, patting him on the back. "Don't beat yourself up for being a tool."

"It doesn't make any sense, though," Logan said. "She loved this job. She wanted to make a career of it. Even if she didn't like any of you . . ."

Reagan noticed that he'd left himself out of his rationalization.

". . . she still wouldn't jeopardize her future career for a few lousy bucks."

"Give it a rest, will you?" Steve said. "She played you for a sucker. She's not the first woman to fuck you over. She won't be the last."

Logan shook his head. "But—"

"Will you stop fucking talking about her?" Reagan shouted.

Both men stepped back and raised their hands in surrender. Jeez, was she really *that* scary?

Dare squeezed her shoulder. "Where did Trey wander off to? Is he okay with all of this?"

"I sent him to Sinners' bus with Ethan." Because she couldn't stand to look at his forlorn expression without being able to comfort him. Trey Mills should never look depressed. He should only look sexy and mischievous and like he didn't have a care in the world. Reagan just had to figure out how to get him back to that place of carefree happiness.

Dare nodded as though he understood, but he looked almost as excited to perform tonight as Reagan felt about it as he flipped his guitar strap over his head and released a deep sigh.

Fucking tabloids. Dare had been hurt by that rash of articles too. He was just taking it better than Reagan had.

"Maybe someone else wrote those articles," Logan said, still on his mission to defend Toni. "Do you have proof that she wrote them?"

Max grabbed him by one arm and shook him. "Open your goddamned eyes, Logan! Did anyone else have access to all that information?"

Logan stared up at him, his blue eyes wide. Max was always so calm and cool. Reagan had never seen him the least bit upset about anything.

"Did anyone besides Toni know all those details?" Max asked.

"You," Logan said. "And all of us."

"Are you suggesting that one of us told the tabloids about Vic?"

Logan cringed. "Of course not."

"We've managed to keep that story a secret for how many years?" Max asked, his nose an inch from Logan's. Reagan was starting to feel bad for the guy. She sure as hell wouldn't want to be on Max's bad side. And Logan hadn't done anything wrong. Except fall for a back-stabbing bitch.

"I don't know," Logan said. "Ten years or so. What does it matter?"

"Because Toni Nichols is the only one outside of the band who learned about my involvement with Vic. And a couple weeks later, that little tidbit is published in the goddamned *American Inquirer*. Coincidence?"

"Maybe." Logan said, slapping Max's hand off his arm.

"She fucked you in more way than one, Lo," Steve said, his voice defeated. "She fucked us all."

"She's not like that!" Logan insisted.

Steve rolled his eyes at him. "I don't mean she literally spread her legs and fucked us. I meant—"

"Of course she didn't," Logan blurted. "She also wouldn't hurt any of us on purpose. She's kind and gentle and loving and . . . and *loyal*."

"You are delusional," Steve said. "You better get your shit together before we fire you too."

Logan crossed his arms over his chest and scowled. "Whatever."

Reagan sidled up to Logan and patted him on the arm. "No one blames you."

"Of course no one blames me," he snapped.

His temper threw Reagan off guard. He was usually so cheerful. This was a side of Logan she'd never seen.

"And no one should blame her either."

"Did you see what she wrote about you?" Steve said. "Besides where she insinuated that we're gay." He leaned in close and made a biting motion next to Logan's ear. "With each other."

Logan shook his head, his normally tanned complexion pale and waxy. "What did it say?"

"It wasn't nice," Dare said. "Let's get onstage. Everything real seems less important from up there."

The five of them shambled under the stage and found their respective places. A few moments later, Steve's drum platform began to rise out of the stage behind Reagan. Her heart would typically be racing with anticipation and excitement. Tonight, however, while she felt obligated to do her best, she wasn't eager to get her place in the spotlight. Maybe she could hide out under the stage and play her guitar out of sight. Before she could hop off her platform and secure a handy hiding spot, the metal plate beneath her shook and began its ascent. She played the proper notes of the song's riff, but found she was abusing the strings as her rage boiled over into her music. *Have to sleep my way into the band, my ass*, she thought as her instrument wailed in perfect harmony with Dare's lead. *I might be a lot of things, but talentless isn't one of them, you fucking bitch.*

The crowd cheered as Max was launched upward out of the stage floor and landed in a semi-crouched position, the note he carried reverberating through the stadium. Max might be capable of impregnating a bandmate's girlfriend, but he was an amazing performer. And even if Dare had hated Max in the past, his skill on the guitar was unmatched. That was what should matter, not their personal lives. Not their looks or who they were fucking. Their talent. Their ability to perform and make music that touched the world.

Logan might have horrible taste in women, but when he played that bass, it made every inch of Reagan's body throb to his infectious rhythm. She couldn't be the only woman in the room who got off on that feeling. And, sure, Steve could be a dick, and she didn't really believe he was gay, but who fucking cared if he was? His drumming was phenomenal. Why did people read that garbage? Why did they slur the celebrities that brought them entertainment? Even if they didn't like metal music and saw no value in its dark, heavy sound and passionate lyrics, the musicians were still people. They had feelings.

I have feelings, she thought, punishing her guitar with an even heavier hand to keep her tears in check.

Fuck them all. It was her life, and she'd live it how she wanted to.

When the song ended, Reagan lifted her head, surprised to find herself live in concert. The crowd cheered with their usual enthusiasm, but she stepped back into the darkest recesses of the stage just outside the perimeter of the brightly lit drum kit to catch her breath and collect her thoughts. Dare offered her a pleased smile and a thumbs-up. She had no idea why.

"That's our Reagan," she heard Max say over the sound system. "A more badass version."

Badass? More like pissed off.

"You can't believe everything you read in the tabloids," Max said.

Reagan shrank back into the darkness several more steps. She'd hoped no one in the audience had read the articles yet. No such luck.

"I appreciate that," Max said.

Who was he talking to? Someone in the crowd? Reagan couldn't hear a thing.

"We made amends long ago," Dare said into his microphone. "It's not going to break up the band."

Apparently the fans were concerned about tension between Max and Dare over Vic. And yeah, she was sure that was far more important to the fans than finding out their temporary rhythm guitarist spread her legs for two men. At least the article hadn't blatantly claimed that she took them simultaneously.

"I can't speak for Trey," Dare said.

Reagan still couldn't hear what the fans were asking, so she eased forward, taking her earpiece out and straining for the thread of the conversation.

Logan was standing off to the side, near the stage wing, staring at the floor and shaking his head. She could only imagine the thoughts swirling through his mind. She felt bad for him. Toni had betrayed all of them, but they'd get over it. Reagan wasn't sure if Logan ever would. He'd fallen for Toni hard. His heart must be breaking.

"For the last time," Steve yelled from behind his drum kit, "I'm not gay. I get more pussy than a crazy cat lady on free-pet adoption day."

"Would you stop listening to Exodus End's music if he was gay?" Reagan yelled at the crowd, her emotions so overwhelming that her hands were shaking. "Our private lives are none of your fucking business! We're here to rock, not have a discussion."

"What do *you* know?" someone yelled from the audience. "You're not even a real member of the band!"

Reagan didn't see which loud-mouthed guy yelled those hurtful words, but they struck her in the chest hard enough to steal her breath. She couldn't argue; he was correct. But it still hurt to always be the outsider.

"Reagan's right—we're here to rock," Max said. "Time to crank, crank, crank it up." He made a twisting motion with his free hand, shaking his perfect leather-clad ass to the beat in his head.

Signaling the start of "Crank," Steve slammed one of his bass drums so hard, Reagan jumped. She hurriedly shoved her earpiece back into place and played the rapid, repetitive riff that carried the hard and gritty song. She watched the jeering crowd, wondering how many of them wished she would disappear so Max could reclaim rhythm guitar. She wasn't sure when she started thinking of the fans as her enemies, but she was no longer playing to delight them. She was playing to show them that she belonged on this stage, that she was good enough. She wasn't a phony, Reagan Elliot was the real deal, and if they still denied her skill after this performance, they were flat out *wrong*.

At the end of the song, Reagan reached for a bottle of water and took several swigs between gasps for air. She'd never played so hard in her life.

"Reagan is on fire tonight," Max said.

She smiled slightly and took another drink. She kept up the same pace through the entire performance. As they took their final bows after the encore, she clenched and unclenched her aching fingers. Trailing behind the others as they exited the stage, she examined her fingertips, which felt unusually raw and sore. She winced at the spots of blood seeping through the crack in her middle finger. She usually expended plenty of sweat while she played, but tonight she'd added a few tears and even some blood. If that was what it took to prove her fretwork spoke for itself, then she'd gladly bleed all over the stage.

"Are you riding with Sinners?" Dare asked as they wound their way down the corridor to their dressing room.

She shook her head. "They've already left."

"Trey didn't stay behind to be with you?"

"He needed a quiet place to think. I sent him and Ethan ahead. I'll meet up with them at the hotel tonight."

"He missed seeing you at your finest," Dare said, his smile wide. She was pretty sure that was pride shining in his eyes.

She shrugged, though it felt damned good that he'd noticed she'd put her all into that performance. "I guess I should always play pissed off."

The after-parties had been canceled out of respect for Sed's loss. No one felt like celebrating anyway, not even party addict Steve Aimes. They trudged toward the bus, ready to put Albuquerque behind them. Reagan couldn't wait to snuggle between Ethan and Trey later tonight and forget how cold the world outside their embrace could be.

She'd just put her foot on the bottom step when the familiar voice of Toni Nichols carried across the parking lot.

"Logan!" she yelled again, struggling in the arms of some security guard who'd caught her around the waist and was doing his damnedest to keep her from getting any closer.

Reagan clenched both hands into fists and turned to take out some of her rage on the one responsible for her foul mood. Dare blocked her path with his arm.

"Get on the bus," he said quietly while Toni screamed for Logan to listen to her, claiming her innocence in a gut-wrenching wail.

Reagan forced her feet up the steps, Dare's hand at the small of her back reminding her in which direction she should be moving.

"Logan," Dare said to the ashen-faced bassist behind him. "Don't fall for her lies. Walk away."

Logan closed his eyes and took a deep breath before stepping onto the bus. The door swung shut behind him and he turned, pressing his forehead against the inside of the door. He closed his eyes, his hand curled, fingertips digging into the surface beside his crumpled face. There was a loud thud on the door's opposite side, and Reagan could hear Toni shouting and the repetitive beating of hands on the side of the bus, but she couldn't hear what Toni was saying. Eventually the bus left the wolf in lamb's clothing behind. And though Logan looked as if they were dragging his heart along the asphalt behind them, Reagan was glad she didn't have to deal with Toni anymore. Damn, the woman was a good liar. If Reagan hadn't known better, she'd have thought Toni wasn't responsible for the mess they were in. But the evidence was irrefutable. The tabloid's mole couldn't have been anyone else. How could a friend be so cruel?

CHAPTER
7

E THAN PUSHED a beer across the table to Trey and slid into the bench across from him. Sed and Jessica had taken a flight home. Brian and his family, along with Jace and Aggie—who apparently did a lot of sewing for her corset business—were in the motorhome that followed Sinners' bus everywhere. Eric and Rebekah had stayed behind to help with tear down, Rebekah making sure the sound system was packed just so while Eric mostly made a nuisance of himself. So besides the driver, tonight it was just him and Trey on the bus. Which was good. Maybe Ethan could find it in himself to talk.

Ethan had read all the articles in the tabloid twice, and while he was called out as the villain—sleeping with another man's girlfriend—and Trey was depicted as a clueless but loveable twit, Reagan had been completely trashed. And not just in the article about her sex life with two men. Her integrity had been questioned. Her talent had been crucified. She was a strong woman, but anyone would crumble beneath that much condemnation.

"We should have waited for Reagan." Trey took a long swallow from his beer.

"She told us to go ahead without her." But Ethan had been thinking the same thing.

"What should we do? It isn't fair that she's taken the fall for something we're all equally involved in."

"What do you suggest?"

Trey gnawed on his lip. "I don't know. Do you think it would help if we came out?"

Ethan felt as if a heavy fist just slammed him in the chest. "Came *out* out?"

Trey nodded.

"As gay?" Just making sure here.

Trey shrugged. "I was thinking we both come out as bisexual, but we could pretend we're gay and claim that Reagan doesn't sleep with either of us. She's just trying to cover our forbidden relationship. We'll pretend she's our beard."

Trey's foot pressed against Ethan's beneath the table.

"I think that would make things worse," Ethan said. And he didn't want the world to know he slept with *both* women and men. His family would never speak to him again. The thought of coming out as gay was daunting enough, but coming out as bisexual? Not happening.

"We should just tell the truth."

"How would that help anything? Reagan would still be sleeping with two different men. They'd just know that we're sleeping with each other too."

"This isn't just about fucking," Trey said. "It's much more complicated than that."

"I know that and you know that and Reagan knows that, but how will the rest of the world see what we have?"

"If they're smart, they'll realize we're in love."

Ethan snorted. "That will never happen and you know it."

"So what do you suggest we do?"

"Stage a huge breakup between you and Reagan. You just found out she's been sleeping with her bodyguard behind your back. You should dump her, if for no other reason than to save face."

Trey slammed his beer on the table. "I'm not breaking up with her because of this."

Ethan shook his head. "I don't mean for real. If the tabloids want a story, give them a story. But don't tell them the truth."

"How am I supposed to act around her if everyone thinks we've just broken up?"

"Distant," Ethan said. "And it won't be easy. I should know."

Trey's hand slid across the table, and he trailed his fingertips over Ethan's knuckles. "I know it hurts you to have to pretend we're not involved when we're in public."

Ethan nodded, his gaze trained on the table in front of him.

"Will it make you feel better if I have to pretend as well?"

Ethan lifted his gaze to Trey's. No, he didn't want Trey to feel the same disconnect that he was forced to endure for the sake of public scrutiny. "Of course not. I just don't see any other solution."

Trey sighed and scratched his nose. "Maybe Reagan has an idea."

"Is she still onstage? We could call her. Ask her if she thinks dumping you is a good idea." Ethan winked at him to let him know he was joking.

Trey snapped his fingers and pointed at Ethan's chest. "I have an idea. We could release a sex tape. I volunteer to be in the middle. It will put all the public's focus on *my* obvious perversion."

Ethan chuckled. "How sweet of you to sacrifice yourself for the common good."

"I promise to yell how much I love you both as I'm fucking her and being fucked by you."

Lust curled low in Ethan's belly as his thoughts fast-forwarded a few hours to when he could be alone with both of his lovers and participate in exactly what Trey was suggesting. Yet Ethan pushed his desire to the back burner to simmer. Trey would sate his lust if Ethan showed his sudden need, but he knew Reagan was bothered when they made love without her. She seemed to be under the impression that if she weren't present, he and Trey would decide she wasn't a necessary variable in their equation. She couldn't have been more wrong.

After an hour of discussing possible answers to their dilemma, neither was closer to coming up with a real solution. Hopefully, Reagan had some valuable input. Trey switched on the TV in the lounge and stretched out on the sofa to watch a baseball game, signaling that he was done talking. Ethan joined him, sitting on the end of the sofa and shifting Trey's head onto his thigh. He smiled when Trey unwrapped a cherry sucker and stuck it between his luscious lips, licking and sucking at it as if it were the best thing he'd ever had in his mouth. If the ornery imp kept it up, the desire Ethan had on simmer would be at a rolling boil in no time and he'd put something a little bigger into that mouth of his. Ethan stroked Trey's bangs from his face, far more interested in watching him than any televised ball game. Usually the tour bus was crowded, so Ethan kept his ever-growing affection for Trey locked inside. But sitting alone with him, he didn't bother with the macho façade or feigned disinterest.

"I love you," he murmured, his fingers lost in the silky strands of Trey's hair.

Trey looked up at him and grinned, his smile lighting up his emerald-green eyes. Even the adorable freckles on his nose seemed to brighten with happiness. "Best news I've heard all day."

Ethan's phone rang, and he would have let it go to voicemail if it had been anyone but Reagan. The sound of her ringtone had him digging through his pocket.

"Hey, babe," he answered. "How'd the concert go?"

"The concert was fine," she said. "The rest of the evening sucked balls."

"Did she say she wants to suck our balls?" Trey asked, his devilish grin drawing a smile from Ethan, but he didn't dare laugh. He could tell Reagan was not in the mood for jokes.

"Did you have another run-in with Toni?" He'd never seen Reagan get physically violent with anyone before. He was pretty sure if Butch hadn't hauled the little journalist off when he had, Reagan would have done a lot worse than shove her.

"Not directly, but can you believe Logan is already trying to patch things up with her?"

"Love is blind," Ethan said, tracing Trey's eyebrow and the small hoop piercing it with one fingertip and then brushing over the freckles he adored on Trey's nose.

"He's as much a traitor as she is as far as I'm concerned."

"I'm sure you'll see things differently after you've had a nice bath and a soothing massage and the two men who are the cause of all your troubles make love to you until you can't move."

She released a soft moan. "That sounds perfect."

"We know what you need."

"I wish I was there with you now. Are you at the hotel yet?"

Ethan glanced toward the front windshield of the bus, but couldn't tell where they were. "Not yet, but we're probably getting close. Do you want to talk to Trey?"

"Yeah. Put him on."

Her conversation with Trey was entirely different from the one she'd had with him. She told Trey about the performance and how the fans made her feel and how bad her fingers hurt and other stuff only mutual guitar heroes could commiserate about. Maybe she needed the two of them in her life as much as Ethan needed both Trey and Reagan in his. They didn't only fulfill each other's excessive sexual needs, but also met different emotional needs. Reagan came to him when she needed to feel safe, and she went to Trey when she needed a deeper understanding of all she was going through in the spotlight.

"Make sure you put something on those fingers," Trey said. "And eat something. You'll feel better."

Trey listened to her say something and replied, "I love you too." A few seconds later he added, "I'll tell him." He ended the call and handed Ethan his phone. "She says she loves you and that since she can't be here, she wants you to give me a blow job while I finish watching my ball game."

"She said that, did she?" Ethan said, slipping his phone back into his pocket.

Trey looked up at him through one partially closed eye. "Yep."

"You sure she didn't say you should give me one?"

"I give them to you all the time, E. You almost never—"

Ethan pressed a finger to Trey's lips. "Reagan's had a rough day. I should probably do what she says without arguing."

Ethan slid a hand down Trey's suddenly quivering belly and unfastened his jeans. "Did she say *why* I should give you a blow job?" Ethan teased, knowing damned well this was all Trey's idea.

"Because I've been thinking about it since we moved over to the couch." His eyes drifted closed, and he sucked in a breath when Ethan's hand circled his partially erect dick.

"So she's a mind reader now?" Ethan said, massaging Trey's cockhead, loving how his touch made Trey tremble.

"She must be." Trey moaned as Ethan's thumb rubbed his rim.

"Are you sure she wanted me to use my mouth and not just my hand?" Ethan asked, his grip light as he stroked Trey's shaft.

"I think she wanted you to do both."

"Pull your pants down for me."

Trey lifted his hips and tugged his pants and underwear down to the middle of his thighs. He was far more obedient than Reagan was, and Ethan rewarded him for his unquestioning cooperation by leaning sideways and licking the tip of his cock. Trey's head lifted from Ethan's thigh as he shifted so he could watch. Ethan knew Trey loved it when Reagan sucked him off, but he always went insane when Ethan did it.

Ethan shifted his hand between Trey's legs to gently massage his balls, and then further between them to brush one fingertip against his asshole.

Trey groaned and opened his legs as far as his tangled jeans would allow. Ethan knew he wanted penetration, but it was much more fun for them both if he toyed with him, teased him, and made him beg.

"E," Trey gasped.

Ethan drew the head of Trey's cock into his mouth, sucking gently.

"Oh God." Trey's head dropped back against Ethan's thigh as he thrust his hips upward, pushing himself deeper into Ethan's mouth. Ethan waited until his hips settled back on the sofa before he began to move his head, sucking gently as his mouth rose and fell over Trey's dick. Trey shifted restlessly, lifting his head again to watch. His belly clenched, well-defined abdominal muscles tightening. His fingers touched the back of Ethan's head.

"So sexy," Trey murmured, and Ethan suppressed a grin. Ethan typically liked to dominate, but he recognized how excited Trey became when he took a more submissive role. Ethan's ass clenched with expectation. Just how submissive did he want to go here? He didn't bottom for Trey often, but he was in an unusual mood this evening.

"We should take this back to the bedroom," Ethan said before sucking Trey vigorously accompanied by several rapid bobs of his head.

Trey's fingers clenched in Ethan's hair, only relaxing when Ethan lightened his suction and slowed his strokes. All the while, he continued to massage Trey's balls and tease his ass with his fingertip. The bus slowed, the tone of the engine lowering as they exited the highway.

"I don't think we have time for you to fuck me," Trey said.

"Do we have time for you to fuck me?" Ethan asked.

Trey jerked out of his mouth and rolled off the sofa onto the floor. He held up his pants with one hand and grabbed Ethan's arm with the other. "We'll make time."

Ethan chuckled as he hurried after him.

Had Ethan been in charge, he would have already been pounding his cock into Trey's ass. Fuck, the man turned him on and drove him to become an insatiable beast. But Trey was a different kind of top. Tender. Meticulous. Generous with his touch. Thorough with his tongue. And the brat didn't force Ethan's face into the mattress and fuck him from behind like an animal. Oh no. He had to make Ethan feel as vulnerable as he felt loved. Trey took him face to face, staring deep into his eyes, sliding into him with perfect, painless, deep strokes. Filling him with his body but at the same time stuffing his heart so full of tenderness that Ethan could hardly stand it. Trey paused every now and then to kiss him, but the hand he had wrapped around Ethan's cock never stopped moving. Even though Trey's thrusts were slow and careful, his hand tugged and stroked relentlessly—faster and faster—drawing Ethan ever closer to his peak. Ethan figured only a musician could play a man's body so perfectly—maintaining two separate and intensely pleasurable rhythms simultaneously. And fuck it all, Ethan was in love with *two* musicians. How blessed was he?

The speed of Trey's hand finally hit Ethan's sweet spot, and he couldn't fight orgasm no matter how much he wanted the pleasure to continue. Deep pulsations of bliss drew a groan from his throat. His entire body went taut, and he erupted with a hard shudder. As soon as Ethan started spurting, Trey's thrusts changed from gentle and deep to hard and shallow.

Dear God, he couldn't stop coming. He lifted his head and forced his eyes open, stunned that gallons of cum weren't shooting from his dick. His belly was covered with his own sticky mess, so his body shouldn't still be shuddering with orgasm. What the fuck was happening to him?

Ethan closed his eyes and stopped trying to fight the pleasure ripping through him. He decided the reason he was coming so hard was because Trey was bumping into his prostate with each perfectly angled thrust. If Ethan survived this, he'd have to try the same technique on Trey in the future.

"Now are you sorry you never let me top?" Trey asked as his tugging hand and driving cock kept Ethan suspended in a euphoric state far beyond his usual point of bliss. "Or are you afraid of coming this long and this hard?"

Afraid? Not exactly. But he couldn't take any more, and he feared the only way to get Trey to stop was to make him come. Finding strength in his sated body, he flipped Trey onto his back, stripped the condom from Trey's cock, and sucked him into his mouth.

"Oh fuck," Trey groaned, clinging to Ethan's head with both hands. Within seconds he filled Ethan's mouth with thick, salty cum. Ethan swallowed and sucked harder, making sure Trey had given him every drop, before he dropped onto the bed beside him and lay gasping, not sure he'd ever be able to catch his breath again.

"You give the best head," Trey said with a breathless laugh. "I love that you swallow."

"And I hate that you don't," Ethan countered.

"Someday," Trey said, shifting his attention to the far wall. "Maybe."

"And someday maybe you need to show me how to get that perfect angle when I fuck you."

"That's a secret I'll never share," he said.

"Then I'll go to the source. Who taught you how to do that?"

The teasing smile on Trey's face vanished, and he sat up, searching the room until he spotted his discarded T-shirt and grabbed it. "We should probably get going." The bus had stopped moving a while ago, but no one had knocked on the bedroom door to bother them.

Ethan tackled Trey to the bed and peered into his troubled green eyes. "Who taught you that? Was it an exotic prince? A world-class athlete? A well-traveled truck driver? Tell me. I won't be jealous."

"Yeah, you will. You're totally the jealous type."

"I'm not."

"It was Brian."

Ethan's jaw hardened. Okay, so now he was a liar. He was totally fucking jealous.

"He did that to me when he took my virginity. I've never been the same since."

The strength went out of Ethan's arms, and Trey easily slipped from his grasp. He rolled to his feet and found his clothes.

"Were you thinking of him while you were fucking me, Trey?" He had to have been at some level. And why was that always Ethan's first thought? He was on a hopeless loop of wondering just how magnificently Brian Sinclair must have fucked Trey all those years ago to keep him hopelessly in love with him for so long.

"This again?" Trey shook his head and jerked his boxers up his legs. "I wasn't thinking of him, but what difference would it make if I had been?"

Ethan hated that he was jealous. He needed to vanquish the hateful green demon inside him. He pressed the heels of his hands into his eyelids and took several calming breaths.

"He should have never let you go," Ethan said.

"But he did. He let me go a long time ago, E. And though I've finally let him go too, we'll always be friends. We'll always joke around and we'll always touch when we play guitar solos together, so you might as well stop trying to glare him dead when we're performing."

Ethan snorted. "You noticed that, huh?"

"Yeah, I noticed." Trey slipped on a sock and rammed his foot into his shoe.

"I don't know why I'm so jealous of him. It drives me crazy when he's anywhere near you."

Trey stood next to the bed fully dressed and stared down at him. "You have cum all over your belly."

Ethan slapped a hand in the sticky goo. "It's all over my hand too."

Trey handed him a container of wet wipes and sat on the bed beside him, watching him clean himself up.

"I don't know how to help you get past your jealousy," Trey said.

Ethan shook his head. "You don't have to. It's my issue, not yours."

"I have to be honest. If Brian ever left Myrna and decided he wanted another go at my ass . . ."

Ethan's hand stopped mopping at his stomach. The one that suddenly housed a nest of angry hornets.

". . . I'd tell him to dream on." Trey grinned at him. "This ass belongs to Ethan Conner and no one else." He pointed to his backside and yelled in surprise when Ethan yanked him into his arms and hugged him fiercely against his chest. Ethan kissed his hair, wondering if it was possible to love someone as much as he loved Trey. Yeah, it was totally possible. He loved Reagan just as much. Which reminded him . . .

"We probably shouldn't tell Reagan I let you top me tonight while she was stuck on the bus with her band."

"She'll just be sorry she missed it," Trey said, his words muffled against Ethan's chest.

"She'll feel left out. And I promised her we'd center our attention on her tonight."

"We will," Trey said. "I bet I can make her come harder than you can."

"I'll take that bet. What prize goes to the victor?"

"Whoever wins gets to be top the next time we're alone together."

Ethan chuckled and gave him a tight squeeze before releasing him. "Then I might have to lose this one," he said.

CHAPTER
8

TREY LIFTED Reagan's foot from the steaming bathtub water and gently kissed the instep before reaching for the bar of soap. Somehow Ethan had gotten the superior duty of washing her breasts, which didn't seem quite fair. Boobs were way more fun to play with than feet. But Reagan seemed to be enjoying their attention. She no longer looked like she wanted to stab everyone around her.

"You're both so good to me," she said, a fresh flood of tears pooling in her eyes. "How did I get to be so lucky?"

Ethan brushed a tear from her cheek and kissed the spot gently. "We're the lucky ones."

Trey ducked his head to hide a grin. Their tough guy was excellent at coddling Reagan when she needed it. Ethan could be tender when called upon or be the rock they were more accustomed to.

Trey wondered how often Reagan had relied on Ethan for support in the past. Trey hadn't forgotten that Ethan had been the one she'd gone to for help when that whacked-out guitarist, Pyre Vamp, had been threatening her. Trey had been right there beside her, but she'd still called on Ethan—no matter that he'd been hundreds or thousands of miles away—whenever she'd been anxious or frightened. She was starting to come to Trey for other problems, though—problems about her career mostly—so he no longer felt left out. She worked hard at keeping their relationship in balance, while Trey just let things happen. He wasn't sure if either method was advisable for keeping all three of them happy, but they were making up the rules and adjusting them as they went along. Apparently, Ethan claiming her top half while Trey was left with the bottom was one of those unspoken rules. Of course, there were plenty of delightful body parts below Reagan's waist. Trey's hands slid up her ankle and calf on their journey to find more interesting prospects than feet. It was one fetish he'd never understand.

"Trey and I were talking while traveling here on Sinners' bus," Ethan said, his voice deep and calming.

Trey stifled a snort. They'd done far more than talk on that bus.

"What about?" Reagan asked.

"How to get the press off your back."

Her face twisted in displeasure. "I don't want to talk about it right now. Maybe by tomorrow everyone will have forgotten."

Trey cleared his throat. If anything, the situation would snowball and the press would hound Reagan even more. If the paparazzi followed her long enough, they'd soon figure out that the true situation was far more scandalous and juicy—tabloid gold— than what Toni had revealed. It seemed strange to him that a reporter would hold back details. But she was pretty clueless about sex, so maybe she didn't fully understand what was going on between the three of them.

"Did Toni know all three of us are involved?" Trey asked. "She made it clear that you were involved with both of us, but there's nothing about Ethan and me hooking up."

"Hooking up?" Ethan grumbled.

"Being passionately in love," Trey corrected, sending him a love-sick look in apology.

"She knows," Reagan said. "She didn't mention that at all?"

"Did you read the article?" Trey asked.

"Most of it," Reagan said. "But it makes me so angry, I can't seem to get all the way to the end without ripping the pages."

"It says you are involved with both of us," Ethan said. "And focuses on that."

"Nice way to put it," Trey said. "Why would Toni leave out the stuff between Ethan and I? She had no problem claiming that Steve is gay—and he's not or I would have tapped that fine ass long ago."

Ethan shoved him, obviously not appreciating his joke.

"But there's nothing in that article about *my* sexual orientation. I'm just the dumb guy who's too stupid to realize my girlfriend fucks her bodyguard."

"Maybe she's saving it for a future article," Reagan said, sitting up in the tub, obviously no longer in the mood to be spoiled.

Ethan shrugged. "Maybe she's only interested in destroying Exodus End. You're in a different band, Trey."

"If that's really what she's trying to do, why would she leak the information now?" Trey asked. "*Before* she was finished with her assignment? Wouldn't it make more sense for her to wait until it was over? She only had another week, right? She might have dug up more scandals if she'd waited. She had to know she'd be fired for releasing information and then she'd no longer have access to all that dirt she was digging up. Her actions make no sense."

"Nothing she does makes sense," Reagan said. "She's an idiot. And cruel."

Reagan stood, water pouring from her succulent body, and pulled the plug. Ethan hopped to his feet and wrapped her in a towel, scooping her into his arms and carrying her out of the bathroom.

Was Trey the only one who wanted to discuss this right now? He used the edge of the tub to pull himself to his feet.

"Grab another towel," Ethan called to him.

"Yes, master," he grumbled and yanked a spare towel from the rack. He entered the suite's bedroom and tossed the towel at Ethan, who caught it against his chest. Instead of going to the bed, Trey settled into a tub chair in the corner.

"What's your problem?" Ethan asked.

"Same as yours. Same as Reagan's. It's not going to go away just because we wish it would. And we can try to hide the truth—which I know will fail—or we can be reactionary when we're found out—which will be terrible—*or* we can figure out what we're going to do now, before more shit about us comes out."

"Maybe it won't," Reagan said. "Maybe this is the worst of it."

"Tell her your plan, Ethan," Trey said.

"I thought you didn't like my plan."

"I don't like it," Trey said. "I fucking hate it, but I think it will work."

"What plan?" Reagan said, sitting on the edge of the bed and drawing her towel more securely around her body. "You've been making plans without me?"

"We discussed plans," Ethan said. "We didn't make any."

"Let's hear it then."

"Trey needs to break up with you for cheating on him," Ethan said. "Very publicly."

Reagan turned in Trey's direction, her face twisting in anguish. "You're going to break up with me?"

Trey slipped out of the chair and sat beside her on the bed, wrapping an arm around her cool-to-the-touch shoulders. "Not for real. I love you. You know that."

"Our other option is that you fire me and send me packing," Ethan said.

Trey lifted his head to gape at him. They hadn't discussed that plan. That plan would separate them both publicly *and* in private.

"She's not doing that," Trey said. "I'll break up with her, and we'll pretend to hate each other when we happen to be in the same room together in public."

"They'll still think I'm a whore," Reagan said quietly.

"They'll think you made a mistake and had an affair with your irresistibly gorgeous bodyguard. Who wouldn't want to fuck him? I mean, look at the guy."

Ethan grinned at his compliment.

"And then they'll get over it," Trey continued. "People love to trash celebrities, but they also like to forgive them."

Reagan stared down at her hands twisting anxiously in her lap. "Even if it isn't real, if you break up with me again, it would destroy me. I couldn't face it the first time, and I'm far more into this now than I was then."

Trey touched her hair. He didn't want to hurt her. He felt her pain in his own chest. As far as he was concerned, there was only one viable solution to their problem.

"There's a third possibility," Trey said. "We come out—all three of us. We tell the truth."

"Absolutely not," Ethan said.

Wide-eyed, Reagan shook her head. "That's a terrible idea."

Trey knew it was their best option and that they'd survive the backlash together if they were united. But he also knew he was put together a bit differently than his two loves. Trey didn't give a shart what people thought of him. He'd been that way since birth. He'd been bullied relentlessly as a kid for his *weirdness*, but if his spirit hadn't been destroyed by close-minded bigotry in his impressionable youth, a bunch of fucking paparazzi weren't going to break him now that he'd finally found everything he needed in life. No way. But Reagan and Ethan did care how the world saw them, so to protect their feelings, he'd try to bend his don't-like-me-or-those-I-care-about-then-go-fuck-yourself attitude.

"So what do you suggest, Reagan?" Trey asked.

"Wait it out. See if it blows over before we do anything rash."

Trey sighed. In other words, be reactive instead of proactive. Yeah, that never worked, but he knew she was currently more affected than he or Ethan was, so he'd let her have her way and keep scraping her off rock bottom until she figured out how to deal with negative publicity. He hoped she was a fast learner, because being caught up in a slur campaign sucked.

"All right," Trey said, shrugging. "We'll try this your way, but think about our options. They might seem more sensible after you've thought about them for a while."

Reagan leaned into his side. "I'll sleep on it." She turned her head to kiss his neck. "But right now, what I really need . . ."

". . . is to be held and told everything will be all right," Ethan said.

Reagan nodded, tears springing to her eyes again. Trey realized Ethan was loads better at comforting her than he was. As Trey was supposedly the more sensitive man in this relationship, he sure hadn't seen that coming.

Ethan tossed back the covers and climbed between them, tugging Reagan down with him. He pulled her wet towel free and threw it to the floor before pressing her entire body against his. She released a contented sigh and melted into him.

"I don't want to think about the outside world when we're together," she said.

Trey watched the two of them finding comfort in each other and wondered if it really would be best for them all if he broke up with Reagan. For real. He knew he could be happy in this relationship, but he wasn't so sure Reagan and Ethan would ever truly relax and enjoy what they had.

Reagan angled her head to peer up at him, a mischievous smile on her sexy lips. "Well?" she said. "Are you going to join us? According to the paper, one man just isn't enough for me."

"And according to *you*?" Trey asked.

"They got that right." She winked at him.

"And you're okay with them knowing?" He was pushing. He needed to stop doing that.

Ethan patted the mattress behind Reagan's back. "Will you just get in here?"

Trey shook his head and removed his boxers before settling in behind Reagan and cuddling into her back. He pressed a kiss to her shoulder, breathing in her familiar scent mingled with Ethan's.

"I'm sorry I'm overthinking this," Trey murmured. "Maybe it is best to let things happen as they will. We can deal with anything they throw our way as long as we're together."

"Exactly," Reagan said, her hand grasping Trey's hip as she squirmed her round ass into his ever-responsive cock. "I don't want to hear another word about it. I'd rather our mouths be occupied with more enjoyable things."

"Such as my dick?" Ethan chuckled.

"Eventually," she said. "But I recall you promising me a massage after my bath. And then making love to me until I couldn't move."

"I did promise her that," Ethan said.

"I don't remember having a vote in this decision," Trey teased.

"Are you refusing?" Reagan said, her fingertips digging into his hip. "Ethan could probably handle both tasks on his own if you're not up for it."

Trey shifted his hips so she could feel how up for it he already was. "Given the opportunity, I would have voted yes."

Trey scooted back a couple of inches to give Ethan access to her back, while Ethan moved away to give Trey access to her front. Still lying on his side, Trey used his dominant left hand to massage her collarbone, chest, and breast. He was sure her nipple was very tense, so he spent extra time massaging that. Ethan's big hand started at the nape of her neck and slowly moved lower to knead her shoulder and her upper back, but then his arm got caught up with Trey's because Trey wanted to make sure Reagan's nipple was thoroughly relaxed. Of course, the more he rubbed, the less relaxed it—and she—became. Ethan cocked an eyebrow at him, sending him a silent signal to continue his journey down Reagan's front, but when Trey merely smirked at him, Ethan leaned forward and kissed him, squashing Reagan between them. She didn't protest, but lifted her leg to rest on Ethan's hip.

"Trey, you're driving me crazy," she said, twisting slightly so her nipple was no longer beneath the persistent attention of his fingertips. He pulled his mouth free of Ethan's and pressed his forehead to Reagan's shoulder.

"Fine," he said, moving his hand to her ribs, which he massaged lightly, and then to her belly, which made her squirm.

Ethan continued massaging her back, moving slowly lower. The muscles on her left side were probably well relaxed. They'd have to flip her on her other side to finish their task. But as Trey's hand moved lower, over her hip and the top of her thigh, he couldn't stop himself from centering his hand between her legs to massage her clit. He was sure there was plenty of tension coiled in the swollen little nub, and he wasn't going to let up until it had all been released.

Ethan scooted down Reagan's body and looped her leg over his shoulder. Trey didn't have to wonder what Ethan was doing. He felt Ethan's tongue glide against his fingertips as he licked Reagan where Trey was touching her. Trey hoped it wasn't too greedy of him to want a piece of that action. He squirmed down the bed and moved his hips until his cock was nestled in Reagan's hot, wet seam. It didn't take Ethan more than a second to figure out what Trey wanted. His tongue brushed the head of Trey's cock, and Trey shuddered. Trey shifted into a more accessible position, pressed firmly against Reagan's back. Ethan's hand pressed Trey's cockhead up against Reagan's clit, and then Ethan took them both into his mouth, sucking, licking, and massaging their most sensitive flesh with his lush lips. It took a truly talented man to give his boyfriend and his girlfriend head at the same time.

"Jesus," Reagan gasped, her hands tangling in Ethan's hair. "That's amazing. Sexy."

"And I thought I was gifted," Trey said, rocking his hips slightly to increase his pleasure.

Ethan's hand shifted, and he pressed Trey's cock into Reagan's opening. She moaned, encouraging Trey to alter his position so he could thrust up into her. He took her slowly to make it easier for Ethan to keep his mouth on her clit.

"Who would ever give this up once they had it?" she said.

"Not me," Trey said.

Ethan grunted his agreement.

Reagan shuddered as she found her peak.

"Who made you come, Reagan?" Trey asked, remembering the bet he had with Ethan.

"You b-both . . ." she sputtered. "Both are responsible. And don't stop. I want more."

She always wanted more. And he loved that about her. It meant he got more as well.

"Fill me," she said breathlessly. "Both of you."

"How do you want us?" Trey asked. She was in command tonight. Both of their dicks were gladly at her disposal.

"You fuck my ass while I ride him."

"Can do." It was one of his favorite positions since he got the added benefit of rubbing his balls against Ethan's and watching his face when he came. E made the sexiest fucking face when he let go.

Trey pulled out to go in search of lube while Ethan shifted onto his back. He dragged Reagan along with him, holding her pussy to his face as he continued to suck at her clit. The sound of his mouth working her over had Trey's balls throbbing with need.

"Oh God, hurry, Trey," she said.

He dug through their bag and found the tube he was looking for. Reagan's ass was really in for a treat tonight. He then crawled up between Ethan's splayed legs and got into position. Catching Reagan by the hips, he pulled her off Ethan's face. Ethan took a deep breath and then pushed up into a partial sitting position so he could watch Trey claim Reagan's ass. Trey made sure they were all lined up properly before he began. It was easy to break something—most likely one of their dicks—if they had their angles wrong.

Reagan bounced her butt against his cock, eager to take him. He usually filled her slowly, allowing her body to become accustomed to his thickness first before he gradually introduced his length, but her impatience was infectious. A breathless moan tore from her throat as he entered her. He grasped a breast in one hand, her pussy in the other.

"What do you want, Reagan?" His voice was low, words spoken close to her ear. She shuddered and shifted her hips forward and back to drive him in and out of her tight ass.

She whimpered when his finger traced her empty hole.

"What do you want, Reagan?" he repeated, his gaze trained on Ethan, who was watching with his mouth agape and his muscles tense.

"E-ethan."

"You want Ethan?" Trey asked, matching her motions to drive himself deeper into her ass.

"Yes."

Trey shifted his fingertips to her clit, rubbing it with alternate fingers as if he were playing his favorite instrument. He kind of was. "So you want me to stop?"

"N-no."

"You want both of us?"

"Yes!" she hissed.

"You need two cocks to satisfy you, one isn't enough?" He wasn't sure why he needed her to admit that tonight. Maybe because he was starting to worry that she'd decide she could be satisfied with only one of them in her bed. Only one of them in her heart.

She reached down, grabbed Ethan's cock, and angled it into her pussy. Ethan winced and grabbed her ass to slide her forward. Trey squirmed closer, not willing to lose his place inside her.

Reagan found a position—her chest nearly touching Ethan's—that allowed her to ride his cock while Trey pounded into her ass from behind. Ethan had completely surrendered to the pleasure—his eyes closed, head thrown back, hands knotted in the covers. Every muscle in his body was taut and twitching. Trey knew he was fighting orgasm for all he was worth. Reagan was moaning, her forehead pressed firmly into Ethan's shoulder as she simultaneously fucked him and opened herself to being fucked. Once Trey found their rhythm, which was always easy with Reagan, he allowed his hand to explore her body. He stroked the silky skin of her back, now slick with sweat, plucked at her nipples, rubbed her belly—loving the way her muscles clenched each time she shifted backward—and eventually found his true goal between her legs. He rubbed her clit, making her cry out as she came, but she didn't slow her motions to enjoy it. She fucked Ethan even harder, faster, encouraging Trey to match her tempo.

Only when he was certain both of his lovers were experiencing as much pleasure as he could give them did Trey let himself truly feel what his body was enjoying: the maddening friction of Reagan's ass and the knowledge that the hard ridge he was rubbing against with each thrust was Ethan's cock inside her pussy. Both sensations felt amazing, but the combination of the two was too intense for him to keep up for much longer. He tried shifting his focus away from his own pleasure to ensuring Reagan's, but his hand was doing a fine job rubbing her clit on its own.

The need for release built inside him so quickly, it stole his breath and made his balls ache.

"Sorry . . . I can't . . . I'm gonna come," Trey said, knowing he was too far gone to stop.

Trey's admission sent Ethan over the edge. He grabbed Reagan's hips and held her still while he trembled and shook through his own orgasm. Ethan's expression of pure abandonment as he let go pulled Trey straight into climax. He pressed his face into Reagan's back and held on tight as bursts of sensation shattered deep inside him. His arms gave out, and he landed on Reagan, pressing her body into Ethan. Ethan labored for breath beneath their combined weight, but he didn't push them away. He wrapped his arms around Trey's back and hugged them both closer. They lay there for a long moment, gathering their wits—if any of them had had any to begin with.

"I really am the luckiest woman alive," Reagan murmured, her voice slurred as if she were drunk.

"And don't you forget it," Trey mumbled.

He'd do everything in his power to remind her that she was a lucky woman, because he'd never be able to let either of them go.

CHAPTER 9

REAGAN REFUSED to leave the hotel room the next day until right before the show. She'd missed a band interview—she always felt like an unwanted accessory during those anyway—and she still wasn't prepared to face the public or more precisely, the press. From her suite window, she could see the gaggle of reporters loitering around the hotel's entrance. They'd been there over an hour. She knew they were waiting for her to leave so they could make a mockery out of her. Trey didn't have to face them today; Sinners' show had been canceled because Sed was making funeral arrangements for his father. And she'd told Ethan that she'd actually feel safer without her bodyguard at her side. He was still brooding over that claim.

She didn't know what to do about any of this. Her stomach was tied into so many knots, she couldn't eat. Her head was full of so many troubling thoughts, she couldn't sleep. So when a knock came at the door, she jumped as if a firing squad had just pulled their triggers.

Butch's smile of greeting was laced with worry. "How are you holding up, kiddo?"

"Not so good. Is there another way out of here?"

"We'll leave through the parking garage. The hotel can keep the reporters off their property—which includes the garage underneath—but they can't keep them off the sidewalk out front."

Parking garage? Perfect. Reagan took a steadying breath and stepped out of the room. A bright flash lit up the corridor from the end of the hall.

"Get out of here," Butch roared, pulling Reagan behind his body.

Reagan trembled behind him until she heard a commotion beyond Butch. Exodus End's security team—which was currently short one man—hauled the protesting photographer into an elevator.

"I swear they come out of the walls," Butch said, stepping behind Reagan and placing a steadying hand on her back to urge her into motion.

She searched the corridor for additional spectators and finding no one but two familiar faces of Exodus End's security crew, she took a shaky step forward.

"A word of advice," Butch said as they headed toward the stairwell.

Reagan had heard about all the advice she could handle already, but she nodded.

"Don't give them the satisfaction of knowing how much they upset you. Pretend like they're not there."

"How am I supposed to do that?" she asked.

"Focus on whatever you're doing. Be as uninteresting as possible."

She chuckled. "Well, that last part should be easy."

"If they do happen to catch you out and about, act like a Hollywood starlet. Like you eat up the attention. Smile and be friendly no matter how much you want to kick them all in the teeth."

"That sounds a bit more challenging." Or impossible.

"You'll be fine. Just give it time. Someone more famous than you will fuck up and the paparazzi's focus will shift to them."

She nodded, wishing he had an exact date and time for the end of her limelight. The man was a master of scheduling. Couldn't he just add a couple of lines to the band's itinerary?

6:03 p.m. The press finds someone more interesting and less sensitive than Reagan Elliot to hound

6:04 p.m. Reagan stops feeling like she's going to hurl

When Butch opened the stairwell door, a member of their security team was standing on the landing waiting for them.

"All clear?" Butch asked.

The guy nodded. "We have someone on every floor." His dark-eyed gaze shifted toward Reagan, and she tensed, wondering what he was thinking. "Isn't Ethan with you?" he asked, and some of the tension drained from her spine.

Butch answered for her. "We figured that since he's part of the scandal, it's best if she isn't seen with him until this all blows over."

Reagan missed Ethan's steadying presence already, but she headed down the stairs, Butch in front of her, the other guard bringing up the rear.

"I feel like the First Lady or something," Reagan said as she followed Butch, her boots echoing on the steps.

He didn't speak to her until they had descended all fifteen flights and she was ushered into a waiting SUV with dark-tinted windows. The first thing she noticed was that other than Butch, who climbed in beside her, she was the vehicle's only passenger.

"Where are the guys?" she asked as the SUV moved forward at a sedate pace. Likely so it didn't draw attention.

"They'll leave through the front door in a few minutes. They have a decoy with them—a woman of your approximate size and coloring with her face hidden. The hope is that the press will follow them as they take the long way to the arena and it will give us time to sneak you inside unnoticed."

Reagan flung herself against Butch and squeezed him until her shoulders ached. "You are the absolute best."

Patting her weakly, Butch turned to look out the window.

"Did I embarrass you, old man?" she asked, grinning as she peered up at him through her long bangs.

"You won't think I'm the best later tonight," he said, returning her squeeze, probably so she'd finally release him.

"What did you do?" she asked, her heart thrumming. He didn't set up some impromptu press conference after the show, had he? She hoped he wouldn't throw her to the wolves and let her fend for herself.

"I just think you should be prepared."

Oh God, he *had* set up a press conference. Reagan started eyeing the door, wondering if she'd survive if she jumped out of a moving vehicle. "For what?"

"I've been helping Logan make amends with Toni all day."

"What?" Why would he do such a thing after the hell Toni had put her through? Correction, after the hell that she'd put all the musicians in Butch's care through.

"He's going to patch things up with Toni after the show tonight. He had me arrange a flight and everything."

Reagan's fear and anxiety were instantly replaced by boiling rage. "You've got to be fucking kidding me," she yelled. "How could he take that back-stabbing little bitch back?"

"Toni wasn't the one who leaked the information to the press."

"Of course she was. Who else had access to that information?"

"We don't know yet, but someone took the information from her personal belongings."

"You have proof of this?" Reagan's outraged roar lowered at least half a decibel. She'd actually be thrilled if it turned out her friend hadn't betrayed her trust, but she wasn't going to buy into the idea unless she had inarguable evidence that Toni wasn't involved.

"Logan's talked to her, and she mentioned something about her diary being lost or stolen."

Reagan shook her head. "So she didn't hand secrets that could ruin my life over to the press. She just left them lying around in some diary so anyone could get their hands on the information."

"I'm sure she's crushed," Butch said, and Reagan swore she saw the sparkle of a tear in his eye. "Actually, I know for a fact she was devastated."

"You feel guilty," Reagan said.

"I shouldn't have told you all about the tabloid the way I did. Everyone overreacted and—"

"We did *not* overreact, Butch."

"I had to literally carry her away from the bus, and I threatened to call the police on her. Have you ever seen her cry?" Butch rubbed at his throat and bit his lip.

"More times than I can count." Toni cried over freaking dog shelter commercials. Reagan crossed her arms and jiggled her foot in annoyance. Just whose side was Butch on?

"I've been with this band since they were kids," Butch said. "Every last one of them is like a son to me."

"I know that, but Toni isn't one of them." And I'm not one of them either, Reagan realized.

"Logan loves her. Crazy, impulsive, never serious Logan Schmidt is in love with that sweet, naïve woman." Butch chuckled softly. "I figured he'd be the last one of the boys to settle down, but Toni has changed him. Made him a better man. Don't get me wrong, he's still the same fun, adventurous, foul-mouthed, ornery little shit that he's always been, but she makes him a better, more considerate, happier version of himself. It didn't feel right to take that away from him."

"You didn't, Butch," Reagan said. "She betrayed us. It's her fault that she was fired, not yours."

Butch took a deep breath. "But I honestly don't think it *is* her fault. She made a mistake, but it wasn't malicious. She didn't mean to hurt anyone, especially not you. She really looks up to you."

"She's only two years younger than me," Reagan said. "You're making me feel old."

"Age is just a number, Rea," he said, cupping the back of her head and showing her a bit of that fatherly affection he showed the rest of the band. "You're wise beyond your years, and she's been completely sheltered."

Reagan snorted. "That's a fact."

"She probably should have known better than to write personal details about her new friends in a journal."

"Damn right she should have."

"But remember who we're talking about here. Did she really know better? Or had that journal been her only confidant for so long that she never considered the possible consequences of what would happen if someone besides her read it?"

Reagan groaned and poked him in the belly. "You suck," she said, narrowing her eyes at him.

"Why do I suck?"

"Because you're making me feel sorry for her, and I really, really need someone to direct my hatred toward right now."

"Then direct it toward whoever took her journal and sold the info to the tabloids."

"I would if I had any idea who it could have been."

Butch smiled and patted her knee. "You're a good kid."

Reagan couldn't help but smile back. Her own father thought she had been possessed by a demon at puberty. She needed a fatherly-type man to tell her she was a good kid every now and then.

"And you're a good person," Reagan said. "Exodus End would be lost without you. *I* would be lost without you."

"Damn straight," he said, and his chest puffed out with pride.

The SUV pulled up to the barrier fences behind the arena. Reagan flinched away from the window when several people put their hands to the glass and tried to see inside.

"That guy right there is a total dick," Butch said, pointing at one of their spectators. "His favorite pastime is to follow celebrities whose relationships are kind of rocky and get them arguing so he can take pictures of their fights. Relationships between celebrities are challenging enough without some shithead egging on arguments."

Reagan shrank into her seat. "So why is he here?"

"He's probably hoping to raise tensions between you and Trey."

"Trey's back at the hotel."

"Then you have nothing to worry about," Butch said. "Tonight. Just know what kind of crap that guy is capable of. He's very good at what he does. Half of the nasty shit that was publicized when Steve was going through his divorce was his doing."

Reagan nodded, grateful that Butch was there to help her navigate the shark-infested waters.

The barrier gates were opened to allow the SUV through. The clutch of paparazzi was much smaller here than it had been in front of the hotel. Reagan hoped that meant the plan to divert them had been successful, but it would also mean that more people eager to get into her business were headed in their direction.

"Now, remember," Butch said as the vehicle stopped feet from the back entrance. "Pretend you don't notice them. Smile. Preferably at me or someone else you're greeting. Don't play the starlet right now, or they might use that as proof that you're proud of your scandalous love life."

"What's wrong with that?"

"No telling who they'll accuse you of sleeping with next."

"Probably you," she said with a smirk.

"Maybe. But more likely Dare or Max or anyone you happen to glance at. You don't want them to have to deal with this shit too, do you?"

"No," she said. "So act like I'm not bothered that they're all a bunch of nosy jack-ass-lanterns and pretend I hope they forgive me for living my life as my own. Got it."

Butch grinned and shook his head. "No need to be a smart ass. You have five steps to get to the door. Use them wisely."

Oh yeah, great. No pressure there.

Butch opened the door and even though the congregated press—or whatever they were calling themselves these days—was standing yards away behind the barrier fence manned by the surliest-looking members of Exodus End's team, Reagan could still hear them yelling their ridiculous questions at her.

"Reagan. Reagan! Does Trey realize that you've had sexual relations with his brother?"

She'd slept with Dare? When had that happened? She was

pretty sure she would have remembered that.

"Is it true that all your live performances are actually recorded and you're just pretending to play?"

Did she look like Milli Vanilli? Better invest in some dreadlocks and bicycle pants to wear with her combat boots to complete her farce of a career.

"Pyre Vamp of Hell's Crypt says you cheated to win Exodus End's Guitarist for a Year Contest and that he should have won. Do you have a comment?"

Reagan stopped one step from the door and spun toward the crowd, her eyes narrowed.

"Yeah, I have a comment for Pyre Vamp," she yelled. "He can go fuck himself! And you all can go fuck yourselves too."

Butch shoved Reagan through the open door and marched in after her.

"What are you doing?" Butch yelled at her.

She was too pissed to shrink away from his rage. She straightened and stood on tiptoe so she could get in his face.

"Do I need to remind you what that Pyre asshole did to me?" She traced an imaginary line around her throat where the bruise he'd left there with a guitar string had once been. "He tried to fucking kill me because he was jealous that I beat him. And now he's telling the press that he won and that I cheated. There is absolutely no truth to that."

"There's no truth to any of those questions they were asking you. Unless you did sleep with Dare . . ." Butch raised both hands. "It's none of my business—"

"Of course I didn't sleep with Dare!"

"So why are you pissed about one lie but not another?"

"Because," she said. "Because I allowed Sam Baily to snow me into letting Vamp get away with hurting me, with almost killing me, and I'm tired of taking shit and not standing up for myself."

"Okay, cool," Butch said, taking her by the arm and walking her quickly toward her private dressing room. She didn't understand why until she noticed several members of the press were inside the building and writing down everything she said. Once they were inside the room and the door was securely shut behind them, he resumed talking.

"I'm not sure Baily's decision on that issue was wise, but now is not time to dig up another scandal. Don't you have enough to worry about?"

"If they focused on that talentless hack and the *truth* about what he did to me, they'd have someone else to harass."

"Depends on which story sells more papers. What do you think people will want to read about, an unattractive failed guitarist's hurt over not getting the chance to realize his dream, resulting in your long-gone neck bruise, or a very attractive rising-star guitarist who's sleeping with Sinners' ornery, much-adored guitarist *and* her dark, mysterious bodyguard?"

She hated that Butch was right. It made her want to kick him. She flopped herself into a chair instead and tried to scowl a hole through his head.

The walkie-talkie on Butch's belt screeched, and he answered the summons. "Yeah?" He sounded almost as pissy as she felt. She supposed dealing with all this bullshit was trying for him as well.

"The guys are here." A somewhat familiar voice came out of Butch's handset. "Do you want them to come directly inside or talk to the press?"

"Give Max five minutes to sweet-talk the press," Butch responded, "but send the rest of them in."

Reagan's jaw hardened. "Why does he get to say whatever he wants to the press?"

"If you want me to throw you outside and let you fend for yourself, I will," he snapped at her.

She was half tempted to take him up on the offer, but she crossed her arms over her chest and shifted her glare of death to the floor.

"Max knows how to work a crowd, Reagan. He's better at it than anyone. He'll keep his head no matter what they ask, and he'll charm them all. It's what he does. When you get to his level of finesse, you can speak to the press, but until then—"

"Keep my mouth shut."

"Please," Butch said with a relieved sigh as he rubbed at his eye.

"Fine. But can I hang out with the guys until the show? I don't want to sit here by myself for hours."

Trey and Ethan usually kept her occupied before a show, but since they were both absent, she knew she'd go mad if she were left to dwell on all the bullshit she was forced to endure.

"I'll ask them." Butch let himself out of the room, closing the door behind him.

He'd *ask* them? What did he mean he'd ask them? Wasn't she part of the band too? She'd always assumed she got her own dressing room because she was female, but maybe it was because she was an outsider. She was feeling supremely depressed about her lot in life when the dressing room door opened and Steve bustled into the room.

"Jesus, it's a paparazzi circus out there," he said. "It wasn't even this bad when they were hounding me through my divorce."

"That's because your divorce wasn't news to anyone." Logan said, following Steve. "It was bound to happen." He sidestepped to avoid the fist Steve swung in his direction.

Dare brought up the rear and closed the door behind him. He crossed the room and squatted in front of Reagan's chair, taking her hands in his and staring up into her face. "How are you holding up?"

She meant to yell about the injustice of it all, but somehow ended up crying instead. As an only child, she'd never had a big brother's shoulder to cry on. She hoped Trey didn't mind that she used his.

"Toni feels so guilty about what happened," Logan said. "Even though she didn't do anything."

Reagan sniffed her nose and pulled away from Dare so she could wipe at her eyes. She'd always dealt better with anger than self-pity. If she felt sorry for herself, she ended up taking no action. If she was angry, she went after the root of the cause. And she had every intention of going after the son of a bitch responsible for this mess. "She should feel guilty."

"I guarantee she didn't sell those stories, Reagan. If she did, I'll serve you my left nut on a platter."

Reagan laughed and shook her head at him. "Your left nut? Why the left one?"

Logan's blue eyes twinkled as he grinned at her. "It's my favorite."

"I don't want to know why," Reagan said, waving her hands. She shifted her attention to Dare, who was still watching her with concern and holding her upper arms. Did he realize how much strength that leant her? "Thanks for the shoulder."

"Don't mention it," he said. "How's Trey?"

"He's fine," she said. "It's kind of annoying how fine he is about all this."

Dare chuckled. "He's only happy when he's being himself. I've been reminding him of that fact for years. To think, my advice finally sank in. Now if the two loves of his life would figure out how to do the same."

Dare's stare made Reagan feel like she was about five years old, had been disobedient, and needed to stand in a corner to contemplate her wrongs.

She squirmed and scowled at him, but she wasn't really cross. Deep down she knew he was right, but following his advice was hard. Part of her still wanted to be *normal*—whatever that was—and love only one man, but her heart refused to cooperate. And her body didn't want that outcome either. Dare ruffled her hair and straightened from his crouched position.

Max entered the dressing room and shut the door against the din of loud conversations in the hall. "I don't know why I always get stuck talking to those fuckwads."

"Takes one to know one," Steve said, helping himself to the snacks that had been set out for Reagan. She noticed that the bouquets of flowers and gifts that usually filled her dressing room before a gig were missing. It hadn't taken long for her admirers to turn their backs on her.

"So what did you say?" Logan asked.

Max grinned. "I used the answer-their-questions-with-more-questions technique. It always confuses them."

Reagan perked up. She needed to learn how to talk to the press without telling them to go fuck themselves. "How does that work?"

Max sank onto the sofa and stretched his arms over his head, giving Reagan a lovely view of his toned and tattooed abdominals.

"Uh . . ." His hazel gaze met hers. "Do you really want to know?"

She nodded. "Teach me, master."

Max smiled, nearly knocking her out of her chair with his natural charm. He didn't smile all that often, which was probably a good thing. Women might walk into traffic or tumble down stairs while distracted by it.

"Okay, so for example, when they ask *is Logan really the biggest pussy who ever cried into his pillow over his mommy . . .*"

"Hey!" Logan threw a cashew at Max, who tilted his head so that it missed its mark.

". . . I say, *are you speaking of an actual domesticated feline or are you insinuating that Logan commonly displays characteristics that are more befitting a cantankerous toddler?*"

"Hey!" Logan turned to Steve. "That was an insult, right?"

"He said, *so you want to know if Logan is a regular pussy or a giant pussy?*" Steve opened his arms as wide as they'd stretch. "I'd go with about this big."

Steve's stretch left his gut wide open for Logan's elbow.

Reagan laughed. "That's so mean."

"Don't worry," Max said. "I didn't answer any of their questions. They probably won't figure it out until they're going over their notes to write their articles."

"What did they ask about me?" Reagan leaned forward in her chair and rested her elbows on her knees. Whatever he responded, she could handle it. She hoped.

Max's smile faded. "They were more interested in my involvement with Vic," he said, his gaze flicking to Dare.

Dare turned away and crossed to the mini-fridge in the corner. "Where's the scotch?" he asked. He pulled out one of Reagan's favorite strawberry wine coolers. "Do you really drink this shit?"

"They're good," she said. "Get out of my fridge." She didn't drink wine coolers on the bus, because she'd known the guys would tease her about her girly beverage of choice, but she'd thought her secret would be safe in her private dressing room.

Her fault for telling Butch she didn't want to be alone.

The door opened again, and Reagan expected to see Butch, but it was the band's manager, Sam Baily, who entered the room. Everyone stopped what they were doing to gawk at him.

CHAPTER 10

AS USUAL, SAM BAILY WAS PERFECTLY PUT TOGETHER, from his ridiculously expensive crocodile loafers to his impossibly unwrinkled gray Armani suit to his immaculately styled gray hair.

"Hey, Sam," Max said, climbing to his feet and offering his hand for a stiff handshake. "We weren't expecting you."

"I heard we've had another run-in with the tabloids," Sam said. "A full issue this time. I'm impressed."

Reagan blinked at him, but was too intimidated to speak. *Impressed?* Why the fuck would he be impressed?

"It's not *good* publicity," Dare said, closing the open fridge door with his foot and twisting the top off a bottle of water. "Every article they published was derogatory."

"All publicity is good publicity," Sam said. "We had a spike in sales yesterday. The record label is very pleased."

"That's because all they care about is making money," Steve said.

"We need to discuss strategy and how to turn this situation to our advantage," Sam said.

"I think we'd rather ignore it until it goes away," Logan said.

Reagan nodded. That was exactly what she wanted to do.

"We take opportunities when they present themselves," Sam said. "Why do you think you're so successful?"

"Talent," Reagan blurted.

Sam smiled at her, and she suddenly felt like prey. "There she is. Our little money maker."

"You're not going to use her that way," Dare said, as if he knew what Sam was going to suggest.

Before she could even thank Dare for sticking up for her, Sam stepped closer and Reagan tried to magically melt into the sofa at her back. When he turned to focus his attention on the guys, she sucked in a relieved breath.

"Most of your fans are males," Sam said. "And it doesn't matter if they're fifteen or fifty— when they see a woman who looks like Reagan and they know she's capable of having sexual relations with multiple men, they start to think they'd have a chance. They fantasize about her. Want to be as close to her as possible. They buy tickets to see her in concert and merchandise with her face on it. They look her up on the Internet and stare at her image while they play with their pathetic peckers, oblivious to all the ad income they're generating for us."

Reagan's jaw clenched tighter with each word the man spoke. "Are you offering me up to the fans as your whore?"

"I didn't have to," Sam said. "It's already happened. We had new shirts printed last night with your image on them and had them shipped overnight so the merch stands could sell them tonight. They're already sold out."

"You can't sell shirts with my image on them!" Reagan yelled.

"It's in your contract," Sam said. "Tonight, when you're onstage, I want you to rub up against the guys and flirt with men in the audience. We're going to try a new segment where you bring an audience member up onstage, strap your guitar on him, and stand behind him while you play a solo."

"I'm not going to do any of that," Reagan said, looking to her bandmates for support. None of them would even meet her eyes. Not even her usual champion, Dare.

When her gaze finally returned to Sam, he smirked. "It's in your contract."

"Acting like a slut so you can sell T-shirts and internet ad space is *not* in my contract," she bellowed.

"Calm down, Reagan," Dare said.

"I'm not going to fucking calm down. This is bullshit, and you all know it."

"The price of fame," Steve murmured from behind the hand covering his mouth.

"We'll let the rest of the garbage that was printed settle down,"

Sam said. "But we can give the tabloids this one angle as a distraction to keep their attention off my talent."

Reagan felt as if someone had slapped her. "You're using me as a publicity stunt?"

"We hired you as a publicity stunt," Sam said. "Or have you forgotten?"

"I've forgotten," Dare said, crossing his arms over his chest.

"So have I," Max said.

Logan stepped beside her and squeezed her shoulder. "She's one of us now."

"Sorry, Sam, we're on her side," Steve said. "You're going to have to come up with something more compelling than Reagan's ass to drive record sales and keep the label from breathing down your neck."

Reagan was too overjoyed by their support to feel the sting of Steve's indirect barb about her ass.

"We're tired of all the publicity," Steve added. "We want to make music, not sell merch."

"It's always been a piece of the puzzle," Sam said, looking completely unruffled by the guys' stand. "It always will be."

"But it shouldn't be the *biggest* piece of the puzzle," Logan said.

"It isn't," Sam said. "That would be tickets sales."

While it was great that they had a manager who was focused on their financial success, Reagan wondered if he was really the right man for the job.

"About that," Dare said. "I had a fan a couple of weeks ago tell me how excited he was to be able to attend our show. His buddies bought him a ticket for his birthday because he couldn't afford it. A lifelong devoted fan couldn't afford a concert ticket. That's a problem, Sam. So I checked ticket prices the other day. Since when do we charge seventy dollars for general admission?"

"Since people are willing to pay it," Sam said. "They're getting Exodus End and Sinners in one show. It's a bargain as far as I'm concerned. The scalpers are getting two or three hundred a ticket these days."

"Don't we get a say in ticket prices?" Logan glanced not at Sam, but at Max, who shook his head.

"Do we have a say in anything?" Steve said, throwing up his hands in disgust.

Reagan couldn't believe how little freedom they had. What was the point of being successful if they had to answer to a bunch of record company executives interested only in counting their money?"

"Where you buy your second mansion," Sam said. "So how's the book coming along? I expected Ms. Nichols to be here with the band. Is she out gathering material from the fans? I'd like to talk to her."

"Uh." Logan's gaze darted to the rest of them. "She went home due to a misunderstanding, but I plan to bring her back after the show tonight."

"What kind of misunderstanding?" Sam asked.

"We thought she was the one who sold all that stuff to the tabloids, but it was someone else."

Sam chuckled. "Of course it was someone else. If her publishing company uses any material gathered for the book for anything other than what is permitted under contract, we'll sue. They'd have to be pretty stupid to risk crossing our legal powerhouse."

Logan licked his lips. "Uh, well, what if the information was accidently leaked or if someone stole it or something like that?"

"It's their responsibility to protect your private information. If they hadn't assured me of that at the start, I would have used a larger publisher for this biography. Were their computers hacked? Is that where those tabloid stories came from?"

"Nope!" Logan said. "Just a hypothetical question."

Hands clasped behind his back, head tilted, Sam studied him carefully for a long moment. "If you find out differently, be sure to let me know. Lawsuit money spends just as well as any other."

Reagan felt positively sick for Toni. Sure, Reagan had been pissed at her and had hated her guts for a few hours. She might have even threatened to sue her in one of her many rants. But she'd never want an entire team of well-paid lawyers to financially destroy her new friend over a simple mistake. Toni was a victim in this mess too. She might not have the added insult of an oily and misogynistic manager who wanted to exploit her sexuality for a few extra bucks, but she'd suffered.

"Well, now that you've finished airing your grievances . . ." Sam said.

"Not even close," Steve said under his breath.

"Let's move on to the real reason it's taken me so long to join the tour."

Join the tour? He wasn't going to follow them around from here on out, was he? If he did, Reagan couldn't be held responsible for any murders she committed.

"I recently signed a new band—Baroquen—and they've just finished up in the studio. Amazing stuff, guys. Wait until you hear it. The label is rushing the release of their first album. It drops late summer."

"*This* summer?" Max asked, and when Sam nodded, he said, "That is a rush."

"What does this have to do with us?" Dare asked.

"They'll be joining you on the second leg of your tour as an opening band."

"Okay," Max said, "but the tour is already full."

Sam shook his head. "They'll be replacing Twisted Element."

"No fucking way!" Steve shouted so loud that Reagan jumped.

"Every fucking way," Sam said.

"They stepped up to fill in for Hell's Crypt when their douchebag of a guitarist tried to kidnap Reagan," Steve said, "and you're going to drop them now?"

"It was great of them to help us out, but frankly, they're not that good," Sam said.

"They're sensational," Steve said, his volume increasing even more.

"I know about your love affair with their drummer," Sam said.

"Oh my God, you too?" Steve yelled. "He's a friend." He looked at the rest of them for support.

Reagan opened her mouth to back Steve's claim, but she couldn't seem to form words.

"That's what I meant," Sam said.

"He's very sensitive about his love affair with Zach," Logan said, giving Steve a playful shove.

"I'm gonna fuck you up later, Lo," Steve threatened. "You can't kick them off the tour," he said to Sam. "This is the opportunity of a lifetime for them."

Sam scratched his nose. "I'm well aware of that. We're opening up that same opportunity to my new talent."

"Fuck that."

"Take a breath, Steve. It's done. I'll tell the guys of Twisted Element tonight."

"This is fucking bullshit." Steve was already storming out of the dressing room. The crowd of reporters outside didn't slow him down as he shoved his way through them like a bulldozer.

"You should practice your tact," Dare said to Sam. "You knew he'd be upset."

Sam shrugged. "He'll get over it."

Reagan doubted that, but she still felt as though she didn't have a say in the workings of the band or tour politics, so she held her tongue.

"Do you have any other fabulous news to offer?" Dare looked like his patience had been tried and was about to lose its battle with calm.

"I booked studio time for November. I hope you've been writing. The new album is due."

"Who has time to fucking write?" Dare snapped. "We're so overloaded with promotional bullshit, we barely have time to sleep."

"I understand you're all under a lot of stress," Sam said. "Isn't Butch taking proper care of you?"

"That man is a fucking saint," Dare said. "Don't use him to wipe the shit off your shoes. You're the one who always pushes us to do more than we can handle."

"You can handle it," Sam said. "You're the hardest-working band in America. That's why you're so successful."

They did work hard. Too hard. And Reagan had seen the strain; she just hadn't realized they were so close to snapping. Especially not Dare, who'd been her rock from the start.

"I'm going to go check on Steve," Logan said.

Reagan wished she'd thought of that ingenious escape plan. But when Logan opened the door and the press started yelling their asinine questions, she realized she couldn't leave. Not unless she wanted to be further insulted.

"I'll work with Butch on the schedule," Max said. "See if there's any give in it."

"You're fucking kidding, right?" Dare asked, offering him a glare that would have sent Reagan sobbing under the sofa.

"We have to write," Max said. "We don't have a choice in the matter."

"That's the problem," Dare said. "We don't ever have a choice. This isn't even our band anymore." He pointed an accusatory finger in Sam's direction. "It's his and the assholes he answers to."

Reagan cringed when Dare stalked to the door and threw it open. "I'm not answering any questions," he announced as he stepped out of the room. The incessant chatter of the milling reporters went silent, and they formed a clear path for him to walk unhindered down the corridor. Reagan wished she could do that. It was as if Dare had superpowers. She hoped they were contagious.

"Are you going to yell at me and stalk out of the room as well?" Sam asked Reagan.

She shook her head, far too intimidated to speak. And she doubted the reporters would obey her commands to leave her alone.

"They really are under a lot of pressure," Max said.

"You don't think I know that?" Sam said, sinking into the sofa.

Reagan was shocked by how old and tired he suddenly looked. It was as if someone had punctured his pompousness and all the jerk in him had leaked out at once.

"Sales still not where they need to be?" Max said, sitting on the coffee table in front of Sam.

Sam shook his head. "A new album will help," he said, "but the youth of America isn't as angry as it used to be. They all listen to pop and techno."

"Not all," Reagan said, surprised she remembered how to speak.

"Do you have any ideas on how to keep the fans Exodus End already has and at the same time attract new ones?" Sam asked.

"Me?" Reagan asked, slapping herself in the chest so hard, it was sure to leave a mark.

Sam chuckled. "Yeah, you. We hope this new all-girl band draws a younger crowd and they stick around for the headliner, but we have no way of knowing if the strategy will work."

"So you signed them to the tour to help us?" Reagan asked, her head spinning. "Not the other way around?"

"Everything Sam does, he does for the band," Max said. "Deep down, the guys know that, but no one likes to work harder for fewer and fewer results. So they take it out on him."

"I didn't realize," Reagan said.

"How could you? You're the new girl," Sam said. "Another promotional stunt to keep Exodus End on top."

"I'd like to help keep them there," Reagan admitted. "But I'm not comfortable being used as a sex object."

Sam sighed. "Maybe instead of trying to get young men to fill the stadium, we should focus on horny women. Max, how do you feel about performing shirtless?"

"I thought Steve was our angle there," Max said.

"Steve isn't very visible back behind his drums, and you no longer have a guitar strap chafing your shoulder—"

"I'll think about," Max said.

Reagan ducked her head to hide a terse frown. She knew how much it bothered Max that his guitar strap was currently chafing Reagan's shoulder instead of his. None of them needed the reminder that he couldn't play.

"You do that," Sam said, patting Max's knee. "And Reagan . . ."

"Try to pretend I'm sexy," she said.

"You are sexy," Sam said. "I'd be a fool not to take advantage of that fact." Sam stood and walked stiffly toward the door. "I guess I'd better deliver the bad news to Twisted Element myself. Assuming Steve hasn't already set them off on a rampage. Would you do me a favor, Max?"

"Probably."

"Try to get the guys excited about having Baroquen join the tour."

"I've never heard of them," Max admitted. He looked at Reagan and lifted an eyebrow.

She shrugged and shook her head. She'd never heard of them either.

Sam smiled, his eyes flashing with excitement. "That's about to change. They're going to be huge."

Sam left the dressing room and barked at the reporters. "The band will have a press conference within the next week and you can ask any questions you like. You're wasting your time hanging around here."

Reagan hoped they listened. She didn't want to have to make her way through that swarm on her way to the stage.

The door closed, and Max released a long sigh. "He's always doing this to me."

"Who?"

"Sam. He puts me in charge of pissing everyone off."

"Maybe you're good at it."

Max laughed, rested his elbows on his knees, and then rubbed at his eyes with the heels of his hands. "I completely understand why Steve is ready to drop the record label, but the reason they're always on our backs is because we're not pulling in as many sales as we did even three years ago. We're on a steady decline and have been since the last album came out."

"I don't see how that's possible," Reagan said. "The arena is packed every night. Fans line up around the block at every promo event."

"Sinners is drawing part of that crowd. I'm not sure we'd sell out if we weren't co-headlining with them. I'm not saying we're broke—we're still the top-grossing band in hard rock—but our margin of success is slipping."

Dread dropped into the pit of her stomach like a stone. "I had no idea. Do the guys know?"

Max nodded. "They're just not too concerned about it. I guess they figure we're still doing well and we're busting our asses trying to keep the fans we have."

"But you're not bringing in new fans," Reagan said, seeing the conversation with Sam in an entirely different light.

"Not many. We haven't found the right hook."

"And Sam thinks I might be the right hook."

"We all think you're the right hook, but none of us want your sex appeal to be the focus of your career, Reagan. You're an amazing musician, not our whore."

"Tell that to the tabloids." Reagan laughed, resisting the urge to hug him for making her feel valuable. She didn't think Max was much of a hugger. She'd seen Toni hug him, but Toni hugged anyone and everyone, oblivious to how uncomfortable it made some of them.

"Don't let them get you down, Reagan. It's not personal. They're just trying to sell papers."

"And you're just trying to sell music."

Max shifted his gaze to the floor. "I can't apologize for doing whatever it takes to save this band from obscurity."

Reagan reached over and touched the back of his hand, her fingers brushing the brace that stabilized his wrist.

"I don't want you to apologize, Max. I want to help." If she had to shake her ass to do her part, she'd shake her ass.

Max turned his hand over and linked his fingers through hers before patting the back of her hand with his good one. "We appreciate your cooperation," he said. "Just don't forget that the music always comes first."

"I won't forget." How could she forget? Before Max had made her see things differently—unlike Sam who just bossed her around and expected her to obey—she'd believed music was her *only* responsibility.

"Will you be okay if I leave you alone?" he asked. "I have some business to attend to."

She didn't want to be alone. God, she was getting as bad as Trey. Maybe his inability to spend even a moment in solitude was infectious. But she didn't want to hold Max back from his business. Whatever needed his attention was likely far more important than keeping her company.

"I'll be fine," she said, "but if you see Cora, could you send her to me? I think I need to make a few adjustments to my costume and makeup for tonight's show."

"Don't overdo it," he said. "Last night when you showed up in your street clothes, with your hair a mess and wearing indignation like a shield, you were the sexiest I've ever seen you."

She drew her eyebrows together, no longer sure what he wanted from her. "I thought you wanted me to get the fans all hot and bothered."

"That's exactly what we're after." Max's predatory grin filled her belly with butterflies. "And all you have to do is be yourself. Drop your guard, let them see what's inside—Reagan in the raw. And I'm not talking about your body. Bare your soul. It's always the sexiest part of a woman."

This was going to be a lot harder than she'd anticipated.

And, jeez, was it hot in there, or was it just him? She nodded and licked her lips, not sure she could form words. Max stood and crossed the room. Reagan tried very hard not to stare at his ass, but her eyes were starved for candy. He paused at the door and turned. Her gaze darted upward. Shit, she'd been caught. He grabbed the hem of his shirt and pulled it off over his head. Her jaw dropped. She'd never seen Max without a shirt; he even wore one in the gym. Beneath his shirt, the man was all hard muscle and beautiful colored tattoos and well-groomed chest hair that tapered into a narrow strip that separated his abs before disappearing into his waistband. He was blindingly gorgeous.

"Do you think this will draw more women to our shows?" he asked, running a hand down his side. It wasn't the cheesy bragging move she expected from a man who looked the way he did. He seemed to be genuinely concerned that women wouldn't find his shirtless look appealing.

"Yeah," she said, "but they won't be there for the music."

"Good point." He pulled his shirt back on over his head. "Let's try baring our souls a little more first. And if that doesn't work, we'll show some skin."

"So is Steve going to perform entirely nude then?" The drummer already played shirtless and barefooted, and he didn't make it a secret that he went commando under those tight pants of his.

Max laughed as he reached for the doorknob. "Don't put any ideas in his head. With the way he flails about when he performs, he'd end up putting an eye out."

Reagan laughed at the mental image of Steve's flailing cock poking him in the eye. "I think you're being rather generous."

Max opened the door and Reagan was relieved to see the crowd of reporters had vanished. Maybe they'd taken Sam's words to heart, or maybe they'd found something better to do than stare at the outside of her dressing room door.

"Do you still want me to send Cora your way?"

"Yeah. Maybe she has some makeup that will cover up the ugly parts of a soul."

Max smiled at her. "You don't need it."

How is that man still single? she wondered as he exited the room and the door clicked shut behind him. In her head, Reagan started going through a list of her single friends, wondering if he'd be open to an introduction. She was still dismissing prospective mates as not good enough for Maximillian Richardson when Cora entered the room lugging a makeup case the size of Texas.

"Girl," she said, her dark eyes wide as she gaped at Reagan. "What did you do to your hair?"

Reagan ran a hand over the tangled mess. "Not a thing."

"That's obvious." She set her case down next to the dressing table in the corner. "Get on over here. We have work to do."

Reagan trudged across the room and plopped down on the bench. She stared at herself in the mirror, rubbing at the dark circles under her eyes with her fingertips. She looked like she hadn't slept at all the night before. But then she pretty much hadn't. Trey and Ethan had kept her occupied for a few hours, but even after they'd both fallen asleep, she'd stared up at the ceiling, a hand on both of the men she loved to remind herself that they were worth any trouble that came with loving them both.

CHAPTER
11

MAKING REAGAN LOOK LIKE SHE WASN'T TRYING too hard to look sexy had taken a professional with a suitcase of supplies almost an hour to accomplish. Seriously? The painted-whore look didn't even take that long.

Cora stepped back and spun the chair to face the mirror. Reagan was a little afraid to check her reflection for the results. When she did find the nerve to look up, her appearance wasn't what she expected. She looked basically the same as she usually did except more vibrant. Cora had skipped the contouring and hadn't used the deep eye and lip colors she'd used in the past.

"Is that what you're going for?" Cora asked.

"I think so." Reagan was a terrible judge of her own appeal. Max had thought she looked sexy the night before, and she hadn't been wearing *any* makeup then. So maybe this was the right look. She liked it.

"Are we doing a wardrobe change too?" Cora asked.

"I guess. You know I'm not good at this stuff."

They tried several combinations of Reagan's normal street clothes and her stage attire, mixing pieces until they decided she'd wear lace-up boots that were a more feminine version of her favorite combat boots paired with the short skirt she usually wore on stage. Cora ripped off most of the tulle that made up the outer layers of the skirt, leaving a few ragged pieces that gave the skirt a grungier look. Cora also took her scissors to the back of the black T-shirt Reagan had put on that morning. The designer created a skull pattern with holes, the eyes appearing red since Reagan's bra strap showed through, the rest revealing areas of bare skin.

"I think it looks awesome," Reagan said, looking over her shoulder so she could see her back in the mirror. "But I'm not sure it's sexy."

"Trust me, girl, it's sexy. Y'ain't gotta show tits and ass to look sexy."

Reagan was relieved to hear that. A knock at the door made her jump.

"Are you decent?" Dare's voice asked through the crack in the door.

"I'm never decent," she said, "but I am dressed if that's what you're asking."

"Can I come in?"

"Yeah, I need a guy's opinion."

"I can offer one of those," Dare said as he opened the door and stepped inside.

Reagan put her hands on her hips—feeling foolish—and then turned to show him the back of her attire. "We're going for sexy without trying too hard."

"That's cool," Dare said, sticking a finger into a hole in the center of her back and making her dance sideways. "Where'd you get it?"

"Cora made it. Is it sexy or just cool?"

"It makes me want to stick my fingers in all your holes." Dare winked at Cora, who snorted.

"I'm gonna make me a shirt like this," Cora said, fanning her neck with one hand.

"Watch it, Dare," Reagan teased. "You wouldn't want me to tell your brother that you're making moves on me, would you?"

"I don't think he'd care." Dare lifted both eyebrows. "Unless they were successful?"

"Dream on."

"Yoo-hoo," Cora called, waving to get Dare's attention. "They'd be successful on me."

Dare chuckled. "I'm tempted, beautiful, but you know I don't mix business with pleasure."

"Fire me," Cora said. "Right now. Fire me."

Reagan rolled her eyes. "Stop joking around, Cora. You know I need you to fix my hair."

"She thinks I'm joking," Cora grumbled, grabbing a brush,

both curling and flat irons, and a variety of hair products from her bag and then arranging them none too gently on the dressing table. "Like I'd rather do her hair than rock Dare's world," she continued under her breath. "The girl's done lost her mind, I tell you."

Still grinning, Dare leaned against the edge of the dressing table.

"What's up?" Reagan asked, wincing as Cora got to work on her hair, also none too gently.

"Sam's arranging the press conference for tomorrow morning," he said. "I figured you'd want to know so you could prepare."

Reagan's body stiffened involuntarily. "Tomorrow morning!"

"Hold still," Cora complained.

"Why so soon?" Reagan asked, though ten years in the future would still be too soon for her to face the press.

"We're going back to LA to attend Phil's funeral before we head to the East Coast for the final leg of the US tour."

"Trey wanted to go back tonight after the show," Reagan said, thinking she was off the hook. "He wants to be there for Sed."

"Trey should go back tonight," Dare said, "but you need to stay here with us."

So not only was she expected to face the press, she was expected to do it without Trey? She trusted him above all others when it came to this notoriety bullshit. How would she manage without him?

"I don't think I can get through this without him," she admitted.

"We're here for you," Dare said.

"Wish they was here for *me*," Cora grumbled. She wrapped the hair at the back of Reagan's head around her curling iron.

Dare's claim meant a lot to Reagan. If she wanted the guys to ever truly accept her as part of their band, she figured she should allow herself to rely on them a little. "I know," she said. "I'll call Trey and let him know he should leave without me."

"You'll see him tomorrow," Dare said, patting her hand.

Reagan nodded, though she was sure the next twelve hours would feel like a lifetime.

"Stop moving your head," Cora protested.

"I'll come get you and escort you to the stage in about forty-five minutes," Dare said. "Do you think you can stay out of trouble that long?"

Reagan grinned but didn't chance a nod. Cora was liable to

brand her with that curling iron if she moved again. "I'll try."

Dare shifted away from the dressing table.

"I'm almost done here," Cora said. "Do you need help with your hair?"

Shoulder-length, straight and shiny, Dare's black hair looked like dark angels continually tended every strand to perfection. "I'm good, thanks," Dare said, "but I'm sure Max could use some help."

Cora sighed forlornly and nodded. "I'll hunt him down in a bit. And Logan too. Get that fro of his under control."

Dare left the women alone, and Cora reached for her flat iron to run through Reagan's bangs.

"Are you really cheating on Trey with your bodyguard?" Cora asked.

Reagan's eyes widened and flicked upward, catching Cora's gaze in the mirror.

"Sorry," Cora said, "that ain't none of my business."

"I'm not cheating on him," Reagan said, concentrating hard on keeping the tremor from her voice. If she couldn't say such things to Cora, she'd never be able to repeat them to the press the next morning. And she *wasn't* cheating on Trey. So she could confidently say that without lying. But if they worded the question a bit differently—*are you involved with Ethan Connor*, for example—she would have to lie, and she was horrible at it. Maybe she could just run away and no one would notice.

After Cora finished with her hair, still grumbling about never getting to work with Dare, she left Reagan alone. As soon as the door closed, she called Trey.

"Everything okay?" he asked.

"As good as can be expected," Reagan said. "I've been hiding out in my dressing room all evening. And Sam's here."

"Did he piss you off again?"

Sam managed to piss her off every time she interacted with him. She'd always considered him misogynistic, but Max had changed her way of thinking about Sam's motives. At least a little.

"A bit, but it's not important. He's scheduled a press conference for tomorrow morning."

"Have you thought about what you're going to say?"

"Not much," she admitted. Just thinking about being under a media microscope made her skin itchy, as if she were breaking out in hives.

"Ethan and I will come up with a bunch of potential questions, and we'll drill you tonight."

"I'd rather you just drill me and skip the questions entirely," she said.

Trey chuckled. "We can do both."

"Actually, you should go to LA without me. Your band needs you there to support Sed."

"I just talked to him. He's holding it together."

Reagan covered her churning belly with one hand. She didn't want Trey to go to LA. She wanted him sitting right beside her when she faced the press. But knowing him, he'd tell the whole world what kind of relationship they were truly involved in, and Reagan doubted she could handle the public outrage.

"I need to do this myself," she said. "Dare wants me to depend on my own band a little more."

"Dare said that?"

"Yeah. I can't expect to be one of them if I go to you with all my band-related problems."

"I get that," he said. "But this isn't just a band-related problem, Reagan. It affects all of us."

Reagan licked her lips, contemplating her options. Dare had a point, but so did Trey. Whose advice should she follow?

"Will you be upset if I do this press conference on my own?" she asked.

"Of course not," Trey said. "If you feel more comfortable without me there—"

"I'd feel loads better if you were here," Reagan admitted. "But I think I need to do this on my own."

"What about Ethan? Do you want him there?"

"No," she blurted. She didn't want the press to give him the third degree. She'd shoulder the burden this time and hopefully diffuse this bomb before it exploded and destroyed them all. "Take him home with you."

"He isn't going to like this," Trey said.

"I'm sure you can charm him into leaving with you."

"If he thinks you might be hurt? Yeah, wish me luck. He's been pacing the floor since you left."

"Let me talk to him."

She heard Trey say, "She wants to talk to you," before Ethan came on the phone.

"Say the word and I'm there," Ethan said. "I don't give a shit what those reporters say about me, but if they insult you, I will make them sorry."

"Ethan, I don't need you here." Which wasn't true or even slightly true. "I want you to leave with Trey tonight, and I'll meet you at home tomorrow."

"Not happening."

Reagan massaged her forehead. She didn't need the added stress of Ethan's stubbornness. "It will make things easier on me."

"I'm not buying it, Reagan," Ethan said. "I know you need someone to lean on right now."

"That's what my band is for. I won't ever be accepted if I don't allow myself to rely on them."

She could hear Trey's voice in the background, but couldn't hear what he was saying.

"She's too upset to know what she needs," Ethan said.

She refused to listen to a one-sided conversation about her inability to make her own decisions. "I'm going now. We're on early tonight."

"Reagan . . ."

"And if you show up here against my wishes, I will be pissed." Hands shaking, she hung up the phone before they got into a heated argument. She didn't want to take out her frustration on those closest to her. Her outlet, once again, would be her guitar, and an arena full of people would be there to witness her fury.

Moments later Dare and the rest of the band came to retrieve her.

"You ready?" Max asked.

She breathed in a deep breath and blew it out to steady her nerves. "Yeah," she said, but she wasn't.

Logan held open the door as they filtered out into the corridor and offered her a gentle smile as she passed. Most of the paparazzi had cleared out of the backstage area, but a few had stuck around to take pictures. At least they weren't shouting offensive questions. The guys surrounded her like a protective shield, and she was grateful, but she didn't understand the tears prickling her eyes. Why did she feel like they were escorting her to the electric chair?

She reached out and fisted her hand in the back of Dare's shirt. He glanced over his shoulder and grimaced before looping an arm around her shoulders and pulling her into his side. Blinking back tears, she clung to his shirt, one hand at his chest, the other at his back. She wished Ethan was the one she was holding on to. Wished it were Trey rather than Max who gave her shoulder a comforting squeeze.

"Take one more fucking picture, and I will break your face with that camera," Steve yelled at someone.

For some reason, that image made Reagan chuckle. Dare lifted a hand to touch her hair, but after observing the perfect artistry that Cora had created, he settled his palm between her shoulders instead.

"Keep laughing," he said. "Don't let them see you cry."

Reagan nodded, but couldn't muster so much as a chortle.

Sam was waiting for them just outside the door that led to the darkened area behind the stage. His lips were pursed, brows drawn together, hands once again clasped behind his back. He shook his head at Reagan, but waited for everyone to pass through the doors— and they'd closed the photographers out—before he said anything.

"You can't even walk from your dressing room to the backstage area without hanging all over a man?" Sam asked. "We'll never be able to present the reputation you claim to want if you behave like this."

What the hell was he talking about? It took her a moment to realize he was criticizing her for leaning on Dare. Yes, Dare was a man, and a very delicious one at that, but she thought of him as a big brother.

"Lay off, Sam," Dare said.

"They have pictures of that little scene," Sam said. "You know how they'll slant this."

"Then you're going to have to slant it a different way for them." Dare nudged Reagan forward.

"I still think making her out to be a total slut is our best option," Sam called after them.

Reagan's stomach clenched.

"And we told you, if you do that, you're fucking fired," Steve said.

Reagan looked from Steve to Dare. She'd apparently missed out on some goings-on while hanging out alone in her dressing room. "What's he talking about?"

"Our strategy for tomorrow's press conference," Max said. "We'll go over it with you after the show."

Great. Something else for her to worry about.

"I won't be there," Logan told her. "I'm leaving for Seattle right after the show tonight."

To be with the woman responsible for this mess, Reagan thought with a snarl. She didn't hate Toni's guts entirely, but what grown-ass woman wrote secrets in a fucking diary?

"You're missing out on a great opportunity, Lo," Steve said, twirling a drumstick that a roadie handed him. "You might have been able to convince them you don't constantly cry for your mommy."

"My mommy could go to the press conference in my place," Logan said. "She lives a few miles up the road."

"Oh yeah," Steve said. "That'll show them. Send your mommy in your place to speak on your behalf."

Reagan laughed. Those two were always going at each other. She wouldn't truly feel part of the band until Steve started ripping on her constantly. The only reason Steve criticized her was for her love of the San Diego Chargers. Surely he could do better than that.

Someone handed Reagan a guitar, and she flipped the strap over her head, settling the instrument into place. She automatically reached for a tuning peg, before remembering that a technician had already tuned it for her. She strummed the strings just to be sure. At first she'd been overjoyed that someone else took care of her instrument on tour, but the novelty had worn off. She kind of missed tuning it herself.

Sam appeared at her side, to chase away her improved mood, apparently. "We're going to call up an audience member following 'Rebel in You.' "

"Fine," Reagan said. "But it has to be a woman."

Steve whistled. "Now we're talking!"

Reagan reached over and slapped his bare stomach. "I'm not playing the sex kitten," Reagan said. "Forget it."

"Fantastic idea," Dare said, a supportive hand on her lower back. "Aspiring female guitarists can look up to her instead of misogynistic assholes looking down on her."

Ha! She wasn't the only one who saw Sam that way. She looked at Max, who'd convinced her she might be mistaken about their manager's sexism. She was happy to see that Max was nodding. "Yeah, I like that idea better," Max said.

Reagan refrained from giving Sam a literal middle finger, deciding her disobedience was enough of a figurative fuck you.

"We'll see how the fans respond," Sam said.

So Reagan had won a battle, but evidently the war was far from over.

Reagan released a ton of pent-up fury into the first song of the show. "Ovation" was one of her favorite songs to play live and while she did interact with her bandmates more than usual, she kept her interactions fun and playful, hoping no one misconstrued their antics as sexual. Of course, there was always some asshole in the audience who volunteered to show her his dick, but she refused to degrade herself or Exodus End's music by responding. Dare, however, never had a problem telling the perverts off.

"How are we feeling tonight, Phoenix?" Max called to the crowd while Reagan replaced her tattered pick with a new one from the tape on Dare's mic stand.

The crowd started chanting *Logan, Logan, Logan*, which had never happened before. Why would they be so interested in the band's bass player?

"It's good to be home," Logan said, waving at the audience with both hands raised high above his head.

Oh yeah, Phoenix was Logan's hometown. Maybe that would take some of the focus off Reagan tonight.

As the performance continued and the crowd's responses weren't much different from those made before the tabloid stories' release, Reagan figured she should start to relax, but they were getting closer to her new guitar lesson segment. What if they couldn't find a woman in the audience who wanted a lesson from her? Would they force her to instruct a guy? She couldn't think of a way to make that look even slightly nonsexual.

Reagan added a mini-guitar solo to the end of "Rebel in You." Not to show off, but to put off the inevitable. But she couldn't delay it forever.

"Hey, Phoenix," Max said as he crossed to stand near her. "Reagan has offered to give a lucky fan a personal guitar lesson right here onstage."

Offered? More like had been forced. But Reagan could make this segment her own. Assuming she could get her nervousness under control. She expected Max to send out a call for volunteers, but a woman had already been selected. When she crossed the stage, Reagan's jaw dropped. The slender brunette was stunningly gorgeous. Her hair and makeup had been done to perfection, probably by Cora—the traitor. Reagan was pretty sure those were her high-heeled boots her *impromptu* pupil was wearing. The smug look on Sam's face as he stood in the wings with his arms crossed over his chest made a muscle above Reagan's eye twitch. She was sure he'd rehearsed this woman's role with her before putting her onstage.

"Uh," Max said, watching the newcomer cross in front of him as she sauntered toward Reagan. Jeez, had Sam told her how to walk too?

"I guess we have a volunteer," Max said, shooting a confused look at Dare, who shrugged.

"And she's a hottie!" Steve called from behind his drum kit.

Reagan ignored him, though she considered tossing her guitar at his face and allowing him to give Hottie the lesson.

"What's your name?" Max asked, holding his microphone out to their guest.

"Felicity."

"Have you always wanted to learn to play guitar, Felicity?" Max asked.

Felicity gave Reagan a look that made her decidedly uncomfortable. It was the kind of look that Ethan gave her right before she found herself being fucked against a wall.

"I have if she's doing the teaching," Felicity said.

The entire stadium erupted into raucous cheers and lewd catcalls.

Jaw set, Reagan nodded. "Well, let's get to it then."

She lifted her guitar strap over her head and handed the instrument to Felicity. Felicity held it as if she'd never even seen a guitar and looked to Reagan for instruction. Reagan decided the sooner she got this over with, the sooner they could get on with the show and once it was over, the sooner she could kick Sam in the nuts. It was that glorious idea that made her smile and take her guitar from Felicity's trembling hands. She stepped up behind the other woman and showed her how to properly hold the instrument. Felicity was a few inches shorter than Reagan, so the strap needed adjustment. Reagan had never realized that the buckle was adjacent to the breast until she had to fiddle with it next to Felicity's tit.

Reagan focused on what she was doing, trying hard to ignore the excitement of the crowd. She was pretty sure Felicity was playing the scenario for all it was worth, but Reagan didn't look at her face the entire time she was adjusting the strap.

Reagan stepped back, almost tripping over the mic and stand that had been moved next to them to pick up their conversation. "Okay, now you just finger and strum."

"Finger?" Felicity said, a naughty pout on her face.

From the amount of noise the audience was making, they obviously liked that visual.

"You walked right into that one, Reagan," Logan said into his microphone.

Reagan snorted. She had. There was no way for this situation not to deteriorate, so she might as well have her own fun with it.

"So you have some experience with fingering?" Reagan said, actually relieved that she'd found her sense of humor.

"A little," Felicity said, using her left hand to stroke her right index finger back and forth.

"I'm an expert at fingering," Reagan said, which drew a shudder of excitement from Sam's over-acting puppet. "We'll see if you can keep up."

Reagan stepped up behind Felicity. There was no way to reach the strings without plastering herself to the woman's backside, so she went for it, knowing Sam was likely enraptured by her actions. But then, so was the crowd.

"We'll start with strumming," Reagan said. "You want to hit the string in that sweet spot over and over again until she wails."

Reagan showed Felicity how to hold the pick and then had her strum the D string repeatedly. "Faster," Reagan said, and Felicity strummed faster. "Oh yes, faster. Right there. Don't stop. Faster." Reagan released a moan and pulled the whammy bar, making the guitar wail. The crowd roared in appreciation, and Felicity shifted in her arms. Was Reagan making her uncomfortable? Good.

"I will never look at that guitar the same way again," Max said.

Reagan grinned. "Strumming is a necessary part of playing, Felicity, but you have to use your other hand at the same time to draw out the guitar's full range of sound. Do you think you can use both hands at once?"

"Show me," Felicity said, her voice breathy with excitement.

Was this woman actually turned on by Reagan's little act or was she just pretending? Reagan hoped Felicity was just following Sam's instructions. Otherwise Reagan would feel bad for toying with the woman.

Reagan covered Felicity's strumming hand to control the rhythm and fingered the proper notes to the intro to "Bite" because it was played on just one string.

"Reagan, teach me to play!" yelled a man in the audience after the final note. "I want to learn how to strum and finger at the same time."

"I give only one lesson per night," Reagan said. "Then I roll over and go to sleep."

She loved that the audience laughed at her joke. Her bandmates laughed too. Even Sam, who was still on her shit list, was cracking up. The only one who wasn't laughing was Felicity. Reagan leaned over her shoulder to try to see her expression and got a rushed kiss on the cheek.

"I hope you didn't take my lesson the wrong way, Felicity," Reagan said. "I like guys."

"I want to get in line to tap that!" a fan yelled.

"I got all the dick I can handle at the moment." Reagan didn't know what possessed her to say that, but the entire stadium erupted into the laughter. This time even Felicity laughed. Maybe Reagan had been approaching the situation from the wrong angle. Maybe instead of being so angry, she should laugh about it. But she wasn't sure if she wanted her love life and her career to be the brunt of some huge joke. Then again, she didn't want them to be a tragedy either.

CHAPTER 12

TREY WAS GETTING a neck ache from watching Ethan pace the floor.

"She doesn't know what she needs right now," Ethan said for the tenth or twelfth time since they'd spoken to Reagan. "What she needs is me." He tossed a hand in Trey's direction. "Us. She needs us."

"I know it's hard to understand band dynamics if you've never been in a band—"

"I was on the force. I know what it's like to depend on your comrades."

"It's not quite as extreme as that," Trey admitted. None of the guys had ever taken a bullet for him. "It's not life or death, but everyone is watching you—judging you—all the time. I worked my way up slowly, so I adjusted to fame gradually. Reagan was thrust into the spotlight. She hasn't had time to adjust."

"You said *thrust.*" Ethan grinned crookedly and cocked a suggestive eyebrow at him.

Trey grabbed the pillow from the bed and smacked him with it, though he was glad something he'd said had broken through Ethan's aura of gravity. The guy needed to loosen up. Trey knew Ethan couldn't stand the idea of anything hurting Reagan—physically or emotionally—but the best thing they could do for her was let her handle the scandals her own way. She was the one who'd been affronted. They'd just been treated like accessories to her scandal.

Ethan tossed his suitcase onto the bed and unzipped it.

"Seriously, E? We don't have time for thrusting right now," Trey said, knowing their stash of lube was in Ethan's bag.

Ethan pinned him with a pair of dark brown eyes narrowed in annoyance. "Is sex all you ever think about?"

"No." He shrugged. "Only most of the time. You're the one who pointed out I'd said *thrust.*"

Ethan pulled his shirt off over his head and tossed the crumpled mass into his open bag.

"And now you're taking off your clothes," Trey said. "What am I supposed to be thinking about?"

"Reagan."

"I would prefer her to be in on the thrusting thing."

Ethan rolled his eyes and tugged a neon-yellow shirt on over his head. SECURITY was written in a bold font across the back. "Do you have a backstage pass for tonight's show?"

"Of course, but we're not going there, so it doesn't matter."

"I'm going," Ethan said, unfastening his pants so he could tuck his shirt into the waistband. "I'd like for this to be our decision, but if it has to be mine and I have to go it alone, so be it."

Trey got distracted by what he knew was in those pants before jerking his attention back to the problem at hand. "Reagan doesn't want us there."

Ethan tilted his head and held Trey's gaze. "I thought you knew her better than that."

"Huh?"

"Of course she wants us there."

"She's going to be pissed." But Trey climbed from the bed and went in search of his shoes. Maybe it wasn't really Reagan who wanted them there. Maybe Ethan was just using her needs as an excuse. But Trey wanted to be there for her, despite her wishes or even what might be best for her. He was actually glad Ethan had forced their hand.

"She won't be pissed. She'll be happy to see us." Ethan looked almost convinced of his assertion, but Trey figured they'd be flayed within an inch of their lives by her sharp tongue. At least they'd both be in the same boat.

"Ethan?"

Ethan stopped with one hand on the doorknob and turned back to Trey. In an instant, Trey found himself wrapped in Ethan's arms, their lips close. "Everything will be okay," Ethan whispered.

Staring up into Ethan's dark eyes, Trey believed him.

What a wonderful feeling. No wonder Reagan was always seeking him out for reassurance.

They took a cab to the arena and prepared for a media onslaught. The area where the paparazzi was likely to congregate was blissfully devoid of nosy photographers. Trey fought the urge to hold Ethan's hand as they went through various security checkpoints. They kept a comfortable distance between them in case they were being watched.

"Where are all the photographers and reporters?" Ethan asked Butch as they finally found their way to the dressing rooms.

"They're resting up for tomorrow's press conference, I'm sure." Butch scowled at him. "Are you supposed to be here?"

"Yes," Ethan said. Without hesitation he entered Reagan's dressing room. Trey nodded at Butch as he followed.

Reagan was sitting on the bench of her dressing table, her hands knotted in her lap and her gaze fixed on the floor. Her bandmates, with the exception of Logan, were perched on various pieces of furniture, looking equally uncomfortable. The band's manager was pacing about, gesticulating as he gave his sermon—or lecture—Trey couldn't tell which. Sam paused to confront his latest spectators.

"Didn't Reagan tell you to leave?" Sam turned toward Reagan, and Trey's hackles rose at the accusatory look he gave her.

"She did, but sometimes she says go when she really means stay," Ethan said.

Reagan sprang from her seat and, apparently not knowing who to hug first, wrapped her arms tightly around both of them. Trey felt a tremble in her body, but couldn't tell if it was the manifestation of fury or hurt.

"I asked you to go to LA," she said, drawing away and lifting her hands to place one on Ethan's cheek, the other on Trey's. She looked from Trey's eyes to Ethan's and back again. "Whose bright idea was this?"

"Uh." Ethan's gaze shifted to Trey.

"Both of ours," Trey said, not sure if he was taking credit he didn't deserve or shouldering some of the burden of her anger.

She smiled and kissed Trey's lips and then Ethan's. "I should be mad, but I'm not. Did the reporters see you arrive together?"

Ethan lifted his brows at Trey, offering his smuggest I-told-you-so look.

"No," Trey said. "I think they've all left."

"Just as well," Reagan said. "Sam's talking strategy for tomorrow. Maybe you'd like to weigh in."

Trey was sure no one would like his views, except maybe his brother, who he waved at when he remembered that the three of them weren't alone in the room. But he'd gladly share his opinions. He didn't want to hide his feelings for Reagan and Ethan from anyone. There was no strategy in that. Just truth.

Reagan slipped away from them and sat on the bench again. Ethan positioned himself behind her left shoulder, his arms crossed, a look of warning on his face. Trey doubted anyone would cross Ethan when he was so obviously guarding his lady, but his stern expression made Trey want to poke him in the ribs until he could draw a smile from Ethan's terse lips. Trey decided to lean against the wall by the door instead. He fiddled in his pocket until he found gold—a cherry sucker. He unwrapped it and stuck it in his mouth to soothe his jitters. The familiar sweet tang washed some of the tension from his spine, and he leaned heavily into the wall at his back.

"Where was I?" Sam asked.

Max scratched at his jaw. "Steer their attention toward her career and away from her, uh . . ." He glanced at Trey and then turned his head to look at Ethan. ". . . unusual love life."

"I think the word he used was *abhorrent*," Reagan said, glaring up at Sam through her long bangs.

"*Aberrant*," Sam said, his gaze flitting to Ethan, who was cracking his knuckles. "I said *aberrant*."

"Not much better," Reagan said.

People *would* call their relationship abhorrent if they knew the truth, but Trey realized they'd be repulsed because they didn't understand or had only enough love to give one person at a time. He just happened to be built a bit differently. He was lucky to have found two others who felt the same way he did.

Trey cleared his throat. "I think we should just tell—"

His words were interrupted by Dare's hastily spoken, "Focus on her music career."

"Yeah, good plan," Steve said, covering his mouth with a yawn. "Can we go now? I'd like to go to bed early since all this nonsense resulted in the after-party getting canceled. Again. And now I have to get out of bed early for some fucking press conference."

"Do you honestly feel like partying right now?" Max glanced

over his shoulder at Steve, who was leaning against the back of the sofa behind him.

Steve drummed on Max's back with both palms and used his head as a cymbal. "I always feel like partying."

"So what do I say if they don't care about my career or interactions with the band and all they ask are questions about my relationship with Trey?" Reagan asked. "Or with Ethan?"

Ethan squeezed her shoulder, and she smiled up at him.

"You can say whatever you want," Sam said. "Your personal life doesn't reflect poorly on the band. It actually draws attention, which is always a benefit."

"You're looking a little tired, Sam," Dare said. "Why don't you and Steve head off to bed?"

Sam stiffened. "I don't know what you're insinuating—"

"That it's time for you to go. You've said your piece, and Steve doesn't care if we make decisions without him."

"Yes, I do," Steve said.

Trey smiled around his sucker. He'd grown up with Dare, so he was well accustomed to the man always getting his way. As children, Dare had used his wits to get everything he wanted while Trey had relied on being irresistibly cute. Trey had always admired his older brother. He was pretty sure Steve had no idea he was being manipulated.

"Well then, why not try acting like you give a shit for once in your life?" Dare said.

"Steve isn't the only one who's tired." Max stood from the sofa and massaged his damaged wrist, loosening a Velcro strap on his brace before adjusting it into a new position. "Why don't we all go back to the hotel and get some sleep? We can talk this out in the morning after we've rested."

Max exchanged a pointed look with Dare, who shrugged. "I'm a little tired myself. Let's call it a night."

Reagan paled. "I still don't know what I'm supposed to say tomorrow."

"It'll come to you," Dare assured her. "Just don't panic."

But Reagan already looked panicked.

They all piled into the limo, including Sam and Butch, and sat in edgy silence all the way back to the hotel. Reagan clung to Trey's hand, and he had plenty to say to her, but he didn't want to say anything in front of Sam. He wouldn't have cared if the others had heard his advice, but he didn't trust Sam and from the tension in the limo, he was pretty sure he wasn't the only one. He'd been hanging around these guys for weeks; they never sat completely silent in the car, no matter how tired they were. When they reached the hotel, Butch was the first out of the car. He tugged Sam aside to ask him how he wanted security to be handled the following day while the rest of them entered the lobby.

"Give us all half an hour," Max said to Reagan. "We'll arrive one at a time so Sam doesn't get suspicious."

Reagan crumpled her brow and stopped walking. "Huh?"

"What's going on?" Steve asked, looking from one person to the next.

"We can't talk candidly with Sam looming over us," Max said. "Meet in Reagan's room when the coast is clear."

"Oh," Reagan said. Apparently, she was as clueless about Max/Dare telepathy as the rest of them were.

"So we're *not* sleeping?" Steve grumbled.

"If you don't show up, that's your decision." Dare stepped into the elevator.

Butch had stalled Sam for as long as possible. They both hurried into the lobby to catch up. Max held the door so they could squeeze onto the elevator with them.

Their manager was keeping unusually close tabs on them. Trey had heard tales, but this was excessive, even for Sam. Trey tried to catch Dare's eye, but his brother was staring straight ahead. Sometimes Sed could be a bit of a tyrant, but Trey was glad Sed was the one who did the majority of management for Sinners. Having someone like Sam breathing down their necks would have driven the entire band insane. Why did his brother's band put up with this guy? Couldn't they tell him to get lost? Or to loosen their dog collars a little?

Butch got off the elevator one floor below theirs, but Sam was staying on the same floor as the band. They filtered off the elevator and said their good nights as each of them split off to enter his personal suite. Sam bypassed his room and continued to trail after Reagan. Trey was glad he and Ethan had decided not to go back to LA tonight; Sam made Reagan anxious. Why was he following them?

"I think you missed your room," Ethan said, coming to a halt and turning to face Sam. Trey urged Reagan to keep walking.

"I just wanted to have a private word with Reagan," Sam said, and for once he was the one who appeared anxious.

"She needs to rest. You can talk to her in the morning."

Mmm. Trey loved that authoritative tone of Ethan's. It did all sorts of tingly things to him.

Sam opened his mouth, likely to protest, but Ethan stepped his feet apart and crossed his arms over his broad chest.

"Um, yes, well, be sure she sees me first thing in the morning."

"If she feels like it," Ethan said, still not budging.

Sam eventually gave up and turned, shuffling toward his room, which was beyond the elevator. Trey opened their suite door, and Reagan hurried inside. Ethan didn't join them until Sam's door had shut behind him.

"Is he always like that?" Ethan asked Reagan once he'd followed them into the room.

"Yeah. Every time I've interacted with him, he's been like that. Pushy. I can't stand the guy."

Trey's phone vibrated in his pocket. A text message from Dare. *Is the coast clear? Or did Sam follow you into your room?*

Trey shook his head. "Dare wants to know if Sam followed us to our room, so I'm pretty sure Sam's like that with everyone, Reagan, not just you."

"So I'm not special?" Reagan said, a teasing grin on her face.

The tension she'd displayed while she was in Sam's presence had already melted away.

"Of course you're special," Ethan said, drawing her against him and rubbing her back with both hands. "How did the show go?"

Trey texted Dare about Ethan thwarting Sam's attempts to follow them into their room while Reagan described the concert and the guitar lesson she'd given a woman Sam had selected.

"I'm glad you decided to have fun with it," Ethan said.

"Maybe I've been taking everything too seriously," Reagan said. "Stressing myself out."

"Yep," Trey said, shoving his phone back into his pocket. "I've been telling you that from the beginning."

"Well, it's hard to relax just because someone tells you to."

"Maybe I should have tried reverse psychology." Trey kicked his shoes off and made himself comfortable on the sofa. "Always be perfect; freak out over every little mistake; try to be someone you're not comfortable being; and whatever you do, don't have any fun."

"Shut up," Reagan said, drawing away from Ethan and flopping onto the sofa beside Trey. "I'd say no one asked you, but I did ask. I just have a hard time following advice." Reagan massaged her temple and closed her eyes.

Trey shrugged, pulling the empty sucker stick from his mouth and wondering how long his favorite treat had been gone. He'd admittedly been distracted at the arena and in the car. "It's better to figure out what works for you on your own anyway."

A quiet but intricate knock sounded on the door. Ethan gave them a confused look before opening it.

Steve slipped inside, humming the *Mission Impossible* theme song. He sidled along the wall and then ducked down behind an end table, still humming. Trey snorted. Were all drummers a little wacky or just the ones he knew? Timing his actions to the pauses in the tune, Steve belly-crawled under Trey and Reagan's extended legs, his wriggling body sandwiched between the coffee table and sofa. He flipped over onto his back and nudged his head up between Reagan's knees, which earned him a slap on the head. Still humming, he shifted to his knees and then sprang to his feet, diving sideways into the open bedroom door on the last crescendo.

"Ow!" Steve hollered from somewhere inside the bedroom.

Trey couldn't stop laughing, even after Steve had completed his very secretive entrance.

"Am I the first to arrive?" Steve asked when he reentered the living room, smoothing his hair and then tying the unruly locks back with a band he wore on his wrist.

"So far," Reagan said. "Did you hurt yourself acting like an idiot?"

"I think I landed on a huge dildo in there or something." Wincing, he rubbed at his side.

"Oh," Trey said. "That's mine. Sorry about that."

"It's all fun and games until Steve lands on Trey's giant dildo," Reagan said, shaking her head.

Steve grimaced and closed the bedroom door. "Out of sight, out of mind," he said under his breath.

Another knock sounded on the door, but before Ethan could answer it, Steve darted in front of him and put his lips to the crack in the door. "What's the secret pass phrase?"

"Is he always like this?" Ethan asked.

"He's usually only about half this obnoxious," Reagan said. "But he didn't get to burn off his crazy at an after-party two days running, and Logan isn't here to balance him out."

"What?" Max's muffled voice said from the corridor.

"Incorrect." Steve opened the door, smacked Max on the top of his head, and closed the door. "Try again. What's the secret pass phrase?"

"Steve, quit fucking around."

"Wrong again." Steve opened the door, tried to smack Max again, but Max was ready. Still, Steve managed to slam the door before Max could barge in.

"I'm going to kick your ass if you don't open this door."

"Ding, ding, ding. Correct." Steve opened the door wide.

Max slapped Steve's shoulder as he passed. "You're an idiot."

"You're just too boring to know how to have fun."

"You've been snorting coke again, haven't you?"

"Incorrect." Steve opened the door again and in impressive linebacker style, he shoved Max back into the hall.

Steve probably would have continued fucking with Max if Dare hadn't walked between them and entered the suite without mishap. The other two trailed in after him, Steve looking more subdued than before, Max less annoyed.

Steve sat on the coffee table while Max and Dare took the two tub chairs. Ethan settled onto the sofa next to Trey.

"So are we ready to fire him now?" Steve asked.

"We can't fire Sam," Dare said. "It's—"

"In the contract," the rest of his band said simultaneously.

"After this tour is over, that damned contract is fulfilled," Steve said.

"It is?" Reagan asked.

Steve nodded. "We have a new contract, but we haven't signed yet. And I have no plans to ever sign it. So either we lose the label, or you'll be looking for a new drummer."

"You've told us that a hundred times. We're all aware of your feelings on renewing the contract," Max said. "But we're not here to discuss what happens after this tour ends. We're here to discuss what's going to happen tomorrow."

"Are you going to find a different label?" Reagan asked Steve.

"No label," Steve said. "We can do everything ourselves. We have the money. We have the notoriety. We have the connections." Steve ticked off each of their assets on his fingers.

"It's not that simple," Dare said. "Stop changing the subject for your own agenda, Steve. We have to figure out how to get out of this press conference tomorrow."

"Get out of it?" Reagan looked from Dare, who seemed very certain of this idea, to Max, whose lip was trapped between his teeth while he shook his head, to Steve, who was staring at Dare in wide-eyed shock.

"I don't think you're ready to talk to the press, Reagan," Dare said. "And they don't want to talk to the rest of us. So we'll keep finding excuses to put them off a week, then another, and then we head to Europe. By the time we get back to the States, the bloodsuckers will have found someone else to harass."

If Trey hadn't already thought his older brother was the moon and stars, his plan to protect Reagan would have launched him into the heavens.

"You don't really think that will work, do you?" Max asked, tossing his hands up. "You have to know this is a terrible idea. If we don't settle our scandals now—*all* of them—the tabloids will blow everything out of proportion."

"If we wait too long, they'll have her giving birth to three-headed bat-boy quadruplets due to her secret love affair with aliens from Uranus," Steve said, looking to his left, probably for the absent Logan to feed on his joke. Steve's Uranus joke went unanswered, which was unfortunate. Trey could have used another laugh. Dare and Max looked so grave as they stared at Reagan, he feared she might have died when he hadn't been paying attention. He squeezed her hand just to make sure it was still warm.

Dare extended a hand toward Reagan. "So when she's ready to tell her version of the truth . . ."

Reagan cringed.

And Trey's heart caught.

Would it really be that terrible for everyone to know he loved her? That Ethan loved her? That they both loved her? Fuck, he was ecstatic about the situation. Why wasn't she? Ethan looked equally morose. He didn't seem too keen on shouting their love from the rooftops either.

". . . it will be far less scandalous than whatever the tabloids print."

"I need to discuss this with Trey and Ethan before I make any decisions," Reagan said. "This affects all three of us, not just me."

"Trey will want to come clean," Dare said. "I have no doubts."

Trey smiled, glad his brother understood where he was coming from, even if his lovers didn't.

"True, but Trey has the support of his friends and family. Ethan's still in the closet," Reagan said. She immediately covered her mouth. "Sorry, I shouldn't have just blurted that out."

Ethan's gaze was trained securely on the floor.

"I didn't realize that," Dare said, his gaze shifting to Ethan. "How will your family take the news?"

Ethan's normally tanned face went ashen as he continued to stare at the floor. "Uh . . ."

"About as well as my dad will take the news that I'm shacking up with two men at the same time," Reagan said.

Ethan closed his eyes and nodded. Trey sighed. He knew he was lucky to have understanding parents, but how would either Ethan or Reagan know how their respective families would react if they never told them the truth? Maybe he should take them both to meet his parents over the break. Maybe if they saw how a supportive family behaved, they'd be less secretive. Trey had to admit, if only to himself, that their mutual tight-lipped attitude was eating at him.

"I'd say the worst way of breaking the news is for them to read it in the tabloids," Steve said. "That's how my mom found out that Bianca and I were getting a divorce. She still uses that to guilt trip me as necessary."

"So we're all in agreement that this press conference isn't happening tomorrow," Dare said.

Reagan nodded without hesitation. It was probably cruel of Trey, but he kind of wanted to see if she'd be willing to stick her neck out for him and Ethan. So far, she'd turtled her neck deep into her shell and didn't seem willing to budge.

"I don't care one way or another," Steve said. "I'm impervious to tabloid bullshit by this point."

"Did you forget that Sam has veto power?" Max asked. "If he says we're having a press conference tomorrow, it's going to happen whether we want it to or not."

"This doesn't involve Sam," Dare said. "I can't believe he fucking shows up here and starts barking orders like a four-star general after getting a boner in New York over some unknown girl band. Fuck his opinion. Fuck his agenda. And fuck his press conference."

Trey caught the smirk on Steve's face at Dare's declaration. He knew Steve was ready to toss their record label and their iron-fisted manager aside, and Dare seemed to be teetering toward agreement with him. Trey wasn't sure if Dare had really had it with Sam's dickhead-tatorship or if he was only interested in protecting Reagan. Or more likely, protecting his brother. Dare had been looking out for Trey since he was a kid. Sure, Sam had helped make Exodus End the sensation it was today, but at what cost? That record label of theirs was sure to run the entire band into the ground if they didn't stop putting so much pressure on them. And if Dare—Mr. Patience himself—was fed up, conditions must be worse than even Trey realized. He'd been so wrapped up in his own issues that he hadn't imagined that Dare might need support. Trey stretched out one leg and nudged Dare's foot with his to let him know he was on his side. Always on his side. Just like Dare was always on his.

"You three had better leave tonight," Dare said, nodding to the trio on the sofa. "I'll tell Sam that Sed needs Trey's support in preparation for his father's funeral and that it's not appropriate for any of you to have to deal with the added bullshit during this tragic time. The rest of us will head for home in the morning and do the press conference on our own to appease Sam if he insists on it. We'll just refuse to answer any questions about Reagan."

"Sam is going to be pissed that Reagan slipped away in the night." Steve grinned, obviously not upset about pulling a fast one on their manager. "Logan's going to be sorry he missed this."

"Max?" Dare turned to the thus-far silent vocalist.

Max shrugged. "Seems like a fine plan to me. There isn't anything in the contract that says our temporary band member has to be present at all required functions."

"Reagan?" Dare asked for final approval.

"I think there's something like that in *my* contract," Reagan said.

"Everyone's always worried about getting sued," Steve said, shaking his head. "There are worse things than being broke, you know."

"Sam won't pull a dickhead move if we use Sed's situation as an excuse," Max said. "Not after Logan got all that positive publicity for supporting Sed in his time of need with that karaoke stunt. Sam won't want to detract from that right now."

Steve snorted. "You know that's the only reason Sam didn't flip out when Logan took off with the jet to go retrieve his little tabloid rat."

"Speaking of dickhead moves . . . You don't think it's shitty to use Sed as an excuse to get out of a press conference?" Trey asked. "He really looked up to his dad. Phil meant the world to him."

"We'll make it up to him," Dare said. "Go get your things, Reagan. You're going home tonight."

The tension drained out of her shoulders. *Thank you* was all she said.

Dare's gaze settled on Trey's face. "You already packed?"

Trey nodded. He'd thought he was leaving with Ethan earlier, so he was ready to go.

"Can I talk to you in private before you go?" Dare lifted his eyebrows and held Trey's gaze for a long moment.

Starting to feel uncomfortable by Dare's intensity—which he rarely leveled in Trey's direction—Trey glanced at Reagan, who was climbing from the sofa, and Ethan, who was assisting her. He wasn't sure why Dare wanted to talk to him alone or why he seemed so serious, but his lovers didn't seem to think Dare's request was suspicious.

"Uh, I guess so," Trey said. He followed Dare out of his suite to the one next door, careful to close doors silently so they didn't alert Sam to their covert mission.

When they were shut securely inside the privacy of Dare's suite, Dare turned and squeezed Trey's shoulder. "How are you holding up?"

"Me? The tabloid didn't say anything negative about me."

"I'm not talking about the tabloid. I'm talking about this fucked-up relationship you're involved in."

Trey sucked in a deep breath and gaped at his brother. Of all the people who knew Trey, Dare was the one he expected to understand what he needed to be happy.

"Don't look at me like that," Dare said.

"Like what?" Trey said, turning away to hide his expression.

"Like I've betrayed you."

Dare always could read him. Trey slid his hand into his pocket, searching for a sucker, but found nothing but an empty wrapper.

"I thought I could count on you to be on my side," Trey said, feeling oddly breathless.

"I am on your side—that's the issue. You didn't tell me Ethan was still in the closet."

Trey shrugged. "He'll come out when he's ready. Besides, he's not explicitly gay. He likes women."

"He likes Reagan," Dare said, "but I've never once seen him turn an appreciative eye on another woman. He'll check out other guys—"

"Are you saying he doesn't really love me?" Trey blinked to keep his emotions in check.

"No. I'm saying he's more gay than you are."

"So what if he is?"

"Don't you think he should own that part of himself? Doesn't it hurt that he doesn't want anyone to know how he feels about you, not even his own family?"

Trey shrugged, but if he were honest with himself, yeah, it bothered him. He would love for Ethan to display his feelings more openly, and even though Ethan made it seem like he hid his feelings because Reagan wanted him to, Trey didn't think he'd show them publicly even if Reagan gave the go-ahead.

"And Reagan." Dare shook his head. "All she thinks about is how this scandal makes *her* feel."

"That's not true. Besides, this attack is against *her* more than anyone. She's been hurt. Humiliated. She has more to lose."

Dare huffed out a breath and grabbed the back of Trey's neck. "The only thing she should be worried about losing is *you*."

"She's not going to lose me, Dare. I love her. I'll always be there for her. And the same goes for Ethan. I'll always be there for him too."

"Are you just going to give and give and give until there's nothing left of you? Who's going to be there for you, Trey?"

Trey chuckled and grabbed Dare's wrist until he released his hold. "I have this obnoxiously nosy brother who looks out for me."

"Yeah, well, that guy wants everyone who cares about you to put you first. And it pisses him off when they don't."

"You're so obsessed with me." Trey rolled his eyes.

Dare grinned and knocked Trey in the head. "Go get on a plane with your underattentive lovers. I'll see you tomorrow. Tell Sed that if he needs anything, just ask. I mean that."

His lovers weren't underattentive, just private. Exasperatingly private. "They're different when we're alone," Trey said.

"I'm sure they are. Sorry if I crossed a line by saying something. I just worry that you're turning into a bystander in your own life."

Trey was still puzzling out those words when he, Reagan, and Ethan climbed into a cab headed for the airstrip where Exodus End's private jet was waiting for them after returning from Seattle.

Was he getting complacent? Dare often saw in him what he didn't see in himself. Was Trey so afraid to tilt the dynamic of his relationship with Reagan and Ethan that he was just allowing it to play out rather than being an active participant? Was keeping his opinions on public transparency to himself the key to his continued happiness, or would it ultimately destroy them?

He had no idea. He was new to this relationship thing. But he was worried that the world would eventually wear them down. He just wasn't sure which of them would crumble under the pressure first. He hoped it wouldn't be him.

CHAPTER 13

ETHAN GAWKED as Trey pulled in front of a massive iron gate and pushed a button on the intercom outside the driver's window. The letter *M* was centered in each gate panel, and a long driveway, flanked by enormous palm trees, snaked toward the hint of the terra cotta roof of a sprawling mansion. Ethan knew that Trey's father was a well-known Hollywood plastic surgeon. He hadn't realized that the guy would be majorly loaded.

"Is that really you, sweetheart?" said a woman's voice from the speaker. "I thought you had another couple of weeks on the road."

"Let me in, Mom," Trey said. "I brought someone you've been dying to meet."

"Is it Reagan?" Her excited voice squeaked through the intercom.

"Hi, Mrs. Mills," Reagan called from the passenger seat, leaning across Trey and waving enthusiastically at the small camera lens above the speaker.

"And someone else too," Trey said.

Ethan instinctively ducked down in the back seat. He hadn't wanted to meet Trey's parents, but Trey had convinced Ethan that he could pretend only to be Reagan's bodyguard today, present only to protect her against pushy photographers and reporters. He wasn't sure how he could convince anyone that paparazzi lurked in the Mills' gated backyard, but it was better than them knowing the truth of his involvement with their son.

"You brought Ethan too?" Mrs. Mills asked.

Ethan froze. She knew about him?

"I thought you said he was too shy to meet us," she continued.

"Open the gate, Mom," Trey said, shifting in his seat so he could peer at Ethan in the rearview mirror. "Before he abandons ship."

A loud buzz sounded before the gate creaked as each panel slid open. Ethan reached for Trey's shoulder, but Trey gunned the engine, tossing an unprepared Ethan against the back seat.

"What did you tell her?" Ethan asked, shifting forward. He was going to strangle Trey.

"Nothing much," Trey said, waving a dismissive hand. "Just that I love you and that you give fantastic blow jobs."

"What!"

Reagan laughed gleefully at Ethan's expense. Before Ethan could get a good hold on Trey, Trey slammed on the brakes, forcing Ethan's seat belt to bite into his shoulder before he was flung against the seat again. Trey shoved the transmission into park while releasing his own belt and then escaped through his door. Trey wrapped his arms around a tall slender woman whose hip-long waves of dark hair were streaked with gray. Her multicolor-striped skirt billowed out around her ankles as Trey lifted her off the ground and twirled her around.

Ethan had expected Trey's mother to be a polished, silicon-enhanced Beverly Hills supermodel or something, so when the Bohemian hippie-type approached the car with a streak of blue paint on her cheek and a welcoming smile on her friendly face, Ethan's head started spinning. This free spirit was Trey's mother?

Ethan couldn't help but smile back as her green-eyed gaze shifted from Reagan to him.

Of course this was Trey's mother. Who else could have raised a spoiled brat who not only accepted oddities in himself and others, but embraced all sorts of diversity?

Reagan exited the car and looked only slightly uncomfortable when Mrs. Mills squeezed her. "You're even more lovely in person," Mrs. Mills said, leaning back and cupping Reagan's face between her palms. "How are you holding up? Are you sleeping okay? Has Trey been supportive?" When Reagan didn't respond immediately, Mrs. Mills turned her head and scowled at her son.

"He's been wonderful. And so has Dare." Reagan glanced at the car. "And Ethan too."

Mrs. Mills gave Reagan another squeeze. "If you need anything at all, you can call me, okay? Stay here if you need to. The BHPD are known for keeping the streets free of paparazzi and have a one-minute response time if called to a resident's house."

One minute? Ethan thought. Impressive.

Reagan smiled and nodded. "I'll keep that in mind."

"Mom, she's fine," Trey insisted. "You don't need to call the cops on her behalf."

Mrs. Mills released Reagan and approached the car. She leaned in through the open driver's window and lifted her eyebrows at Ethan.

"Are you going to come out and give me a hug, or do I have to come in there after you?" she asked.

Ethan hadn't made a move to even release his seat belt, much less approach the woman.

"Uh." Warmth rushed up his throat and flooded his face. Was he blushing? No way. The temperature inside the car must be rising from the heat of the sun. "I . . ."

Mrs. Mills opened the back door, and cooler air rushed into the car. "I guess I'm coming in."

Ethan fumbled with his seat belt—because as uncomfortable as hugging a virtual stranger would be, having her climb in on top of him would be doubly so. She stepped back to let him escape the confines of the car and then gaped up at him when he stood before her.

"Wow," she said, laying a hand on her cheek. "You didn't tell me he was such a hunk, Trey."

"Yes, I did," Trey said, dropping an arm across Reagan's shoulders and drawing her against his side. "Tall, dark, and handsome were my exact words."

"The cliché doesn't do him justice," Mrs. Mills said.

Ethan chuckled and opened his arms to draw her against him for a hug. She lingered, taking a moment to squeeze his biceps and pat his pecs.

"Do you ever do nude modeling?" she asked.

Ethan was pretty sure his jaw hit the pavers beneath his feet.

"Mom!" Trey shook his head at her.

"What?" She shrugged. "I'm an artist. I want to see him naked for the sake of *art*."

Ethan was definitely blushing now.

"I'm not buying it," Trey said. "You want to see him naked for the sake of eyes. Yours."

Reagan laughed. "Nice gig you've got there, Mrs. Mills."

"Oh, for heaven's sake, call me Gwen." Gwen winked at Reagan and looped an arm through hers. "Speaking of gigs, tell me all about yours. What's it like to be a rock star?"

"Didn't you raise two of them?" Reagan walked with Mrs. Mills to the house.

"They don't share much about the whole rockstar experience with me," she said.

"Maybe that's a good thing," Reagan said, her laughter carrying into the house as Mrs. Mills led her inside.

"Sorry for tricking you like that," Trey said, taking Ethan's hand and staring down at their entwined fingers. "She wanted to meet you both, and . . ." Trey shrugged. "She's cool. I promise she's cool."

"Does she know the truth about the three of us?" No mother on earth could be *that* cool. Not even Ethan's mom, whom he absolutely adored.

Trey nodded, his sultry eyes flicking up to meet Ethan's through a fringe of long black bangs before he looked down again. "If they love you, parents accept such things. They just want you to be happy."

Ethan captured Trey's chin between his thumb and forefinger and tilted his head to stare him in the eye. "I'm not telling my family about any of this, so get it out of your head. Okay?"

"Is that why you think I brought you here?" Trey asked.

Ethan knew that was part of the reason. To show him—and Reagan—that their relationship *could* be accepted by loved ones. But Ethan's family wasn't anything like Trey's family. Ethan's half brothers would never accept that he was gay. He knew what several of them had done to a gay classmate back in high school. He knew because he'd watched them do it and he hadn't told anyone. And Joshua had been too scared to tell anyone. No one crossed the Mendez brothers—that hadn't changed since high school. He might be able to confide in his mom, but she might let something slip, and then they'd know the truth about their oldest brother. No, it was better if his family never knew.

"I'm happy for you," Ethan said, drawing a silky lock of Trey's bangs between his fingertips, "that you have and have always had this great support network. But not everyone is as lucky as you are."

Trey smiled and lifted a hand to his cheek. "You can borrow my support network anytime you need it."

How could Ethan not have fallen for this generous, caring

man? And how could he be expected not to kiss him in his parents' driveway? He was still kissing him when a car pulled up beside them.

Ethan jerked away and watched over his shoulder as an unassuming man climbed from a Mercedes. He was of average height, with an average build and thinning brown hair, but Ethan would know that mouth anywhere. He'd just kissed one with an uncanny resemblance.

"Hey, Dad," Trey said. "You're home early."

"Mom said you'd brought a couple of someones home for us to meet. But if you're trying to keep this under wraps, you might want to reconsider kissing your boyfriend out in the open. There's a photographer with a wide-angle lens parked across the street at the end of the drive."

Ethan's heart skipped a beat, and he turned to glare down the driveway. The slope prevented him from seeing the photographer.

"Unless he's sitting on the roof of his car, he won't get a clear shot," Trey said. "Don't worry."

"This photographer was a *she*," Dr. Mills said, "and she was still setting up. Just thought I'd warn you."

"I hate those damned photographers," Ethan growled.

"Better get used to it if you're dating my son."

Ethan doubted he'd ever get used to being watched, but he'd endure it for the sake of being with Trey.

"Let's go inside," Trey said. "You can remind me how irresistible you find me in the house."

Ethan gaped at him, the uncharacteristic blush on his face burning hotter than ever. How could Trey say things like that in front of his father?

"Did you bring the other one?" Dr. Mills said. "Your woman?"

"Mom already commandeered her."

Dr. Mills chuckled. "Gwen has been going on about her for weeks. Shattering a music glass ceiling and all that."

Trey lifted a pierced brow at his dad. "There are dozens of women guitarists in the industry."

"Are they part of one of the top-five-grossing metal bands in the world?"

Trey shrugged. "Well, no."

Dr. Mills clapped Trey on the back. "Your mother will have Reagan spearheading a new activist movement if you don't rescue her soon."

Trey rushed toward the house as if he planned to pull Reagan from some nasty wreckage. Ethan started after him, but Dr. Mills caught his arm, forcing him to walk calmly beside him toward the open front door.

"You look a bit shell-shocked," Dr. Mills said.

Ethan's tongue tied itself into a knot. "I . . . well . . . isn't it unusual . . . I mean . . ." What did he mean? Trey's parents seemed wonderfully open, but frankly, Ethan found their acceptance of their son's unusual lifestyle mind-bogglingly odd. He supposed he shouldn't be surprised. Dare was as okay with Trey's proclivities as their parents appeared to be, but Dare was young and open-minded. Dare was a rock star who'd probably seen just about everything there was to see. Trey's parents were, well, *parents*.

"You can't change who people are on the inside," Dr. Mills said. "Though I do get paid a hefty fee for changing them on the outside." He laughed and slapped Ethan on the back. "You can let your guard down here. Except in the front drive. Do you think I should call the cops? They'll make the photographer leave the neighborhood."

Ethan caught a glare at the bottom of the drive. The sun reflecting off a camera lens, he decided. "The tabloids aren't going to go away until they've destroyed us or they get bored with their three new toys, are they?"

"Not unless you can convince them there isn't a story here," Dr. Mills said.

Ethan rubbed a hand over his jaw. Now there was an idea. But how exactly did he pull that off?

"I suggest you come out with the truth, honesty being the best policy and all that."

Ethan chuckled. "You sound just like your son."

"Which one?"

"Both of them, actually, but especially Dare."

"I guess their mother and I did something right."

If Ethan had openly been anything like Dare or Trey, his mother and stepfather would have disowned him.

Dr. Mills ushered Ethan inside and closed the door behind them with a comforting click. No photographers there, just an amazing assortment of colorful and bizarre artwork. Brilliant sunlight filtered down from a glass dome in the ceiling, highlighting paintings and sculptures and fragments of colored tiles forming murals on the foyer walls and pillars and floor. Even the tiered table at the center of it all appeared to be a mixed-media sculpture of some sort, with a giant saw blade at its center, several additional smaller blades forming additional platforms, and an eclectic set of chairs ranging from antique wood to a child-size red PVC chair to form the piece's many legs. It reminded Ethan of some deadly alien insect.

"My wife won't be happy until every inch of this enormous house has her stamp on it." Dr. Mills set his briefcase down on the largest saw blade. The sharp edges were covered with a protective clear plastic. Ethan imagined Trey running around this dangerous-looking thing as a child and shuddered.

"Gwen, sweetheart," Dr. Mills called into the cavernous house. "Come out, come out, wherever you are."

Ethan was still gawking at one of the wall murals, finding that up close, the tiles were interspersed with bottle caps and bolt washers and bits of broken compact disks that added shine to the fish scales in the design.

"This is remarkable," Ethan said.

"Trey inherited all of his talents from his mother," Dr. Mills said.

Probably not all of his talents. Ethan stifled a wry grin. He was pretty sure that talented tongue of Trey's was a learned skill, not an inherited one. Then again, Dr. Mills seemed a very happy man. Maybe Trey had inherited such skills from his mother.

Disturbed by the direction of his thoughts, Ethan wandered into the parlor off the left of the foyer. Trey found him there a few minutes later, examining the fireplace mantel.

"I was wondering where you were," Trey said. "Genevieve is making a cherry cobbler. You won't want to miss it."

"*You* won't want to miss it," Ethan said, patting Trey's back. "You must have had a very . . . uh . . . *colorful* childhood."

Trey tilted his head as he studied the faces along the sides of the mantel. They'd been fashioned from chips of colored bricks and were easily identifiable as Trey at various ages on the left side and a progressively aging Dare on the right.

"You know, she didn't start going crazy with the house until after Dare and I were grown and out on our own." His smile was a little sad. "I think she misses us."

"She'd probably like a few grandchildren in her future," Ethan said.

"That's up to Dare." Trey laughed. "And believe me, she hounds him about it constantly."

"Where's Reagan?" Ethan asked.

"Listening to my mom gab. The poor woman lived in a house full of boys and men her entire adult life. She's overwhelmingly happy to have a woman in the family." Trey wrapped an arm around Ethan's shoulders and leaned in close. "Though I'm sure she'll love you just as much. Assuming you stop isolating yourself."

"Is that what I'm doing?"

"Isn't it?"

Ethan shrugged. "There's a lot to see in this house. Amazing things. I've never seen a home like this before."

"There's no other place like it." Trey slid a hand up Ethan's chest until his palm covered Ethan's heart. It began to thud at the promise in Trey's eyes. "Do you want to check out the pool behind the house? Mom's murals started there. You can see how her work has progressed with time."

"I'd like that."

"And I can see you without your shirt on."

Trey's other hand slid up under Ethan's shirt, his fingers skimming over Ethan's bare belly. The muscles there tightened as unanticipated waves of lust clenched deep inside Ethan.

"Trey," Ethan protested as his touch grew bolder. "Not here."

"Would you like to see my bedroom?" Trey deftly unfastened the button of Ethan's pants.

"What are you—"

Trey nipped the sensitive flesh at Ethan's throat, causing Ethan to suck an excited breath through his teeth.

"I feel safe here," Trey said. "I want you to feel that way too."

"What I'm feeling," Ethan said, drawing Trey's seeking hand from his pants, "is uncomfortable. Your parents could walk in at any moment."

"That's why I wanted to show you my bedroom," he said. "I'll lock the door."

"Trey . . ."

"If you don't want to fuck me . . ."

Oh, but he did. Just not here.

". . . I'd settle for a hand job."

Trey took Ethan's hand and led him away from the childhood shrine fireplace mantel and back into the foyer. Ethan could hear voices and laughter from deeper in the house, but they didn't go in that direction. They followed a set of curved marble steps to the second floor. Ethan might have paid more attention to the series of paintings along the hall's lengthy wall if Trey hadn't been walking backwards in front of him, holding his gaze as securely as he was holding his hand. The naughty imp was going to get far more than a hand job if he kept looking at Ethan with that fuck-me-hard expression on his face.

Trey opened a door near the end of the hall and tugged Ethan inside. He closed the door quietly behind them and locked it with a barely audible click. The room was large, its deep-red walls decorated with large posters of rock bands—many that Ethan didn't recognize. A collage of photos hung over a sturdy black dresser. Ethan recognized a teenaged Trey and Dare, and in almost every shot, someone he wished he didn't recognize—Brian Sinclair. Familiar but unwanted jealousy clawed at Ethan's gut, and he jerked his gaze away from the images of fun and friendship and easily recognizable love.

"He took my virginity in this room," Trey said, standing beside Ethan now, smiling fondly at the photographs.

"Is that why you brought me here?" Ethan asked, backing away. "I don't want to hear this."

Trey caught his arm. "I need you to hear it, Ethan. I've never told anyone the details of what happened that night, not even my brother. But I want you to know, because . . ."

Trey blinked back a sudden flood of tears and Ethan crushed him against his chest. "Don't do that."

Trey sniffed against Ethan's shoulder. "Sorry."

Ethan's arms tightened around him. "No, I'm sorry. You can cry on my shoulder any time you need to."

"I shouldn't be this emotional," he murmured. "I'm over Brian now. Our past shouldn't matter to me anymore."

Ethan's embrace tightened. He wished he could believe that Trey was truly over Brian, but he could almost guarantee that Trey's past with his first love would always matter to him. And that was okay. Ethan was the one holding Trey now; Brian hadn't wanted him. Ethan was sorry that fact had hurt Trey so many times in the past, but he was secretly glad that his competition for Trey's affection had never taken the heart so recklessly thrown in his direction.

"Tell me what you brought me here to say," Ethan said, struggling to keep his embrace from crushing Trey.

"Brian used to spend the night here a lot when we were in school. His dad wasn't home much and his mom was *cold*—there's no other way to describe her. My parents are . . . You've met them. They're free with their affection. Brian was like another son to them."

"Did you have feelings for him from the beginning?" Why was he asking that? Did he really want to be as jealous of the teenaged Brian as he was of the adult version?

"Since fifth grade?" Trey pulled away so he could see Ethan's eyes. Humor teased the corner of Trey's sensual mouth. "I'm not that obsessed."

"When?"

"I don't think it was until that night. Or maybe the second."

"How many times—"

"Just those two." Trey grinned crookedly. "Not for my lack of trying. I can't count how many times I threw myself at him. I made a complete fool of myself."

"Didn't he get tired of rejecting you?"

Trey chuckled. "I guess not. Maybe he liked the attention."

"He probably misses it," Ethan said.

"He's probably relieved." Trey laughed. "We were always better as friends than as lovers. I can't deny that."

"I won't be upset if you tell me he sucks in bed."

Trey laughed and kissed him. "At the time, I thought it was amazing, but now that I've had you . . ." His lips caressed Ethan's jaw.

"I'm sure you've had better."

"Never." Trey's lips moved to Ethan's throat. "You and Reagan are the best thing that's ever happened to me."

"Same here."

Trey went still, his voice low and calm as he said, "It started like any other night. Brian and I practiced guitar for a while. We had dinner with my family. We came up to my room to play a video game or something. We decided it would be fun to sneak some booze, so I lifted a bottle from my dad's liquor cabinet. We drank vodka—a lot of vodka—and were goofing around on the Internet. We ended up watching porn. Not too unusual for a couple of fifteen-year-old boys left to their own devices."

"If I'd have had internet as a teen, I'd have never left my room," Ethan said with a chuckle.

"Brian got really turned on by this chick getting fucked in the ass. I don't know if he'd never seen anal before or what, but the tent in his pajama bottoms was impossible to ignore. I told him he could whack off in front of me if he needed to. We were friends. it was no big deal. I really didn't think it was a big deal until he pulled it out and started stroking it. I'd never been so turned on in my life, even though I was confused by my excitement. I wanted him doing to me what that girl in the video was having done to her. So I offered to touch him with my hand in a sock, because, you know, I wouldn't be actually touching it, so that was okay."

Ethan chuckled. "That's totally not gay."

Trey grinned at him. "I know, right? He was really getting into it—me jerking him off with that sock—and I was so hard, my stomach was in knots. He liked what I was doing even more when I pulled off the sock. Even more when I kissed his dick, licked it, sucked it, got my first taste of his pre-cum."

Ethan remembered his first homosexual experience all too well. But he'd been on the receiving end. His partner had sucked him off in the front seat of their police cruiser while they'd been staking out a suspected meth lab.

"I pulled my pants down, wanting a little reciprocation, you know," Trey said.

"Naturally."

"Next thing I know, he presses me against the side of the bed, holds my wrists behind my back, and shoves his cock in my ass. He kept saying, *pretend you're a girl, pretend you're a girl*. I didn't want to pretend I was a girl. I wanted him to reach around and stroke my dick while he fucked me, but he wouldn't touch me."

"That's disappointing."

"I don't know; he's hung. He fucked me to orgasm even though he didn't have any idea what he was doing."

"You're supposed to tell me that he sucks in bed, remember?"

"If that experience hadn't opened my eyes to the pleasure of being fucked senseless, I'd say it wasn't perfect, but I'd be lying. I came so hard, I swear I blacked out for a few seconds. And when Brian recognized how much I liked being fucked, he came inside me. I thought he'd liked it too—as much as I did—but he completely freaked out afterwards. He hid in the bathroom for over an hour. Meanwhile, I dipped my fingers into the load I'd blown all over the side of my bed and shoved my fingers up my ass so our cum could mingle inside me. How fucked up is that?"

"It's more fucked up that he left you there. What did he say when he finally came back?"

"Nothing. I pretended to be asleep. The next day we acted like nothing had happened between us."

"That must have been hard for you."

Trey shrugged. "Not really. I just blew it off as a onetime mistake. It was our second time together that really fucked with my head."

"Did he pretend you were a girl that time?"

Trey shook his head. "He looked me in eyes the entire time. It was like he was trying to decide if he wanted to be with me—as a couple. I gave him my fucking heart that night and when he'd finished me and finished himself, he said, *we can't ever do this again.* I didn't think he was serious. What we'd shared had been so beautiful. So perfect. It was the most powerful connection I'd ever felt with anyone. But Brian was serious. We never did it again. No matter how many times or in how many ways I tried to make him mine, he was true to his word."

"You probably don't want to hear how much I hate him right now."

"Don't hate him for knowing what he wanted. Or rather what he didn't want. He's always stood beside me through everything." Trey grinned crookedly. "Unfortunately, he never stood behind me again. Did I mention that he's hung?"

Ethan squeezed Trey's ass in both hands, drawing a tormented groan from his lover's throat. He knew Trey was trying to make light of a matter that had scarred him deeply.

"Better hung than I am?" Ethan lifted his brows in challenge.

"Yep, and just as thick."

"Are you trying to make me jealous?"

"Just stating facts."

Ethan scowled. Trey stroked the tense muscles in his face.

"Do you know how I said I'd never felt a stronger connection with anyone than when Brian was staring into my eyes as he fucked me?"

Ethan looked away, unable to stand the look of love in Trey's eyes when he knew it was directed at well-hung Brian Sinclair.

"I've felt an even stronger connection since then," Trey said. "With Reagan." Trey grabbed Ethan's jaw and forced him to meet his gaze. "And with you. Brian secured my devotion for ten years with that connection. How long do you think I'll be devoted to you when I feel an even stronger connection with you multiple times a day?"

"I'm hoping forever," Ethan said, his voice gruff with emotion.

"Forever and a day," Trey whispered.

"What happens when I'm too old to fuck you?"

"First, I hope that never happens. Second, you don't honestly think the only time I feel connected to you is when you're buried balls deep in my ass, do you?"

"You made it sound that way."

"Every time our eyes meet, I feel it. Every time I hear your voice, I feel it. Every time we touch, I feel it. Even when I think of you, I feel it. I feel it with Reagan too."

"Have you ever told her this?"

"She knows. I'm sure she knows."

"She might need a reminder." Ethan stroked Trey's hair back from his face, beard scruff scraping against Ethan's fingertips. "Do you need a reminder too?"

Trey pressed his lips together, his green eyes going shiny with repressed tears. He nodded slightly.

"I love you," Ethan said, knowing his words weren't as eloquent as Trey's had been, but he had no idea how to explain his deep and complicated feelings in a way that would do them justice.

"Yeah, but do you ever wish I was a girl?"

Ethan smiled. "Not even for a second. I'm glad Reagan's a girl, though."

"So am I. We should probably go find her. Everyone is going to think we snuck away for a little private time."

"Isn't that what we did?"

Trey nodded. "I probably should have included Reagan in this conversation, but there are just some situations I feel you'd understand better than she would."

"She's very understanding about such situations. When she caught me with Joseph, she was heartbroken, but she didn't kick me out of the apartment. She encouraged me to talk to her about my feelings."

"*You* talked to someone about your feelings?"

Ethan couldn't help but laugh at Trey's flabbergasted expression.

"Well, no, I didn't. But it wasn't because I didn't want her to know how I was feeling. I didn't understand my feelings myself at the time. I've always wondered if she'd have been so accommodating of my shitty behavior if she'd caught me cheating with another woman instead of a man."

Trey scowled. "Let's not find out."

His distrustful words punched Ethan in the gut. "Once a cheater always a cheater? Is that what you're getting at?"

"Should I be worried?"

"Never. I blew it once with Reagan, and it was the stupidest mistake I ever made. I refuse to fuck this up, not when I have everything I could possibly want or need with the two of you in my life." Well, except a career that didn't make him feel like a mooch, but Ethan would figure that out once he felt Reagan could tour the world safely on her own. He scowled at the direction of his thoughts. If she was on her own, that meant she'd be without him for lengthy stretches of time. Perhaps Ethan would put more effort into being an essential member of Exodus End's security team. He was disappointed in himself for not taking more initiative already. Being complacent wasn't like him. He blamed his lack of ambition on being in love with two people at once. It was challenging enough to keep one's head out of the clouds and feet on the ground when in love with one person; he currently had a double dose of the loopies going on. And then there was the sting his ego had taken for being kicked off the force. They'd called him not a hero but a liability. A *liability*. Just because he'd rearranged some woman-beater's face. Ethan supposed lawsuits were far more frightening than criminals to some people. He wasn't one. He didn't regret beating the shit out of that asshole. Even knowing the consequences, he'd have done the same thing again. He just wished he could help more people. But his current state of affairs didn't lend itself to that impulse.

"Ethan." Trey shook his shoulders.

Ethan blinked hard to force his gaze to focus. "What?"

"You're off in your own little world there. What are you thinking about so hard?"

"Nothing much. Work mostly."

Trey's ornery grin refocused Ethan's attention at once.

"Is that what you call following Reagan around all day?"

"I do get paid to do it," Ethan said, trailing Trey out of his stuffy bedroom and into the breezy hallway.

"Some guys have all the luck."

Ethan could hear someone in the distance calling for Trey. "I think we've been missed," Ethan said.

"They can't expect me to pass up a chance at being sucked off by the gorgeous tough guy my mother wants to see naked."

"But I didn't—"

Trey laughed at Ethan's expression.

"We were gone for quite a while," Trey teased, hurrying out of Ethan's reach. "You could have sucked me off three times over in that time."

"Trey," Ethan whispered harshly. "Don't make your parents think that I did *that* to you under their roof."

"Did what?"

"Blew you," Ethan said under his breath.

"Would you be mortified?"

"Yes!" he hissed, chasing Trey down the stairs so the fool wouldn't have time to make embarrassing announcements before Ethan could stop him. Why did he put up with this guy?

When Trey stopped short at the foot of the steps, allowing Ethan to capture him, he knew exactly why he put up with Trey. The man was irresistible. He was also loving, generous, and fun, not to mention as sexy as sin.

Ethan held Trey's back securely against his chest and pressed his face into the crook of Trey's neck. Ethan's heart pumped vigorously as he found that the prey he hadn't realized he was stalking was at his mercy.

"You'd better get that hard-on under control," Trey said. "I guarantee those approaching footsteps are my mother's."

Footsteps? Ethan had been so wrapped up in Trey, he hadn't even heard the soft cadence echoing lightly off the mosaic tiles of the foyer.

"There you two are," Gwen said, her smile never faltering as she took in her son in a compromising position with another man. "The cobbler just came out of the oven. I know you prefer it warm."

"With melting vanilla ice cream on top," Trey said, covering Ethan's forearms with his hands so he couldn't pull away.

"Obviously," his mother said. "Reagan said if you didn't turn up soon, she was going to eat both your shares."

"Sounds like something she'd do."

Feeling a tad uncomfortable but, surprisingly, not mortified, Ethan followed Trey and his mother toward the kitchen at the back of the house.

"She's delightful," Mrs. Mills said. "So enthusiastic and vibrant and witty. I can see why you fell for her." She peeked over her shoulder to catch Ethan's eye. "Why both of you fell for her."

Ethan shifted his gaze to the wall, unable to believe that Mrs. Mills really thought their relationship was acceptable.

"You forgot to mention she's talented," Trey said. "And apparently she's even better on cello than electric guitar."

"It's a fact," Ethan said. She tried to hide her love for the instrument her father had forced her to take up as a child, but when she played, the bond she had with the music—*classical* music—was magical.

"You've heard her play?" Trey asked, hesitating for a step so that Ethan would walk beside him instead of behind him.

Ethan smiled. "Many times."

"Unfair." Trey scowled.

"I don't think she's played cello at all since she signed with Exodus End."

"Maybe she'll play something for me," Gwen said. "Your rock music gives me a headache."

Trey laughed and hugged his mom with one arm. "You poor woman. Having to put up with two budding rock stars in your house must have been pure torture."

"Why do you think we built the pool house?"

Trey's jaw dropped. "So you didn't have to listen to us play? Does Dare know you hate us both?"

"I could never hate you, sweetheart, but I was going through so many earplugs with you and your friends always jamming in the main house."

"Earplugs!"

Ethan chuckled, suddenly missing his own mother. She was a great woman—similar in many ways to Gwen. If not for his brothers, Ethan would have liked her to meet Trey. She'd have a great time teasing him. But Ethan doubted she'd keep his secret from the rest of the family, and he didn't want his stepfather and brothers to know he was a disgusting faggot. He could hear them using that odious word in his head, because they'd used it in reference to other gay men. Ethan wasn't sure how he'd react if they referred to Trey in a derogatory manner. He'd likely go off the deep end. Best to not risk it, he decided.

Reagan was seated at the dining table, one undoubtedly of Gwen's design. The top consisted of an enormous old door—maybe from some medieval castle—and the legs appeared to be fashioned from the bottoms of lamp posts. Each chair around the table was unique. Ethan settled into the one that seem inspired by an Andy Warhol painting of soup cans.

Reagan was talking animatedly to Dr. Mills about killer whales in captivity. Ethan hadn't realized she was passionate about wild animals being protected in their natural habitats.

"Try thinking of them as ambassadors for their species," Dr.

Mills was saying. "Thousands of people see their performances each year, cementing a bond with the animal, so they become aware of the animal's plight and are more likely to do something about it. If you never saw a killer whale for yourself, you probably wouldn't give them a second thought."

"Just so you know," Trey said, sitting across the table from Reagan, "no matter which side you're on, my dad will take the opposing side. The man loves to argue and will not back down until he thinks he's won."

"That's not true," Dr. Mills said.

"You see?" Trey said. "He even argues about arguing."

Gwen set a plate in front of Trey, and his father stole his spoon. "I'll teach you to argue with me, son."

Trey picked up a gooey cherry with his fingers and popped it into his mouth. "Like that's going to stop me," he said.

Dr. Mills turned to Ethan, his green eyes, so like Trey's, wide and inquisitive. "Reagan tells me that you used to be a police officer. Why did you quit?"

Ethan supposed he'd eventually have to participate in the conversation. That didn't mean he was prepared to answer prying questions.

"Dad," Trey admonished. "Ethan doesn't like to talk about himself."

"So that would make him your exact opposite, wouldn't it?" Dr. Mills teased, drawing a chuckle from Ethan.

Trey snatched his spoon from his father's hand and scooped up some melting vanilla ice cream. Ethan picked up his spoon to sample the sweet-looking dessert. He didn't care for sweets in general, but if eating would allow him to avoid revealing his darkest secrets, he'd endure.

About halfway through dessert—the conversation had turned to all the places they'd be traveling to when they headed overseas in a few weeks—Dare breezed into the room.

"We weren't expecting you!" Gwen said, obviously delighted to see her eldest son.

"Does that mean I should get lost?" Dare asked, dropping a kiss on her upturned cheek and another on Reagan's.

"Sit down," Gwen said. "I'll get you some cobbler."

"I see you're spoiling the brat again," Dare said, grinning at Trey, who'd long before finished his cobbler and now repeatedly leaned across the wide table to steal cherries from Ethan's plate.

"It's a tough job," she said as she went into the kitchen.

"Well?" Reagan said, her rosy complexion going grayish.

"What?" Dare asked, sinking into the chair next to Trey.

"How did the press conference go?"

"Oh, that," Dare said. "It was fine."

"That's all you're going to tell me?"

"Max diverted all your questions to Steve, who insisted he was too hung over to respond."

"How pissed was Sam?"

"Pissed, but he kept his mouth shut. We opened by telling everyone that the entire band would rather be in Los Angeles supporting a dear friend in his time of need."

"I tried to call Sed this morning," Trey said. "He really is torn up about this. So much so that I was allowed to talk to Jessica because he didn't think he could talk."

"We should go see him," Reagan said. "Even if he thinks he doesn't want us to."

"Did Toni get ahold of you?" Dare asked Reagan, who scowled at him.

"No."

"Logan called this morning. Toni's little sister is in the hospital."

"What? Is she okay?"

"Something's wrong with her heart, but I think she'll be fine. Logan feels terrible about missing the funeral tomorrow, but thinks Toni needs his support more than Sed does."

"Of course she does. Toni adores her sister. I'm sure Logan is a tremendous comfort to her." Reagan stood from the table and pulled her cellphone out of her pocket. "I need to call her."

"I thought you hated her for leaking your secrets to the tabloids," Ethan said.

"If it was really her, and I now honestly doubt that, I'll chew her out later. I'm sure she can use a friend right now, but she's probably terrified to call me."

Ethan smiled at her. Reagan might be too forgiving for her own good sometimes, but he knew firsthand how wonderful it was to be granted her forgiveness. Ethan was blessed to have two amazing loves in his life. He would do everything in his power to ensure no one ever took them away from him.

CHAPTER 14

REAGAN HADN'T ANTICIPATED that meeting Trey's parents would make her gloriously happy. Within moments of meeting Gwen Mills, Reagan felt that she was the mother who had been missing from her life. She admired Mrs. Mills's strength, kindness, openness, and her creativity. She was a woman Reagan could look up to, and they shared a deep love for Trey. Dr. Mills reminded her of her own father, with several important exceptions. He wasn't judgmental, and from what she could tell, he wasn't an overbearing, controlling hardass. So perhaps their differences outweighed their similarities. Reagan did miss her dad—they'd been through a lot together—but as much she'd been afraid to call him when she'd been hired to go on tour with a metal band, she was terrified to contact him now. What if he'd read the tabloid stories about her? She knew he'd never forgive her for leading an alternative lifestyle. Maybe it was best if he thought she was the cheating whore those stories made her out to be.

Reagan excused herself from the table, went outside through the French doors off the kitchen, and after gawking at the intricate tilework of the swimming pool—undoubtedly more of Gwen's incredible work—dialed Toni on her cellphone. Toni didn't answer, so Reagan left a message.

"Toni, Dare just told me that your sister is in the hospital. I hope everything is okay. If you need someone to talk to or anything at all, please call me. I promise I won't yell at you about the tabloid situation. I've cooled down since the last time you saw me, and I'm thinking more rationally. If you were the one who leaked the information, I'd very much like to hear your explanation. I'm sure you had a very good reason. And if it wasn't you, well, I owe you an apology. After your sister is better, we'll straighten this out. Focus on taking care of yourself and your family. I just wanted you to know you still have a friend."

Reagan hung up, her heart heavy. She didn't have any siblings, but she could imagine how devastated Toni would be about Birdie's health concerns. Because of Toni's current home situation, Reagan doubted Toni would come back on tour with them even if they did clear her of wrongdoing. Reagan had so enjoyed her company, and Logan would likely be unbearable without Toni to moon over at every opportunity.

"Did you talk to her?" Trey asked.

Reagan turned to offer him a weary smile. She hadn't realized he'd joined her outside. "I left a message."

His lower lip poked out as he assessed her. "You look depressed, baby."

She felt depressed.

"You know I can't have that." His ornery grin sent off alarm bells in Reagan's head. He cocked his head to one side, long black bangs shifting to cover one eye. He had a laser-like focus on the pool behind her. "I think a little swimming will cheer you up."

"I didn't bring a suit."

He blinked, and when his eyes focused on her and the corner of his mouth turned up, she knew she was in trouble.

"You won't need one," he said.

He made a grab for her, but she sidestepped and darted in the opposite direction. "Don't you even think about throwing me in that pool, Trey Mills."

"Too late. I've already thought about it."

Reagan raced around the edge of the pool until she heard Mrs. Mills call, "No running!" She slowed her escape to the fastest walk she could manage.

"Terrance Charles Sol Mills, you leave her alone this instant," Mrs. Mills yelled.

Trey continued to stalk Reagan with a long stride. Apparently he wasn't willing to break his mother's no running rule. "I will not leave her alone in any instant. Not until she's laughing."

Reagan released a half-hearted chuckle in an attempt to save herself.

"A real laugh," Trey said.

Reagan had to admit that last one had sounded fake. "Tell me a joke," she said, squeaking and jumping forward when Trey's fingertips brushed her shoulder.

"I don't know any good ones. Do you Ethan?"

Reagan looked to Ethan for assistance, but he was too busy grinning to rescue her. She should have kept her attention on her escape route. Confronted by a low wall backing a raised flower bed and benches, she stopped short.

Trey folded her in his arms and tipped them both into the pool with a splash. Clear, cool water enveloped her, but did nothing to cool her anger. She surfaced, sucking a breath into her lungs, and blinked water out of her eyes.

"Damn it, Trey," she sputtered. "I'm drenched."

"You sure are," Trey said, tossing his head back and laughing as if she were the funniest sight he'd ever seen.

"She isn't laughing," Ethan pointed out.

She scowled at Ethan standing at the edge of the pool. "You're supposed to rescue me. Isn't that your job?" But she knew Ethan wouldn't jump in after her unless she was truly in danger.

"Now I have you all to myself," Trey said, squeezing her tight.

She tried to struggle, but the feel of his arms around her was too soothing.

"I've got you," he whispered. "Everything is going to be okay."

"But—"

"Everything is going to be okay, Reagan. I promise."

Now fighting tears, she pressed her face into the crook of his neck. She was used to going to Ethan when she needed someone to make her feel secure, but Trey was pretty good at it too. He was good to her. Good for her. She would never feel complete without him in her life.

"Hey, I'm feeling left out over here," Ethan said from the side of the pool.

"There's an easy solution to that problem," Trey said. "Join us."

Reagan chuckled under her breath. Yeah, right. Ethan wasn't the type of guy who'd jump into a pool fully clothed. He was much too serious for such silliness.

At the sound of a loud splash, Reagan gasped and jerked around, staring in wide-eyed wonder as Mr. Tall Dark and Serious surfaced behind her. "Ethan!"

She burst out laughing at his wide-eyed, baffled expression. He seemed to be wondering how he'd ended up in the pool.

Trey sent a splash in his direction. "I don't think you're wet enough."

Soon they were all splashing and shouting and laughing together. Reagan loved how Trey brought out Ethan's playful side. Hell, before Trey had come into the picture, she hadn't known Ethan possessed a playful side. They were good for each other and good for her. She wasn't going to let the opinions of others take that away from her.

"This is good to see," Dare said, lounging in a chair on the pool deck, sipping what appeared to be lemonade. "I haven't seen any of you smile for days."

"Is that so?" Trey said, trudging through the water in his sodden clothes.

"I was getting concerned," Dare said.

"You should be more concerned about yourself," Trey said. Without warning he grabbed the end of Dare's lounger, tipping him and his glass of lemonade into the pool.

Consummately cool, Dare somehow managed to look like he'd meant to slide into the pool fully clothed. He even prevented his drink from spilling as he dropped into the water. He took a casual sip, set the glass down poolside, and then launched toward Trey, catching his ornery little brother off guard.

"Reagan, help!" Trey shouted just before his head went under water. Dare held him under with one hand and reached for his lemonade, taking another sip as he held Reagan frozen in place with a steely glare.

"You're on your own, Trey," Ethan said.

"For heaven's sake, Darren," Gwen said calmly, "don't drown him."

"Someone has to keep him in check," Dare said, allowing Trey to surface. "I swear the brat could get away with murder. All he'd have to do is train *the look* on judge and jury, and they'd let him go free."

"This look?" Trey asked, his head tilted just so, his gaze sincere, his mouth slightly twisted with amusement.

Reagan was yards away, but she wasn't immune to *the look*. She was already prepared to give Trey anything his heart desired.

"That's the one," Dare said, and he shoved Trey under the water again.

"I thought I was the only one who couldn't resist that look,"

Ethan said, shaking his head.

"There are few who can."

Trey's head bobbed above the surface again, and he drew a deep breath. "Mom!" he cried before Dare shoved him under again.

"Darren Edward Lunar Mills behave yourself," Gwen demanded.

Reagan sniggered, not at the usage of Dare's full name—though that was pretty funny—but at how he immediately obeyed his mother's demands. Dare whispered something to Trey, which made Trey glance nervously at Reagan, before Dare pulled himself out of the water and peeled off his dripping wet shirt.

"You baby him, Mom," Dare said as he flipped his lounger upright and spread his shirt out over its back. "You've always babied him."

Gwen offered her eldest a smile that reminded Reagan so much of Trey it made her laugh. "Well, he's my baby. And he'll continue to be my baby until *you* give me grandchildren."

"I'd better buy him a pacifier then," Dare said as he settled back in his lounge chair with his glass of lemonade.

"Reagan," Gwen said, "don't you have any nice friends you could set him up with?"

Reagan snorted on a laugh. Dare Mills needed no assistance finding dates. When she figured out that Gwen was sincerely asking for her aid, she said, "I'll see what I can do. But I'm pretty sure all of my friends would die on the spot if I told them I got them a date with Dare Mills."

Gwen scowled. "He's not all that bad."

Reagan's eyes widened. "I meant they'd die because he's so famous and good looking and rich and talented and kind and polite. Any girl would be lucky to have him."

Trey cleared his throat behind her, and she cringed. "Any girl but me," she amended.

"I've always thought he was a catch," Gwen said, concern marring her brow. "So why doesn't he ever bring a nice girl home to meet us?"

"I will when I find the right one," Dare said.

"Well, hurry up about it," Mrs. Mills said, crossing her arms over her chest. "It's getting harder and harder to find diapers in Trey's size."

"Mom!" Trey protested.

When laughter exploded from Ethan, everyone joined him—

even Trey. Gwen invited them for dinner, but the visitation for Sed's father was that evening and the three of them were planning to go.

Reagan tried to prepare herself for going from such an uplifting day to an evening focused on loss. She wasn't sure her nerves could handle such a shift.

"You be sure to come visit while you're on break from the tour at the beginning of June," Mrs. Mills said, offering Reagan a loose hug against her damp clothes.

"I definitely will, Mrs. Mills. It was wonderful to meet you."

"Is it too presumptuous of me to ask you to call me mom?"

"Jeez, Mom," Trey said, leaning in to peck her on the cheek, "you've only known her for a few hours. You'll scare her away."

Reagan covered Trey's face with one hand and smiled brightly, her eyes swimming with tears. "I'd be delighted to call you mom." So that meant she had two moms now. Not her own—that family-deserting bitch could die for all she cared—but Ethan's mother was wonderful to her as well.

Mrs. Mills—*Mom*—turned to Ethan, who was standing off to the side as the others said their goodbyes. "Ethan, you can call me mom whenever you feel comfortable enough to do so."

He nodded, a pleased smile curving his lips upward.

"This is about as comfortable as Ethan gets," Trey said, patting Ethan on the ass. The affectionate gesture made Ethan's body more tense, not less so.

"I wish I'd gotten to spend more time with Dr. Mills," Reagan said.

"Some starlet had a wrinkle emergency," Trey said with a laugh.

"Breast implant emergency," Mom corrected in a serious tone.

"My apologies. A *boob-job* emergency. Dare," Trey called into the house, "we'll see you there."

"Okay!" Dare returned from somewhere inside the enormous home.

"I'll be there too," Mom said, "and I'll be careful not to let on that I know about the three of you." She cupped Trey's cheek in her hand and gave him a smooch on the lips.

"Thanks for understanding, Mrs. Mills," Ethan said, but Trey was pouting again.

"If you're not going to call me mom, at least call me Gwen," she said.

Ethan nodded. "Thanks for understanding, Gwen."

When they backed out of the driveway through the open gate,

a photographer snapped dozens of pictures of their car, no doubt trying to capture a shot of whoever was inside. She even chased after them on foot for half a block.

"Fucking ridiculous," Reagan said, shaking her head at the side mirror. The woman had stopped her chase, but was still taking pictures through a gigantic lens.

"We're taking my car to the visitation," Ethan said from his scrunched position in the back seat. "I have darker tint on my windows."

Trey rolled his eyes. "I say we have a public three-way on the hood of the car and get this all out in the open."

"That *would* do the trick," Ethan said with a throaty chuckle.

Reagan whirled in her seat to gape at him. "You're not actually considering sex in public, are you?"

"In public, no," Ethan said. "But if we parked in a garage somewhere . . ."

"You can't seriously be horny right now," Reagan said, shaking her head at him.

His dark eyes smoldered as they held hers. "Playing in the water—you both with your clothes soaking wet and clinging to your bodies . . . How could I not be horny?"

"Detour!" Trey did a U-turn and headed back toward his parents' house.

"Absolutely not!" Reagan said, reaching for the steering wheel. "I will not insult your parents by fucking their son *and* his boyfriend in their garage."

Trey took a right at the next corner. "Different detour."

The low rumble of Ethan's voice drew Reagan's attention to the back seat.

"Droplets of water dripping from Trey's hair, sliding down his neck into the T-shirt plastered to his chest. God, how I wanted to lick those drops from his skin." Ethan's eyes were closed as he shared his fantasy. "The outline of Reagan's bra barely covering a pair of hard nipples. I can practically feel the texture of her wet shirt against my lips and taste the chlorine in the water as I suck her breast through her clothes."

"You okay back there?" Reagan asked. She couldn't help but notice the appreciable bulge in the front of Ethan's damp pants.

"Dare, stripping off his wet shirt, the sun kissing his golden skin as I—"

"What?" Trey slammed on the brakes, sending Reagan's

shoulder biting painfully into her seat belt. A squirrel darted across the street in front of the car. "You were fantasizing about my *brother*?" Trey's harsh gaze focused on the rearview mirror.

"Everyone fantasizes about your brother," Ethan said.

Trey turned to Reagan. She couldn't lie. Before she'd fallen for Trey, she'd had a few Dare-ing fantasies of her own—most of them involving both brothers simultaneously. "It's a fact. He's almost as fuckable as you are."

"But not quite, right?" Trey started forward again at a slower speed.

Reagan squeezed his thigh, knowing he needed his ego stroked. And maybe a few body parts as well. "Not even close. You're infinitely more fuckable than Dare ever thought of being."

"Well, I wouldn't go that far," Ethan said. Reagan scowled at him over her shoulder and found him laughing silently. Ethan was joking again? What the hell? If he wasn't careful, he might acquire an actual sense of humor.

Grumbling under his breath about never being the best at anything, Trey turned right again, his destination obviously home.

"You're so sensitive." Ethan leaned over the front seat and caught Trey's earlobe in his ear.

Reagan suddenly wanted to find the nearest garage—be it Trey's parents' or the pope's. There was something so erotic about Ethan and Trey being intimate that it pushed all her lust buttons.

"That's what I love most about you." Ethan's hand slid down Trey's chest and belly, stopping just short of his crotch. "I wouldn't trade you for ten Dares." Trey gasped as Ethan's hand stroked him through his damp jeans. "Well, maybe for ten, but no less."

Trey grunted and slapped Ethan's hand away.

"You're so mean," Reagan said.

She heard Ethan's seat belt click. He shifted from behind Trey's seat to behind hers and whispered, "That's not mean. Mean would be if I took advantage of you while he's driving and made him watch but not let him participate."

Ethan was really in a mood. A mean and horny one, Reagan decided, as both his hands covered her breasts and his mouth sucked at her throat. Perhaps she should have scolded him or tried to escape, but her nipples were already hard and straining against the harsh touch of his fingertips, and her belly fluttered with anticipation. One of Ethan's hands slid down Reagan's stomach and deftly unfastened her shorts.

"Ethan!" she gasped in surprise when his hand delved inside, but she didn't stop him. She didn't want to stop him as his finger slid between her lips and over her throbbing, swollen clit.

"Are you thinking about how good it feels to slide your dick into this sweet, slick pussy?" Ethan asked Trey.

"You really are cruel," Trey said, keeping one eye on the road and one on the wicked things Ethan was doing to Reagan's eager body.

Ethan's finger rubbed over Reagan's clit. Pleasure and excitement danced along her nerves. Her heart thundered in her chest, and her breaths came in excited gasps.

"Don't make me come, Ethan," she protested as her pleasure built rapidly. She regretted that request when he eased off her clit and shifted his fingertip to delve into her aching center.

"God, her pussy is hot and wet, Trey," Ethan said, his low voice drawing shudders of delight from Reagan. "Do you think it needs a fast fuck?"

"I know it does," Trey said, his mouth twisting into an ornery smile.

Reagan's eyes opened wide when Ethan unfastened her seat belt. "What are you doing?"

"Being cruel to Trey," Ethan said, his voice so hypnotic and reassuring that she actually helped him get her into the back seat. "But very generous to you."

He stripped her shorts off and tossed them onto Trey's lap. "That's as close as your dick is getting to what it wants right now."

Reagan fumbled with Ethan's fly, so excited by the thought of being filled with his hard, thick length that her fingers wouldn't work properly.

"Let me help you with that," Ethan said, freeing his cock from his pants.

"Yes," Reagan said, shifting onto his lap and grasping the back of the front seat with both hands.

Ethan scrunched down in his seat to center himself between her legs, pushed her thong to one side, and pressed his cockhead inside her. She moaned, her face pressed against the seat back, as she lowered her hips and took him deep.

"Mmm. Her pussy is always better than I remember," Ethan said, his hands stroking her belly and breasts as she rode him. "Is it that way for you, Trey?"

Reagan lifted her head to peek at her neglected lover in the driver's seat. He was massaging her discarded shorts into his crotch while navigating traffic like a Nascar driver.

"You didn't answer me," Ethan said.

"Fuck you," Trey muttered under his breath.

"No, baby, fuck you," Ethan said. "I'm going to hold your hands behind your back and fuck that hot ass of yours until you come. You can beg me to touch you, but I won't."

Just thinking about Ethan pounding into Trey had Reagan working Ethan's cock and trying to soothe the ache deep within her. She never could seem to reach that ache unless she was filled with both of them. Ethan helped her by fingering her swollen clit until she exploded. She cried out, her fingers digging into the thick leather of the seat, her pussy clenching around Ethan's cock.

He groaned. "That's it, baby. Take what I give you."

"Thank you," she whispered, still breathing hard, her body trembling with shattered bliss.

"This isn't fair," Trey said, stopping at an intersection and turning his head to look at the pair of them scrunched low in the back of his brand new car. "When do I get relief?"

"It won't happen easy. Reagan will want to help you by sucking or stroking or fucking that gorgeous dick of yours—and I can't blame her—but I'm not going to let her touch you. I'll be the one to make you come. By penetration only."

Trey huffed out a breath, pressing Reagan's shorts so firmly into his crotch that it had to hurt. Poor guy.

"You really are cruel to him," Reagan murmured.

"That's what he wants. Isn't it, Trey?"

Trey swallowed hard, but he nodded.

"He wants to relive that first time with Brian over and over again."

Reagan straightened—Ethan's stiff cock still buried inside her—and focused on Trey. His face had gone pink and the knuckles of one hand white as he gripped the steering wheel.

"I didn't tell you about that so you could use it against me," Trey said, his voice taking on a breathless quality.

"Tell him about what?" Reagan asked, angling her head to stare at Ethan.

Ethan's tan complexion was unusually pasty. "Shit, I'm sorry, Trey," Ethan said, the sexy timber of his voice replaced with its usual pitch. "I didn't mean it that way. I just . . . I just want you to have what you need. I thought you liked that."

"What are you talking about?" Reagan asked. She'd apparently missed an important piece of information.

"Forget it," Trey said.

"Did you tell Ethan the details of your affair with Brian?" she asked, her chest aching at the idea of him confiding something to Ethan that she hadn't managed to pry out of him with both hands and a crowbar.

"I said forget it," Trey said. He threw her shorts into the back seat. "Put those on."

Ethan had gone soft anyway, so she slid off his lap and wriggled into her shorts. "Did he tell you about Brian?" she asked Ethan, wincing at the accusatory tone of her voice.

"It's not a big deal," Ethan said.

He couldn't possibly believe that.

"If it's not a big deal, why wouldn't he ever share it with me?" Reagan said, flopping into the seat behind Trey, fastening her seat belt, and crossing her arms over her chest. Yeah, she was pouting. So what.

"I thought Ethan would be more understanding because he's a guy," Trey said, pulling to a halt in front of their apartment building. They'd decided to find a new place for the three of them after they finished their summer tour, but for now they were still stuck in their crummy neighborhood. Trey's BMW practically had a Steal Me sign affixed to the bumper.

"So because I'm a woman, I can't possibly understand how it feels to love someone you shouldn't?"

"It's more the first ass-fucking thing that you wouldn't understand," Trey snapped as he hurried out of the car. They'd all been too upset to notice the photographer hiding in the low palms around their front walk. He was taking pictures of Trey before he'd even slammed the car door.

Reagan left Ethan rearranging his fly while she jumped out of the car to confront the frizzy-haired man. "Will you just go away and leave us alone!"

Trey dashed up the stairs and was already shoving his key into the door when Ethan emerged from the back of the car. The photographer's eyes widened—most likely because Reagan had been in the back seat with him, not in the passenger seat with her supposed boyfriend—and then he started snapping pictures. A wide grin spread across his oily face.

"Give me that camera," Ethan said, placing his hand over the lens and tugging.

The slightly built guy refused to release his hold on the camera and started moving backward. "I'm in a public area, within my rights to photograph anything or anyone for editorial—"

"As Reagan Elliot's bodyguard, I feel you are threatening her well-being, and I'm within my rights to punch you in the fucking mouth."

Reagan cringed, knowing Ethan was prone to get violent when he was protecting someone. "I'm okay," she said, wrapping a hand around Ethan's arm and tugging. They really didn't need more attention drawn to them, and if Ethan started punching paparazzi in the mouth, they'd end up with a heap more of the kind of attention they didn't want. "Let's just get ready. We don't want to be late for the visitation."

"The visitation for Sed Lionheart's father?" the photographer asked, relinquishing his camera to Ethan, backing away, and reaching into his pocket to pull out a cellphone.

Reagan's stomach churned, and her heart was pumping so hard, she could hear blood rushing through her head. If a bunch of paparazzi showed up at the visitation, it would be her fault for blabbing without thinking.

"Don't you fucking dare," Ethan said, charging forward after the fleeing man who was jabbering breathlessly into his cellphone as he darted around the parking lot in a chaotic pattern.

"Ethan!" Reagan called. "Don't make this worse. Please!"

Sending the photographer a look dark enough to blot out the sun, Ethan set the camera on the ground and returned to Reagan's side. "Let's get inside."

Reagan nodded and reached for Ethan's hand, but thought better of it when she noticed the frizzy-haired dude had already collected his camera. Ethan followed a safe distance behind her until they were inside the apartment. He pulled all the curtains shut while Reagan went in search of Trey.

She found him in the bedroom in his recently changed underwear, searching through the few clothes he had left in her closet. His clothes, still slightly damp from his dip in the pool, lay in a discarded heap on the floor. Hangers scraped across the bar as he jerked each article of clothing into the next. With a frustrated sigh, he yanked a pair of slightly faded black jeans from a hanger and shoved a foot through one leg. Reagan moved in close behind him and pressed her hand to the center of his bare back. His breath hitched, but he didn't acknowledge her, only stuffed his other leg into his jeans, pulled them up, and fastened them with shaking fingers.

"Sweetheart, what's bothering you?" Reagan asked. "You can tell me anything." *Including the details of your brief affair with Brian.* But she wouldn't push him to spill his guts. Maybe Ethan did understand Trey better than she did. Maybe that was why she hadn't been enough for him. Would never be enough for him.

"I just . . . I need to be with Sed," Trey said, pulling a gray-and-black-plaid button-down shirt from a hanger. "He supported me through a lot of shit and now—when I might actually be able to return to the favor—I'm playing chauffer to a pair of insensitive jackasses who only care about fucking." He stuck his arms through the shirt's sleeves, but didn't bother fastening the buttons as he yanked on one sock and then the other.

Reagan blinked at him, too stunned to defend herself or Ethan. Did he really see them that way? If he'd wanted to be with Sed, he should have told them. It had been his idea to spend the morning at his parents' house. Before she could gather her thoughts enough to point that out, he grabbed his shoes and stormed out of the bedroom.

She heard Ethan say, "Trey? Where are you—" before the slamming of the front door cut him off.

The front door opened again, and Ethan was yelling after Trey from the landing's balcony. Reagan hurried to stop him. That ridiculous photographer was probably still milling about outside. They didn't need this little spat displayed across every checkout stand in the nation.

She grabbed Ethan's arm and tugged, trying to draw him back inside. Trey's car was already backed out of its parking spot. The tires squealed as he sped forward, bumping over a curve when he turned into traffic to the alarming sounds of several car horns.

"We have to go after him," Ethan said, pulling his arm free and starting toward the stairs.

She grabbed his arm again to stop him. "We will go after him, but we have to be calm about it." She jerked her head toward the frizzy-haired man in the parking lot who was snapping pictures of them from ground level. She had no idea how they'd spin this tale in the tabloids, but she was certain it wouldn't be flattering or sympathetic to their pain.

With a snarl, Ethan gave the photographer a one-fingered

salute and spun to go inside. Reagan plastered a smile to her face so fake that she feared she'd magically turned plastic. She followed Ethan inside and closed the door, leaning against its back and drawing a steadying breath. Her entire body was trembling, and her heart was full of longing for Trey. She hated that he'd rushed off hurt and angry, hated it even more that some stupid photographer made her feel like she couldn't comfort him. And that Ethan definitely couldn't comfort him.

"Fuck," she muttered under her breath.

"Hurry up and change," Ethan said as he used a hip to burst through his bedroom door. His arms and damp T-shirt were suspended over his head. "I'm so sick of those damned photographers," he grumbled. "If they know what's good for them, they'll stay the fuck out of my way."

Reagan knew the feeling. She was sick of them too. She also knew this would get a lot worse before it got better. Scrubbing her face with both hands, she went to her bedroom in search of something suitable to wear, her thoughts bouncing around in her head like unselected lottery balls.

Maybe Trey was right. Maybe this would go away—or at least diminish—if they were open about their complicated relationship. And maybe her father wouldn't murder all three of them and bury them in the desert in an unmarked grave. Maybe he'd publicly execute them and display their dead bodies instead.

CHAPTER 15

TREY PUSHED through the crowded room, offering quiet greetings to the people he knew, but he was looking for one familiar face. He didn't see Sed anywhere, but he did notice a highly recognizable, crazy hairstyle—black with a distinctive yellow strip—near the front of the room. He hurried to Eric's side, hoping Eric could point him in Sed's direction, certain their rock of a lead singer could use a little support. Hell, Trey could use a little support himself. He wasn't in the mood to interact with anyone else.

"Where's your shadow?" Eric asked in greeting, nodding at the empty space behind Trey. "And your shadow's shadow?"

Trey shrugged, as if he didn't care that he was at odds with Reagan and even more so with Ethan. He didn't know why he'd reacted so strongly to Ethan revealing his secret to Reagan. It wasn't that Trey didn't want Reagan to know the details of his brief affair with Brian—that wasn't the issue. The issue was . . . Trey wasn't sure, exactly, but a dark feeling was gnawing away at his insides. In the car he'd been absolutely livid, and he wasn't sorry he'd let the pair of them know he was upset. Trey just wished he understood why he felt utterly betrayed by Ethan's slip. The three of them were supposed to be partners. *Equal* partners. Equal partners shared everything with each other and didn't exclude anyone. Didn't they? He'd thought so. Now he wasn't so sure.

"Where's Sed?" he asked Eric.

"I think he went outside for some air," Eric said. "I wouldn't bother him right now. He's not dealing with this well."

That was why Trey planned to bother him. "Thanks."

He turned to hunt for Sed outside, but Eric caught his arm. "Aren't Reagan and Ethan coming?"

Trey shrugged again and pulled away from Eric's loose grip. When he turned, Rebekah was standing in his path. "About time you got—" Her cheery smile faded into a concerned scowl. "Are you okay? You look pretty down."

"How am I supposed to look when a friend's father dies?"

He had known Sed's father—and he was saddened by his passing and especially concerned by how much it must hurt his only son—but Trey had troubles of his own, and he didn't want to talk about them with anyone, except maybe Dare. A quick glance around the room and at the line that was filtering past the open casket told Trey that his brother had yet to arrive.

Rebekah gave Trey a quick hug. "He's with God now. You'll see him again when it's your time."

Trey didn't find her words comforting in the least, but he nodded, and when she released him, he continued on his way. When he finally located Sed behind the building, part of him wished he hadn't. Sed's muscular, tattooed arms were wrapped around a sobbing woman in a trim black skirt suit—Sed's mother, Trey realized on second glance—and though the words Sed repeated to her sounded strong, his face was a crumpled mask of despair.

"It's going to be okay, Mom," Sed told her. "I'll take care of everything."

"How could he leave us now? Doesn't he know we need him?"

Monica's angry words surprised Trey. It wasn't as if the man had committed suicide. She had to know he hadn't wanted to leave his family behind, broken and grieving.

"We would always need him. Now. Ten years from now. A hundred years from now."

"I just . . ." She shook her head and sniffed loudly. "I don't know what I'm going to do without him. I already miss him so much." She tilted her head back and looked up at her son, who towered over her.

"It's going to be okay," Sed repeated. "I'll take care of everything."

She smiled through her tears. "You're so much like him. A mighty rock in turbulent seas, standing strong against whatever the waves crash against you."

Sed's smile was terse—tired—but Monica didn't seem to

recognize that the waves were weathering her mighty rock more than usual. "You should go find Elise and Kylie. They're worried about you."

"I don't want your sisters to see me like this." Monica pulled a tissue out of her pocket and dabbed at her eyes and nose.

"They can handle it," Sed said. "They're like Dad too. And like you. It'll give them strength to stand beside you when you need them."

She nodded and they exchanged a lengthy embrace before she drew away and turned toward the door. She offered Trey a wavering smile as she passed, and all Trey could do was choke out a gruff, "I'm so sorry, Monica," before she vanished inside. He never knew what to say in these situations. He felt useless—even burdensome—as if everything he said or did would make things worse. Perhaps he should leave Sed to stare at the perfectly manicured lawn without saying anything.

"She brought me out here to give me this," Sed said, extending his arm behind him in Trey's direction. Did he even know who he was offering the crumpled paper to? He hadn't glanced Trey's way since Trey had stepped outside. "I want to read it, but my vision gets all blurry when I try. Would you?"

Trey stepped out of the shadow of the building and took the paper. What was it? His father's will? Some old love letter to his mother? Trey smoothed the page against his chest and when he read the scrawled title at the top of the page, his throat closed off. *Wedding Toast for Sed.* Trey swallowed against the knot in his throat. Sed was marrying Jessica soon, and now his father would miss the wedding.

"Are you sure you want to hear this now?" Trey asked Sed's back.

"I'm sure. If I can't handle it, I'll tell you to stop."

Sed continued to stare at the lawn, and Trey was glad. He wasn't sure he'd be able to read if Sed got all emotional and he had to stare that in the face. The man wasn't only his family's rock, he was the band's rock too. Trey, Jace, Eric, and even Brian had always depended on Sed's infallible stability.

Trey glanced at the funeral home, deciding he wasn't the best person for the job. "Maybe Jessica should—"

"I asked you."

"Fine." Trey lifted the page and cleared his throat. "Wedding toast for Sed," he read. "Believe it or not, this big guy was a little baby once."

"I don't believe it," Eric said from behind Trey. "No woman could squeeze out a head that size."

Trey scowled at the interruption, but Sed just laughed. "My mom did have to have a cesarean."

"You see?" Eric said. "He was never a *little* baby." He tried to snatch the paper from Trey's hand, but Trey smashed it against his chest. "What are you reading?"

"The toast Sed's dad wrote for his wedding."

"Sed's wedding?" Jace asked from somewhere behind him. This was turning into a regular band meeting.

"Yeah." Sed nodded. "Continue."

Trey was a bit surprised that Sed wanted him to keep reading now that Eric and Jace had shown up, but they did share a tour bus for most of the year, so why not?

Trey lifted the page—Eric standing close behind him to read over his shoulder—and continued. "I remember when his mother and I brought him home—"

"There you guys are," Brian interrupted as he dashed up behind them. "I was starting to wonder if I was at the right funeral home."

"Shh!" Eric said, waving a hand at Brian. "Trey's reading the toast Phil wrote for Sed's wedding."

"Oh," Brian said, stopping short. His smile of greeting slipped from his handsome face, and he offered Trey a questioning look. In a glance, Trey understood Brian's anxiety, his turmoil and his concern—his need to be part of whatever was going on here. He also understood his affection for Sed and for the other members of his band. His guilt. What did he have to feel guilty about?

Trey tore his gaze from Brian—why did the man always bring him peace and unsettle him at the same time?—and started reading the page over again.

"Believe it or not, this big guy was once a little baby. I remember when his mother and I brought him home. We were so afraid we were going to mess him up."

"I'd say they did a pretty good job at that," Eric quipped.

Jace shook his head at him, and Eric ducked his head and folded his hands at his waist. Even though they all knew that Eric dealt with uncomfortable situations with jokes, now was not an appropriate time for Eric to unleash his inner clown.

"He grew so fast," Trey read. "First words. First steps. First temper tantrum. There were many more tantrums in store for his mother and me. I'm sure Jessica has dealt with a few of those herself."

Sed chuckled. "More than a few."

Trey smiled and kept reading. "I tried so hard to push him into sports. Baseball and basketball, track and swimming. Hell, he even tried soccer. Yet all he ever wanted to do was sing. But when you have a kid built for athletics—look at the guy, he's a tank—you don't want him involved in that sissy stuff." Trey glanced up, expecting Sed to look hurt for his father calling his chosen profession "sissy stuff," but Sed had a smile on his face and was nodding in agreement with his father's words. "You want him to kick some ass. He eventually took up football. Not because he was any good at it or because he liked it, but because he wanted to make me proud."

Somebody in the group sniffed, but Trey pressed on.

"I was proud of him. I *am* proud of him. Not because he scored a touchdown—*once*." Eric chuckled and slapped Sed on the back. "Not because he's successful or rich and famous or too damned good looking for his own good. Not even because he has a voice that makes the angels in heaven envious. I'm proud of him because he's my boy. And now he's a grown man. A man smart enough to marry a strong woman who doesn't put up with his bullshit. Congratulations, Jessica. He's your problem now."

A laugh burst from Sed, but it ended on a sob. He pressed the heels of his hands into his eyes and took a strangled breath. Leaning close, Jace touched his arm. Jace had lost his father at a young age. He must understand what Sed was going through. Maybe that was why Sed grabbed him in a crushing hug, his body quaking with silent weeping. Trey exchanged a glance with Brian and Eric, and the three of them wrapped Sed in a tight embrace.

They stood in a huddle, lending strength and drawing upon it, until a gentle voice interrupted their public display of less-than-manly affection. "Are you okay, sweetheart? I've been looking everywhere for you."

Sed's body relaxed as he turned his head toward Jessica. "I'll be okay," he said. "I had Trey read Dad's wedding toast to us because I was too emotional to read it myself."

"I could have read it to you," Jessica said. She squirmed into a narrow opening between Jace and Brian to add her hug to their huddle.

The guys all let go of him at once, and Sed released his stranglehold on Jace—who took several deep breaths upon gaining his freedom—and wrapped his arms around his fiancée, burying his face in her long strawberry-blond hair.

"I'll read it to you," he said. "Later, when we're alone."

After that cue to leave, Sed's bandmates filed back into the funeral home with Trey bringing up the rear. They all had women to lean on now. He supposed their old habit of depending on each other for comfort had become obsolete. Except Trey still wanted to confide his troubles to Sed. Only now wasn't the best time to burden the poor guy with his trivial problems.

"Trey?" Sed called after him, and Trey turned, his shoulders slumping with relief. Sed had recognized his turmoil. Good old dependable Sed. "Can I have that back now?"

Sed nodded at the paper fluttering in Trey's hand. With a sullen nod, Trey retraced his steps and returned the wedding speech to its owner. "Sorry. I'm sure you'll treasure it always."

Sed's eyes scanned Trey's. "Did you need to talk to me about something?"

Jessica turned to examine Trey as well, her lips pursed with concern.

"It's nothing," he said, his gaze shifting to the meticulous lawn that had so enraptured Sed earlier. Maybe once Sed's life settled down, Trey would feel comfortable sharing his woes, but he felt like an ass for even considering unloading on him just then.

Sudden shouting from around the corner of the building made Trey cringe. He recognized Reagan's and Ethan's raised voices, and a knot formed in the pit of his stomach. His hurricane had arrived.

CHAPTER 16

T HE LAST THING ETHAN WANTED to deal with was another goddamned reporter, so of course half a dozen swarmed around Reagan as soon as she stepped out of the car near the mortuary. Did these people have no shame? Someone had died, and yet they carried on as if the only matter of any importance in the entire universe was the question of who Reagan Elliot was fucking.

"Stop following me," Reagan insisted. Her short heels clicked against the pavement as she trotted across the parking lot toward the enormous white building.

Ethan slammed his door and hurried after her. He'd told her to stay in the car until he could let her out—it *was* his job to guard her body, after all—but she'd mistakenly thought there weren't any paparazzi around when they'd arrived. As they'd driven through the entry gate, she accused Ethan of being overprotective and silly. As soon as she'd set foot on the curb, however, several photographers had literally jumped out of the bushes. Others had climbed out of an SUV parked several spaces down the row. All of them were snapping pictures and shouting questions at her. He wasn't sure how they'd gotten through the gate. Surely they wouldn't claim to be guests just to get a scoop on a story.

"Are you and Trey Mills breaking up?" a woman with sleek black hair asked.

Reagan stopped trying to escape and turned to face the woman. "Why? Is that what he said?"

Ethan found himself behind half a dozen reporters

surrounding Reagan like a swarm of flies on shit. And based on the devastated look on Reagan's face, she was feeling like that particular fly attractant at that moment. He waved, trying to gain Reagan's attention and prevent her temper from making her do or say something she'd regret. Ethan was positive that even if Trey was considering a breakup—which seemed impossible—he would never make that information public. She didn't really believe Trey would break up with her—with *them*—did she? Yes, Trey had been distraught when he'd left the apartment, but he loved them both. Ethan would never doubt that.

"Maybe he did," the reporter said. "How is Trey coping with the knowledge of your affair with your bodyguard?"

Ethan's stomach sank as half the reporters turned disgusted looks on him. The other half were waiting for Reagan's reply.

"It's none of your business who I sleep with," Reagan spat.

Ethan cringed at Reagan's all-but admission of guilt.

"Trey was seen leaving your apartment an hour ago," the black-haired woman said. "He was obviously upset. Maybe he'd feel better if you found a different bodyguard. One you *aren't* having an affair with."

Several additional disgusted glares were tossed in Ethan's direction. He wondered how offended they'd be if they knew the truth. He was trying very hard to keep a handle on his temper. He'd lost it with that photographer waiting in front of their apartment building, but he was more prepared for the invasion of their privacy this time. With a little jostling—involving a bit of brute strength—Ethan managed to squeeze through the throng of busybodies and get a hand on Reagan's upper arm.

"Excuse us," Ethan said, his voice calm but authoritative as he addressed the press. "Miss Elliot is already late for a somber occasion. We appreciate your cooperation in allowing her to attend the visitation without further interruption." What he really wanted to say was *fuck right off, assholes*, but he'd try a less combative tactic fist.

He tugged on Reagan's arm gently to get her feet moving again. For a moment or two, Ethan thought the paparazzi were tactful enough to leave them be. No such luck.

"*Miss* Elliot," the black-haired report said snidely. "Do you use what's between your legs to control every man in your life or just—"

Ethan knew the woman was trying to goad Reagan into revealing something—and maybe Reagan realized that too—but he didn't blame her for flying toward the rude woman in a rage. Ethan caught Reagan's flailing body around the waist, lifting her feet off the ground as she reached for the woman who'd insulted her. Every camera around them was snapping successive shots. Photos of Reagan struggling for her freedom, her face contorted with hurt and anger. Photos of Reagan taking wild swings at the object of her fury. Photos of Reagan spewing curses so loud and blasphemous that deaf sailors in the middle of the Atlantic would have blushed.

Ethan leaned close to Reagan's ear to talk soothing words of sense to her and got a head butt to the nose for his troubles. The damned thing had been broken more than once, so it didn't take much force to make it bleed. Ethan supposed that meant there would be pictures spread across newsstands of him with a bloody nose as he struggled to control a small woman with an enormous temper without hurting her.

"Reagan," Ethan bellowed. "Chill the fuck out!" She stiffened as if he'd head-butted *her* in the nose, and then covered her face with both hands. Her piteous sob squeezed his throat, choking off his airflow. He realized she was more hurt than angry and as pissed off as she'd been seconds ago, he could only imagine how her passionate heart ached.

He scooped her into his arms, probably revealing a bit too much of her thigh as his arm slipped beneath her knees. "It will be okay," he murmured to her, fighting the instinct to brush comforting kisses to her forehead and temple.

He shifted her into a more secure position, and her arms went around his neck for stability. Her tears soaked the crisp black fabric at his shoulder as she sobbed uncontrollably. Ethan turned to carry her toward the mortuary, praying that the assholes didn't have the audacity to follow them inside, and noticed the crowd emerging from the open front doors of the sprawling colonial structure. Sed headed the group. His strong face was such an angry shade of red, Ethan wondered if he'd kissed the sun.

"How did you get inside the gate?" Sed asked the nearest photographer.

"It was open, so we came in," he said, nodding in the direction of the iron gate at the end of the drive. Ethan knew better. When he'd arrived he'd had to identify himself as a guest of Phillip Lionhearts's visitation. Still, they hadn't checked a list for his name. He assumed they were a little more careful about who got in to funerals for celebrities.

"See your way back out, you're not welcome here," Sed continued. The three members of his band flanking him nodded in agreement. Trey was conspicuously absent. Ethan had recognized Trey's car when they'd pulled up, so he had to be around somewhere. He probably wanted to avoid the press.

"This doesn't concern you," the black-haired reporter told Sed. "We're just trying to get Reagan Elliot to answer some of our questions."

"It *does* concern me," Sed boomed, his face now an alarming shade of purple. "Reagan is my guest. She came to offer her support to me as a friend. My father died unexpectedly two days ago, and I sure as hell don't want to deal with this right now. This is private property, and you've been asked to leave. You can do so now or explain to the police why you're trespassing."

"Let me down," Reagan said quietly to Ethan.

Ethan had been so caught up in Sed's interactions with the press that he'd failed to notice Reagan had stopped crying and was tugging at her skirt to cover her thighs. He set her on her feet and dabbed at the blood trickling from his nose with a shirt cuff. Reagan smoothed her skirt with both hands before straightening. She approached Sed and gave him a huge hug—which inspired another flurry of photos.

"I'm so sorry this mess followed me here," she said, staring up into Sed's troubled blue eyes and laying a palm on his cheek amid additional shutter clicks. "Let's go inside. Out of sight, out of mind."

Sed smiled and nodded. He placed a hand on one side of Reagan's head and pressed a gruff kiss to the opposite side. Ethan had seen Sed do the same to Trey and to just about anyone he considered a friend, but the excited murmuring among the paparazzi as they jotted their notes and took their fucking pictures worried Ethan. What twisted angle would they assign to Sed's tender show of friendship? Ethan followed Reagan and Sed's other guests into the mortuary fantasizing about grabbing a sledgehammer and destroying a truckload of expensive cameras. He was less inclined to admit that he wouldn't mind taking the same sledgehammer to a few fingers as well. But he no longer solved his problems with violence.

As he stepped under the entryway's roof, he noticed Trey standing in the shadows near the open front door. Reagan was caught up with offering her condolences to Sed, so Ethan broke off from the group to speak to Trey. Before he could reach him, Trey slipped around the corner and disappeared into an alcove just inside the front entrance.

Ethan's heart thudded. Did that mean he didn't want to be bothered? Too bad. Ethan wasn't going to let him hide. Ethan had a whole lot of apologizing and groveling to do. He wasn't sure this was the time or the place, but he needed to start now.

Trey stood against the wall—his back pressed to the smooth surface, his chin ducked so that his long bangs hid his expression.

"I really am sorry, Trey. I didn't know you wanted to hide your affair with Brian from Reagan."

Trey's head lifted. His crumpled brow and set jaw told Ethan he'd gotten his apology all wrong.

"I don't want to hide anything from Reagan." He reached for a box of tissues and pulled a sheet free. Handing it to Ethan, he asked, "Why is your nose bleeding?"

"Reagan bumped it with her head. I thought it was accidental, but seeing as I'm a huge jerk, maybe she did it on purpose." Ethan wiped at his nose, finding the bleeding had almost stopped.

"You are a jerk," Trey said.

"I probably should have warned you about that before I made you fall in love with me." Ethan had hoped his jest would provoke an ornery grin, but Trey merely sighed.

"You should definitely wear a warning label."

"I didn't mean to hurt you. How can I make it up to you?" He reached for Trey, wanting so badly to touch him that his belly ached, but people were milling about everywhere, so he dropped his hand.

"Do you really want to know how to make it up to me, or are you just offering out of stupid courtesy?"

"I really want to know."

"Kiss me."

Ethan grinned. "If that's all it takes, I'll take you to bed and kiss you for hours."

"Not in bed—here, in front of everyone. One deep, demanding, unquestionably sexual kiss. That's what I want."

Ethan glanced around, hoping by some miracle that everyone in the vicinity had been stricken with complete blindness. If he kissed Trey here and now, there'd be more than one witness. And he was pretty sure the unfamiliar person watching them from near a pillar was an incognito member of the press.

"I can't do that, Trey. Not here."

Trey closed his eyes and nodded. "I figured as much. You don't even love me enough to claim me as yours."

He pushed off the wall and brushed against Ethan's arm as he passed. With his heart trying to crawl out of his throat, Ethan grabbed Trey's arm and spun him to face him. One kiss was all he'd asked for. One kiss. And yet, as Ethan searched Trey's troubled green eyes, he couldn't bring himself to do it. He was terrified of the backlash. An easy kiss had never been so daunting. A simple kiss had never been so complex. He had to trust that Trey would understand why he couldn't grant his small request. "I'd die for you, Trey," Ethan told him, squeezing Trey's arm so he'd know how much he meant it. "I'd *die* for you."

"Dying is easy," Trey said. "Living with who you are is the hard part."

He pulled away and before Ethan could regain his attention, Trey brightened and waved at his brother and parents, who'd just entered the building.

Living *was* the hard part, especially if he ever had to go on without Trey in his life. How would Ethan ever find the strength—the courage—to be the man Trey needed? Be the man Trey deserved?

CHAPTER 17

REAGAN WAS AVOIDING the inevitable. Trey hadn't spoken to her all evening. If their eyes happened to meet, he immediately looked away. She could feel an argument simmering—a big one—and since a funeral visitation wasn't the place for it to boil over, she chatted with acquaintances, offered her condolences to the deceased's family, and didn't feel too conspicuous when dabbing away the occasional tear with her soggy tissue. Ethan was avoiding her for different reasons—too many inquisitive eyes on them at all times—but she could feel his presence, and his concern, from across the room.

When she couldn't stand the tension any longer, she used the genuine headache pounding between her temples as an excuse to make an early exit.

"I have some Tylenol in my purse," Jessica offered kindly from where she sat beside an ashen-faced Sed with a comforting hand on his lower back.

"Don't trouble yourself," Reagan said. "I've burdened everyone enough already today with my entourage of paparazzi." She rolled her eyes.

Sed shook his head, his terse expression softening into a smile. "I enjoyed telling them to fuck off."

"And you did a very good job getting them to do it."

"Not really," Sed replied. "Do you see that woman over there introducing herself as my cousin Martha?"

Reagan recognized the black-haired reporter from earlier,

except now she was wearing a hat and wide white-rimmed sunglasses. Reagan's jaw dropped at the woman's audacity.

"I don't have a cousin named Martha."

"That's the reporter from earlier. The one who asked if I use what's between my legs—" Realizing that her voice had risen by several inappropriate decibels, Reagan slapped a hand over her mouth to control her tirade. She took a deep, calming breath and said, "I better go. I'm sure *cousin* Martha will follow me out."

"They're so hurtful," Jessica said glumly, probably thinking of her own embarrassing stint in the spotlight when she and Sed had been filmed having sex in a Las Vegas tourist spot. "And prying."

"I hope they hurry up and find someone more interesting to pester." Reagan winced as her building headache produced a blinding throb. She massaged one temple with her fingertips, providing only limited relief from the pain.

"You look like you need to lie down," Jessica said. "We appreciate your stopping in, but don't feel bad for leaving."

"If you need anything . . ."

Sed nodded in appreciation and turned his attention to Steve Aimes, who'd just arrived. Cousin Martha's gaze shifted to Steve, and then the reporter inexplicably slipped out of the room. Well, hell, if all it took was one glance at Steve to get these people to leave her alone, Reagan would be cozying up to the drummer on a regular basis. She'd heard that he'd had a few run-ins with the paparazzi, but she hadn't known they were actually afraid of him. She'd already said her goodbyes, however, so after a quick greeting to her new paparazzi-repelling hero, she went in search of her ride. She found Ethan leaning against a wall, arms crossed, and looking all sorts of surly.

"I have a headache," Reagan told him. "Will you take me home? Or are you going to catch a ride with Trey? I think I can drive myself if you give me your keys."

"I'll drive you," Ethan said. "I don't think Trey is ready to leave yet."

She spotted Trey sitting shoulder to shoulder with Sed. Trey said something that made Sed smile—an expression she hadn't seen from Sed since she'd arrived. Now that Reagan thought about it, Trey had been at Sed's side every moment *except* when she'd been with Sed. Trey wasn't very subtle about letting her know he wasn't interested in talking to her. She didn't want to cause a scene by confronting him here, so she blinked back a few more tears and started toward the exit. What she really wanted to do was collapse against Ethan's chest and sob out her agony, but she couldn't do that. Not with all the prying eyes around her.

"I think he just needs time," Ethan said quietly to Reagan's back.

She smiled at a gaping stranger when their gazes connected and then clenched her teeth when the same woman whispered to the woman next to her behind a concealing hand. Now Reagan had two strangers staring at her as if they'd been thoroughly scandalized. If she'd been anywhere but a mortuary, she might have marched across the room and told them both off. Instead, she swallowed her anger and pride and a heap of hurt and simply pushed the door open to go outside. Seeing the reporters standing just outside the fence with their camera lenses poking between the iron bars as they waited for her to do something photo-worthy made her stumble over her feet. Ethan placed a hand on her back to steady her, and she flinched away from his touch. Even the slightest attention from him made her wonder how she'd be portrayed in the media.

Fuck, she hated this.

She was acutely aware of the lack of pictures being taken as she walked woodenly to Ethan's car and even more aware of the flurry of shots as he opened the car door for her and assisted her inside. Her head had been pounding before, but now it felt as if someone were trying to remove her brain through her hair follicles, and her stomach churned in protest of the pain and the anxiety tightening her muscles into knots. She curled forward, her arms wrapped securely around her belly, and took deep breaths to stave back her nausea. If she puked for the cameras, they'd probably insist she was pregnant with Ethan's love child. Or maybe they'd twist the false tale into her being the future mother of non-identical sextuplets, each with a different father or something equally ridiculous.

Ethan climbed into the driver's seat and slammed the door. "Are you okay?" he asked, laying a comforting hand on her shoulder.

Terror poured ice into her veins, and she slapped his hand away. "Don't touch me!"

"Reagan?"

She cringed at the hurt in his voice. Trey had already wounded him; he didn't need her adding salt to his wounds, even if the salt came from her own tears.

"I'm sorry. Just . . . I want to get out of here. Please."

"It's okay. I'll take you home."

"No." She shook her head, tightening her arms around her stomach as bile rose up her throat. "They'll be there too," she whispered.

"Where should we go, then?"

"A place where no one knows who I am. A place where I feel safe." She wasn't sure such a place existed, but Ethan must, because he backed out of his parking space and drove away from the mortuary without another word.

After several blocks, Reagan asked, "Are they following us?"

Ethan glanced in his rearview mirror. "Yes."

"Why won't they leave us alone?"

"You know why," Ethan said. "Maybe Trey is right. Maybe we should just come out with the truth. At least all this bullshit will be for something we believe in. I'm sick of seeing you suffer over lies."

Reagan's cellphone began to ring. She scrambled to pull it from her purse, hoping it was Trey. They needed to talk and come up with a game plan that suited them all. This—whatever it was that they were doing—wasn't working.

She glanced at her display, and immediately her churning stomach dropped into her shoes.

"Aren't you going to answer that?" Ethan asked.

Reagan's first instinct was to not answer, but maybe hearing his voice—even if it was the condescending tone he used when she disappointed him—would bring her a little peace. He couldn't possibly make her feel any worse. He was home. He was safe. Maybe he was exactly what she needed.

"Hi, Daddy," she said, surprised at how normal her voice sounded.

"You'd better hightail your ass back to Arkansas right now, young lady. I knew I should have had your legs sewn together before you left."

Or maybe he was exactly what she *didn't* need.

She'd underestimated her father's influence over her mood. He *could* make her feel worse. And *she* could hang up on him. After ending the call with a shaky finger, she blocked his number, shoved her phone back into her purse, and stared at her trembling hands.

"Did he tell you that you're just like your home-wrecking bitch of a mother again?" Ethan asked, his voice terse with anger.

"I hung up on him before he could get that far." But her father knew that she was involved with two men. He couldn't have the details right, but he *knew*.

Reagan had never been more mortified.

CHAPTER 18

TREY STUCK it out with Sed until the last guest had left, partly because he felt obligated to be there for Sed and partly because he didn't want to go home. An altercation was waiting for him there, and he hadn't yet decided if he was going to stick to his guns or back down and wait for his pair of reluctant lovers to open their reality to the outside world. Trey understood why Reagan wanted to keep the truth about their relationship a secret. He even understood why Ethan wanted to hide his sexuality. What concerned Trey was that neither of them were willing to go to bat for this relationship—for *him*—and if he felt this miserable about it now, how would he feel after weeks of secrecy? Months of hiding who they were? He was sick just thinking about it.

Trey typically went with the flow; he didn't like to churn up controversy. His goal wasn't to be different. He just was. He'd accepted his personality and his quirks long ago. With the exception of his fixation with Brian, Trey moved past life's stumbling blocks easily, but when his heart was involved—his whole heart—he couldn't walk away. He'd given his heart to two people, and he would not let go of them. He was prepared to fight for Ethan and Reagan, but without a united front, the three of them would be destroyed by the bigots of the world. In his opinion, they needed to stand together. And while Reagan and Ethan seemed to have formed an alliance of secrecy, Trey was on an entirely different page and he knew nothing would change his mind about what needed to be done. He didn't want his happiness to end so quickly after he'd found it, but he had to admit that he wasn't happy. He could be happy again. They all could be happy again. He just didn't know how to get back the glorious euphoria that they'd experienced together before the tabloids insisted that Reagan was cheating on him with Ethan and that Trey was supposed to be devastated by that false revelation.

"Why are you still hanging around here?" Sed asked. "Go home and sleep. The funeral is early tomorrow. You need to get some rest."

"I think that's what I'm supposed to say to you," Trey said, but he made no move to rise from the folding chair he'd parked his butt in while Sed said goodnight to his mother and sisters. Even Jessica had been convinced to go home, as the stress of the day had exhausted her so much, she'd been nodding off against Sed's shoulder.

"I can tell you want to talk." Sed sat in the chair beside him, rested his forearms on his thighs, and linked his fingers. "So talk."

"I shouldn't burden you with my stupid problems right now."

The corner of Sed's mouth twitched in a hint of a grin. "But you're going to anyway."

Trey chuckled. Sed knew him all too well. Trey always went to Dare first—mostly for validation since they usually had the same opinions about issues—and Sed second, for a different perspective. Sed would shoot straight with him. Trey used to go to Brian with his problems, but his comfort level with his best friend had diminished since he'd confessed his love to him and been made to see what a fool he'd been.

"I'm not sure how to handle this situation with the tabloids. I think we should just tell it like it is. Don't you think that would be for the best?"

Sed scratched behind his ear. "That depends."

"On what?"

"On what your partners think."

Trey hadn't been expecting Sed to side with them. Maybe Trey should just stick to seeking Dare's advice after all. "They're afraid of what people will think or what they'll say."

"Most people would be afraid." Sed slapped him on the back. "You're a bit of an oddity in that regard. And they're probably more afraid of what people will do. People can be quite cruel to those they perceive as different."

"Homosexuality has become accepted by most of society." Trey shrugged. "It's not that big a deal anymore."

"You're not talking about homosexuality, you're talking about bisexuality. You're talking about polyamory. These practices still aren't considered normal. People won't understand."

"We can make them understand. What Reagan, Ethan, and I have together is beautiful. It's perfect." Perfect when they weren't at odds with one another.

"It's also strange. How can you love two people with all your heart at the same time? If you give your all to one, there's nothing left for the other."

Trey shook his head. "That's not how it works."

"I see you with them every day, Trey, and it still doesn't make sense to me. Do you really think you're going to convince a bunch of strangers that your relationship is ideal?"

"I don't get why it's so hard to believe that I can love two people with all that I am. What if you have two kids or six? Do you divide your love for them into sections, or do you love each of your children with all your heart?"

"That's different." Sed shook his head.

Trey released an exasperated breath. If he couldn't get Sed to understand, how could he ever expect the tabloids to get it right? They'd likely confuse his perfect relationship into an even bigger scandal.

"So you think we should keep everything a secret until the media storm blows over?" Trey asked.

"I don't think you want to be the poster child on this issue. It might sound heroic and you might think stepping up and out will solve your problems, but being in the spotlight will be hell—hard on you, hard on your relationship, hard on everyone who supports you."

Sed was telling him to back down. If Sed didn't think Trey could handle the pressure, he was probably right.

"Now, if Reagan and Ethan are willing to support you through this, you'd probably be okay. But I don't see them waving their freak flags any time soon."

"So I probably shouldn't wave mine with such enthusiasm," Trey said flatly.

"That's up to you, but I don't think it will bring the happiness and relief you expect. Relationships are about compromise, and with three people in a relationship . . ." He closed his eyes and shook his head. "Not sure if there's enough compromise in the world to see you through." Sed's phone dinged with a text message, and he dug the phone out of his pocket. He smiled at the display as he read. "Jess is worried about me."

Of course she was. Trey was being selfish asking Sed for advice at a time like this. Plus, as sound as that advice was, it just didn't sit well with Trey. It did make him think, though, which was important when he'd been so focused on taking action. If he took the step he wanted to take, they'd never be able to return to where they were now.

Trey patted Sed's back. "You'd better go home before she sends out a search party."

"If you need me to stick around—"

"Nope. I'm going too. Sorry I laid this on you right now. I know you have more important things to worry about than my love life."

"I don't mind." Sed climbed to his feet. "Gave me something to think about besides everything my father will miss and all that my future kids have lost before they're even born."

Trey's heart ached for Sed. "They'll get to know him through you."

"It's not the same."

Trey followed Sed to the exit, trying to come up with the right words to say. Nothing felt right, so he ended up saying nothing.

"I'll see you tomorrow," Trey said.

"If you ever need a place to crash . . ."

Trey blew out his cheeks. It seemed Sed didn't have much confidence in his ability to keep his relationship together. Or maybe he was just being nice. Sometimes Trey overthought things. "Thanks for the offer, but I'm good."

By the time he reached Reagan and Ethan's apartment, he was convinced that they'd make everything work out. If he had to compromise, then he'd compromise. He'd push, but he'd compromise. He could do that. And when they were ready—*if* they were ever ready—they'd announce their relationship to the world together. Strength in unity and all that jazz.

His confidence faltered when he noticed Ethan's car wasn't in the parking lot, and it crumbled at the lack of light glowing in the windows. They weren't home. They'd taken off from the wake without a word to him and then disappeared together. So much for unity.

Trey had a moment of panic when he discovered his phone wasn't in his pocket before he remembered he'd tossed it into the glove box hours earlier. The battery was completely drained, so he plugged it into his car's USB jack and waited for it to collect enough charge to boot up. While he sat there, he noticed movement behind his car. He didn't have enough time to register what was going on before a bright flash of light went off just outside his window, blinding him. He blinked to clear his vision, glad he'd been delayed in the car for a few minutes. No telling what they'd print about how he'd showed up at Reagan's apartment that night only to find she was out cheating with her bodyguard lover *again*. He kind of hoped she was. After the three of them set things straight between them, Trey was very much looking forward to some rigorous make-up sex.

His phone finally came on, and he searched through his messages, looking for anything from either Reagan or Ethan. He paused when he came to a new voicemail from Brian, but after a second of hesitation, he flicked past it until he found what he was hoping for.

The message was from Ethan. He played it, putting the phone to his ear instead of playing it over his speakers so that the photographers still skulking around his car wouldn't overhear.

"It's E. Reagan said I shouldn't bother calling you because you're behaving like an ass, but she's just upset. She's in Brian's bed sleeping off a migraine. I'm sure she'll see things differently when she wakes."

Brian's bed? What the hell?

"Sorry we barged into your apartment without an invitation."

They'd gone to his place—the two-bedroom apartment he'd shared with Brian until his long-time roommate found a wife and fathered a child. Trey found it impossible to stay there by himself without falling into a deep depression, so he didn't go often. It made sense that Ethan and Reagan would seek shelter in the place. It was a gated community, and the security team was good about keeping unwanted visitors from entering the premises. He was glad he'd added Reagan and Ethan to his occupancy list and given them Brian's unwanted set of keys and his card to the parking gate.

"We tried shaking the paparazzi, but gave up and went into hiding." Ethan was quiet for a moment before he added, "We need to talk. If there's any way we can make this work . . ." He released a raspy sigh. "I love you. Even if no one else in the world ever sees it, you need to see it. You need to believe it. So please, Trey, come home. We can talk. Or you can talk and I can just hold you." Ethan chuckled. "This is the longest phone message I've ever left, so you must mean a lot to me. I'm trying to be more like you. More open and free to be myself. But it's going to take time and patience on your part. I hope you think I'm worth the effort."

"You are," Trey said, even though Ethan couldn't hear his words. Trey had been so drawn in by what Ethan was saying that he'd forgotten he was listening to a recorded message.

"I'll see you soon," Ethan said. "Don't make me stalk you. I'll do it."

Trey laughed. Ethan knew how much he hated being pursued by discarded lovers. But he'd never give up Ethan voluntarily. And if that meant they had to keep their love a secret for the rest of their lives, Trey would do his best to restrain his affection for the man when in public. He'd just have to save his devotion for when they were alone. Which is where Trey wanted to be more than anything—alone with Ethan and Reagan.

Trey shifted into reverse, almost striking the photographer standing behind his car. He ignored the angry swearing thrown in his direction, ignored the headlights in his rearview mirror as he navigated the near-deserted streets, ignored a red light to get the paparazzi off his ass. Surprised that his illegal and potentially dangerous maneuver had worked, he turned down a residential street and took a less-traveled route to his apartment. Proud and relieved that he'd managed to lose the journalists, he groaned aloud when he noticed several suspicious vans parked outside the entrance to his community. He was surprised when photographers didn't jump out of the vans and start snapping pictures of him when he slipped his access card into the reader at the gate entrance. Were they sleeping on the job or looking to harass only Reagan?

When he let himself into his apartment, the television in the living room provided the only light and sound. He gasped when a strong hand grabbed him around the throat.

"Trey?" Ethan asked, his hold slackening.

Trey rubbed at his neck. "Who else would it be?"

"As sneaky as these reporters . . . Ah fuck it." He drew Trey into his arms and against his strong body. Ethan's heart thudded so hard, Trey could feel it in his own chest. "I wasn't sure I'd see you tonight. Or ever again."

"After that stirring message you left on my phone?"

"No idea what you're talking about," Ethan said.

Trey tilted his head back to look up into Ethan's eyes. The words he was saying and the sappy expression on his face didn't coincide.

"I guess it was some other guy who called," Trey said, lifting a brow at him. "I better find out who it was, because he said all the right words, and I need to get close to him before this lovesick daze wears off."

"It was me," Ethan said, his dark eyes searching Trey's. "Did I really say something right?"

Trey nodded.

"Miracles do occur. I'm sorry about what I said about you and Brian back in the car."

Trey cringed. He'd all but forgotten what had started the tension between them in the first place. "Do you have to bring that up now?"

"I can't stop thinking about how many times I disappointed you today. I'm still so fucking jealous of Brian I can't stand it. To know that you loved another man with such ferocity—"

Trey covered Ethan's lips with his fingers. "Stop while you're ahead."

"And when you asked at the mortuary, I *wanted* to kiss you," Ethan continued, his words slightly garbled by Trey's fingers. "I always want my mouth on you, but . . ."

"You're afraid."

Trey knew Ethan was a fierce man—he wasn't afraid of anything—but he swallowed hard and nodded. His fingers tangled in the shirt at Trey's lower back to pull him closer. Trey touched Ethan's face and held his gaze.

"Coming out isn't so bad," Trey said. "It's always far worse in your head than it ever is in reality."

"Easy for you to say. You have the kind of family who would support you through anything. Not all of us are that lucky."

"You don't talk about your family much," Trey said, tilting his head. "Are they really that terrible?"

"I can't complain. Mom loves me with all her heart, and I think she'd come to terms with my bisexuality. Not sure she'd cope with me never giving her grandchildren. She adores Reagan and is always going on about what cute babies we'd make together. My stepdad holds me at arm's length, but he's not all that affectionate with his own sons, so I'm not really worried about his reaction. It's my brothers. They've always treated me like one of them even though I have a different father. Maybe because I'm the oldest and I was always around. But no matter how close we were in the past, I know they won't accept this about me."

"Why do you say that?"

Ethan's gaze shifted above Trey's head. "They despise homosexuals. Hate them on a pathological level. There was this gay guy in school that they harassed and bullied relentlessly. They hurt him, Trey. Bad enough to eventually land him in the hospital. But he was too scared to tell on them and even though I knew who was responsible, I couldn't rat out my brothers. They were family."

"Not to defend what they did, but they were kids when that happened, Ethan. Surely now that they're adults—"

Ethan shook his head. "There's no telling what they'd do if they found out I'm one of those perverted freaks they hate."

"You're afraid of them?"

"Not of what they might do to me, but of what they're capable of doing to you. If they ever hurt you . . ."

"I'm not afraid. They're in Texas, we're in California. Soon we'll be in Europe. They're not a threat."

Ethan nodded slightly, but Trey was certain a deeper issue was eating at the man slowly emerging from his self-inflicted emotional repression.

"Do you really think they'd try to hurt me?" Was Ethan truly that scared of them on his behalf, or were they his excuse to keep his secret under wraps?

Ethan shrugged. "I honestly don't know."

Maybe deep inside, Ethan was a lot like him and that was why they connected. "Or is it more like the issue I had when I came out to my family?"

"You had issues?"

Trey nodded, his arms tightening around Ethan. "The thing I feared most when I came out was that I'd be a disappointment to them. I didn't want to let them down. I wanted to live up to their expectations, and I thought I knew what those expectations were."

Ethan absorbed his words for a moment and then nodded.

"But then I figured if they still spoke to me even though I didn't go to medical school and follow my father's illustrious and lucrative medical career with my own, the bisexual thing probably wasn't too much of a letdown."

One of Ethan's eyebrows arched. "So you didn't just come out as gay, you came out as bisexual?"

Trey smiled. "I came out as *me*, that's all. If people can't accept you for who you are, then you don't need them in your life, am I right?"

"I'll really be limiting my circle of friends and family, don't you think?"

Trey shook his head. "All the important people in your life will stand by you. *I'll* stand by you."

Ethan stuck a finger under Trey's chin and lifted his face to offer him a tender kiss. "I know that. And I'm sure that with my hesitation to come out, I'm a disappointment to *you*."

Trey shrugged. "Not a disappointment. Yeah, it stings a little, but I'll give you all the time you need. Even if you never tell a soul."

"I don't deserve you."

"I agree," Trey teased, his lips fighting a grin. "What are you going to do to convince me you're worth my heartache?"

"Tell you I love you."

The intensity in Ethan's gaze made Trey's belly quiver. What he wouldn't give to have the world see that this man loved him with all-consuming passion.

"I like that," Trey said. "What else?"

A gasp of surprise and excitement escaped Trey when his back thudded against the wall. Ethan dropped to his knees at Trey's feet, gazing up at him as his fingers unfastened Trey's pants. By the time Ethan had them lowered to his ankles, Trey was fully erect with anticipation.

Ethan slid a hand between Trey's legs, gently cupping his aching balls and massaging his back entrance with one fingertip. Trey loved how Ethan knew exactly what he needed and got right down to business. Trey sucked an excited breath deep into his chest as Ethan's tongue traced the rim of his cockhead. The finger tracing his asshole in the same maddening pattern dipped inside as Ethan took Trey's cock into his mouth. Ethan's suction was so tight, his rhythm so swift and perfect as he bobbed his head, that Trey lost all senses except pleasure.

Trey's ass twitched as his hips began to thrust involuntarily. Ethan's throat tightened around the tip of Trey's cock as he accepted the entire length. Trey groaned and forced his eyes open, admiring a slightly blurry vision of the man he loved getting throat-fucked. Having Ethan on his knees at his feet was more than a heady experience; Trey felt utterly euphoric. A mixture of tender love, sexual bliss, and exhilarating power flooded him as Ethan gave all and took nothing in return.

Trey struggled not to come, wanting the feeling to last forever, but his body couldn't resist the strong and relentless tug of Ethan's mouth and throat or the teasing motion of his tongue or the gentle pressure of Ethan's hand on his balls. When Ethan's fingers pressed deep inside him, rubbing his prostate with practiced precision, Trey let go. Watching Ethan swallow his load drew a moan of tortured delight from Trey's throat. The man might never kiss Trey in public, but lord did he make up for that lack when they were behind closed doors.

Weak from his explosive release, Trey slid down the wall, gratefully accepting Ethan's hungry kiss when they were face to face at last. The taste of himself on Ethan's tongue made him more than ready to reciprocate Ethan's gift of ecstasy.

Trey reached for Ethan's belt and unfastened it. "I'm going to suck you off so hard, you'll forget your own name."

"I have a better idea," Ethan whispered, gasping when Trey's cool hand found the hot, thick length of him inside his clothes. God, he was hard. Trey couldn't wait to taste him. Still, he was intrigued.

"Better?" Trey asked.

"Let's see if we have the cure for Reagan's headache."

Trey grinned, his heart thudding with excitement. "That *is* a better idea."

CHAPTER 19

DEEP, FAMILIAR VOICES DREW Reagan from an uneasy rest. She lifted her head from her pillow, but it was too dark to see anything but Ethan's outline. She squinted into the darkness, wondering if she was seeing things. There were two men in her room. She didn't know whether to be pissed or relieved.

"Trey?" she croaked, her throat scratchy from sleep. She'd probably been snoring.

"Hey, baby," Trey whispered. "Can we join you, or are you still convinced that I'm behaving like an asshole?"

"I didn't say you were behaving like an asshole," she said.

"Uh, yeah, you did," Ethan said.

"I said you were being an ass. And you are. You completely ignored both of us all evening."

"That's what you said you wanted me to do."

She threw her pillow in his general direction. "Don't twist my words to make up for your rude behavior."

The mattress sagged beside her, and Ethan placed a cool hand on her forehead. Funny how she could tell Ethan's touch from Trey's even when she couldn't see them. "How's your headache?"

"A little better, but I'm really thirsty."

"You want a beer?" Trey asked. "I think there are still some hiding in the back of the fridge."

"Water would be better."

"Got it," Trey said.

Reagan winced when light from the hallway flooded the room

as he opened the door. She sighed in relief when he closed it again.

"Light still bothering you?" Ethan asked.

"Not as bad as it did earlier." She reached up for his hand. "Did you make up with Trey?" She hoped so. The only thing worse than experiencing heartache herself was watching a man she loved struggling with it, and when they were both hurting, she couldn't stand it.

"We're better," Ethan said. "He's pressuring me to come out to my family."

Reagan snorted. "That's because he's never met your brothers. God, after we'd broken up and I thought you were gay, I remember how hard it was to watch you listen to their constant homophobic jokes. And when I tried to defend gays without revealing your secret, I thought they were going to kick my ass."

"I wouldn't have let them touch you," Ethan said.

"I know. I didn't really think they'd kick my ass. They're normally great guys. They're just a little homophobic."

"More than a little. I don't want Trey anywhere around them. If their hatred and hurtful remarks are directed toward me, I think I can handle it, but I fear what they'll do to him if they think he's responsible for what I am."

"That's ridiculous. You can't change that part of who you are. You can deny it, maybe, and not act on it, but you'll never be able to change who you're sexually attracted to or who you fall in love with."

"I know it's ridiculous, but you know what my brothers are like. Best to keep my sexual desires a secret and keep Trey as far away from them as possible."

"So you're not ready to reveal the truth about our relationship to the press?" She was relieved that Ethan was on her side, even if she did feel bad for Trey. She knew he wanted the world to know he was in love—one person or two or even ten, he didn't care who knew. And truth be told, she admired that about him.

"I'm not. Are you?"

She shook her head, sending a sharp pain into the center of her brain. She distinctly remembered that feeling of horror she'd felt when her father had called earlier. And Daddy didn't know half of what he thought he knew about her affairs. "No."

"So how do we keep Trey happy? He's used to getting his way."

Reagan chuckled. "He *is* a spoiled brat."

"He deserves to be spoiled."

Reagan grinned. Ethan had it so bad for the guy, not that she blamed him. But she found Ethan's sappy side adorable, and he was displaying it now more than ever. "So we'll spoil him. That should keep a smile on his face."

The door opened a crack. "Are you through discussing me among yourselves?" Trey asked.

"Who said we were talking about you?" Reagan asked, scooting into a seated position with Ethan's assistance.

"Why wouldn't you be?" Trey said, brushing his long bangs back with his free hand. "I'm just that awesome."

"Someone's full of himself," Ethan said.

"Someone," Trey countered, "would rather be filled with you."

"Back of the line, Mills," Reagan said, wrapping her arms around Ethan's neck. "I'm first."

"You sure you're up for this?" Ethan asked, pressing a gentle kiss to her forehead. "You had a splitting headache earlier."

"My headache was caused by stress. And being here with the two of you has washed that all away."

"For now," Trey said, offering her the glass of water he'd brought.

She released her loose hold on Ethan to take the glass and swallowed a drink, the cool liquid soothing her scratchy throat. "Don't burst my bubble of happiness here, Trey. It gets enough holes poked in it *out there*." She flicked her wrist toward the offensive *out there*, and water sloshed over her hand.

"Won't happen again," Trey promised. "Tonight we're the only three people on the planet."

Reagan wished they had more than one night alone together. They were all heading to New York City after the funeral the next morning, and as much as she loved performing onstage with Exodus End, there wasn't any place to hide in the spotlight.

"Maybe it would be best if you found a different bodyguard for the tour, and I stayed home," Ethan said.

"No!" Reagan and Trey said in unison.

"I don't care if she finds a different bodyguard," Trey said, "but I wouldn't be able to stand not seeing you every day." He crawled up onto the bed with them and wrapped his arms around both their backs, leaning his face in so their cheeks were touching. His breath tickled Reagan's lips when he said, "It was hard for me to stay away from you both today."

"You made it look easy enough," Ethan grumbled.

"It was terrible," Trey said, turning his head and stealing a kiss from Reagan. Somehow he'd managed to get between her and Ethan. "I'm first."

Ethan rescued the glass of water from her hand just before Trey tumbled her back into the nest of pillows she'd been sleeping in.

"Excuse me," Ethan said, his hand sliding between her belly and Trey's, "but I believe she requested the double chocolate-covered Macadamia nut surprise."

Reagan scrunched her eyebrows together. "What's that?" She didn't remember requesting anything.

"Nice," Trey said, ignoring her question. "Raw or toasted?"

"Raw or toasted?" Ethan asked her.

"I don't know what you're talking about," Reagan insisted.

"We should surprise her," Trey said.

It was too dark to see their faces, so she didn't know if they were joking or serious. "Turn on the light."

"I thought the light bothered your head," Ethan said, leaning over Trey's shoulder to kiss her.

"Not knowing what the two of you are up to bothers me more."

"It's just a little double chocolate-covered Macadamia nut surprise, Reagan," Trey said. "Everyone does it."

"Then why haven't I heard of it?"

"It's hard to explain," Ethan said. "Better if we show you."

She trusted both of them, but her brain was racing through possibilities of this previously untried act. It had to be something pertaining to their balls, she decided. Would their nuts literally be covered in chocolate or was that a euphemism for something dirtier?

Reagan was stripped of the panties and T-shirt she'd worn to bed and spread out on her back. As if the two of them were synched for her pleasure, Ethan drew her right nipple into his mouth while Trey delighted her left with that exquisite tongue piercing of his. Pleasure rippled down her belly, anchoring itself in her pussy as a deep throb of longing. A soft sigh escaped her, and her toes curled, her back arching in surrender to her body's forbidden indulgence.

Trey's arm shifted across her thighs, and Ethan's mouth freed her nipple, a broken sigh brushing against her dampened flesh.

Trey released her flesh as well. "Is your dick this hard for me or for her?" he asked gruffly.

"For both of you," Ethan said.

"Fuck her for as long as you like, but save your cum for me. I want you to mark me as yours on Brian's bed."

Reagan wasn't sure why that got them so hot and bothered, but the two of them were instantly tearing at each other's clothes and exchanging deep, heated kisses over her neglected chest. She cleared her throat.

"So the, uh, double chocolate-covered Macadamia nut surprise is two guys sucking your tits at the same time? I've got to say I'm underwhelmed." Though there was nothing underwhelming about the two of them going at each other like maniacs. She just wanted to be one of the maniacs.

Both men chuckled as they drew apart. "Sorry, love," Ethan said. "We haven't gotten to your surprise yet. I was just a little distracted by Trey finally figuring out that he can use my jealousy of Brian to make me burn for him."

"Damn," Trey said. "How could I've been so dense?"

Reagan laughed at the sound of Trey slapping his forehead. Or was he slapping Ethan's ass? She couldn't be sure.

"Has he ever come on your dick?" Ethan asked. "Watched his own fluids drip down your shaft and balls and ass."

"Nope," Trey said breathlessly.

"Mmm," Ethan said, obviously visualizing what he was saying. "Has he ever—"

"Hey," Reagan interrupted. "Can you stop talking about what Brian *hasn't* done to Trey and start talking about what you *are* going to do to me?"

"We already told you," Trey said. "The double chocolate-covered Macadamia nut surprise."

"It will blow your mind," Ethan said, giving Trey one last kiss before returning his attention to Reagan's breast.

Either that display of their excitement for each other or her own anticipation made the sensations even more pleasurable; her body shuddered in response to the firm tug of Ethan's lips. She moaned when Trey's mouth captured her other nipple. She was already on fire when their hands began to explore her quivering belly and trembling thighs, so when they tugged her legs apart and began their thorough exploration of all the hot achy flesh between them, she ignited into a raging inferno of need and desire. Ever impatient, Trey slid two fingers into her drenched pussy. She cried out when two of Ethan's joined them. They worked their fingers inside her— in unison, in opposition—while their thumbs massaged her clit and their little fingers took turns teasing her ass. Even after they brought her to orgasm and she was screaming her bliss into the dark room, they continued to touch her as partners in her pleasure. Perhaps they were too busy kissing each other to notice her pussy was clenching around their joined fingers or maybe they liked to drive her insane. Unable to stand the torment any further, she clamped her legs shut on their hands.

She heard their mouths separate somewhere over her belly. Both were breathing nearly as hard as she was.

"So *that* was the double chocolate-covered Macadamia nut surprise," Reagan said. "I definitely enjoyed that. No wonder everyone is doing it."

"That was just a warm-up for the real surprise," Ethan said.

Strong hands gripped her hips and turned her onto her side. Her leg was looped over a shoulder, and Trey's tongue flicked against her already over-sensitized clit. She knew it was him, because that mind-blowing tongue piercing of his was working its magic.

She gasped when another tongue brushed over the tingling flesh of her ass.

"Oh wow," she breathed, her fingers twining through Trey's long bangs. She needed something to ground her while she got a double dose of oral pleasure. Was it selfish of her to wish there was a third tongue available to delve into her aching, empty center?

"Oh God," she groaned, as with a little shifting of heads, their tongues converged, struggling to gain entry into her pussy. The feel of them working against each other to enter her sent her over the edge. She cried out, gasping with renewed excitement as they separated again, Trey meticulously teasing her clit and Ethan dominating her ass with more and more enthusiasm as his excitement grew.

"I can't take anymore," Reagan moaned as her body teetered close to another wave of release.

Apparently that was their cue to meet in the middle again, proving her a liar when she tried to suffocate Trey by pushing his face into her pussy while their writhing tongues fucked her wildly and sent her flying again.

When her muscles went slack, Trey collapsed beside her struggling to find air while Ethan brought her down with slow and thorough licks to her quaking pussy and trembling ass.

"I think she needs the double yogurt-covered Macadamia nut surprise before we advance to chocolate," Ethan said, his tongue swirling softly against her back entrance. Did he know how quickly that made her crave more? He must.

"Whatever you think is best," Trey said between huffs of breath. "It's your dick. If you think you can handle it—"

"I'm more worried about your tongue," Ethan said, shifting his body over Reagan so he could reach Trey. She was pretty sure he was offering Trey a consoling pat, but it was too dark in the room to be sure.

"No worries," Trey said, an ornery grin in his tone. "My tongue is in excellent physical condition."

Ethan chuckled. "I can attest to that."

"Wait," Reagan said, still breathless. "That wonderful thing you just did to me, that *wasn't* the surprise?"

"Another warm-up," Ethan said.

"Mercy," Reagan said under her breath, but she was eager to enjoy whatever they had in store for her next.

After several minutes of relaxing touches and deep sensual kisses shared by all, Ethan switched on the bedside lamp. It gave off a dim glow.

"Does that worsen your headache?" Ethan asked, his dark eyes full of concern. She blinked back an unexpected flood of tears. What had she ever done to deserve the fierce, protective love of this wonderful man and the passionate, heady affection of the man currently kissing her neck in a way that made her toes curl.

"No," she murmured, touching Ethan's face. "My headache is completely gone."

She was glad he'd turned on the light, so she could see him when his expression softened into a gentle smile.

"Good."

"Let's never be at odds again," she said, voicing her deepest wish. "With the world, yes, I can handle that. But not with each other."

"Finally, she makes sense," Trey said, his sensual lips finding her jaw, the corner of her mouth, and then Ethan's lips.

"I'd prefer that as well," Ethan said, but the crinkle between his dark brows made her wonder if he truly believed it was possible. Well, she'd just have to make him believe by being as wonderful to both of them as they were to her. Assuming the naughtiest of their trio didn't stir up trouble.

"Trey?" she asked, fisting his silky hair in one hand to temporarily halt his ever-seeking lips.

"I'm a lover, not a fighter," he murmured, tugging against her hold at the risk of scalping himself, solely so he could nibble on

Ethan's earlobe. She released her grip and smoothed his hair, sorry to have caused him pain. Trey *was* a lover and Ethan was more of a fighter, so which was she? She'd be a little of both, she decided.

"Time for that surprise," Ethan said, the sexually charged timber in his tone bringing appreciative moans from both her and Trey.

The three of them were always perfectly in sync in the bedroom. Perhaps they should never leave it.

Reagan was shifted until she knelt over Trey's face. She grasped the headboard in both hands to steady herself, and gasped when his tongue found her clit. Ethan moved in beside her and grabbed her breast. The contrast of Trey's gentle licks to Ethan's harsh pinching made her so wet and hot, she whimpered.

"Open her for me, Trey," Ethan demanded.

God, why did that hard tone of his make her throb with need?

Trey's hands slid up her thighs, his little fingers spreading her pussy lips. Cold air bathed the aching heat there and made her realize how much she needed to be fucked. Not by a pair of exquisite tongues, but by a huge, thick cock—hot and hard.

"Are you thinking about how much you'd like me to fuck that wet, empty pussy?" Ethan growled into her ear.

The man was a mind reader. The stinging slap he delivered to her ass made her entire body tense and ache with need. She ground her clit into Trey's tongue for the rougher stimulation she craved. Bless that tongue piercing and every tingling nerve-ending in her clit.

Ethan slapped her ass again. A little harder. A little better. "Answer me!"

"I forgot the question," she admitted.

"Are you thinking about how much you'd like me to fuck that sweet, empty, hot, dripping-wet pussy?"

"How do you know it's hot?" she asked. "You haven't touched it."

Instead of sliding a finger—or better yet, his cock—inside to determine how hot she was—she'd estimate inferno level on a scale of cold to hot—he slapped her ass again. A spasm delighted her pussy with the first hint of release.

"Are you sassing me?" Ethan asked, the threat in his tone making her even hotter.

"Depends," she said, rocking gently with the motion of Trey's skilled tongue.

"On?" Ethan asked.

"If I sass you, will you spank me some more?" She offered him a challenging grin over her shoulder, and received three hard, successive slaps on the ass for her sass.

Her eyes drifted closed and her mouth dropped open as her orgasm exploded. She cried out, vaguely aware of Ethan shifting behind her, and then she became completely aware of him as the head of his cock entered her clenching pussy. She slammed back against him, filling herself with him, but was immediately sorry when her hasty action separated her clit from Trey's soft licks and the flick of the metal ball near the tip of his tongue.

"Easy, baby," Ethan said. "We've got you."

He shifted her forward until they had her exactly where they wanted her, Trey licking her, Ethan fucking her. Ethan's hands were like steel on her hips, holding her still so he could pound her pussy raw without crushing Trey's face.

"Are you satisfied?" Ethan murmured in her ear.

More was the only word she could form. Probably because it was echoing through her head with each hard thrust.

His chuckle sent prickles of pleasure down her spine. "Are you ready to get in here with me, Trey?"

"Mum-humph," came Trey's response from somewhere beneath her.

Ethan's strong arms lifted Reagan, and Trey pulled himself into a seated position in front of her. She wrapped her arms around him and kissed him thoroughly, tasting her cum on his lips. "I love you," she said. "I love you both."

"I think she's remembered why she puts up with us," Ethan said, rearranging his body so that he was flat on his back and she was straddling him but facing Trey. Ethan's thick cock never left her pussy. They usually had to get her really worked up to get her to agree to let them both inside her pussy at the same time, and today they'd done a more than thorough job of getting her there. Her pussy was demanding that they both fill it.

Trey shifted forward, and Reagan stared down at the spot where Ethan was already within her, thinking it looked impossible for them both to fit inside her but knowing how fucking fantastic it felt when they made it work.

"Lift her," Trey said.

Reagan gasped in protest when Ethan lifted her hips until his cock slipped free. Fascinated, she watched as Trey moved up against Ethan and pressed their cocks together—underside to underside—

holding their mind-boggling combined thickness in one fist. Eyes wide, she watched as her pussy stretched to accommodate them both. When they were halfway in, Trey removed his hand and both cocks slid deeper. All three of them were moaning by the time she was completely filled.

"Can you thrust, Trey?" Ethan asked.

"I think so," Trey said breathlessly. "You feel amazing. Both of you."

Ethan angled Reagan's hips so that she was leaning back slightly. Trey tugged out, wincing as his cock rubbed Reagan's front wall and Ethan's cock simultaneously. "We probably should have lubed up first," Trey said.

But after a few slow and easy strokes, Reagan was so wet, he was able to fuck them both with little resistance. Every time Trey's cock pushed as deep as it would go, Ethan moaned. It felt best for Reagan when Trey was a few inches from falling free. Apparently it felt great for Trey the entire thrust in and out. He was drenched in sweat, his eyes closed, his body trembling as he took her at the same time he rubbed his cock up and down Ethan's length inside her.

Reagan squeezed her eyes shut, allowing herself to feel every sensation shaking her body.

"It's time for your surprise now," Ethan said, panting in her ear.

There couldn't possibly be more. She was incapable of experiencing additional pleasure. She whimpered when her very delighted, very full pussy went inexplicably empty. Trey had her lovers' combined cocks held together in one fist again. When she felt the head of his cock against her ass, her eyes flew open in shock. She fought her way out of their embrace and scrambled away.

Nope. Hard limit.

She was not up for getting double penetrated in the ass. No way.

"Not happening," she said, surprised her over-sated body could move with such haste as she scuttled over the edge of the mattress and onto the floor.

Ethan sighed. "I was sure we had her turned on enough to try it."

"We'll try harder next time."

Try harder? Reagan blinked at them from her uncomfortable seat on the hardwood floor. A seat that would have been far more uncomfortable if they'd succeeded in their plot against her ass.

"They would never fit."

Trey grinned his most devilish smile and offered her a naughty wink. "Oh, they'll fit. I know that from experience."

"And you liked it?" Reagan asked, pulling herself up with two fists locked on the bedding. Trey's hand had started stroking the two cocks gripped in his hand, and Ethan obviously liked that. Maybe even more than Reagan liked to watch it.

"Not as uncomfortable as fisting." Trey winced.

Reagan's gaze shifted to Ethan's large fist, and she cringed. If they ever engaged in that business, she did not want to be a witness. A woman had to have boundaries. At least a few.

"Do you want to get back in here?" Trey asked. "We'll both stick with vanilla, or Ethan can go vanilla and I'll go chocolate."

Ah, so that was the double chocolate part of her surprise. She still wasn't clear on the nut part.

Ethan groaned, his body tensing as he found release at Trey's hand. Mouth wide with surprise, Trey looked down between them. Thick cum pulsed from Ethan's tip, drenching the underside of Trey's cock and dripping down over his hand.

"Ethan," Trey said, his tone chastising. "You came without me."

"C-couldn't help it." He grabbed Trey's hair in his fist and pulled him close for a deep, passionate kiss. "My cum on your dick is so hot." He was panting.

"It's dripping down my balls too," Trey whispered.

Ethan groaned and kissed him again, even harder this time. Reagan wasn't sure why Ethan was so turned on by seeing his cum on Trey. He must have come on the guy a thousand times in the past. But seeing the two of them so passionate for each other made her burn for them both.

"Can I get some of that?" she asked, nodding to the spectacular pair of cocks still pressed together in Trey's fist.

"Don't think I can handle tight pussy right now," Ethan said, still shuddering with the aftershocks of his release.

"Climb on, baby," Trey countered. "Maybe it will teach him not to come without me."

Reagan grinned, always loving to torture Ethan right after he came. His cock became so sensitive that any stimulation drove him insane.

"Hold still," Trey insisted when Ethan began to squirm.

Facing Trey, Reagan slipped between them and straddled their hips, finding the most comfortable kneeling position she could in their tangle of legs. She sighed heavily as Trey helped her sink onto his tip. She paused while he worked Ethan's tip inside her as well and then pressed her hips down to take them both.

"Fuck." Ethan's breathy curse caused Reagan and Trey to exchange devious grins.

She moved slowly, keeping them deep within, her strokes short and grinding. They felt so good inside her, filling her to her limit, that she didn't have to move much to find pleasure. She was almost to her peak when Ethan's spent cock slipped free. Trey didn't miss a beat. He wrapped both arms around her and turned her onto her back, thrusting into her with the deep, penetrating rhythm that always existed as an undercurrent between them. As his face contorted with pleasure, he opened his sultry green eyes and stared into hers. That was all she needed to send her over the edge. Their gazes remained locked as they found release together. As the waves of pleasure ripped through her body, a warmth simultaneously spread through her chest. God, she loved this man. Loved *both* of the men in her bed. And maybe someday she'd be strong enough not to care who knew it.

In the afterglow of loving, Trey did his best to snuggle against her and Ethan at the same time. "You two should move in here with me," he said. "It will keep the paparazzi away and you have to admit, it's a lot nicer than your place."

Reagan tried to think of a reason why they shouldn't, but her higher order brain processes weren't functioning. Never make decisions on an empty stomach or while in bed with two men after three orgasms or . . . how did that idiom go again?

After a moment, Ethan asked, "Why did we originally decide to stay at our place?"

Reagan tried to laugh but apparently that part of her wasn't working either. She might as well forget trying to speak. Sleep seemed to be the only action she was capable of as her eyelids opened and closed dreamily, eventually settling on closed.

"So it's settled," Trey said. "You're moving in with me."

"I'm for it," Ethan said. "Reagan?"

She answered with a snore.

THE NEXT MORNING REAGAN AND ETHAN MADE a run to their old apartment for clothes and a few personal items they couldn't live without while Trey headed for the funeral. Only a few close friends of Sed's family would attend the actual funeral, and though Reagan felt a measure of relief that she could be out of the public eye for a few more hours, she felt guilty that she wouldn't be there to support Trey while he offered his support to Sed. Trey had seemed fine with the situation. He'd been humming under his breath while Ethan stood behind him and properly fixed his tie for him. He'd kissed them both goodbye several times and had left with a smile on his face. A smile that she realized he hadn't shared with them for days.

"I think Trey's happy that we're moving in with him," Reagan said. "He was like his old self this morning."

"Could be that," Ethan said, grinning at her from the driver's seat. "Or maybe it was all the amazing sex we had last night."

She laughed. "I guess that would put a smile on anyone's face."

"I think he's happy because we got to be completely alone for the first time since we went on tour together."

Reagan shook her head. "But he doesn't want to isolate our relationship from the rest of the world like we do."

Ethan didn't respond as he maneuvered through traffic, his eyes frequently checking the rearview mirror.

"Is someone following us?" Reagan asked, the bubbly feeling of love and happiness in her belly instantly twisting into a queasy knot.

"I'm not sure, but whatever. I'm done pretending they'll go away if I wish for it hard enough."

"Maybe they'll disappear if I wish for it even harder then," Reagan muttered under her breath.

"I do think Trey would be content isolating our relationship from the rest of the world," Ethan commented on her earlier statement. "I just think he's come to terms with the idea that doing so is impossible and so we might as well get it all out in the open so the leeches on our backs will fall off in a search of newer, juicier blood."

Reagan's knotted stomach twisted even tighter. She might be able to keep their secret if she was just holding her ground against Trey, but if both of her men were against her decision to be tight-lipped, she'd eventually start blabbing. She knew she would.

"Are you starting to agree with him?"

"Not in the slightest." Ethan turned into the parking lot of their apartment complex and cursed when several cars turned in after them. "I don't think our relationship would survive it."

Reagan feared the same. She also feared that her career wouldn't survive it, nor would her already troubled familial ties. And though she'd be willing to give up both her career and her family if she were guaranteed eternal happiness with Trey and Ethan, she was too afraid that she'd lose everything instead. Then where would she be?

"We have to get through this," Reagan said, "and come out on the other side still holding on to Trey."

"I'm not letting him go."

Reagan smiled and nodded. "Me neither. Let's pack our bags and wait for him at home."

A loud knock on her window made her jump.

"Trey Mills was seen heading to Phillip Lionheart's funeral alone," a reporter yelled at her through the glass. "Is this really the best time to slip away for some alone time with your bodyguard?"

Is that what this looked like to them? Fuck! Reagan's lips had gone numb, not that she knew what to say to make this situation right, but she couldn't take any more. She knew she shouldn't care what these strangers thought of her, but she did care. They thought she was the type of woman who would desert her boyfriend—while he was at a funeral—to fuck some other guy. Tears flooded her eyes, and she buried her face in her hands, unsuccessfully stifling a sob.

Ethan's growl of rage alerted her to impending doom just before he tore the door open and jumped out of the car.

"Look, you stupid motherfuckers," Ethan yelled. "She wasn't *invited* to the funeral, that's why she didn't go. And we did not come here to have sex. We came to gather her clothes so she could move in with Trey."

The paparazzi surrounded him like a pack of hungry wolves spotting a defenseless fawn who'd been separated from his mother. This was going to be bad if Reagan didn't do something, but her hands were trembling so hard, she couldn't get her door to open no matter how many times she pulled at the handle.

"I'm her bodyguard, nothing more. Yes, you will see me around her a lot. Yes, I do have to touch her on occasion. I'm trying to protect her from people like you. So back the *fuck* off so I can do my job!"

Ethan shoved through the crowd and tried to open her door.

It wouldn't open for him either. Through the window, he pointed at the engaged lock, and she laughed at her stupidity. When she was finally free of the stifling car, Ethan placed a steadying hand on her elbow and escorted her—rather coolly—toward the stairs.

"Is it true?" someone called after them. "Are you really moving in with Trey?"

"It's true," she called, walking faster. The staircase—*sanctuary*—was just ahead.

"And this Ethan guy isn't anything more to you than a bodyguard?" another voice called.

She pretended she hadn't heard the question. Ethan was much more to her than a bodyguard. He was her best friend. Her lover. Her heart. Her soul. Her everything. And Trey was all of those things to her as well.

"Tell them I mean nothing to you," Ethan said in her ear.

She blinked back the fresh flood of tears that came to her eyes. "I can't," she whispered.

"It's okay," he assured her.

"He's *just* my bodyguard. Leave us alone," she yelled before racing up the stairs.

Once they were closed inside the apartment, she collapsed against Ethan's chest and broke down, repeating, "I'm sorry. I didn't mean it," over and over again.

"Shh, babe," Ethan whispered to her. "It's okay. I know you didn't mean it."

But wouldn't her life be a whole lot easier if she had?

CHAPTER 20

NORMALLY TREY WOULD HAVE BEEN glad to be back on the road with his band. He typically loved the excitement of the entire glorious affair, adored the camaraderie between himself and his bandmates, and couldn't wait to meet eclectic people in exciting places—even if he no longer seduced those people. But even though they were in New York City—one of his favorite stops on any tour—he just wasn't feeling the love, and the reason was no mystery to him.

The funeral had been a somber occasion and he was glad that the road gave Sed concerts, events, and fans to distract him from his grief. But Reagan and Ethan were different when they were on tour. At home they'd both been happy and fun and horny and open, the wonderful people he adored. Here the two of them were forlorn and guarded and withdrawn and cranky, which made him glum. Trey didn't do glum. He admitted to pouting on occasion, but he wasn't sure how much longer he could stand feeling this low.

"You look miserable," Brian said as he sat beside Trey on the tour bus sofa. He'd talked with Trey a million times before on this same sofa, but there was an impossible to ignore difference this time. Brian held Malcolm in his arms and was feeding his tiny son from a bottle. "Girl trouble? Boy trouble?"

"Both," Trey admitted. He slicked back Malcolm's soft hair, and his heart went all mushy. "Let me hold him." He needed someone he could publicly shower with affection, and his wide-eyed godson was easy to love.

Brian handed over the squirmy bundle, but he didn't rise from the sofa. Trey was uncomfortably aware of how close Brian was sitting next to him. His scent, the cadence of his breaths, his mere presence—all familiar and comforting and unsettling. Would Trey ever shake that feeling of connection with Brian? It was so fucking confusing. He wasn't in love with the guy anymore, but he'd always love him. Why?

"So what's the trouble?" Brian asked, watching Malcolm eat his lunch. When the baby's gaze landed on his doting father, he smiled around the nipple in his mouth.

"They're different on tour," Trey said, making a face at Malcolm to compete for one of those smiles. Curious brown eyes shifted to Trey, and he was gifted with an adorable giggle followed by more sucking.

"Aren't we all?" Brian said wearily.

Trey lifted his gaze to Brian's and got lost in a pair of intense brown eyes so similar to his son's that Trey's heart ached. "Uh, no," Trey said.

Brian chuckled. "Well, maybe not you. But some of us get the jitters before a performance and hide behind our talent. Some hide behind a huge ego, others hide behind jokes, and then there are those who hide period."

Trey knew Brian was talking about the members of his band, but he never saw them that way.

"Everyone is hiding from something," Brian added.

Were they really? "Why?"

"To keep from getting hurt."

Trey shrugged. "You get used to it."

"You're lying to yourself," Brian said.

Maybe he was, but if a guy spent his entire life hiding from heartache, he couldn't possibly live a full life, a rich life, or the self-indulgent life Trey craved. He wanted it all exactly the way he desired.

"I'm being selfish again, aren't I?" He knew it was a flaw of his, but knowing it didn't change his behavior. If he knew what he wanted, he went after it, persistently and without ever giving up. Lord, Brian must know that about him more than anyone on the planet. There was still a part of him that fucking wanted Brian, and Trey hated that he couldn't get completely over that unfulfilled desire. Did he crave Brian because he was the one thing Trey had wanted but never attained? Or was he just stupid?

Brian rested a hand on Trey's knee. "You're the most selfless selfish person I've ever met."

Or was Trey struggling to get over the guy because Brian always felt comfortable touching him? A hand on the knee, leaning against him when they played guitar. sitting close enough to him that their arms brushed on occasion. Straight guys just didn't do that around each other. They erected a solid imaginary box around themselves and were only willing to let another dude inside said box in rare instances, typically those punctuated with some measure of physical violence to offset the touchy-feely stuff. Hell, even his brother was more likely to slug him than hug him. Trey had puzzled over this oddity about Brian for years. It was an enigma that Trey would probably never unravel. Not that he'd ever minded Brian touching him. It was just goddamned confusing.

Someone climbed the bus steps and paused at the end of the corridor. "There are my three favorite men in the world," Myrna said.

Trey couldn't help but smile. He did adore the woman, even if she had officially pulled Brian out of his reach. If Trey hadn't thought she was the perfect woman for Brian, he probably wouldn't have ever stepped aside. He'd probably still be trying to turn the guy's head and would have missed out on having Reagan and Ethan in his life. Maybe stuff really did happen for a reason.

"Am I still your number one?" Trey asked Myrna with a teasing grin.

Both guys stared at the legs accentuated by a pair of black stilettos as she stepped over Brian's outstretched legs and sat on Trey's opposite side. She ruffled his hair as if he were her favorite pet and said, "Of course you're number one, Trey, but this little guy is a very close second." She leaned in and kissed Malcolm on the forehead, and he lit up like the Rockefeller Center Christmas tree as he stared adoringly at his mother.

"Hey," Brian protested. "What about me?"

"Coming in third isn't so bad," she teased.

"That's not what you said last night," Brian countered. "I distinctly remember you referring to me as God several dozen times."

"I did?" Myrna asked, her pretty hazel eyes wide and innocent in her lovely face. "I must have been completely delirious."

"On orgasms."

The sweetness left her expression as she examined Brian's face.

"I came to tell Trey that Reagan is looking for him, but perhaps I should ask him to babysit instead."

"Reagan's looking for me?" Trey asked, suddenly uncomfortable sitting between the couple with all the fuck-me vibes flowing between them. Huh. Maybe he *was* getting over Brian, if being the meat in a Sinclair sandwich made him uncomfortable rather than sexually excited.

"Yeah, Logan just got back, and he brought that Toni chick with him," Myrna said. "I was like what the fuck? Wasn't she the one who started the tabloid fiasco in the first place?"

"It's complicated," Trey said, handing Malcolm to Myrna. "I'd better go see what Reagan needs."

Myrna showered Malcolm with kisses and as soon as Trey stood, Brian slid in close to his little family to blow raspberries on Malcolm's bare feet. Was there anything cuter than a happy, giggling baby? Too bad Trey would never have one of his own.

He left the three of them behind as he exited Sinners' tour bus and hurried to the Exodus End bus parked just behind it. He was surprised to see Ethan standing outside the bus. He was wearing his bright orange SECURITY shirt, which looked great with his bronze skin and dark hair. His expression was unreadable behind his dark sunglasses, but his body was all sorts of tense. Trey wouldn't mind taking the time to release the tension from those distracting, bulging muscles. However, he doubted Ethan would appreciate him jumping his bones just then.

"Myrna said Reagan was looking for me," Trey said.

Terse nod.

"Is she on the bus?"

Another terse nod.

Trey sucked at the small hoop that pierced the corner of his mouth. So that was how they were going to play this?

"I was wondering—does Brian put up a bro box when he's around you?" Trey asked.

Ethan's biceps bulged as his already tense frame tightened further. "A bro box? What's that?"

"You know. That area of personal space around a straight guy that's uncomfortable to cross. And if you do cross it, you're liable to get punched."

Ethan slid one hand across his jaw, drawing Trey's attention to the dense, dark stubble that he hadn't shaved that morning. They'd been in a rush to catch a flight back to New York for that night's concert and had been distracted by activities much more pleasurable than shaving.

"Yeah," Ethan said. "He does put up a bro box—or whatever you want to call it—when he's around me."

"Oh," Trey said, worrying the hell out of the hoop at the corner of his mouth. He knew Ethan was staring at the action of his tongue from behind his mysterious dark sunglasses. "I thought maybe he didn't have a bro box with anyone. I guess I'm the only guy he lets into his space. Do you think that's odd?"

"Are you fucking kidding me?" Ethan grumbled.

"Yeah." Trey grinned. "Just trying to get a rise out of you."

"That wasn't nice."

"And it's not nice to ignore me, E," Trey said.

"It's impossible to ignore you," Ethan said. "I know if I talk to you, I'll end up looking at you, which will make me fantasize about you and lead to embarrassing bulges in these unforgiving slacks. Is that what you want?"

"I mostly want what comes out of those pants." Unable to resist, he rubbed a hand along Ethan's flank as he moved past him, up the steps, and onto Exodus End's tour bus. The man did know exactly how to remind Trey that he was desired.

"It's her!" Reagan jabbed at the crumpled tabloid spread across the counter. Toni was standing beside her, shaking her head.

"No, not that one. The other one." Toni pointed to a photograph on the page. "*That's* the woman who convinced my mother to steal my data and leak your information to the press. That's the woman who had the connections with the tabloids and wrote the articles. Her name is Susan."

"Okay, fine," Reagan said, "but *that's* the reporter who was at the visitation for Sed's dad. Her hair is different, but I'll remember that face until I die."

"Her?" Toni's eyes went wide. "Are you sure?"

Trey moved in close behind the two women so he could see what they were looking at.

"What are they doing with Steve? That is Steve, isn't it?" Reagan scanned the bus interior, presumably for the man in question, but when she noticed Trey, she gave him a quick hug. "Isn't it great?" she said to Trey, her smile lighting up her eyes. "Toni was duped."

"There is nothing great about being duped," Toni said glumly. "To think you can't even trust your own mother."

"Steve!" Reagan called. "Are you still on the bus? I need to ask you something."

A bunk curtain along one side of the bus slid open. "It's about damn time you figured out Steve's dick in your bush is worth the two dicks you already have."

"Say what now?" Reagan said, sending him a frosty glare.

"Come here," Toni said. "We need to ask you about these two women."

"Only two? I prefer an even three."

Toni snorted. "Three isn't even."

"Feels even when one's sitting on my face, another is riding my cock, and a third is licking my balls."

"Will you stop?" Reagan grabbed Steve by one arm and maneuvered him in front of the tabloid. "You can go find some pussy or three after you help us figure this out."

Steve looked down at the picture Toni was pointing at and crinkled his nose. "Why did you show me that? I won't be able to get hard for days." Reagan punched his arm. "Ouch. Hours, then. No need to get violent over a little lie."

"Who are these women?" Reagan said.

"Bianca in a wedding dress and me in a tux didn't give it away?" Steve shook his head at their obvious stupidity.

"Who's the other woman with you? I recognize Zach, but who is she?"

"That's Tamara, Bianca's younger sister."

"Are you sure her name isn't Susan?" Toni asked, her shoulders slumping.

"Of course I'm sure. I'll never forget her. She was always trying to get in my pants."

"And you didn't let her?" Trey asked with a laugh.

"The chick was vile," Steve said. "A man has to have standards."

Reagan poked him. "She's a bit chubby, but she isn't *vile.*"

"I don't mean the way she looks—her nasty personality. She was determined to break me and Bianca up before we were even married and when that plan backfired, she followed me around trying to catch me doing something wrong. I still think she's the one who broke the story of my affairs to the press. She always had it out for me, ever since I rejected her advances. I probably should have let her suck my dick to keep her mouth shut."

"Ew. Don't say that," Toni said. "She *is* vile. I really don't like her. Well, I don't like Susan. Does Tamara have a twin sister?"

"No." Steve shook his head. "Bianca is her only sister."

"I saw Bianca at the visitation," Reagan said. "She wore a black wig, but I know it was her. She was asking all sorts of prying questions and even snuck inside. Later, when you arrived, she left as soon as she saw you. I thought it was because she was afraid you'd go ballistic because she's paparazzi."

"I've never gone ballistic," Steve said.

Trey laughed. "Nope. Throwing a full sheet cake at the paparazzi isn't ballistic at all."

"It was my birthday," Steve said. "And I was tired of their bullshit! Did I mention it was my birthday, for fuck's sake? They couldn't leave me alone even on my fucking birthday."

"Don't worry, they hate me more than you at the moment," Reagan said.

Steve laid an arm across her shoulders and gave her a reassuring squeeze. "They don't hate you, dove. And they didn't hate me. They just want to make a lot of money by fucking up our lives."

"Feels like hate," Reagan said.

When Trey took her hand, lacing his fingers with hers, she offered him a tired smile. She had so much life in her. It was terrible to see her defeated by a bunch of assholes who didn't know her.

"So why would Bianca be at the visitation in disguise?" Toni asked. "Is she a reporter?"

Steve shrugged. "Not that I know of. Maybe she's assisting her vile sister, Tamara or Susan or whatever she's calling herself these days. I'm sure they're still trying to get back at me for crimes I've already paid for a thousand times over."

"If they have it out for you," Reagan said, "then why are they focusing on me?"

"You're prettier than I am?" Steve said, batting a pair of long lashes surrounding soulful brown eyes.

Reagan chuckled. "Are you sure about that? You definitely have better hair than I do."

Steve twisted a long wavy strand of hair around one finger. "I'm thinking about cutting it."

"No!" The two women shouted in unison.

"Maybe I should grow mine out," Trey said, stroking a long strand of bangs behind one ear. Steve was getting all the attention and if it took a thick head of chest-length, wavy hair to turn the ladies' heads, he was willing to give it a go.

"You'd look like a girl with long hair," Reagan said. "You don't have the jawline for it."

Ouch.

"The style you have suits you best," Toni said, flushing prettily. "It makes you look . . ."

"Sexy as fuck," Reagan supplied, and Trey smiled, his ego regaining its usual luster.

"Yeah, that," Toni said, waving at her reddened face with one hand. She whispered out of the corner of her mouth to Reagan, "Does being around all these hot rock stars make you perpetually horny?"

Reagan laughed. "Why do you think I have two lovers?"

Trey clung to the kernel of hope offered by her openly admitting she had two lovers. She was only repeating something both Toni and Steve already knew, but it was a start. Baby steps, he reminded himself, even though he was prepared to take a running leap off the cliff.

"Have you given any thought to breaking the real story?" Toni asked. "I could write it and slant it in a way that flatters the three of you. You'd have final approval and everything."

Reagan blinked at her. "Are you seriously asking for my permission to get the scoop on my relationship with Trey and Ethan?"

"I wouldn't sell it to the tabloids," Toni said hastily. "I was thinking something more reputable. Like *People*." Toni lifted one eyebrow. "Or *Rolling Stone*?"

Steve chortled. "Now wouldn't that piss off the paparazzi?" He slapped Reagan on the back repeatedly. "Do that. You should totally do that."

"No fucking way," Reagan said. "I don't want the world to know. Not ever."

"Never?" Trey muttered under his breath.

"No. Stop pressuring me about it!" Reagan snapped. "Just pretend you love only me in public and Ethan will pretend he doesn't love either of us and everything will blow over eventually."

"That's not fair to Ethan," Trey said. Or to him. He wanted to openly express his feelings. He'd never be able to keep them bottled up inside for long.

"It's what he wants. What both of us want." Reagan snatched the tabloid off the counter, crumpling it in one fist, and then shoved it into Steve's chest. "Find out why these bitches have it out for me.

I want some ammunition before I confront them."

"Uh, okay," Steve said, his eyes wide, expression confused.

"And if you write an article about me," she shouted at Toni, who flinched, "I'm putting you back on my bitches-I-plan-to-destroy list."

"I would never do that without your permission," Toni said, her voice squeaky.

Reagan rounded on Trey, her fury strangely exciting. "And *you!*" She pressed her hands to her forehead, making him fear she was cooking up another one of those stress headaches. "I hate that our secrecy hurts you. I just . . . I don't know how . . . I don't know how to keep Ethan from being hurt without hurting you."

Trey hadn't realized how much she was struggling to balance his feelings with Ethan's until that moment. He'd actually suspected that she didn't get how their secrecy hurt him, thought she'd just been ignoring his desires because they didn't suit her agenda. His feet-dug-into-the-dirt, head-up-his-ass approach wasn't working anyway. He needed to let it go.

"I think I'll be okay with this public ruse on one condition," Trey said.

"If you say a double chocolate Macadamia nut surprise, I'm going to throttle you."

"What's that?" Toni asked Steve.

"No idea."

Trey chuckled. "Well, not that precisely, but along that vein. We need more alone time together. We skip the after-parties and the tour events and with the exception of rehearsals and live performances, we're off tour. We'll completely disassociate from it on our days off."

Reagan snorted. "But we *never* get a day off. Sam will never let that fly."

"Which is exactly why you should do it," Steve said.

Reagan rolled her eyes at him. "You know damned well I can't."

So she wasn't willing to sacrifice anything for him. Not her privacy. Not her reputation. Not her career. Not her family. Not even her goddamned days off. Trey could understand why she'd resist compromising important things, but she was rarely included in Exodus End's promotional machine and when she was included, she was either miserable about the way she was treated or she was ignored. Wasn't he worth even that little inconvenience to her, for fuck's sake?

"Then maybe we should take a break while we're on tour," Trey said, his stomach a writhing jumble of nerves. He knew temporary breakups often led to permanent breakups, and that was the last thing he wanted. But maybe if they stopped trying so hard to make this work while they were in the spotlight, they'd all be happier. And honestly, he wanted to see a little fight in her. For him.

Fight for me, goddamn it. Even if it's just a little.

"A break?" Reagan's voice cracked. "What do you mean by a break?"

"I mean we should stop seeing each other as a couple—a *threesome*—while we're on tour."

She huffed at him like a dragon awoken from a long slumber. "I can't believe you even thought that, much less said it."

"Uh, I'm gonna go find Logan," Toni said, sidling toward the door. "See you later."

"I think this conversation requires your third wheel," Steve said. "I'll vamoose and send him in."

"A few minutes ago, you said you could be *okay* with a public ruse, and now you want to break up?" Reagan massaged her eyes, but wasn't able to stop several tears from falling. The fire he'd stirred was already diminishing, and he much preferred dealing with that then the sad Reagan, the broken Reagan. Especially knowing he was responsible for her turmoil.

"No," Trey said, pulling her into a tight embrace, glad she didn't resist. "I *don't* want to break up. I want to be with you and with Ethan forever. That's why I think it might be best to put our relationship on hold while we finish out this tour. The stress of it is going to tear us apart for real."

"What did I miss?" Ethan said, his question punctuated by the closing of the door at the front of the bus, which sealed them off from the outside world.

Reagan sniffed. "Trey wants to break up."

"What?" Ethan's tone was raw.

"That's not what I want at all," Trey said. "You're not listening." Realizing he'd blundered his idea of a solution, he scrambled for a better way to explain. "I just said that while we're on tour, it might be best to take a break."

"You want to fuck other people?" Ethan asked, his voice booming in the small space.

"No." Trey shook his head. "I don't want to fuck or love

anyone but the two of you. I don't want to break up. I want us to be friends—"

"Oh God," Reagan sobbed, her body quaking in his arms.

Wow. He was really fucking this up.

"We are not breaking up," Ethan said. "Why would we do that when things are going so well?"

"Things are going well?" Trey said, not bothering to disguise his snide tone. "I just asked her to take her days *off* to go home with us so we can be alone together outside the chaos of this tour, and she's worried what fucking Sam Baily will think. She doesn't want to sacrifice anything for either of us."

"Love isn't about sacrifice," Reagan said. "It's about compromise."

"Compromise requires sacrifice on someone's part," Trey countered. He looked to Ethan for backup, but Ethan's attention was focused on the floor, his jaw set, mouth twisted in a harsh frown. "If no one is willing to sacrifice anything, it's not a compromise. I'd give up everything for the two you."

"Everything?" Reagan didn't sound convinced.

"Is that what you want? Me to stop playing guitar and leave Sinners? Renounce my family and friends? Go into hiding as your love slave, appreciated only for my skills in bed?"

"Of course I wouldn't ask that of you. And you shouldn't ask it of me!"

"He's right," Ethan said quietly. "We need to take a break from each other."

Ethan lifted his head, but Trey couldn't see his eyes behind his sunglasses. He wished they'd shatter, the way his heart just had. He didn't want Ethan to agree with him—or Reagan, for that matter. He wanted them to tell him he was a fucking idiot and they'd do anything to keep him in their lives. That was what he wanted. He'd thought he was making that pretty clear. But maybe they weren't willing to give him what he wanted. Maybe they didn't care what he wanted.

"What?" Reagan said, struggling to free herself from Trey's now loose embrace so she could glare at Ethan. "You can't possibly think that's for the best."

"I do," Ethan said. "There aren't many tour dates left here in the States. Then we get those two weeks off before we head to Europe. Trey stays on his tour bus and you stay on yours and I'll leave for the rest of this leg of the tour. We'll meet back at home during the break and decide what to do from there."

"Leave?" Trey said, shaking his head. He really had made a mess of things. "You can't leave."

"I need you," Reagan said. "To protect me."

"From what?" Ethan said. "That asshole who threatened you, who hurt you, isn't a threat anymore."

"From the press!"

Ethan laughed softly and cupped her cheek with one hand. "The best way to protect you from them is by leaving. Don't you see that?"

"No." Reagan shook her head, knotting her fingers in his shirt.

Ethan wrapped his fingers around her wrists. "I don't want to be apart from either of you, but Trey's right. Something needs to be sacrificed—by all of us—to make this work. And this is my sacrifice."

What kind of stupid sacrifice was that? Reagan would be terrified to continue on tour if Ethan left her now. She depended on him far more than he could possibly realize.

"I didn't mean for you to leave," Trey said. "You can still be Reagan's bodyguard." Besides, how could they all realize within hours of their temporary separation that they couldn't live without each other if Ethan was fucking *gone* gone?

"I love you," Ethan said, kissing Reagan's lips. "I'll see you when you get home."

"Ethan?" Her plea tore at Trey's heart. How could the man possibly walk away from her?

"And I love you," Ethan said to Trey.

His feather-soft kiss of farewell twisted Trey's throat in a vice so tight, he couldn't force a single word out.

"Promise me you'll put up *your* bro box when you're around Brian."

An uneasy laugh—more like a gasp—escaped Trey. He'd wear his bro box like a suit of armor if it would make Ethan stay.

"You can't go," Reagan said. "Ethan?"

But with a final touch to Reagan's cheek and to Trey's chin and a look of longing for each of them, Ethan went.

CHAPTER
21

SACRIFICE.

Leaving had felt like hell on earth to Ethan, but it needed to be done for Trey's sake and even more so for his own. He'd taken a flight from New York to San Antonio. He'd intended to go home to Los Angeles and sort his shit out there, but while waiting in line at the ticket counter, he'd decided it was past time for him to man up. And make a real sacrifice. One he hoped he wouldn't regret making.

This was the right decision. He couldn't come up with any other way to make things right. Ethan had been avoiding this conversation for years. It was time. Past time. He knew he had to tell his family on his own, no matter how lonely it felt to have no one at his side while he broke his mother's heart, earned his stepfather's hatred, and lost his brothers' respect.

While waiting for a rental car, he called both Reagan and Trey's cellphones but neither picked up—not that he was surprised—so he texted them a group message. *I'm back on the ground. I love you both. Counting the days until we're together again. Thirteen to go. Already feels like an eternity.*

No immediate answer from either of them. They were probably at some crazy party or making love without him.

He didn't want to tell them he was in Texas. Not yet. The flight had given him plenty of time to talk himself out of his self-elected mission, but he couldn't erase the image of Trey begging for someone to believe that he was worth some sacrifice. So sacrifice was on Ethan's agenda, because someone as wonderful as Trey should never have to ask to feel worthy.

The harried attendant finally found Ethan a *suitable* rental car—if baby blue Volkswagen Beetles were suitable—and he headed toward his mother's house. Every mile he journeyed closer to his family strengthened his resolve. He should be coming out for himself—and he was to some extent—but if he lost his nerve, he knew he could do it for Trey. Because Trey was worth it. Trey was worth any sacrifice.

Ethan hadn't just been spouting words when he'd told Trey he would die for him—he'd meant that—but he'd much rather *live* for him. In the back of his mind, Ethan hoped that if he found the strength to reveal his secrets to those he loved, those he might lose over this revelation, then Reagan would find the strength to do the same. She should talk to her father for Trey, yes, but also for herself. Ethan had known Reagan for years, and he'd never once seen her lose her backbone, not until Sam Baily had made her feel small and then again when that goddamned tabloid had been published. He wondered if fame was worth the price. Maybe to her. Probably to Trey. But it sure as hell wasn't worth it to him.

It was late when he pulled into the driveway of the small adobe house. The window of the front room flickered from the light of the television inside. The wrought-iron bars over the two front windows and door were more decorative than protective, but they reminded him where he came from. He wondered if he'd become a police officer because he'd never felt safe in his own neighborhood or because he'd learned to be a badass at an early age or because his mother had an unusual fondness for police television dramas. Or maybe it was because he liked serving justice. He just needed to learn to serve it with a little less fist.

Maybe it was time to go back to the force. Assuming he could convince the LAPD to give him a chance. His temper wasn't what it had once been. He was no longer consumed by uncontrollable rage when confronted by injustice, although he still wanted to do something about it. Reagan had softened him up, he decided. Why else would he be thinking about returning to the force and leaving his personal anger at the door?

His key didn't work, so he had to ring the bell. While he waited for someone to let him in, he examined the bushes flanking the door, deciding they could use a trim.

"*¿Quien es?*" his mother's voice asked and he heard the

unmistakable click of a pistol being cocked behind the closed door. "Who's there?" she repeated in English.

"It's just me," Ethan said. "Sorry I didn't call first. I thought I'd surprise you."

"Ethan?"

"*Si, soy yo.*"

He listened to a series of locks being turned, slid or unlatched before his mother threw open the door.

"Ay *mijo*, I missed you." She tossed her short, plump figure into his arms, and he hugged her fiercely, wary of the pistol wrapped in her tiny hand with the butt pressed into his side. Her thick black hair smelled of cumin and cilantro and crispy flour tortillas. He hoped that meant she'd been cooking. His stomach rumbled, and his mouth watered in anticipation of being delighted by her culinary skill. Madre Rosa's Mexican Restaurant was the local fave for a reason.

"When did you get a gun?" Ethan asked. She pulled out of his arms, grinning up into his face and reaching up to pat his cheek.

"You are so skinny," she criticized, ignoring his question. "Come to the kitchen. I'll feed you."

She'd get no arguments out of him. He closed the door and threw the various locks while she tucked her pistol into a nearby side table.

"Is that loaded?" he asked, still rattled from seeing his mother with a gun. He'd seen one in his stepfather's hand before, and he owned one himself, but what could his sweet little mother need with a gun?

"Si, is loaded. Come. You look hungry." She headed through the small living room, where the television was airing a late night talk show, and into the kitchen. Ethan trailed after her.

"Mamá, you didn't answer me. When did you get a gun? *Why* did you get a gun?"

"Carlos gave it to me. So much crime in town." She began pulling ingredients out of the cabinet and refrigerator. "It's okay though. I protect what is mine."

"Carlos?" What business did his brother have in giving their mother a gun?

Mamá turned, found him standing uncomfortably in the doorway, and scowled at him.

"Si. Sit, sit," she insisted. "I'll feed you."

"We need to talk about this. Where is Papá? Does he know you have a gun?"

"Papá is away most nights. Working late shifts. He will come home if I tell him you're here." She grinned at him. "He will be happy to see you. Now sit, please. You must eat."

"Late nights? Are you keeping the restaurant open late now?"

Mamá opened a cabinet and pulled out a large bowl. "We'll catch up later. Sit."

Ethan sat and watched her mix flour, salt, baking soda, water and lard into her signature dough. The woman never used a measuring cup, yet her tortillas always came out perfect. Ethan made tortillas from scratch on occasion, but they were never as good as hers. When she pulled out a huge cast iron skillet that had been seasoned for decades, he decided that pan was her secret ingredient.

"Mamá, you don't have to cook for me. I already ate at Taco Bell." He waited for the explosion. Nothing got her riled faster than one of her boys eating at fast food's attempt at Mexican fare.

"No," she said, whirling around to stare daggers at him. His thinly veiled grin didn't fool her. She set her lips in a thin line, pulled her skillet off the stove and slid it back into the oven where she stored it. "I wish you told me you were full before I mixed the masa." She lifted her bowl and headed for the trash.

"I was just joking," he said hastily. "I dream about your tortillas, Mamá. Please don't throw them away."

"What else do you dream about, mijo?" she asked. She set to work dividing the dough and rolling it into small balls. "I worry since you left the police. You worked so hard to make it through school. So hard. It made your Mamá proud."

So she wasn't proud now? Ouch. "I told you I'm doing security work with a rock band. Remember?"

"This satisfies you?"

Not really. It kept him close to Reagan and Trey, however, so it wasn't a bad gig for an ex-cop.

"I've been thinking about trying to get on with the LAPD, but how likely are they to hire me with my track record?" He'd been branded a vigilante cop. He wasn't sure he'd ever shake that label.

"Maybe they will give you a chance to prove yourself," Mamá said. "You are no longer so angry and have better control of the temper."

He had changed from that young punk with a badge. Being fired had been his wakeup call. He'd admittedly been drunk on power, so focused on righting wrongs that he'd ignored some of the laws he was supposed to be enforcing. Specifically the law against beating the shit out of assholes just because they deserved it.

"Besides," Mamá continued, letting most of the tortillas dough balls rest while rolling one out with a wooden pin and dropping it into her skillet, so Ethan wouldn't have to wait. "They used you as an example, Ethan, because so many think police are our enemy. Someone had to be the escape goat."

"Scape goat," he corrected automatically.

She offered him a sad smile over her shoulder. "Whatever this is, I wish it had not been you."

"I deserved to be fired," Ethan said. "I was out of control."

"You also deserve second chance." She plopped the first tortilla onto a towel and set it in front of him with a stick of butter.

He'd had a second chance. It was the third chance they hadn't given him.

He rubbed one end of the butter over the hot tortilla, rolled it up, and bit into it. His eyelids fluttered in bliss. Freshly made warm tortillas with melted butter . . . Was there anything more delicious in the entire world? Perhaps Trey's cherry-flavored kisses might give them a run for their money, but little else did.

"Do you want a second chance?" Mamá asked, sitting beside him and taking his free hand. "Or is there something else you dream of?" She lifted her dark eyebrows and smiled hopefully. "Babies?"

Ethan laughed. "That's what *you're* dreaming of."

"I have all sons but no grandbabies!"

"Why don't you harass Carlos or Miguel for grandchildren?" Ethan glanced down at his empty towel and wondered where his tortilla had disappeared to already. Surely he hadn't scarfed it down that quickly.

"You are my oldest, mijo" she said. "And you have a lovely girlfriend. Marry Reagan and make your mamá happy." She reached over and patted his cheek. "Don't you want to make Mamá happy?"

"Reagan doesn't want babies."

His mother was completely unaware that they'd broken up for almost a year—though they'd stayed friends and roommates the entire time. And now that they were back together with an additional romantic partner, having babies was completely out of the question. Which reminded him why he'd traveled so far to see her in the first place.

"All women want babies," Mamá insisted. "We cannot help it. Give Reagan time. She will want them someday."

Ethan blew out his cheeks, his heart thudding with apprehension. He had no idea how she would react to being told he was bisexual and hopelessly in love with a man and a woman. He might as well get this over with.

"Mamá, I have something to—"

The doorbell rang and then a loud pounding began on the front door.

"¡Mamá! ¿Estás bien?" More loud pounding. "¡Mamá! Open the door."

"What is *his* problem?" Mamá asked as she rose from her chair and left the kitchen. Ethan trailed after her to see why his brother was freaking out on the doorstep.

When she opened the door, Carlos said, "Why did you open the door without your gun?"

"I knew it was you, *tonto*."

"Whose car is in your driveway?"

Despite the rapid-fire questions, Mamá didn't lose her cool. "It belongs to a very handsome man, who came to visit." She pressed a splayed hand to her throat and batted her eyelashes.

"Oh really? Only a faggot would drive a blue Bug."

"Long time no see," Ethan said, trying not to let his brother's vulgarity bother him. Carlos still had the round face of his youth, though the soul patch beneath his lower lip was new. As was the bandana fashioned from a golden kerchief. The color immediately set off alarm bells in the cop lobe of Ethan's brain. Had his brother joined a gang? Carlos seemed uncommonly interested in their mother's safety, and if his stupidity had put Mamá at risk, it wasn't gainfully employed law enforcement officers Carlos needed to worry about. It was his older brother.

"*¡Qué onda, güey!*" Carlos nudged Mamá aside so he could enter the house, wrap Ethan in a loose hug, and pound him enthusiastically on the back. Ethan pounded right back. "When did you get here?"

"Less than an hour ago."

"You're driving a Bug? Around here, lesser crimes than that will get a dude shot."

"It's a rental."

"That doesn't make me feel any better about it."

"Come," Mamá said. "I'll feed you both while you catch up."

"Where's Juan?" Ethan asked, trailing after his brother and looking for additional signs of gang affiliation. Carlos was wearing a black tank top, but had no depictions of crowns or any tell-tale lettering. Ethan didn't see any beads in black and gold or gang tattoos, and Carlos didn't have lines shaved into his eyebrows. So maybe he wasn't gang affiliated. Ethan prayed his suspicions were wrong. One golden bandana didn't mean he was a killer, did it?

"Juan's down in Laredo. He's got a woman there," Carlos said, slumping into a chair at the kitchen table.

"A woman he never brings to meet his mamá," Mamá said, rolling tortillas from the masa she'd allowed to rest.

"It's complicated," Carlos said and grinned, rubbing his nose with the back of his hand.

"Why didn't you bring Reagan, Ethan?" Mamá asked.

"She's on tour for another two weeks," Ethan said.

"You still haven't told Mamá that you two broke up?" Carlos asked. Ethan kicked his brother's shin beneath the table, and Carlos cringed before kicking Ethan back.

Mamá spun to glare at her eldest. "What? Why didn't you tell me this?"

Ethan raised both hands in surrender. "We're back together."

"I thought she was banging that pretty rockstar guy now." Carlos leaned in close and whispered so that Mamá wouldn't overhear. "And just banging you on the side."

Carlos had seen the tabloid? Shit.

"It's complicated," Ethan said. Hey, if that kind of vague excuse worked for Juan, surely it would work for him as well.

"Reagan has a new man?" Mamá asked, her brow knotted with concern.

Yes and no. Ugh. Why did Carlos have to show up before he explained his situation to his mother? He'd wanted to gauge her reaction to the news before he considered revealing anything to the rest of the family. He never doubted that his mother would always love him unconditionally; he wasn't so sure his brothers would be able to stomach the news. And his stepfather? Yeah, he'd probably never be welcomed back into this house again, but if it came to that, Trey and Reagan were worth that sacrifice to him, even though the mere thought of being estranged from his family twisted his heart.

"If you ask me," Carlos said—though no one had—"her new guy is a queer and just using Reagan to hide his perversion. Have you seen him? He's prettier than ninety percent of the women I know. Am I right?"

"Don't use that word," Ethan said.

"What? Perversion?"

"Queer."

"Do you prefer fag? Or maybe the more formal faggot?"

Ethan's body tensed, as did his fist. "I prefer Trey. You know, his name."

"So you actually know that *culero*?" Carlos asked, his eyebrows raised so high they disappeared completely beneath his bandana.

"Yeah, we're close. Don't rely on what the tabloids say for information about my life or Reagan's or anyone's for that matter."

"What tabloid?" Mamá asked.

Fuck. He'd assumed that if Carlos had seen it, then Mamá had as well. Ethan's well thought out plan to break the news to his family wasn't going the way he'd envisioned at all.

"It's nothing, Mamá," Carlos said. "Don't worry about it. It's mostly about Reagan anyway."

"Reagan's in the paper? Where can I see this?"

"She wouldn't want you to see it," Ethan said. "The things they said about her hurt her badly."

"And why do you not do something about this?" Mamá had taken on her you're-about-to-get-an-ass-whopping-from-a-tiny-Mexican tone. "Your duty is to protect her."

She was right. As her boyfriend and her bodyguard, he was duty-bound to protect Reagan. But how did he fight public opinion? Perhaps now was a good time to change the subject.

"So what's with the bandana?" Ethan asked Carlos. "Are you tangled up with the wrong crowd?"

Carlos pulled the bandana off his head and stuffed it into the pocket of his jeans, leaving his black hair in complete disarray. "No. Just fashion."

"If the wrong people see you wearing that *fashion*—"

"This is bad, no?" Mamá asked. "Not a safe color to wear. I tell him this."

"No one bothers me when I wear it," Carlos said.

Ethan stared Carlos down, but he didn't flinch. He knew when his younger brother was lying—when they were kids, Ethan had usually been a part of those lies—and Carlos wasn't lying. Not about this. "So you wear it for *protection*?" That was hard for Ethan to comprehend.

Carlos looked away and nodded curtly.

"It might get you arrested," Ethan said. "Or if the Latin Kings know you're misrepresenting their colors, you'll face far worse than incarceration."

"Then you need to talk Mamá into leaving this terrible neighborhood. It isn't safe here. Especially since Papá left her."

Ethan's jaw dropped. "What?" His mother had said Papá was working late, but she'd made it sound like he was coming home soon.

The litany of Spanish and Spanglish swear words his mother produced as she slapped at Carlos with her spatula made Ethan's face burn. In all his twenty-nine years, he'd never heard her cuss.

"Don't you think he would have figured it out eventually?" Carlos asked, shrinking into his chair but not attempting to defend himself.

At the smell of burning tortilla, Mamá whirled back to the stove. "Don will come back." She tossed the burnt tortilla into the trash and laid a raw one in the skillet. "He always does."

"He's not coming back, Mamá."

"But he must!"

Ethan exchanged a worried glance with Carlos before rising to his feet. He stood behind his mother at the stove and gently took her upper arms in his hands. "Why didn't you tell me?"

"Why didn't you tell *me* that you and Reagan are over?"

"We're not over," Ethan said gently. "We got back together."

"So will I and my Don." She straightened her spine and flipped the tortilla, her attention focused so sharply on the pan in front of her that Ethan was surprised her razor-like gaze didn't cleave the iron in two. "I will wait."

"Mamá, he found some woman in San Marcos," Carlos said. "He's not coming back."

"No," she said firmly. "I do not accept this. He must."

"What about the restaurant?" Ethan asked. His parents had been partners since the restaurant had opened almost twenty-five years ago.

"Dad ran it into the ground buying expensive stuff for his little *puta*," Carlos said.

Mamá dropped her head as if ashamed. "We had to sell."

"So he could buy the puta a ring," Carlos muttered under his breath.

"What? Why am I the last to know any of this?" Ethan yelled.

"You're the one who left town. It's not like you could have done anything to prevent it."

"Papá's coming back," Mamá said. "After his midwife crisis."

"Midlife crisis," Ethan corrected automatically.

"Things will get better," she said. "Once he figures out I'm best."

"You can't stay here just waiting for him to come back," Carlos said. "It's not safe for a woman to live in this neighborhood by herself."

"I'm not afraid," she insisted.

"How would you like to visit California for a couple of weeks?" Ethan said. "Just until Papá gets his head out of his a—I mean, remembers how much he loves you." Ethan wondered if the old man might need a bit of reminding.

"I will wait for him *here*. This is my home."

Ethan glanced at Carlos, who was rubbing his face with both palms. He had the feeling that Carlos and his mother had had this same conversation more than once.

"I wouldn't ask you to leave your home forever," Ethan said, his promise punctuated by the wail of passing sirens. "Just come for a short visit. You can fatten me up while Reagan's away on tour."

"You are skinny," she said, setting the last tortilla on the stack next to the stove.

"He doesn't have an ounce of fat on him," Carlos said.

Ethan worked very hard at the gym to make that a reality. Exodus End's personal trainer Kirk made sure of it.

"You could stay here with me instead, Ethan," Mamá said. "Until Don comes home. He should miss me soon."

"Maybe you going away and *not* waiting for him would bring him to his senses," Carlos said.

She shifted out of Ethan's light hold and went to the refrigerator to pull out toppings for their tortillas. She reheated seasoned pork, rice, and refried beans. Ethan helped her by chopping tomatoes, jalapeños, onions and fresh cilantro for pico de gallo. He squeezed lime juice into the fresh salsa and sampled it with a bite of tortilla. A little salt, some pressed garlic and several more samples later, he declared it finished. Mamá pinched his cheek and gave him a look of adoration for his efforts.

"I sent a text to Juan," Carlos said, still lounging at the dining table. "Didn't tell him *why* he should visit Mamá's house ASAP, but he should be here soon."

"I thought he was in Mexico," Ethan said.

Carlos's gaze flicked to Mamá's back before he said, "He finished his business early." He made a circle with his index finger and thumb and thrust a finger of his opposite hand in and out of the hole.

"He should find good Catholic girl to marry instead of buying cow for free," Mamá said, never missing a beat. The woman had raised seven sons—she knew a thing or two about a man's evening business with his woman. "He moved out after school, day after high school. He's still in town for now, but with his woman living far away, is only a matter of time before I never see him either. All my sons leave me."

"Wait," Ethan said. "Why didn't anyone tell me Juan moved out? He's just a kid." Hell, Juan had only graduated from high school a little over a month earlier. Ethan's other four brothers were spread out over the country due to job or school commitments, but Carlos had stayed close to home, and Ethan had just assumed Juan was still living there. Poor Mamá. She really was alone.

"You moved out right after high school," she pointed out.

Well, yeah. Seven boys ranging from the ages of nine to nineteen sharing two bedrooms had been tight quarters, even worse than living with five or more grown men on a tour bus. But Juan was the baby of the family and he'd had a room to himself all through high school. Mamá needed someone to stay with her now. She'd gone from living in a house busting at the seams to being entirely alone. No wonder she wanted grandchildren so badly.

By the time Juan arrived, they were well into their late meal. Carlos and Mamá were in a heated discussion about politics. She argued with him in Spanish since she could better express complex opinions in her native language. Ethan was happily stuffing his face, wondering if his mother would be as fond of Trey as she was of Reagan. She loved her sons; surely she had room in her heart for one more. And as happy as he was to see two of his brothers, he wanted to broach the subject of his unusual lifestyle with Mamá first and decide later if his brothers could handle the truth about him. He was still guessing they wouldn't be the least bit mature or open-minded about his relationship. If he'd been in love with two women, he'd have been their hero. But a woman and a man? They'd consider that a different level of strange. He was sure of it.

"Ethan?" Juan said in greeting. "What are you doing here?"

"Visiting for a few days." He rose from his seat to give his youngest brother a hearty hug and pound on the back.

"You scared me, *cabrón*," Juan said, slapping Carlos on the head. "I thought someone broke into the house again."

"*Again?*" Ethan sat down hard in his chair. "What happened, Mamá? Were you hurt? Threatened? Robbed?"

"Is nothing," she insisted. "Sit, sit," she said to Juan. "I have enough for you."

Juan sat and watched Mamá fix him a pork soft taco. He was old enough to live on his own, yet the woman still babied him.

"It *is* something," Ethan insisted. "And I want details. It's like I moved to LA and everyone forgets I'm part of this family." If he wasn't satisfied that his mother would be safe here by herself, he would find a way to convince her to move.

"Non," she said, "is nothing, mijo. Carlos gave me gun. It will not happen again. I'm ready this time."

Imagining his tiny mother fighting off hardened criminals with a pistol did not put Ethan at ease.

"You should get a dog, Mamá," Juan said. "A big ol' Rottweiler."

"Or one of you should stay with her permanently," Ethan said.

"Us? Why not *you*?" Carlos asked, pointing at Ethan.

"Because I have a life in Los Angeles." Duh.

"And we have lives here," Juan said around the food in his mouth.

"What about Miguel? Raùl? Pedro? Arturo?" But that wouldn't work unless Miguel quit his job, Raul and Pedro dropped out of school, and Arturo was discharged from the air force. Maybe Ethan did need to step up here.

"I don't want any of my boys to give up happiness for me," Mamá said, making Ethan another soft taco even though he was stuffed.

Of course she would say that; almost any mother would put her children's happiness before her own. But did she mean it? Wasn't she afraid to stay there by herself? Or maybe she was more afraid of change. Or did she really believe that Papá would come back only if she stayed? Ethan had come to clear the way for his life with Trey and Reagan, but his mother's safety was more important at the moment.

"Mamá, you know it's more likely that you'll be killed by your own gun than you'll successfully defend yourself with it," Ethan said, hoping statistics would make her see how foolish she was being.

"I will not . . . how you say?" Her brow wrinkled with concentration. "*Suicide* myself."

"That's not what I meant," Ethan said, though that oft-spouted statistic did include gun-related suicides. "Accidents happen all the time."

"I will not accident myself either." She began removing dishes and leftovers from the table with angry huffs and jerky motions. She snatched a half-finished taco out of Juan's hand and threw it into the trash. When Mamá was upset, Mamá didn't feed anyone.

"Go now," she said as she scoured a plate in the sink. "It's past time for bed."

"I'll get the dishes, Mamá," Ethan said.

"I said go," she snapped.

"You want me to leave too?" Ethan said. "I came all this way to see you."

"Yes, you go. I'll show you. I'll show you all I am not weak. I am not afraid. This is *my* home. No one will take it from me."

Ethan tried to take the sponge out of her hand, but she slapped at him.

"I say you go," her English slipping in her outrage. "You go now."

"Mamá, don't be mad."

She narrowed her eyes at him. "Do not treat me like child. Or helpless old woman. You go. I mean this, Ethan. Go."

"You can crash at my place," Carlos said.

What choice did he have? He could sleep in a baby blue Bug in the driveway, he supposed, or stay at a hotel, but he wanted to spend time with his family. He didn't want to leave his mother angry. It took a lot to infuriate her, but she held onto her ire for a long time. He knew if he didn't obey her, she'd become completely irrational. It was better to leave and let her cool off than stay and fuel her fire. He was certain she'd be more rational in the morning.

"I'll come see you tomorrow, Mamá," he said, kissing her cheek even though she stiffened and leaned away from him. "Will you feed me?"

"You're not that lucky," she said.

Ethan watched her scrub another dish, sorry that he'd upset her. "I don't think you're incapable of taking care of yourself, *Madre*. I'm just worried about you. Sleep well." He forced another kiss on her and then followed his brothers out of the house.

"Don't forget to lock up," Carlos hollered just before Juan pulled the door shut.

The three of them stood listening to the various locks being set before they were satisfied.

"Want to head to Oak Hills?" Juan asked.

Ethan didn't feel much like drinking or trying to pick up inebriated women, which was why Juan went to bars. He'd had a false ID since he was fifteen and hadn't let it go to waste.

"I have to pass tonight, bro," Ethan said. "Traveled all day. Ready to crash."

"*Mi sofá es su cama*," Carlos said, slapping him hard on the chest.

A car took off at the end of the street, tires squealing, and Carlos ducked behind the nearest obstacle—which happened to be Ethan's car—until it had disappeared onto the next block.

When Carlos stood straight again, Ethan lifted an eyebrow at his brother. "Problem?"

"Nope," Carlos said. "You'd better take your car. If you leave it here, it probably won't have tires when you return."

"It's not so bad here," Juan said.

Carlos shoved him. "Says the man who voluntarily goes to Laredo for pussy."

"Mamá has bigger balls than you do," Juan said.

"When did Papá leave?" Ethan asked, feeling safe to ask for details now that Mamá was out of earshot.

Carlos scratched behind his ear, one nervous eye still on the road. "About a month ago, I'd say."

A *month*? He talked to his brothers and Mamá regularly, but no one had ever hinted at Papá leaving. "Why didn't anyone tell me?"

"She said there was no need. She really thinks he's coming back."

"He's not coming back," Juan said. "And I'm sure she's low on funds. I try to give her money, but she's too proud to take it. I don't think she can pay the mortgage on her own."

Maybe that was part of the reason she was afraid to leave.

"Papá will pay it," Carlos said.

"If he remembers," Juan said. "He's dick deep in a honey pot these days. He's not thinking clearly."

Ethan turned to look back at the house with a more critical eye. A few of the terracotta roof tiles were missing, one of the porch lights had burned out, and a window on the side of the house was boarded over.

"Isn't that Mamá's bedroom window?" Ethan asked, nodding toward the plywood covering.

"That's where they broke in," Carlos said. "While she was sleeping. She's lucky they didn't kill her."

"Just some kids looking for drug money," Juan said with a shrug. "The cops picked them up a few days later."

So Carlos was overparanoid and Juan was completely unconcerned. Perhaps Ethan could provide the middle ground their mother desperately needed to get her life back on track. Not that he'd tell her it *wasn't* on track. She'd probably crack him upside the head with her cast iron skillet if he did that.

"You should move back in with her," Ethan said to Juan.

"That's a great way to score lots of women," Juan said. "No thanks, bro."

He said goodbye to the self-centered little cuss, climbed in his adorable fucking rental car, and followed Carlos to his apartment that was far too far from Mamá's house to be any comfort to him. She truly was alone there. But how would he ever talk her out of leaving her home? Though he wasn't sure she was in as much danger as Carlos made it out to be, he didn't think she was safe there either. He'd do a little digging the next morning with friends on the local police force. He wasn't sure how much information they'd be willing to share, but he could ask. Just as he pulled into an apartment complex parking lot behind Carlos, his phone rang. It was almost midnight, but he wasn't the least bit upset that Trey was calling him so late.

Ethan connected through his Bluetooth. "Are you finished giving me the silent treatment?" he asked in greeting.

"I can't sleep. I miss you," Trey murmured in a sleepy voice that made Ethan think of bed and how much he wished he was sharing one with Trey and Reagan at the moment.

"I miss you too."

"Are you lying in bed thinking of me?"

"Wishing I'd never left."

"Then come back," he said. "I don't understand why you left in the first place. Reagan says she'll never forgive you for deserting us."

She'd forgive him. She was the most forgiving person he'd ever met.

"I'm in Texas," Ethan said.

Silence met Ethan's ear, and he could imagine the look of confusion on Trey's face. "Why?" he asked eventually.

"I came to visit my mother. And my brothers. I'm going to tell them."

"About us?" Trey sounded much more alert now.

"Yeah," he admitted, feeling relieved to share his burden with Trey. He had planned to surprise him with the news, but was glad he was bad at keeping secrets. "It's proving to be more difficult than I'd anticipated."

Ethan parked in a vacant visitor spot, but left the car running.

"I know it's hard, E, but I promise you'll feel so much better afterward," Trey said. Ethan was glad Trey didn't give him an out, didn't tell him he could forget about it if the process became too uncomfortable. "And when you come back, no matter the outcome, I'll be waiting."

Ethan smiled, his chest warming at the idea of Trey waiting for him.

A loud knock sounded on the car window and Ethan jumped, thinking he was under attack until he recognized his brother staring in at him.

"I've got to go," Ethan said, figuring his brother could probably hear his conversation through the car window. "I'm glad you called. I'll talk to you soon."

He disconnected before Trey could say something incriminating, such as *I love you* or *I wish you were here sucking my dick.* Contact with Trey had strengthened Ethan's resolve once again. Not enough to tell Carlos about Trey's true importance to him just yet. But Ethan was pretty sure he was ready to tell his mother. Tomorrow. Or if she was still upset, he'd tell her the next day.

Ethan opened the door and unfolded his legs from the ridiculously small car.

"Who were you talking to?" Carlos asked. "Your girlfriend?"

"No," Ethan said, going to the trunk for his overnight bag and slinging it over one shoulder.

"You sure? You had this goofy, lovey-dovey look on your face."

Whoops. "Whatever," Ethan said, shoving Carlos in the shoulder. "You're seeing things, hombre."

"I must be," Carlos said. "Sounded like you were talking to a man."

"I was," Ethan said and left it at that.

The apartment complex was small but well kept. The three-story beige buildings formed a large rectangular U-shape flanked by sidewalks and red-mulch beds containing desert plants. Brightly glowing street lamps provided a measure of nighttime safety. Balconies hung from the upper floors, and he and Carlos passed a small swimming pool in the center of the courtyard before Carlos led him to a ground floor apartment and unlocked the door. The place was small, but much cleaner than Ethan expected. Ethan deposited his bag near the sofa—his cama for the night—and kicked off his shoes, making himself comfortable with a loud sigh. Even though Ethan was exhausted, he enjoyed watching late night talk shows and munching Fritos and bull-shitting with his brother. No matter how long it had been since he'd last seen Carlos, they always clicked instantly, as if no time had passed at all. Perhaps he should give the oldest of his brothers the benefit of the doubt, spill his guts, and hope for the best. But then he remembered how Carlos so freely used the word faggot and had referred to Trey—a man he'd never met—as queer. Ethan wondered how he'd feel if Carlos referred to *him* that way. Ethan never cared what anyone thought of him, with the exception of his family. He never wanted to disappoint them again. He was pretty sure they'd think this was a much bigger deal than being fired from the police force.

Ethan wasn't sure when he'd nodded off, but the sun filtering in through the back patio door woke him the next morning. He lifted his head from the back of the sofa and massaged his neck as his muscles protested the uncomfortable sleep position. Carlos was asleep beside him, curled around a sofa pillow, his face smashed against the armrest. A weather anchor on television predicted another hot one while Ethan rubbed the sleep out of his eyes and wondered if Carlos had any coffee.

He was rummaging through cabinets in the tiny kitchen when a knock sounded on Carlos's front door.

"Carlos? You in there, man?" yelled a man with a deep voice before he knocked again.

Carlos sat bolt upright on the sofa, his eyes wide but unfocused. Ethan didn't recognize the voice, so he headed toward the door to investigate.

"Carlos, get in the fucking van!" the unknown visitor shouted. "Did you forget we have to be in Laredo by four?"

Ethan was almost to the entryway when Carlos sprang from the sofa and dashed in front of it, barring the exit—and the man on the other side—from Ethan's curiosity.

"Who's that?" Ethan asked, nodding toward the door behind Carlos. Carlos held his arms splayed wide, as if he could actually stop twice-his-size Ethan from opening the door.

Carlos's gaze shifted to the floor, the far wall, and the kitchen before settling on Ethan's chest. "No one."

"Carlos!" No One shouted before rattling the door handle. "We can't be late. Come on."

"I'll be right out," Carlos yelled back. "Wait for me in the van."

"I'm going to kick your ass if you fuck this up, man."

"I'll be right out!" Carlos repeated. Footsteps receded from the door, and Carlos let out a deep breath. He sucked it in again when Ethan grabbed his arm. Ethan's my-brother-is-up-to-no-good senses were tingling.

"What's in Laredo?" Ethan asked, knowing that the border town of Laredo wasn't the safest place on the continent.

"None of your business," Carlos said, yanking free of Ethan's hold and running for his bedroom. He shoved some clothes into a bag and pulled a small black case from beneath his bed before heading to the door. He grabbed a set of keys off a hook and tossed them at Ethan, who caught them in one hand.

"Make yourself at home, but lock up behind you," Carlos said. "I won't be back until tomorrow."

"What's in Laredo?" Ethan asked again, but Carlos was already outside.

Ethan followed him, determined to stop his brother from heading down a dangerous life path, but the short little shit was surprisingly swift. By the time Ethan caught up with him, he was already in the passenger seat of a beat-up white van. A large black man in mirrored sunglasses sat behind the wheel, and three additional Latinos were crammed into a the second row. They all wore yellow bandanas.

"Carlos?" Ethan called after him, fear for his brother squeezing his throat.

"Go!" Carlos shouted, and the van sped off with a belch of noxious fumes.

Ethan waved a hand in front of his face and coughed, his eyes automatically fixed on the van's New Mexico license plate. He committed the plate number to memory before turning to go back to Carlos's apartment. How pissed would his brother be if he started snooping through his belongings for clues? Not as pissed as his mother would be if Carlos got himself killed in a gang war.

CHAPTER 22

"H E'S DOING *what?*" Reagan shook her head, unable to take one more turd piled on the mountain of shit she was currently dealing with.

Inexplicably fully clothed, Trey sat on the mattress beside her. He sported jewelry in every piercing except her favorite one. Why did he look like it was time to take the stage? It wasn't even time to wake up yet.

Trey's smile faded, and he lifted an eyebrow at her as if he didn't have a clue why was livid. "He's telling his family about his sexual orientation."

Which meant one less roadblock to the world knowing everything. She knew where this would lead. Trey and Ethan would unite against her or at least against her wish to keep their relationship under wraps, and she'd be the only one left fighting for their privacy. Just thinking about the fallout exhausted her. She'd counted on Ethan staying on her side.

"Why would he do that all of a sudden?" Reagan asked. If coming out had been on his mind, surely he'd have mentioned it. Then again, this was silent-suffering Ethan they were talking about here.

"He's doing it for me. For himself." Trey presented a palm to her. "For us."

"*Us?* If this was for *us*, he'd have consulted *us* before he left for Texas."

"He's allowed to do something for himself, Rae," Trey said,

mouth tight. Reagan could see a rare glimmer of fury behind his green eyes. "And you should be supportive. This isn't an easy thing for him to do, you know."

"I know that. Better than you know it. His family, his community, they aren't so open to things like this." Much like her own. Mr. Rich Boy from Southern California had no idea how close-minded much of the world could be. "Besides, you've never even *met* his family." Last time she'd visited, his brothers had made countless derogatory gay jokes, and she knew it had bothered Ethan to have to pretend they were funny. Hell, it had bothered her, to the point that she'd told them several times to knock it off.

"I hope to remedy that soon," Trey said. "And you *don't* know better than me. You have no idea how hard it is for a man to come out as gay."

"Bisexual," she corrected, crossing her arms over her chest.

"Even worse. Especially at his age."

His stare of disapproval pissed her off.

"And with the added difficulty of the woman he loves against it."

"I'm not against it. It's just . . ." She stared down at her hand, where her fingers were picking at the sheet tangled around her naked waist. "The timing is bad."

"You're right; he should have told them sooner. But I'm sure he'd rather his family find out directly from him and not have to read about something that personal in a fucking tabloid."

"He can just deny any bullshit story the tabloids print," Reagan pointed out. That was what she planned to do. *If* she ever answered another of her father's calls. She still had him blocked.

"Maybe he doesn't want to deny it anymore."

And that was exactly what Reagan was so worried about.

"Maybe," Trey continued, "he's realized there are things more important than what other people think about him."

"Maybe," Reagan said through gritted teeth, "he's going to regret revealing this secret but then find he won't be able to take it back." She was sure Ethan hadn't thought through all the potential repercussions.

Trey sighed and slid a hand across his face. "Well, if he can't count on you for support, he can count on me."

She felt as if he'd slapped her. She'd never argued with Trey before, so wasn't sure how he was so good at cutting her to shreds. "He can count on me. He can always count on me!"

"You say that, Reagan, but I just don't see it." Trey pulled on his shoes and stood. "I have a date. See you later."

"A date?" What the fuck? She squinted at the clock on the bedside table. "At nine a.m.? Really?"

"The truth doesn't matter," he said, his back to her as he strode to the door. "As long as Reagan doesn't get her feelings hurt."

She stumbled from the bed, dragging the sheet with her. "What's that supposed to mean? Are you going somewhere that would hurt my feelings?"

"I prefer to keep that a secret." He let himself out of the hotel suite, the door clicking shut behind him.

Trey was twisting her wishes and desires into something they weren't. Yes, bending the truth was important in certain instances. Yes, she wanted to keep certain details about her personal life a secret. But she didn't want lies and secrets to be a part of her *private* relationships. Angry enough to spit fire, she wrenched open the door and peered down the corridor. Trey was just stepping onto the elevator at the center of the hallway.

"Wait!" Reagan said. "We are not going to leave it like this, Trey Mills. I'm not finished talking to you."

The elevator door closed, and the car began to descend. Reagan dashed out of the room, wondering why there was a cool breeze on her backside until she realized the sheet she'd taken from the bed was doing a fine job of concealing her front while leaving her ass fully exposed. The security guard standing just outside their suite, who was watching her in the absence of her very personal bodyguard, grinned as she hurriedly rearranged her cover and sprinted for the stairs. If she hurried, she could catch Trey in the lobby before he headed to his *date*, or wherever the lying jerk was really going. Assuming he *was* lying.

The marble steps were hard and cold against her bare feet as she sped down five flights of them. She burst through the exit door and crashed directly into a broad back. Reagan's hands flew out to catch her fall, and her sheet fluttered to the floor. She landed on her ass with a hard thud. The man she'd careened into turned and looked down at her through mirrored sunglasses.

"Are you okay?" Sed asked, just as the first camera flash went off.

Reagan was too stunned to react, but luckily Sed had his wits about him. He reached for the edges of the sheet and hurriedly wrapped them around her as best he could. Cameras were going off all around them as he helped her to her feet and reached behind her to tug the sheet down to cover her bare ass.

"Are you okay?" Sed asked again, finally bringing her out of her daze.

She scanned the lobby, her eyes growing wider and wider in horror as each face registered. Why were so many reporters there?

"Hey, Reagan," Eric Sticks said, one side of his crazy hair spiked the way he wore it on stage. "I think you're a little underdressed for the occasion."

Brian and Jace tried to form a screen in front of her. They both looked ready to perform as well—Brian with his heavy black eyeliner and the fingerless gloves he wore only onstage, and Jace actually vertical before noon. Maybe it was nine p.m. and she'd slept an entire day away.

She gasped when Trey pulled her into his arms and kissed her deeply. The hoop in his lip felt foreign against her mouth, and if she hadn't been so stunned, she might have punched him in the nose. She hadn't forgotten how pissed off she was for him toying with her before she was fully awake.

"Sorry I forgot to kiss you goodbye," he said, staring into her eyes with such love and adoration that her heart caught in her throat.

Cameras were going off in every direction, and it occurred to Reagan that he was doing damage control. She'd have words with him later. Maybe. She did melt when he looked at her like that, and the protective hand at her waist made her forget she'd chased him downstairs because he'd claimed to have a date.

"Go back to bed," he murmured, his loving gaze turning hot. "I'll see you later."

She swore she heard several female reporters giggle and sigh.

Jerry, Sinners' oft-absent manager, lifted one arm to try to gain everyone's attention. "The press conference will start in the ballroom in ten minutes!" he yelled over the din.

Press conference? Oy! She'd charged directly into a den of wolves.

"I'll see you soon," Reagan said, letting her genuine affection for Trey show as she gazed up at him. She was glad he'd come to her rescue in sight of the press—they'd have torn her apart again if they knew she and Trey were arguing, especially about Ethan—and she felt like a fool for chasing him downstairs in nothing but a sheet. But she was still perturbed at him. It felt like he didn't care that the tabloids were trying to destroy her. Didn't care that she was hurting.

Didn't care about how she felt at all.

She let him kiss her again. Even let herself enjoy it. The spotlighted lovers separated, making sure the world knew they parted reluctantly. Trey disappeared into the conference room with his band while Reagan took the elevator with her useless bodyguard back to the fifth floor.

Trey wouldn't say anything revealing at that press conference, would he? Her stomach twisted into a knot, but she didn't go back downstairs to eavesdrop. She trusted him. For the most part.

Instead of going back to bed as publicly instructed, Reagan took a shower, got dressed, and then called Ethan. She would support him as much as she could when he came out to his family. It wasn't like he was holding his own press conference to tell the world that Reagan was only satisfied when she had two cocks inside her. He was telling his mother and maybe his brothers that he'd been hiding part of who he was from them. They probably wouldn't take the news well, but they'd treat it as a secret and not go blabbing to the press. Now that she was over the initial shock, she realized that just because Ethan was telling his family, that didn't mean he'd freely share his personal business with the world. He wasn't like Trey.

Ethan didn't answer immediately, and she was preparing to leave a message when his breathless voice came on the line.

"Hey," he said. "I'm glad you called."

"Trey told me you've gone to Texas."

"Yeah."

Her original plan to offer her blessing seemed trite now that she had him on the phone. He didn't need her blessing to talk to his family. Hell, he probably didn't *want* her blessing, or he would have asked for it before he left. This wasn't about her at all. This was about him.

"How's your mom?"

"Not so good, actually," Ethan said.

Reagan's heart thudded. "Is she ill?"

"No, nothing like that. My stepdad left her for another woman."

"What?" How could any man up and leave a woman as wonderful as Rosa?

"Not only that, but before he left, he ran the restaurant into the ground and they had to sell it, so she's currently without an income. Living on her savings."

"Oh my God."

"And to top it all off, her neighborhood is in decline. I don't think she's safe here."

Reagan wasn't sure how that shitty neighborhood could get any worse. "Is she okay?"

"A couple of weeks ago some hoodlums broke into her house and robbed her at knifepoint, so Carlos gave her a gun. Of course, no one tells me these things when they actually happen."

"Ethan, you have to get her out of there," Reagan said, her heart racing.

"I'm working on it. She doesn't want to leave her home—not that she'd ever be able to sell it for a decent price in this shithole of a neighborhood—and she thinks Papá will come back if she stays put."

"Maybe he will," Reagan said, certain the man wasn't that stupid. Don would have to come to his senses eventually and realize what he was giving up by leaving Rosa.

"I highly doubt that. He's shacking up with this other woman."

"I feel so bad," Reagan said. "I wish I could be there for her."

"If I can get her to agree, I'm going to have her move in with me in Los Angeles."

"That will be nice." Reagan's brows scrunched together. "At our old place or Trey's?"

"Our old place."

"Isn't it going to be crowded with the four of us living there?"

"I thought you and Trey could live at his place and I'll live at our old place."

She blinked. Surely she'd heard him wrong. "You don't want to live with us?" So when he'd left, he'd actually *left* them? "Ethan . . ."

"I never said that. Maybe once the press is off your—"

"I'll tell them," she blurted, finally realizing that she might lose one or both of the men she loved if she kept their relationship a secret any longer. "I'll tell them everything."

"Is that a threat?" Ethan said, his voice sounding confused.

"A threat?" Reagan also sounded confused, because she was. "No. I'd rather the press know than lose you."

"Don't do that," he said. "I can't find the guts to tell my own mother, so how in the hell am I going to deal with the entire world knowing?"

"You haven't told her yet?"

Ethan released a sigh. "I figured she has enough to worry

about. Carlos spilled the news to her about you being in a tabloid, so of course she went and got a copy first thing this morning."

Reagan's face went numb. Another person she cared about would think poorly of her. Think she cheated on her boyfriend. Think she'd fucked her way into Exodus End. "Oh."

"She's livid on your behalf."

"Livid?"

"She doesn't believe a word of it."

Unlike her own father, who figured the tabloid had downplayed her promiscuity. "I appreciate her faith in me."

"She also put a curse on Trey for stealing my girl." Ethan chuckled.

Well, that wasn't fair. "You should tell her, Ethan. She'll be able to handle the truth."

"Don't you think I should wait until I've talked her into leaving here? I think Carlos might be caught up in some gang. I went through his stuff after he left this morning and can't find any evidence, but—"

"Ethan! You didn't really snoop, did you?"

"Damned right I did. My mom might not be the only one who needs saving here."

Reagan smiled. The guy loved "saving" those he cared about— and even random strangers on the street. "Ironic how you're invading your brother's privacy and trying to protect mine."

"I just want everyone safe and happy."

Which reminded her . . . "Trey and I had a fight this morning, and I ended up making a complete ass of myself."

"What were you fighting about?"

"The same shit we've been fighting about all week."

Ethan sighed. "This isn't going to go away no matter how much we want it to, is it?"

"It has to, Ethan. It can't follow us forever."

"As long as we're together, it will."

"If you say we should break up for my benefit, I'm going to reach through this phone and strangle you."

"I wasn't going to say that."

But she was certain he thought it.

"I thought," he said, "if I went away for a while, you and Trey could sort out your differences."

"We need you here, Ethan. We only work well in threes."

Ethan was silent. She shouldn't ask him to return so soon when he had family matters to fix. "Maybe I can talk Mamá into coming to see you perform. Where are you next?"

"Uh. I'm pretty sure we'll be in Atlanta on Tuesday and Little Rock on Wednesday." Little Rock. Ugh. She was not looking forward to playing so close to home. What if someone she knew showed up and revealed that she'd been a total band geek in high school?

"Little Rock isn't too far from Texas. Maybe she'd agree to go to that show. Or maybe she'd like to see both shows. I'll ask her. Do you think you can stop fucking things up with Trey until then?"

"I can try. Do you think you can save your brother before then?"

"I will. If I don't talk to you sooner, be sure to call me Monday and tell me how you're dealing with things."

"Monday?" She screwed up her face trying to think of anything she should be concerned about that day. "What's Monday?"

"The new tabloids hit the stands."

She had been feeling loads better. Now? Not so much. "Gee, thanks for reminding me. I guess an already shitty day *can* get worse."

"Sorry. I figured you'd be dwelling on it. Pretend I didn't bring it up."

If he'd been there, she'd have given him her "you're fucking kidding me, right" look.

"I've got to go. I love you."

"I love you too," Reagan said, her mind churning out all sorts of potential stories about her that might grace the next tabloid headlines. Would they dwell on what had happened in the hotel lobby less than an hour ago? She knew there would be something about her and Ethan together at the apartment during Phillip Lionheart's funeral, but what other photos did she need to worry about? Hugging Sed? Leaning on Dare? Being carried by Ethan? She was making much too easy for the tabloids to prove she was a slut.

"And tell Trey I love him and that he shouldn't call me at midnight, no matter how much he misses me."

"He called you at midnight?"

"He did. Tell him I'll call him as soon as I come out to my mother. That will give me incentive to do it."

"Aww, you do love him, don't you?"

"As much as I love you. Differently, but as much."

She understood exactly what he meant. She loved both men differently yet equally. Both of them had her entire heart. They didn't have to share that the way they had to share her body.

"Are you going to make up with him?" Ethan asked. "You know he can't stand for people to be cross with him."

"Yeah, I'll make it up to him. I owe him one after he made it seem like I was naked in the hotel lobby because I couldn't live without his goodbye kiss."

"What? Naked in the lobby?"

"I'll tell you about it sometime," she said, projecting a teasing tone into her words. "You have to go, remember? Tell your mom I said hi and that I can't wait for her to see me perform live." Reagan figured Rosa would be more likely to attend if she thought Reagan was the one who'd invited her.

"I'll tell her. And do try to stay out of trouble."

"I try, but it keeps finding me."

He chuckled. "Nothing's changed there."

When Trey returned over an hour later, Reagan was working on a riff that had been plaguing her for weeks. She just couldn't get it right. She envied those who seemed to pull fresh musical scores out of a magic hat. Writing music never came easy to her. Sometimes she'd think she'd come up with a new and innovative melody, only to realize she'd twisted parts of a score from her classical music background into something a bit more metal. She was pretty sure her new riff was trying to morph itself into a line from Beethoven's Eighth Symphony.

Trey's cheeks were red, and an ear-to-ear grin was plastered to his face.

"Something funny?" Reagan asked, finding herself smiling at him.

"Inside joke with Eric."

His band shared all sorts of inside jokes and poignant memories with each other. That connection was currently lacking between her and her bandmates. They were making memories now, but she missed having a history with them. She'd probably always feel like an outsider.

"Whatcha writing?" Trey asked.

"The riff that tried to kill me."

Trey nodded. He was quite familiar with the riff. He'd even tried to help her get it right a few times.

"Any progress?"

"It's getting worse, not better." She played the set of notes she'd just modified.

"It sounds phenomenal to me."

"You don't think it sounds like Beethoven's Eighth Symphony?"

Trey shook his head, a wide grin making him look even more attractive than usual. "It might if I knew what that sounded like."

She played the familiar string of notes from the composer's score on her guitar.

"Oh that." Trey nodded. "Yeah, I've heard that before."

Everyone in the free world had probably heard that before.

"Play your riff," he said.

She played her composition again, and Trey cocked his head to focus his attention on the sound.

"There's what, two notes the same?" he said. "You're overthinking again."

"The rhythm is similar too."

"Reagan, I think it's okay for you to use a three quarter time beat."

"In metal music?"

Trey chuckled. "It's been known to happen."

"So how did the press conference go?" She tried to keep the anxiety out of her voice, but the tremor in her words gave her away. Was it possible to contract a press phobia? Because she was pretty sure she had that going on.

"Our new album drops tomorrow," he said, "so we kept their attention focused on that as much as possible."

"How could I have forgotten?" she said, slapping herself in the forehead. "How exciting for you guys! I know everyone is going to love it."

"The first single has done well," he said.

"Of course it has. 'Sever' is absolutely amazing. I wish I could write music the way Brian does."

Trey laughed. "Maybe you should try boning Myrna."

Reagan screwed up her face at him. "How would that help?"

"Brian had a huge case of writer's block until he started banging her. As Sed once put it, fucking her is magically delicious."

"Myrna is great and all, but I think I'll pass."

Trey shifted to sit beside her on the sofa and took her guitar. After carefully setting the instrument on the coffee table, he pulled her onto his lap.

"I'm sorry about earlier," he said, resting his chin on her shoulder and pressing his cheek against her jaw. "I shouldn't have teased you. I had no idea it would upset you so much."

"I overreacted," she admitted. "Running after you in a sheet? What the fuck was I thinking?"

"You looked sexy," he said, kissing her jaw.

"I looked like a fool. A *naked* fool. I wonder how much of me they'll blur out when they publish those pictures."

"Maybe they won't publish them at all."

"And maybe I'll stop worrying so much about it." Both equally unlikely. She'd forgotten something as important as Sinners' new album dropping. She couldn't focus on anything but the fucking paparazzi and how cornered they made her feel.

"Let's go do something," he said. "Get out of this room and away from it all for an hour or two."

"Like what?" she asked.

"We're in New York—I'm sure we'll think of something."

Her heartrate picked up again. "The paparazzi will follow us."

"Good."

Good? What could possibly be good about that? Her stomach was in knots and when he set her on her feet, her leg muscles trembled so badly that she had to put a hand on his shoulder to steady herself.

"Should we wear disguises?" she asked, sure that Rebekah would have a wig she could borrow. Sinners' soundboard operator was always playing dress-up with her husband. However, Reagan wasn't sure what sticky stuff she might find in such a wig. She was pretty sure Eric Sticks was a cum factory.

"Nope. Just you and me in the city of love."

"I think that's Paris," Reagan said.

"Every city is the city of love with me around." He wiggled his eyebrows suggestively, and she couldn't help but laugh. And God, it felt good. She was pretty sure she hadn't laughed since they'd returned to the tour.

"I'll get my boots," she said, figuring she'd probably freak out at the first sign of the press, but at that moment, she was relaxed and looking forward to hanging around with Trey.

"I'm going to call Ethan real quick."

"No!" she said, remembering that she was supposed to have given Trey a message.

He paused with one finger hovering over the screen of his smartphone. "Why not?"

"I talked to him while you were out. He said to tell you that he'll call you after he comes out to his mother. It will give him incentive or something like that."

"Oh." Trey released a sigh. "He still hasn't told her?"

"He ran into some problems." She told him the news about Don leaving Rosa, the restaurant folding, and Ethan's concerns for Rosa's safety as well as his brother's possible involvement with a gang.

"Those are definitely problems."

"He's going to invite his mom to Atlanta or Little Rock this week to watch our show."

Trey's smile brightened his entire face and half the room. "So he's coming back?"

"He hopes to."

"Awesome."

Reagan finished tying her boot and stood. "That doesn't mean you're allowed to come out to the press."

"You worry too much," he said, holding a hand out to her. "Let's go cause a stir."

Reagan wasn't sure what he meant by that, but she slid her hand into his and followed him out of the hotel suite. The lobby was blissfully empty of reporters, though Reagan did spot a guest at the front desk who looked an awful lot like Jack Nicholson.

"Are you hungry?" Trey asked as soon as they stepped onto the sidewalk outside the hotel.

Her stomach answered with a rumble, and she laughed, covering her belly with one hand.

"That would be a yes," Trey said. "What sounds good?"

Reagan spotted someone with a camera across the street. She tried to convince herself that it was only a tourist, but the giant lens was definitely pointed in their direction. She fought the panic choking her as she turned away from their spectator.

"Room service," Reagan said.

"Nope. I'm not letting you hide today."

Damn.

"What are my options?" she asked, glancing down the street and noting a multitude of banners, flags, signs, chalkboards, and flashing neon encouraging them to come in for a meal.

"That's the thing about New York. If you want it, they've got it."

"Let's go that way and stop at whatever catches our eye." Spontaneity used to be Reagan's forte. It felt good to don it again, even if it was just choosing a restaurant on a whim. Her fear of being in public had changed her and not for the better. She hoped she'd soon get past the near-crippling fear. She didn't want to forever dread venturing out into public places.

Trey gave her a sappy look and captured her lips for a heartfelt kiss. She wasn't sure what had him so affectionate today—hell, who was she kidding, the man was always affectionate—but she clung to his shoulders and kissed him back. She tried to ignore the excited clicking of the photographers across the street, but decided it wasn't possible and pulled away.

"There's one thing the tabloids love as much as a scandal," Trey said, taking her hand again and strolling down the sidewalk. "And that is a celebrity love story."

"So that kiss was just for show?" she asked.

He chuckled and brought her knuckles to his lips for an additional kiss. "Nope. That kiss was just for me. You might make me hide my feelings for Ethan in public, but I don't have to do the same when it comes to you, right?"

"I suppose not." Though it did seem highly unfair to Ethan. On the other hand, Ethan wasn't one for public displays of affection. Back when they'd been dating exclusively, he'd felt uncomfortable holding her hand in public, forget kissing her. She'd been okay with his reluctance at the time since he always made up for it whenever they were alone together. He still did.

"Good. Prepare to be lavished with attention."

She'd had far more than enough attention centered on her over the last week, but this was different. This was attention she craved. Coveted. And she loved Trey all the more for fulfilling that need, even if she hadn't recognized it before he'd mentioned it. This, she decided, was one of the many benefits of loving two men who were so different from each other. She could have everything she needed from this relationship, and she did. She had it all. The absurd pressure the tabloids put on her had almost made her forget that.

"I miss Ethan," she said as they were seated at a table for two.

Reagan was pretty sure that Trey had insisted on Greek food for brunch because the restaurant had a small outdoor seating area, which kept them in the spotlight.

"Am I not being charming enough? I'll try harder." He was smiling that ornery grin of his, so she knew he was joking, but she was sorry if she made him feel as if he wasn't enough. That wasn't how she felt at all. And she hoped it wasn't how he felt either.

"You're perfectly amazing," she said.

"Perfect?"

"Obviously. When I'm with you, I feel like I have everything," she said, glancing over her shoulder to see if anyone was listening. She leaned closer and lowered her voice, just in case. "And when I'm with Ethan, I feel the same way. But when the three of us are together . . ." She didn't have the words to describe it.

"Synergy," Trey said, picking up his menu and scanning the restaurant's offerings.

"Exactly," she said. "I'm so glad you get it."

"Of course I get it," he said. "I'm a part of it."

So maybe it didn't matter that the world couldn't understand what they had. *They* understood. "Do you think Ethan feels that way too?"

"What? That three halves make infinity?" His eyes lifted from the menu, and their gazes locked. "I know he does. Getting him to express it?" He shook his head, and they both laughed.

"He's getting better," Reagan said. "He's much more open than he used to be."

"Really? Because I don't feel like I've even got my shucking knife into that shell of his, much less managed to pry it open."

"You're approaching him all wrong, Trey. His shell is spiral shaped." She made a twisting motion with one finger, and they laughed at Ethan's expense once again.

"I wonder if his ears are burning," Trey said, flipping his menu over and examining the reverse side.

"He knows we love him."

"Can I get you something to drink?" a server asked, completely shutting down Reagan's ability to speak of Ethan.

After they ordered, they sipped beer—before noon!—and dipped triangles of pita bread into the most flavorful hummus Reagan had ever tasted.

"It looks like baby shit, but it's so good," Trey said, helping himself to more of the yellow-beige mush.

"If Malcom's poo is ever that color, please take him to the doctor. I think it means liver failure."

"It is that color sometimes," Trey insisted. "Maybe you should change the occasional diaper and see for yourself."

"I've never changed a diaper in my life." It wasn't like she'd had younger siblings. And while the other teenage girls in her class had time for babysitting, her father had insisted she spend all of her free time practicing the cello. She told Trey as much.

"He was tough on you, wasn't he?" Trey said.

She shrugged. "I was supposed to live the dreams he never made happen."

"One of these days, you need to play the cello for me. I know Ethan has heard you play it. I feel left out."

"I'll play for you if you promise I won't ever have to change a smelly diaper."

"Deal."

They shook on it, and Reagan figured she got the better end of the bargain.

They'd both ordered a gyro and were digging into their delicious meal when a shadow crossed their table. Expecting to find a camera in her face, Reagan was surprised to find Eric standing next to them.

"Trey!" he said, excessively exuberant, even for Eric. He leaned down and gave Trey a mighty hug with one arm. With his free hand, he slipped something into Trey's hand, and Trey shoved it into his pocket.

"Eric!" Trey returned, his greeting equally obnoxious. And suspicious.

Eric stood straight and saluted Trey with one finger. "Later."

Reagan watched him march away with a decided spring in his step and shook her head to clear her confusion.

"What was that all about?" she asked Trey, who was pouring more tzatziki sauce on his gyro.

"What was what about?" He licked a drop of sauce from the side of his finger, and Reagan's center clenched with instant arousal.

Uh, what had she been saying? "Eric just now. He seemed uncommonly excited to see you, even for Eric."

"He's always excited to see me," Trey said.

"He gave you something, and you slipped it into your pocket." Reagan nodded toward the small lump in his pocket.

Trey paused with his half-eaten gyro near his mouth. "You're mistaken," he said.

"I saw it happen," Reagan insisted, leaning far out of her chair to reach for his hip.

Trey dropped his gyro and slapped a hand over his pocket. "You don't want to pull that out in public."

"What is it?"

"Honestly?" When she nodded, he said, "It's a ring."

"A ring?"

"Uh, yeah. A cock ring. We'll put it to good use later."

He leveled his most sultry gaze on her, but she wasn't so easily distracted. "Why would Eric go out of his way to bring you a cock ring?"

"I asked him to."

Okay, yeah, that made perfect sense. In some alternate universe maybe.

"He had a spare," Trey added. He cautiously removed his hand from his pocket to reach for his gyro again.

Reagan couldn't help but be totally fixated on his pocket. If he really had a cock ring in there, she was sure he wouldn't have any problem showing it to her.

"I want to see it," Reagan said.

"I'm just supposed to whip it out here at the table? That ought to make for an interesting tabloid cover." He nodded to the table behind her, and she stiffened.

Was there a reporter sitting behind her? A photographer? Both? Suddenly queasy, she shoved the remains of her gyro to the center of the table.

"Don't let them ruin your meal," Trey said, pushing her food back toward her.

Them? Just how many of them were sitting behind her?

"Pretend like they aren't even there."

Okay, yeah, that was possible. Again only in some alternate universe.

"So," Trey said, before taking a sip of his beer. "How do we get our hands on a cello?"

She wasn't sure if he was diverting the conversation to safe topics for her benefit or for the likely eavesdropping paparazzi nearby.

"I'm sure you're as good at playing cello as you are at playing electric guitar." He was talking louder than usual. Leading the reporters, maybe? "When did you first start playing stringed instruments?"

"I first started playing stringed instruments when I was three years old," she said loudly, letting him know she knew why he was acting so odd. Interview by eavesdropping—she could play that game.

"So would you say you're an expert at the cello?" Trey asked, his words well enunciated.

"I don't know. Maybe you should ask the judges of all the contests I won."

"So the Exodus End Guitarist for a Year contest wasn't the first instrumental contest you won?"

Reagan rolled her eyes, and Trey laughed. God, this was annoying. "No, the Exodus End Guitarist for a Year contest was not my first victory."

"Was it the first you won by sleeping with all the judges?"

Reagan's jaw dropped, and she spun around to find the table behind her empty. She slapped at Trey for tricking her, and he was too busy laughing to fend off her half-hearted attack.

No longer worried about phantom reporters, Reagan finished as much of her gyro as her stomach could hold. After she declared herself full, Trey paid their ticket and they continued on their journey to explore all of New York City in fewer than six hours.

They didn't stay around Times Square for long. Too busy. Too touristy. They headed toward Central Park, walking hand in hand. After a few antsy minutes of checking over her shoulder and scanning potential hiding places they passed, Reagan began to forget that reporters might be watching their every move.

"I'm surprised Ethan hasn't called yet," Trey said. "He must be having a rough time telling his mom."

"Pretty sure he's using his self-assigned detective work as an excuse to put it off."

"Do you think he misses the police force?" Trey asked.

"I know he does. Maybe I should fire him and encourage him to apply for a real job."

"I'm sure he loves watching you for a living. I wouldn't be in any hurry to give up that gig, and I'm sure he's not either."

"Well, I'm sure he's bored out of his mind."

"I honestly don't want him working such a dangerous job," Trey said, his brow crumpled with worry.

Reagan squeezed his hand. "I won't fire him, but I won't stand in his way if he wants to quit."

After they did quite a bit of walking around a lake, enjoying the nature of the area, Trey drew her to a halt before a giant fountain. The wide and perfectly round pool surrounded a bronze angel perched upon the top of several tiered layers. The sound of trickling water soothed Reagan, until she noticed Trey wasn't enjoying the scenery. He was staring at her with an unreadable expression. She'd have thought he looked nervous, but Trey was never nervous about anything. Reagan studied him, trying to gauge his emotions, only to notice that they were being surrounded by reporters with cameras. And not just the point and click kind either. She'd seen a few of them here and there as they'd enjoyed their day, but this was a mob. Where had they all come from?

Trey decided that that moment was the perfect time to kiss her, but she was too anxious to enjoy it. He then sank his hand into his pocket and produced the ring Eric had given him earlier that day. Only it wasn't a cock ring. It was a diamond.

Confused, she blinked up at him. Her gaze stayed on him when he dropped to one knee.

"Reagan, you complete me as no woman has ever completed me. I love you now and will love you when I draw my last breath." He smiled up at her with happiness shining in his gorgeous green eyes. "Will you marry me?"

CHAPTER 23

TREY WAITED for Reagan's response. Seconds seemed like hours.

Say yes, he thought, hoping to sway her decision telepathically. *Say yes.*

She pulled her gaze from his to take in all the reporters surrounding them—reporters who seemed as anxious to hear her answer as Trey was—and then stared into his eyes again. It had never occurred to him that she might say no. Maybe she thought the only reason he was asking her was to change the public's focus from a negative to a positive one. But she should know him well enough to realize he didn't do anything he didn't want to do.

"Yes?" she said, and the word was far more a question than an answer. Good enough for him. They'd sort out her hesitation later, when there wasn't a huge crowd of onlookers.

He slid the engagement ring onto her finger. She examined it as if confused by what it signified. A little more enthusiasm on her part would have been appreciated.

"Wait," she said, shaking her head slightly and blinking hard. "Did you just ask me to marry you?"

"I did."

"Oh."

Oh?

"Oh!" Her face lit up with delight, and she dropped to the ground, her body colliding with his. As her arms tightened around his neck, he lost his balance and they tumbled onto the red brick pavers covering the ground. He laughed as she kissed him repeatedly, each smooch punctuated by the word yes.

There were so many camera flashes going off that he had to close his eyes or risk permanent blindness. People he didn't know were clapping and cheering.

Reagan eventually buried her face in his neck, and he shifted a hand to the back of her head, fingers sliding between locks of her silky hair. He kissed her tenderly on the forehead and said, "You had me worried for a minute there."

"You should be worried," she whispered close to his ear. "Because I'm going to kill you."

She shifted, pushing up on both arms to suspend her body over his. A gleam shot from her eyes. He couldn't tell if it was murderous or a gleam of pure joy. He could tell that her knee was uncomfortably close to his balls.

"Let's get married in June!" she said.

"Next year?"

"Next month."

The smile disappeared from his face as a murmur of excitement raced through the crowd of reporters and spectators.

"That soon?"

"Why not?"

He saw the challenge in her eyes. Was she trying to get back at him by putting him on the spot the way he'd put her on the spot with that marriage proposal? She probably expected him to refuse.

"That doesn't give us much time to plan," he said, widening his smile, "but yeah, let's do it. Let's get married before we go to Europe next month."

Her smile wavered slightly, and she collapsed on top of him, hugging him as if she'd never let him go. Or maybe she was just practicing her strangling technique.

Having obtained their scoop—two of them, actually—the reporters began to disperse. Trey had intentionally invited legitimate reporters, not the paparazzi, hoping that having the news of their engagement and wedding—*wedding!*—in a reputable magazine like *People* or *Us* or *Rolling Stone* would silence the tabloids permanently or at least make readers question the legitimacy of their articles.

Reagan released him, and he lumbered to his feet, reaching for her hand to help her up. Her new ring caught the light as she placed her hand in his. The rock was gorgeous. Rebekah and Eric had done an excellent job choosing something outlandishly large and expensive. Which was fine. He wanted Reagan to have the best. He wondered if Ethan would wear a diamond. Doubtful. Trey would present something more masculine to Ethan when he asked him to marry him. Of course, Trey would have to go against his instincts and ask Ethan a bit more privately than the way he'd asked Reagan. Unfortunately, he didn't think there was a way he could legally marry them both, no matter how much his heart and soul yearned for that level of commitment.

"I can't believe you did that," Reagan said as they meandered through the thinning crowd, accepting congratulations and handshakes and pats on the back.

"I'm just glad you're so behind the idea that you want to make it official in a few weeks. Sed is getting married on that first Saturday we're off. We'll have to schedule our wedding for the following weekend. I wouldn't want to steal their thunder. Jessica would skin me alive."

"She'll have to get in line," Reagan murmured.

"Hey," Trey said, "I was prepared for a long engagement. You're the one who can't wait to make this official."

"You were supposed to baulk at the idea."

"Why? I really do want to marry you."

She looked up at him, squinting at him in the sunlight. "You do?"

"I wouldn't have asked if I didn't."

"What about E—" She pressed her lips together and looked around to see if anyone was listening. No reporters were trailing them for the first time that day. "What about Ethan?" she whispered.

"I want to marry him too," Trey said.

"You can't marry both of us."

"My heart can." He lifted her hand to his lips and kissed it softly. "It already has."

She blinked several times—forcing back tears, if he wasn't mistaken.

"It's impossible to stay mad at you, Trey Mills. Do you know that?"

He grinned. "Yep."

AT THE ARENA, the backstage area was blissfully devoid of reporters. The women congregated in Reagan's dressing room to admire her new rock and sigh dreamily about her surprise wedding proposal. Pleased with how the proposal had turned out, Trey went to hang out with his band and the few VIP fans who were allowed backstage. He really wanted to call Ethan, his parents, and the emperor of the freaking universe to share the news of his good fortune. Everyone was in a celebratory mood for the first time this week, and he was more than a little drunk by the time they headed for the stage.

"Are you sure about this?" Brian asked as they made their way down a crowded corridor.

"Tonight I'm playing live in Madison Square Garden next to Master Sinclair. I'm sure everything is right in my world."

"You haven't known her long," Brian pointed out.

"How long did you know Myrna before you knew she was the one you wanted to spend the rest of your life with?"

Brian scowled. "Less than a day. But that's different."

"How so?"

"I'm not gay."

Wow, that was pretty hurtful.

Trey stopped walking and scowled at Brian. "You're gay-*ish*." Several people turned to gawk at them. Had he said that really loudly? Shit. His voice tended to carry when he'd had one too many beers. "Happy all the time!" Trey said to cover his publicly inappropriate words, no matter how true they were. Brian was closer to straight than Trey would ever be, but on the hetero-homo scale, Brian wasn't on the one hundred percent heterosexual end of the spectrum. Surely he recognized that as much as Trey always had.

Eric pushed Trey in the back to get him moving forward again.

"He's just sad that you won't try to kiss him anymore," Eric said. "The rest of us are over the moon about it. You no longer reek of desperation."

Trey elbowed him in the arm.

"Hey!" Eric said. "Don't damage the goods."

"Maybe Jessica would like a double wedding." Sed scratched at his jaw. "We basically have the same guest list, and as much as I'm paying for that reception dinner . . ."

"Don't even mention it to her," Trey said. "She deserves to be alone in the spotlight on her wedding day. And I'm pretty sure my wedding is going to be a media orgy."

"I don't know," Jace said, glancing around the corridor. "The paparazzi have all disappeared. I think they've lost interest."

"Is that why you asked her?" Brian asked. "To get the paparazzi off her ass?"

"I asked her because I love her." Which was true. That getting the paparazzi off her ass part was an added benefit. And their agreement not to publish pictures of her losing her sheet in the lobby had clinched the deal for him.

"So Ethan is okay with this?" Brian continued.

"He doesn't know yet." Trey smiled. "But I'm sure he'll be pleased."

"Yeah, your relationship is definitely strong enough for you to marry Reagan. That's why he left you both yesterday, am I right?"

Trey had never seen Brian act so . . . so . . . jealous? Was that really what this was? Or was he genuinely concerned that Trey marrying Reagan was a mistake. "He's coming back on Wednesday," Trey informed him. "Why do you care so much anyway?"

"Because you always think with your heart and not with your head, Trey."

"He thinks with his little head regularly," Eric said.

Sed slapped Eric across the back of his head so Trey didn't have to.

"Hey!" Eric said. "Don't damage the goods."

"You have goods in there?" Sed asked, eyeing his head skeptically.

"Is she pregnant?" Jace asked, completely out of the blue.

"What?" Trey stumbled over his feet when all four of his band members stared at him expectantly.

"No," he said. "Of course not. Why would you ask that?"

"You just seem in a bit of rush to get married," Jace said. "I thought maybe she was pregnant."

"He would make a good father," Sed said. "Have you seen how he dotes on Malcolm?"

"Yeah, but only because I can give him back," Trey said. "What's with you guys tonight? If I wanted my balls busted about this, I'd call my mother." Though he was sure his mother would be happy for him. His mother was always delighted when he was happy.

"You haven't told Gwen yet?" Brian asked, shaking his head as he slipped a guitar strap over it and settled his signature black and white electric guitar into place.

"It's on my to-do list."

Jake handed Trey the new orange guitar he'd bought a few days ago at a signing. He'd barely broken it in, but he already loved it. Probably never as much as he'd loved the yellow and black guitar he'd smashed onstage in a fit of frustration, but its replacement was a solid instrument.

"Congratulations," the guitar tech said, giving Trey a one-armed bro-hug and slapping him on the back.

Trey ducked to avoid being poked in the eye by the pointed spikes of Jake's mohawk hairstyle.

"Thanks! Good news travels fast," Trey said.

"The crew watched the whole thing on *Entertainment Tonight*. For a minute there, I thought she was going to say no."

He'd had a similar fear.

"Who could turn down Trey?" Eric asked, thudding him hard on the back.

The cellphone in Trey's pocket began to vibrate. Since he had a few minutes before he had to be onstage, he pulled it out. His heart swelled at seeing Ethan's name on the display. Ethan had finally done it. He'd come out to his mother. The barriers keeping the three of them apart were falling away.

Trey accepted the call, but before he could get his congratulations past his lips, in a cold hard voice Ethan said, "You asked her to marry you?"

CHAPTER
24

E THAN HAD KEPT himself busy for most of the day. He'd
discovered that none of his brothers had been in trouble
with the law, that it wasn't as easy to run a New Mexico
license plate as he'd hoped, and that his mother's neighborhood *had*
become rather sketchy over the past year. The number of crimes
reported had more than quadrupled in that time. He'd arrived at
Mamá's house just after noon, and she'd immediately insisted on
feeding him lunch, which proved she couldn't stay mad at her oldest
son for long. He'd then tackled some chores that were difficult for
an aging, though still feisty, woman—trimming hedges, repairing the
roof, cleaning out a slow drain, replacing the broken window in her
bedroom, and adding some bright-as-the-sun security lighting to the
exterior of the house. When he'd finally sat down for the delicious
dinner she'd prepared—her tamales were to die for—he felt he'd
earned a meal. She'd insisted they watch *Entertainment Tonight*, which
didn't interest him in the least, but he was too exhausted to care.
Until a segment about a very familiar couple filled the screen.

"Oh, look, Ethan," Mamá said, pointing excitedly at the
television. "That's Reagan. Look, it's Reagan."

Ethan's heart dropped, and he prepared himself to listen to all
kinds of derogatory statements about the woman he loved.

". . . over the past week, allegations of her affairs with various
men. So everyone was surprised when her current boyfriend, a
guitarist in the hard rock band Sinners, popped the question in
Central Park."

Ethan blinked at the TV, not responding to his mother's questions about the man who'd stolen Reagan from him. Trey was on one knee presenting a ring to Reagan. Ethan's ears were buzzing too loudly for him to hear Trey's proposal, but going by the way Reagan tackled him to the ground and kissed him, she'd obviously said yes. She appeared so overjoyed, puppies could take lessons from her.

"I can't fucking believe this," Ethan said, pulling his phone out of his pocket.

"Ethan, watch your language," Mamá said. She placed a comforting hand on his knee. "You still love her then?"

"Of course I still"—*fucking*—"love her!"

"Oh, mijo, I'm so sorry." She tried to take his phone. "You shouldn't call her when you're so upset."

"I'm not calling her, I'm calling him. He should have at least warned me that he planned to ask her to marry him."

While Mamá gave him a puzzled look, he dialed Trey's number. A quick glance at the clock told him that Trey would be onstage in a few minutes, so it was unlikely that he'd answer. When he did, Ethan forced words out through the tight fist squeezing his throat. "You asked her to marry you?"

"I was hoping to tell you before you found out secondhand. I didn't know they'd air the story tonight."

"Why is there a story at all, Trey? How long have you been waiting for me to leave so you could do this behind my back?" It wasn't the actual proposal that upset him. It was that they'd done it with absolutely no input from him.

"It wasn't like that. I planned it on a whim. Sinners had a press conference this morning and the reporters started asking about Sed's upcoming wedding and we had to keep diverting questions about me and Reagan and I'd just had enough. I figured if we were engaged like Sed and Jessica, the press—the *real* press—would focus on that instead of all that bullshit that ridiculous tabloid printed. And it worked, E. All the paparazzi have cleared out since I asked her."

"You planned it this morning?"

"Yeah."

"And you couldn't find a moment in your day to give me a call and at least warn me that this was happening?"

"Reagan said you'd call me after you came out. That I wasn't under any circumstances to call you first."

Ethan took a deep breath, recognizing the anger building inside him. *"That's* your excuse?"

"Get on the stage," Ethan heard someone say in the background.

"I'm in the middle of a very important phone call," Trey said to them.

There were sounds of a scuffle and then a somewhat familiar voice—maybe Jake, the guitar technician—said, "He'll call you back." And then the call disconnected.

Ethan sighed in frustration and called his other lover. The one that still had an hour before she had to be in Trey's position.

"Ethan!" she answered, sounding like she was having the time of her life. There was a whole lot of feminine giggling going on in the background. "How did your mom take the news?"

"Not well. She doesn't understand the real reason why I'm so pissed at the two of you. Why I'm hurt." Ethan was pretty sure he'd never admitted to being hurt to anyone in his entire life.

"Huh?"

"Did you think I'd be okay with you two getting engaged behind my back? Don't you think you should have consulted me before flaunting your happiness all over national television?"

"Television? Wait, what are you talking about? Didn't you call to tell us you finally came out?"

Ethan slapped himself in the face and tried to wipe his frustration away. It didn't work. "I'm sitting here having dinner with my mother." He glanced at Mamá and found her staring at him, eyes wide, hands mangling a dish towel. "And what do we see on *Entertainment Tonight* but my boyfriend asking my girlfriend to marry him. On national fucking television."

"What are you talking about, mijo?" Mamá asked quietly.

"We were on TV?" Reagan asked.

"Yes! Do you really think that's the best way for me to find out about this?"

"Oh, Ethan, he should have called you. I should have called you. We suck. Both of us. We were going to tell you everything the next time you called. We figured that would be well before the media announced our engagement."

And now for the million-dollar question. "So does this mean I'm no longer a part of your relationship with Trey?" His voice cracked, and he closed his eyes, taking breaths to steady himself for whatever she'd tell him.

"Of course not. This is just a publicity stunt, Ethan. It has nothing to do with how we really feel."

"So you don't want to marry him?"

"I do. I want to marry you too."

"It doesn't work that way."

"I know," she said, all the happiness completely gone from her tone. He couldn't help but think he was responsible for that. It was his fault she was no longer celebrating her engagement to Trey, and he couldn't stand to hear the turmoil in her voice.

"I'll let you get ready for the show."

"Ethan," she said, her voice raw with emotion. "If you'd asked me first, I would have said yes."

"I wasn't aware that you were in such a rush to get married."

"Neither was I." She laughed, and the sound made him think that maybe things would be okay. But not as long as he was in Texas. He had to get back to them. When he left them to their own devices, they gave in to impulse and made rash decisions. They needed someone sensible in their relationship. They needed him. And he wasn't about to step down unless they forced him to go. He should have never left in the first place. Hell, he couldn't even remember why he'd left.

Then he caught sight of his mother's ashen face where she sat on the sofa staring at nothing, and it all came back to him in a rush.

"I'm going to talk to Mamá now," he told Reagan. "It's time."

"Past time," she said. "Hurry back to us."

"I will. You two can't be trusted without me there to balance you out." He was teasing, so was glad when she chuckled.

"You can't leave us anywhere."

He disconnected the call and shoved his phone into his pocket. He was pretty sure his mother had the gist of the situation from hearing his side of the conversations, but she needed to hear the entire truth directly from him. It would mean a lot to him if she would stand firmly in his corner.

He sat next to her on the sofa, staring straight ahead, because seeing any doubt or hurt on her face would have made the task unbearable.

"There's something I need to tell you," he said.

"I'm not sure I want to hear this."

"Probably not," he said, "but I'm going to tell you everything I've been keeping a secret for the past couple of years. I hope you'll understand." He felt asking for her blessing was too much, but if she understood and accepted him for who he was, that would be enough.

"Ethan . . ."

There was a knock at the front door. Ethan cursed, Mamá chastised, and Juan let himself into the house. "Your door was unlocked," Juan said, approaching the sofa and kissing Mamá's cheek. "Carlos would be furious." He slammed a fist into Ethan's shoulder, but Ethan was in no mood to horse around. "Do I smell tamales?" He took a deep whiff and then gasped in surprise when Ethan stood from the sofa, lifted him from the floor, and sat him next to their mother on the sofa.

"I wanted to tell her alone, but since my brothers have the worst possible timing, I'll just tell you both." And let the chips fall where they may.

"Tell us what?" Juan glanced from Ethan to Mamá and back again. Couldn't he see the turmoil in their mother's eyes? No, he'd always been clueless about such things. No matter.

"Reagan is getting married," Mamá said. She tilted her chin down and stared at Ethan. "To your *boy*friend?"

"What?" Juan looked at Mamá as if she'd grilled hotdogs on Cinco de Mayo. "Ethan has a boyfriend?"

"I'm not exactly straight," Ethan said, unable to stop himself from hedging.

"You're gay?" Juan's jaw dropped.

"I'm not exactly gay either."

"This makes no sense," Mamá said.

Ethan pulled a hand through his hair and started pacing. He should have thought more about how to say this. It didn't help that he had an audience of two instead of one.

"About seven years ago, I had this partner," he said, deciding to start at the very beginning, long before even Reagan had come into the picture.

"While you were with the police?" Mamá asked.

Ethan nodded. "He was openly gay."

"Hernandez." Juan spat the name as if it were bitter on his tongue. Juan had been all of twelve at the time. Ethan was surprised he remembered him.

"Yeah," Ethan said, though the name wasn't important. "I found myself attracted to him, and after several months things progressed and . . ." His gaze shifted to his mother. Awkward. "It wasn't a romantic relationship. Just . . ." Way, way awkward. Especially when his mind was replaying their times together like a gay porn reel. ". . . physical."

"Uh, you fucked a guy?" Juan asked, twisting his face in disgust.

Mamá slapped her youngest. "Do not be vulgar. Go on, Ethan."

"We didn't last long, a few weeks, and I started dating a new woman."

"Lisa?" Juan asked. And when Ethan nodded, Juan added, "Ah yeah, she was fine. I'd like to lick her honey." So that horn-dog thing of Juan's had started young.

Mamá slapped him again.

"She was gorgeous," Ethan said, "and I couldn't get enough of her. At first."

Juan covered his ears with both hands. "Don't say it."

"I sought out another man. Again nothing romantic. It was purely physical."

"You cheated on Lisa with a man?" Mamá asked.

"No, it was after we broke up. Right before I was fired from the force. But I did cheat on Reagan with a man."

"I'm going to throw up," Juan said.

"I don't know why I cheated on her. I loved Reagan and still do, I just . . ." He'd needed some cock in his life. But he couldn't exactly say that to his mamá.

"Despicable," she said. "Does Reagan know this, that you cheat? Like your papá, you cheat!"

Ethan nodded, feeling like slug slime on the bottom of Mamá's shoe. "She caught us together." *Fucking in the shower.* "And that's when we broke up. But we decided to stay roommates and friends."

"You can't be friends with a chick you've banged," Juan said knowledgably. "Not possible."

Didn't Ethan know it? Those long hellish months of living with Reagan, but not as a couple, had nearly done him in. Watching her move on to other men had seemed a cruel and unusual punishment for his infidelity. But she probably hadn't seen it that way.

"So I tried to be exclusively gay during that time, but what I really wanted was to be with a woman," Ethan said. One woman and only one woman. "But whenever I tried to be with another woman, it felt like I was cheating on Reagan and I couldn't do it."

"Ah, mijo, you are so confused."

"I used to be. Until I met Trey. Trey is unlike anyone I've ever met before. Trey is like me."

"Disgusting?" Juan was actually taking this much better than

Ethan had assumed he would, so his barb didn't sting. Much.

"Bisexual."

"Only women can be bisexual," Juan said. "And, *guey*, that is some hot shit right there."

Mamá slapped him again. She apparently needed to strike harder. Her punishments did no good.

"Go on," she said to Ethan.

"The three of us got together. At first it was just physical between us. And I was okay with that, I thought. But I still had feelings for Reagan, and a person can't be with Trey and not fall in love with him."

Mamá smiled. "You're happy now."

He nodded because his throat was too tight to get out the yes that was on the tip of his tongue.

Mamá rose from the sofa and reached up to cup his face. Her dark eyes sparkled with tears as she stared into his eyes. "That's all Mamá wants for her boys. Happy life. Happy always."

"So explain how the physical part of this works," Juan said, twisting his fingers into various configurations.

Mamá turned to scowl at him. "Stop that or I'll send you home."

Ethan was starting to see why Mamá needed her own place. If she moved in with Juan or Carlos, she couldn't send them away when she was perturbed with them. She could starve them, however.

"I need to get back to the tour," Ethan said. "I'm away for one day and they get engaged."

"So sorry they hurt you," Mamá said as she slipped her arms around Ethan's waist to hug him.

"I'm not hurt." Not too much. "They need me there. They're both a little reckless. Especially Trey." He chuckled, feeling so light-hearted he wanted to dance. Or at least fidget a bit. His mother knew that he was in love with a man, and with a woman, and she had yet to kick him out of her house in disgust. .

"I will meet this man you love, no?" Mamá asked.

"How about on Tuesday? There's a show in Atlanta—"

"Tuesday!"

"I'll fly you anywhere you want to go for a concert. You can see Reagan again and meet Trey. Or visit us in Los Angeles when we're on a break from the road."

"Does Carlos know you're queer?" Juan asked.

Mamá spun around so fast that Ethan had to take a step

backward. She grabbed Juan by one ear and pulled him off the sofa. "I don't like that word," she said. "You will never say it in my house again."

"I'm sorry," Juan said, wincing.

"Don't apologize to me. Apologize to your brother."

Juan's gaze focused on Ethan, but he didn't meet his eyes. "I'm sorry," he mumbled. Mamá released his ear, and he scrambled to safety. "If you want to screw men, that's your business."

Mamá groaned in frustration and threw her hands up. "Why are you like this? I raised you wrong?"

"It's okay," Ethan said. "Not everyone will understand me or accept who I am." He was sure everyone felt like an outsider at times, if not for their sexual orientation, then for their quirks or their appearance or their ideas. Trey had come to terms with that fact long ago. Ethan was just starting to align with his wisdom.

"Your brother should accept you—he's your blood," Mamá said. "Where Carlos?"

"He's in Laredo," Juan said, "with his . . ." He glanced at Ethan nervously. ". . . uh, bros."

"Again with this?" Mamá said. "Will he ever get a real job?"

Mamá *knew* Carlos was heading down a dark and dangerous path and she hadn't bothered to mention it to Ethan? Or ask him for help in steering Carlos in a better direction?

"Does he do this often?" Ethan asked.

"Several times a week," Mamá said, shaking her head. "He wants his mamá to die of shame, that's what he wants."

"It's not so bad," Juan said. "You support Ethan and his weird lifestyle, so why can't you support Carlos too?"

"Is an embarrassment!" Mamá snapped.

"Why would Mamá support Carlos being in a gang?" Ethan asked. "What is he trafficking? Drugs? Humans?"

Mamá and Juan gaped at him for a long moment, and then Juan burst into raucous laughter.

"Carlos in a gang?" Juan wrapped his arms around his gut, but that didn't diminish his mirth. "That chicken shit? Oh, that's a good one, Ethan. I'll have to tell him you think he's in a gang."

"Then . . ." Ethan was at a total loss. "Why is he riding with a bunch of dudes in yellow bandanas to border towns?"

"He plays trumpet in a mariachi band," Juan said. "You thought he was in a gang?" He shook his head, still chuckling. "No wonder the police fired you."

Ow, that barb stung. A lot.

"They wear ridiculous sombreros and beg tourists for money," Mamá said, crossing her arms. "So disrespectful to our heritage."

"Mamá hasn't actually seen him perform," Juan said. "Her friend Gloria—"

"Gloria is no friend of mine," Mamá said, pretending to spit on the absent ex-friend. "Puta."

Ethan's eyebrows shot up. Wow, she must be beyond upset if she was calling other women names.

"The puta brought Carlos's shameful profession to Mamá's attention." Juan leaned close to Ethan and whispered, "He's actually doing quite well with it. They've got a manager now and everything."

"Big black guy?" Ethan asked.

Juan nodded. "Dimitri."

"From New Mexico. Drives a beat-up white van."

"That's him."

So all the pieces fit. Ethan felt like an ass for suspecting his brother was up to no good, but why had he tried to hide the truth from him? Probably for the same reason Ethan had hidden his sexuality. He hadn't wanted his brother to disrespect his life choices.

"I'd like to see him play sometime," Ethan said. "Mamá, you should come with me."

She shrugged and headed for the kitchen. "I'll make sweets now."

Juan exchanged a knowing glance with Ethan. "She forgives us," Juan said. "She feeds us."

CHAPTER
25

S INCE THEY PLAYED back-to-back shows in New York, Reagan got to spend an entire long weekend in one place. Her lush hotel suite started to feel like home, with the exception of Ethan being absent. He'd picked a bad time to find himself in Texas. The three of them could have spent quality time in the room together. To pass the hours before Sunday night's show, she and Trey went with Logan and Toni to visit the 9/11 Memorial. As Reagan read each name engraved along the walls of the manmade waterfalls, an ever-increasing weight of despair pulled on her heart until she had to stop and let the tears fall. Toni passed her a tissue and dabbed at her own eyes with a second one.

"I remember the day it happened," Toni said. "Watching it on TV. It was tragic. Horrible. I couldn't believe it was real. But standing here, where these people lost their lives . . ." She sniffed loudly. "And for what?"

Reagan's throat was too tight to respond, so she just nodded and wiped away fresh tears. Trey turned her in his arms, hugging her gently and rubbing her back with both hands. He didn't encourage her to stop crying, but simply lent her something solid to cling to until she got her emotions in check. Though they'd been joking around when they arrived, they were humbled and somber when they left.

They caught a cab back to Times Square for a bite to eat before they headed to Madison Square Garden for their second sold-out show. While Reagan gawked at billboards and chaotic crowds, it

occurred to her that no one had harassed them while they'd been
out in public all day. She got the feeling that while people looked at
her and at Trey, they didn't really see them. Or maybe they just
weren't famous enough for anyone to bother them. She supposed
that was a benefit of being in one of the largest cities in the world.
There was so much interesting stuff going on there that no one gave
a single fuck about her personal shit. Maybe she should move to
New York. LA did have warmer weather, however.

At that night's show, Reagan was again volun*told* to instruct a
pretty young woman in the art of playing guitar. Apparently Reagan's
job wasn't to fill in for Max. Apparently her job was getting strangers
worked up about the prospect of watching two attractive women get
it on. She had half a mind to give the audience what they wanted and
toy with her student, but that would mean that Sam had won another
battle. He might be able to force her into doing this staged publicity
stunt, but he couldn't make her like it or even pretend to like it. By
the time she got offstage, she had made some great music and was
enjoying herself enough to forget about the guitar lesson segment.
Women were exploited for their sexuality all the time; she wasn't
sure why it bothered her so much that she was being used in that
capacity. Sam had made it clear that they planned to use her as a sex
symbol. Sooner or later he'd figure out she wasn't an ideal candidate
for his campaign to give the fans boners. She tried to glare a hole
into his back as the band followed him to the limo, but he didn't fall
over dead.

"There's a little surprise waiting for you inside," Sam said to
Max as he waited for a member of their security team to open the
door. Seeing all the strong, competent men in their yellow security
shirts made Reagan sigh. She missed Ethan terribly.

"A good surprise?" Max asked.

"The best I've found in over ten years," Sam said.

Max peered into the car and immediately stepped back. His
gaze landed on Steve, who was bullshitting with Logan about how
much pussy he planned to conquer at the after-party. Reagan had
promised Toni she would keep an eye on Logan that night—*again*—
because he tended to get in trouble when he was with Steve. *Everyone*
tended to get in trouble with Steve. Was that why Max was eyeing
him oddly? Did he fear he was about to get everyone into trouble?

"Maybe this isn't such a good idea," Max said to Sam.

"Nonsense."

Curiosity getting the better of her, Reagan nudged Max aside and looked into the limo. Five young women sat toward the middle of the long car. Dressed all in black from their Victorian lace-up boots to their lace gowns to their leather corsets, they ceased talking through their black-painted lips their black painted lips paused in conversation and turned heavily lined eyes on Reagan. Though they were dressed enough alike to look like a matched set, each woman had a contrasting hair color—green, white, red, blue and purple— beneath a layer of coal black. The longer Reagan looked at them, the less identical they appeared, but they were obviously part of some group.

"I figured it was high time you all met each other," Sam said. "You'll be spending a couple of months in their company while you tour Europe."

Realization struck Reagan, and she nodded a greeting at the five women of Baroquen before stepping away from the car and studying Steve. Did Sam really think it was a good idea to force them all into a car together for their first meeting? Steve was still pissed that Twisted Element had been replaced on the tour by some unknown goth metal girl band. And Steve was not the kind of guy to mince words. He was sure to be vocal about his displeasure, even if their new tour mates weren't at fault for anything other than Sam's belief that they were talented.

"Maybe you should take a cab," Max said to Steve.

"*You* take a cab," Steve said. He climbed into the limo. "Right on. The hookers are already here."

Reagan winced and scampered into the limo, dodging five sets of eye daggers that were being hurled in Steve's direction. "Hi," she said, settling next to the severe-looking woman with the underlayer of shockingly purple hair. "I'm Reagan." She knew how intimidating it could be to be in the presence of mega-stars like Exodus End. She hoped that by extending the hand of friendship she could decrease the animosity that was sure to follow. At least from Steve.

The woman smiled and said, "We know who you are."

Sam sat next to Reagan beaming an ear-to-ear smile. She'd never seen him so happy. The rest of the band entered the car, forcing Steve to sit as far from the as-yet-unintroduced newcomers as possible.

"I call dibs on Red," Steve said, eyeing each woman appreciatively.

The goth woman with a mix of black and red locks in her long layered hair blinked at him. "Excuse me?"

Dare elbowed Steve in the ribs and then cupped a hand around his mouth to whisper in Steve's ear. Steve's jaw dropped, and he shook his head. "Is it too late to take that cab?"

"Stop being a drama queen," Sam said, which earned a smirk from Red. "This is that band I was telling you about. Baroquen."

"Nice to meet you," Reagan said, still hoping her olive branch was big enough to counter any stupid insult about to come out of Steve's mouth. "I haven't gotten a chance to listen to your music yet, but Sam says you guys rock."

"You'll get to hear them tomorrow during your satellite radio performance," Sam said. "It's all arranged."

"You gave them our air time?" Max asked, looking none too pleased by the news.

"Not all of it. They're just playing one song."

The woman with blue hair leaned forward. "If it's a problem—"

"No problem," Sam insisted. "Let me introduce you all." He started with the quiet mint-green-haired woman on the far end. "Sage plays guitar." Sage lifted a hand in greeting. "Lily plays drums." The woman with the white underlayer nodded. Next Sam indicated the red-haired woman that Steve had called dibs on. "This is Roux. She plays keyboard and sings harmony."

"Keyboard?" Steve said. "What kind of metal band has a keyboard?"

"We're more a mix of punk, goth, progressive, and hard rock than true metal," said the purple-haired woman next to Reagan. Roux gave Steve the finger, which made Reagan snort.

Up next was the blue-haired band member. "Azura"—Sam introduced her—"on guitar."

"Wait," Dare said, obviously trying to keep the women straight. "I thought Sage played guitar."

"I do," Green said. "But so does Azura."

"So which is lead and which is rhythm?" Dare asked, his eyes moving from the green-and-black-haired woman to the blue-and-black-haired one and back again.

"Depends on the song," Azura said. "We mix it up in every song. Sometimes I start a solo, and she finishes it. We play to our strengths."

Sage nodded.

While Dare puzzled out a pair of guitarists who didn't have a set lead versus rhythm role, Sam introduced the final member—the purple-haired woman seated to Reagan's left. "And Iona is lead vocalist. She also plays bass."

"I play bass," Logan said, his knockout smile having its usual affect as several of the women sighed aloud. He was always good looking, but when the man smiled, panties got wet and hearts skipped beats.

"Well aware of that, gorgeous," Iona said with a smile that made Reagan switch into cock-block mode for Toni's sake.

"He's seeing someone," Reagan said out of the corner of her mouth.

"So am I," Iona said, her smile never faltering as she blatantly checked Logan out.

"How can you possibly think our fans will like this group of goth girls better than Twisted Element?" Steve asked Sam, apparently already beyond the limits of politeness.

"I don't think that," Sam said. "I think the opposite of that. Baroquen appeal to a younger fan base. A fan base Exodus End currently lacks."

"So you think teenaged goth kids will flock to see these wannabes and when we play them some real music, they'll become our insta-fans?" Steve asked, shaking his head.

Roux snorted. "Already living up to that asshole reputation of yours, eh, Aimes?"

"His best friend is in Twisted Element," Reagan said defensively. On a regular basis Reagan thought that Steve was an asshole, but these newcomers weren't allowed to judge him before they even knew him. "How do you expect him to feel about them getting fired so you can take their place on the tour?"

"We didn't ask for Twisted Element to be fired," Roux said. "But we'd be fools to turn down this gig."

Azure squeezed Roux's leg and fixed her attention on each member of the band across the car from them. "We are incredibly lucky to have been given this opportunity," she said. "We won't let you down."

Reagan wasn't sure whose side she should be on. On the one hand, she adored the men of Exodus End and she wanted them to be happy—all of them, even Steve. On the other, like these ladies, she knew what it felt like to find yourself unexpectedly on tour with superstars. The experience was both exhilarating and intimidating.

"Twisted Element was allowed to finish out this leg of the tour," Sam said. "They should be glad their mediocrity was allowed on your stage in the first place."

"Mediocrity?" Steve said, his animosity turned on the deserving party now.

"Really, Sam?" Dare said, shaking his head. "Must you always push his buttons?"

Sam's little smirk hinted that he thoroughly enjoyed pushing Steve's buttons.

"Did you really give up some of our unplugged satellite segment?" Max asked. "You know how important it is. The reach is nationwide. Hell, it's global. This isn't some local radio station you're talking about here. It's *satellite* radio, Sam."

Sam lifted both hands in surrender. "We'll discuss this later," he said. "Tonight I want you all to have a good time. Get to know each other. Stir up some interest."

"Do they always go at it like this?" Iona asked, never taking her eyes off the band who seemed to be falling apart at the seams. A person would never realize how much tension existed in the group from watching their concerts and interviews, but when in their company for more than a few minutes, you couldn't miss it.

"Only when Sam is around," Reagan said quietly so she wouldn't be overheard. She wondered if the guys realized that unfortunate truth. Steve obviously did, but she wasn't so sure about the others.

The limo pulled to a halt, and the door opened. Butch popped his head into the car. "You all ready? There's a line of fans about a block long. You can bypass it and go straight upstairs to the party if you're not in the mood to sign autographs."

"Always in the mood for adulation," Steve said, hopping out of the car. The sounds of cheers, screams, and whistles echoed from the avenue outside.

"Did he say adultery?" Roux asked.

Azura chuckled. "He said adulation, babe. That dirty mind of yours is playing tricks on you again."

Logan, Dare, and Max climbed from the car to further exclamations of fan delight. When Reagan started to follow them, Sam put a hand on her knee. "Leave the guys to their autographs," he said. "Take Baroquen up to meet Sinners and the other opening bands. Fourteenth floor. If you feel like hanging with the big guns, the Exodus End party is up in Glasshouse 21, so later you can head up to the twenty-first floor. It's up to you."

"It is possible that someone wants my autograph," Reagan said.

Sam laughed. "I thought you hated being the focus of

attention."

She glanced at the five other women in the car, staring at her as they waited for her to make her move.

"Just negative attention," she said as she slid from the car. No cheers greeted her ears when she appeared on the sidewalk. Everyone was focused on the four *real* rock stars slowly making the rounds, giving their fans an experience they'd never forget. She immediately looked for her bodyguard before remembering that Ethan was in Texas. A few familiar—but not Ethan—security team members rushed her inside to the elevators.

The Baroquen women turned heads as they followed her into the silver and glass building. Reagan felt invisible as people waiting for the elevators whispered about the five *new* rock stars in their midst. Maybe it was because Reagan wasn't dressed outlandishly and the rest of the women in her party looked like they'd stepped out of a gothic movie screen, but she'd never felt more disregarded in her life.

At the after-party, it was much the same. The other women were obviously people who should be met and apparently fawned over. Reagan didn't have to introduce them to anyone who noticed them—and everyone noticed them—as people came forward to introduce themselves.

"You look annoyed," Trey said in her ear.

"Why is everyone going crazy over them?" she asked, crossing her arms in front of her hopelessly lacking bosom.

"They look interesting."

"And I don't?"

"Jeans, T-shirt, and combat boots; no makeup; ordinary hairstyle—you don't exactly draw attention."

"Gee, thanks." She turned to walk away.

Trey caught her arm and pulled her against him. "You draw my attention."

She supposed that was what mattered to her. She didn't want the world to fawn over her the way they were fawning over the five "interesting-looking" women that made up Baroquen.

"If you want to draw attention to yourself—"

"I don't," she said, wrapping her arms around Trey's waist and burying her face in his throat. "It just didn't sink in that if I *looked* like a rock star, people might be more likely to *treat* me like one."

"They would," he said, his hands sliding up her back. "But then they'd probably no longer treat you like a serious musician."

"They treat me like a serious musician?" Since when?

"We live in a sexist world, Reagan. It's rare that a woman is treated seriously in this business."

"And even rarer for a woman to find a man who understands what she's going through." She leaned away and stared into his eyes. "Wish I could find one."

"You!" He poked her in the ribs, making her laugh.

Music began to blare from the DJ booth, signaling the official start of the after-party. Reagan pulled Trey onto the dance floor—he liked to dance almost as much as she did—and moved as if no one was watching. Because they weren't. Let the new girls bask in all the attention; Reagan didn't want it. She just wanted to have fun, love hard, laugh often, and play her guitar like she meant it.

E ARLY THE NEXT MORNING, REAGAN STOOD outside a newsstand on a quiet for New York City street and waited for the owner to open shop.

"Is this really necessary?" Toni asked, knuckling one eye like a sleepy toddler. "The sun isn't even up yet."

Reagan had laid quite a guilt trip on Toni to get her to wait with her to purchase the first copy of each tabloid and entertainment magazine issued today. She wasn't going to let her friend back out now.

"I want to know what I'm up against," Reagan said. "No more surprises. I hate surprises."

Toni grinned. "You liked the surprise Trey gave you Saturday."

Actually, she hadn't appreciated being put on the spot in front of all those reporters. She would have much preferred a private and romantic proposal between the two of them. Or rather the three of them. She was so glad that Ethan would return to the tour soon. She tended to get into trouble when he wasn't around. She was also glad that he'd finally found the courage to come out to his family. He'd seemed in great spirits when she'd talked to him after the show last night, and Trey had been so excited for Ethan that he'd high-fived everyone he encountered for several hours. No one had any idea why they were high-fiving Trey, but not a single person refused to celebrate with him. Fortunately, two out of three of them had supportive parents. Just thinking about telling her father that she preferred polyamorous relationships made Reagan want to hurl.

The gate rattled as a short balding man lifted it to expose the interior of the newsstand. He glanced nervously over his shoulder at the two women staring at him expectantly at four thirty in the morning. "Can I help you ladies?"

"I want a copy of all the new tabloid issues," Reagan blurted. "And anything entertainment related that's been released in the last week." Just in case she'd missed something.

"Don't you think you'd feel better about all this if you didn't seek it out?" Toni asked.

"The delivery trucks haven't dropped off the new issues yet," the man said. "You'll have to come back later."

"When do they show up?" Reagan asked.

"Before six, but not before five."

"Let's go back to bed," Toni suggested. "Maybe he'll save you a copy of each publication, and we can pick them up later."

"Yeah, I can do that," the man said. "No problem."

"We'll wait," Reagan said. "Can I browse your current stock?"

"I'm not open yet."

Reagan dug through her purse and found her wallet. She began removing twenties and handed them to the guy until he smiled in satisfaction.

"I know you're not running a library here," she said, having just forked over enough cash to buy every rag she was interested in as well as most pop-culture magazines. Reaching over the workout monthlies, she pulled out copies of several magazines that might potentially have stories about her or Trey or Exodus End and handed them to Toni. "Start looking," she said. "For anything about anyone on the tour."

"Reagan," Toni said, her voice strained with fatigue. "These magazines usually only print stuff about *real* celebrities. You know, actors and pop stars and rich heiresses and princesses and super models. Rock stars usually only get page time when they die from an overdose."

"Or get married."

"Maybe if they're marrying a supermodel or an A-list actress."

"Just do it," Reagan said, reaching for copies of outdated tabloids—except for the *American Inquirer*. She already knew what that piece of trash had written between its covers.

The proprietor grabbed an issue of the overlooked tabloid and started to hand it to her. "You missed one." He paused to look at the cover and though she was in her stage makeup in the cover shot, there was no mistaking that the woman on the front page was

Reagan. "Hey," the man said. "This is you."

"The one and only." She grabbed the tabloid out of his hand and added it to the bottom of her stack.

She and Toni sat on the sidewalk to the side of the newsstand, using its lights to illuminate their pages, and examined every outdated magazine and tabloid from cover to cover.

"There's nothing here," Toni said as she slapped her final magazine onto the discard stack beside her.

"I figured as much. *AI* did break the stories after the other rags had already gone to press. I just wanted to make sure." She took great pleasure in shredding the offensive copy of *American Inquirer* while they waited for the new issues to drop.

When the deliveries finally arrived, Toni was dozing with her head against the side of the newsstand and Reagan was standing with her hands outstretched to receive any new copies as they were stocked. She examined each cover in turn, relieved to see headlines unrelated to her or to the people she cared about. There might be snippets buried in the pages, but at least there wasn't a full issue devoted to her alleged debauchery or her naked slip in the hotel lobby. Thank God. Maybe this whole thing would blow over after all.

She rubbed her neck and reached out for one more tabloid from the vendor. Damn, damn, damn. She and Ethan were splashed all over the cover of *American Inquirer*.

"Caught Again! Reagan Elliot and Ethan Conner on their Funeral Rendezvous"

She'd kind of expected that one, but not the smaller headline beneath.

"Is Reagan Elliot Actually a Lesbian?"

That query would have made no sense to her if it hadn't been accompanied by a picture of her giving guitar lessons onstage to an obviously enraptured woman at Sam Baily's request.

"Ergh!"

"Trey Mills Heartbroken over Reagan's Cheating Ways"

There was a picture of Trey forcing his way into his car, and he did look heartbroken. She was pretty sure that photo had been taken the night he'd stormed out of the apartment and sped off on his own.

"Is Reagan Wrecking Homes Before Sedric Lionheart Can Even Say I Do?"

The photo of her hugging Sed was zoomed in too close to tell they were surrounded by guests at his father's visitation. Un-fucking-believable!

"It's all about me!" she bellowed.

"Keep telling yourself that, kid," the newsstand guy said.

Well, maybe it wasn't *all* about her, but the *American Inquirer* certainly was.

Toni started awake, blinking at the sunlight hitting her face. "What?" she asked, her voice slurred with sleep.

"Another issue of *American Inquirer* devoted to making my life hell." Reagan fluttered the paper at her groggy friend.

"If it's any consolation," the man said, "not that many people read *American Inquirer*. It hasn't been around long."

"If one person reads it, that's one too many," she spat.

Toni pulled herself to her feet and took the paper from Reagan's hands. "I'll read it and summarize for you."

"What?" Reagan shouted. "You don't think I can handle it?"

"You obviously can't handle it," the salesman said with a sly smile. "I assume you want to buy every copy from my stand."

"I don't care if other people buy it," she shouted, angry that a perfect stranger could read her so well.

"I'll take them all," Toni said.

"You don't have to do that," Reagan said, suddenly on the verge of tears. Her emotions were all over the place, and she fucking hated it. But she loved that Toni was so supportive.

"I need kindling for a fire," Toni said, squeezing Reagan's arm before exchanging cash for a stack of papers. "Let's go back to the hotel. The bus will be leaving right after the satellite radio segment. We can read these when we're bored."

"But what if someone at the station asks me about something that's printed in there?" She nodded at Toni's stack of papers.

"You say no comment."

As simple as that? Reagan took a deep breath. Yep, as simple as that. Reagan nodded, glad she'd brought Toni with her. Reagan didn't like to admit she needed a friend to lean on, but if Toni hadn't been there, she'd have collapsed both physically and emotionally.

Toni took all the papers and magazines from Reagan and sent her to her room to collect more important things, such as her luggage, her guitar, and Trey.

"Why are you leaving so damned early?" Trey mumbled when she shook him awake.

"We have to go to the studio for a segment on satellite radio.

And we're heading for Atlanta directly afterwards."

"Is Sinners involved in that?" he asked, burying his head under a pillow.

"Not the radio show." Was he really going to abandon her when she needed his support? Of course, she hadn't yet told him that *American Inquirer* had struck again, so he didn't realize she needed him beside her. Except he should realize she *always* needed him beside her. Wanted him there. She fiddled with her new engagement ring as she said, "I thought maybe you'd like to read the newly released article about how devastated you are about my continued affair with Ethan." She scowled and shook her head. "During a funeral."

"We're tabloid-famous again?" he said, shifting to sit on the edge of the bed.

She nodded, sucking her suddenly trembling lip into her mouth. He wrapped a comforting arm around her shoulders as a tear slipped down her cheek.

He brushed her bangs out of her face, but she knew if she met his gaze, she'd have a total breakdown.

"We'll get through this week's printed garbage," he said, "and next week will consist of all happy news about how you're engaged to the sexiest, most charming, most talented man alive."

She laughed. "That *is* happy news."

Trey palmed her face and urged her to meet his dreamy eyes. She almost forgot why she was upset until he asked, "How did you hear about the new stories already?"

"I waited at the newsstand until the new issues were delivered."

"Why would you do that to yourself?" he asked. "Next you'll tell me you've been googling your name on the Internet."

Reagan's heart sank. "Have people been saying bad things about me online?"

"Nope," Trey said, shaking his head. "Not a one."

"Oh God," she said. Of course the Internet trolls and hundreds of self-righteous assholes had been talking about her online. She was sure they'd be even crueler than the tabloids because slander was rampant online and no one had a mind to stop the spread of speculation and outright lies. Why hadn't she thought to look there? "What are they saying about me?"

"You are forbidden to find out," Trey said.

"I have a right to know," she said.

Trey wrapped his arms around her, trapping her arms at her

sides. "You will not go online, Reagan. I'll restrain you if I have to. If I'd known you were going to get up before the sun to torture yourself with tabloids, I'd have restrained you before I fell asleep. You're making yourself miserable."

"*They're* making me miserable," she reminded him.

"But instead of going out of your way to avoid the negativity, you're intentionally seeking it. Why did you get up so early to buy a paper?"

A paper? Okay, yeah, she'd let him believe that. The truth was far more neurotic.

She shrugged. "I don't know." It had seemed like a good idea at the time. If she had a heads-up on what the soul-sucking strangers were feeding on, she'd know what to expect when they followed her around barraging her with uncomfortable questions. That was the rational explanation she'd been trying to get behind, but it wasn't the truth. The truth was far harder to admit. "Maybe I . . . Maybe I deserve this."

Trey leaned away and took her chin in his hand, but she couldn't meet his eyes. "Reagan," he said gently, "how can you possibly think you deserve this?"

She shook her head, unwilling to share her innermost misgivings with anyone. Not even Trey.

"I thought you were happy in this relationship," he said.

"I am."

"Are you sure? You don't seem happy. If it isn't worth it to you—"

"It is. Everything *feels* right about loving you and loving Ethan, but . . ." How did she say what she was thinking without making Trey believe she wanted to end it? Because she didn't want to end it, no matter how many voices whispered to her that what she was doing was morally wrong. And no matter how much something deep inside her fucking agreed with those voices, with one voice in particular—her father's. "I wasn't raised this way."

Trey tilted his head and stared at her, searching for understanding.

"Raised what way?"

"To sleep with two men at once. To *love* two men at once."

"Were you raised to be true to yourself? To trust your heart and follow it?"

She wished she could say she had been. She knew Trey had been raised that way. "No," she said, twisting her engagement ring around her finger. "I was raised to not embarrass my father. To do what he said and be who he wanted me to be."

"Ah," Trey said, "so that's why you left home as soon as you could. So you could be who your father always wanted you to be? I thought you went to Los Angeles to find yourself."

"I did," she said. "I'm just not sure I like what I found. The rest of the world doesn't seem to like it much."

Trey pressed his forehead against hers and shook his head. "You don't know how wrong you are. You are loved. By thousands."

"And I'm hated," she whispered. "By thousands."

"They don't know you," he said. "Not really."

She grasped that idea and clung to it tightly. Maybe if she could force herself to believe that the negativity surrounding her wasn't directed at her personally, she'd get through this.

"I do a lot of social media stuff with Sinners fans," he said. "I could help you find your fan base online if you want."

"Too risky right now," she said. Instead of finding fans, she might find haters. "Maybe the craze will calm now that I'm engaged to the sweetest, most charming, most talented man alive."

"You forgot sexiest," he said, capturing her lips in a tender kiss.

She tended to forget everything when he kissed her like that, except that he was sexy.

A timid knock sounded at the door. Instead of diverting Reagan's attention, the knock made her kiss Trey more desperately, press herself closer to him, and hold him tighter. Out there, people hurt her. Here she was safe, cocooned in love and understanding. The only way the moment could have been more perfect was if Ethan had been with them.

"Reagan," Toni called from the other side of the door before knocking again. "It's almost time to go. Are you ready?"

She shook her head, wondering why she'd gone out that morning when she could have been blotting the outside world from existence with the shining star that was Trey Mills. She ran her hands down his hard chest and flat belly as she intensified their kiss. He caught her hand just before she found his cock beneath the sheet tangled around his naked hips.

"You touch that and you're going to miss your ride," he warned. His low, sexy voice danced up her spine and made her shiver with desire.

"Reagan?" Toni called, a little louder.

Trey offered no resistance when Reagan tugged against his

loose hold and found his half-hard cock with her hand.

"Guess I'm going to miss my ride," she said, her smile part amusement, part challenge.

"She'll meet you downstairs," Trey called out to Toni.

Reagan giggled when Trey flipped her onto the bed and went straight to work removing her jeans and panties. He settled between her splayed thighs on his belly and rubbed the tip of his nose over her mound and the ridiculous *lunch-with-arrow* tattoo she had there— the consequence of losing a stupid bet. "A bit early for lunch," he murmured, nipping the inked words sharply, "but my mouth is already watering for a taste of you."

She whimpered, clinging to his silky hair as his tongue delved into her "lunch" box. He released her tension quickly with deft licks, teasing kisses, and hard suction. She was almost worked up enough to come a second time, when he moved up her body, peppering kisses across her belly. He nibbled at her nipple through her shirt and bra and then lifted his head to watch her face as he fit his body into hers. The man had a rhythm like no other—a rhythm that synchronized perfectly with hers and filled her with pleasure and excitement, but also contentment. Gaze locked with hers, he took her higher and higher still until she shattered completely. She rocked her hips, trying to help him find release. His eyes drifted shut, and he bit his lip, strands of black hair sticking to the sweat on his throat and face. He thrust harder, then faster, then slow again. He shifted her hips slightly. Fucked her shallow and then deep. Gyrated his hips. Pounded into her.

"Come on," he whispered.

"Are you having difficulty?" she asked.

"I think I'm trying so hard to come that I can't," he said. "Maybe if you were on top."

He tugged off the rest of her clothes while she rode him. She got herself off with her deeply satisfying churning motions, but Trey still couldn't find his peak.

"You need Ethan, don't you?" Reagan asked with a grin. "You need his big hard cock pounding your ass."

"No, I—" He groaned when Reagan crawled off of him, exposing his hard, wet dick to the air. She suckled its head gently, making Trey twitch, and then mounted him backwards, sinking down slowly. His fingers dug into her hips, thumbs pressing into her ass cheeks as he helped her find the rhythm he preferred.

She peered at him over her shoulder and found his eyes

squeezed shut and his gorgeous face tense with concentration. Poor guy. He really was missing Ethan. Reagan stuck two fingers into her mouth, wetting them with saliva, and slid them down his balls. Trey jerked so hard when her fingertips brushed his ass that he nearly unseated her.

"Easy," she whispered, massaging his entrance until one fingertip breeched him.

He shifted beneath her, bending his knees and opening himself to her penetration. She pushed her fingers into him as far as they would go, and he released a groan of satisfaction so sexy that her pussy pulsed in response.

"Tell me when I find your sweet spot," she said, thrusting and withdrawing her fingers slightly. She curved them upward and tried again. Trey never had to help Ethan find it, but then Reagan didn't have a prostate of her own for comparison's sake.

"Almost," he said, releasing an excited gasp. "A little . . . A little deeper."

She knew when she found it without being told. He cried out, his cock jerking inside her so hard that she felt his rhythmic pulses of pleasure.

"Don't stop," he pleaded.

She didn't want to. His excitement was infectious. She concentrated hard on riding his cock and penetrating him the way he liked it until he finally let go. His ass tightened around her fingers, and his hands grabbed her hips to hold her on him as he writhed beneath her. She peeked at him over her shoulder again, finding his face taut with release and his belly tightening in ever intensifying contractions as he completely let go. That was exactly what she liked to see, her man lost in rapture. Her fingers were no substitute for Ethan's big, thick cock, but they'd gotten the job done.

When Trey finally relaxed and took a deep, sputtering breath, Reagan found herself tossed on the bed beside him and spooned up against his heated flesh as he snuggled against her. "You're perfect," he said, kissing her jaw. "I don't know why I was struggling so hard to come."

"Because you miss Ethan," she said. "I miss him too."

"I do miss him, but I think it might be because I really, really need to take a piss." He kissed her shoulder and hopped out of bed.

She giggled at the moan he released just before the sound of water striking water drifted from the bathroom. With a resigned sigh, she reached for her discarded clothes, wondering if the bus had waited for her or if she'd be thumbing a ride to the studio.

"Are you coming with me on Exodus End's bus?" Reagan asked, finding it difficult to put on her panties because her legs were still shaking from overexertion. She gave up with them still around her ankles and collapsed back onto the mattress.

"I just came with you in that bed," Trey said, turning on the water in the bathtub. Soon she could hear the spray of the shower. "But I'll come with you there too. Join me in the shower?"

"I don't think we have time for that right now."

"I'll behave."

If behaving meant touching every inch of her—sometimes with soap in hand, but more often not—then Trey was remarkably well-behaved in the shower. Most likely, though, their prolonged stay in the steamy water was causing additional tension in her band while they were forced to wait for her. Or maybe they had left without her. She couldn't blame them if they had. She was being uncommonly selfish this morning.

She was surprised to find all her bandmates as well as Butch and Toni congregated in the hotel lobby when she traipsed off the elevator. She had her bag slung over one shoulder, the handle of her guitar case in one hand, and Trey's hand clutched securely in the other.

"We were considering sending up a search party to find you," Butch said.

"Until Toni told us she thought you were having . . ." Steve covered his mouth with a bashful hand and whispered in a very good impression of Toni, ". . . *sex*."

"They were obviously having . . ." Logan copied Steve's teasing motion and whispered, ". . . *sex*." Which earned him a slap on the arm from the subject of their teasing. Toni was so flushed, Reagan wondered if she might get heatstroke from embarrassment.

"I found Trey naked in my bed," Reagan said with a shrug. "Couldn't help myself."

"So you're riding with us today?" Dare asked his brother.

"If I'm allowed," Trey said, glancing at Butch, guardian of the clipboard, for approval.

"I guess it's okay, as long as you don't have . . ." He covered his mouth with one hand and whispered, ". . . *sex*."

"Not you too," Toni squeaked in outrage, taking a swing at Butch, but slapping his clipboard instead of his laughing, mustached face.

Logan wrapped her in his arms and kissed her hair. "We're just teasing, baby."

"I know you're teasing," she said, "but why do you always have to tease *me*?"

"Because it's fun," Steve said. He followed Max toward the exit. Teasing was beneath Max. At least Reagan assumed that was why he was always so serious. Trey tugged at her hand and propelled her toward their ride, another limo.

"We aren't taking the bus?" Reagan asked.

"It's parked outside the city," Butch said. "Doesn't do well in New York City traffic. The car will drop us off at our rendezvous point after the radio segment."

"You mean I could have slept in?" Trey asked.

She squeezed his hand, sorry—but not really—that she'd all but forced him to come with her.

Reagan's guitar and bag were shoved into an already full truck, and they headed toward the radio studio.

"I figured the goth hookers would be riding with us," Steve said.

Reagan kicked him. "Don't be horrible to them, Steve. None of this is their fault."

"They look cool," Toni said. "I want to interview them for the book."

"They are absolutely not going to be part of our biography," Steve said.

"Then maybe I'll write a book about them and leave you out of it." Toni stuck her tongue out at him.

Steve shrugged. "Not much of a threat there."

"Did you bring the tabloid, Toni?" Reagan asked. "I want to read it."

"Butch made me put it in the trunk," Toni said.

"You have no business getting all upset before you're on air," Butch said.

Reagan scowled at him. She was sick of people thinking they knew what was best for her. Even if they were right.

The radio station had put out quite a spread of breakfast items for them to eat while they waited to go on the air. All the station's DJs, including those with the day off, made an appearance. Even though they'd all met hundreds of famous musicians throughout their careers, they still gushed all over the members of Exodus End. They were nice to Reagan and Trey as well, but it was obvious who was idolized. Steve was having a grand time flirting with a thirty-something radio host when Baroquen arrived. Sam was with them, so Reagan couldn't tell if the sudden iciness coming from Steve's direction was directed at their manager or the sexy group of women who headed for the buffet table. Max turned away from the women as well, but Logan launched himself directly into their midst, recounting the fun they'd had the night before.

"He partied with *them* last night?" Toni asked Reagan, clutching the waist of her newly tailored red top. Fitted at the waist, it hinted at just enough cleavage to make her look sexy but not tawdry. Aggie had done a great job helping Toni create a more suitable wardrobe.

"Yep," Reagan said. And she'd been so busy dancing the night away with Trey that she couldn't guarantee that Logan had behaved himself the entire time. Women naturally flocked to him because he was gorgeous and friendly and a hell of a lot of fun. But he loved Toni. Reagan didn't doubt that. "Go over there and claim your man."

Toni shifted her gaze to the floor. "I don't want to get in his way. He's working."

"If you don't make it clear that he's yours, someone will try to take him from you."

"I trust him."

"And you should, but do you trust *them*?"

"I don't know them."

Reagan gave Toni a little shove. "Go over there and kiss him or something. He's yours."

Toni tugged at the hem of her shirt, straightened her shoulders, showing her impressive bosom to full advantage, and stalked over to the buffet table. Reagan had been so wrapped up in Toni's problem—if the meek were to inherit the earth, Toni was sure to get a fair portion of it—she'd failed to notice that two members of Baroquen were getting a bit too close to Trey for her liking. Reagan wasn't the least bit shy about claiming what was hers. She slid up against Trey's side and settled her left hand on his chest, making sure the new diamond on her finger was in plain view.

Trey kissed her hair while Reagan boldly met the gazes of the two predators stalking him. Or at least that was what she'd thought they'd been doing until Azura said, "Congratulations on your engagement. We saw it on the news this morning. Why didn't you mention it to us last night?"

Reagan smiled, her defenses shattered to dust. She really did want to like these women. It was nice to have other female musicians among them. And as long as they kept their distance from her man—men, when Ethan returned—then they'd get along fine. "I don't like to talk about myself," Reagan said. "But thank you."

"Are you really getting married next month?" Sage asked. "That's so quick. I'm terrified of marriage."

"You won't be when you find the right person," Reagan said. *Or persons.* Thinking about Ethan pulled at a place inside her heart reserved specifically for him.

"Reagan," Butch called, "time to head to the studio."

Reagan shifted so she could see past the green-and-black-haired guitarist smiling goofily at her. The members of Exodus End and their entourage of disc jockeys had already left the room. She brushed a kiss across Trey's cheek and moved away from his side.

"You're sure you're okay with introducing us to Master Sinclair," Azura asked Trey as Reagan hurried toward the door.

Reagan smiled to herself. She remembered when she'd met Trey and how excited she'd been at the prospect of meeting Sinners' lead guitarist. She supposed she wasn't the only guitarist with a colossal crush on that man's talented fingers.

An acoustic guitar was placed in Reagan's hands the moment she entered the studio. Except for messing around, she'd never really played Exodus End's songs on acoustic. The technique for playing an electric guitar was entirely different. Reagan's stomach sank as she realized she was about to make a complete fool of herself before an audience bigger than she'd ever played in front of before. At least she didn't have to look at them cringing in their cars and homes and offices as she butchered their favorite tunes.

"Um, what are we playing?" Reagan asked Max.

"Same thing we always play acoustically."

"Which would be?" Reagan asked.

Max stared at her, his green-and-gold-flecked hazel eyes unreadable. "You've never played 'Bite' on acoustic, have you?"

"Bite"? On acoustic. How in the hell did anyone play that fast riff on an acoustic guitar? Reagan shook her head, playing the string of music through her head and staring hopelessly down at the guitar in her hands.

Max grabbed Butch's arm. "She's never rehearsed this."

Butch's mustache twitched as he studied his clipboard, as if by staring at it, it would magically say Reagan learns to play "Bite" on acoustic guitar. "Shit," he said. "Do you think you can wing it, sweetheart?" he asked Reagan.

Hell no, but she nodded. "I'll try."

"I can play acoustic," Max said.

"You're supposed to rest your wrist," Butch reminded him. "We don't want another setback."

"I can play acoustic," Max insisted.

Reagan handed the guitar to Max, who took it eagerly—Reagan had never seen Max eager about anything before—and flipped the strap over his head. Her breath caught. She'd been seeing him as only a vocalist for so long that she'd forgotten how perfect and natural the man looked with a guitar settled against his pelvis.

"I'm not needed at all," Reagan asked. "Am I?"

Which to some extent was a relief. She wouldn't have to answer awkward questions the hosts cooked up. To a greater extent, however, it was a concern. If Max could play, she was out of a job.

"Let me ask Sam," Butch said, already pushing his way out of the overcrowded room to find the boss.

Max squeezed Reagan's shoulder. "I'll teach you to play it on the way to Atlanta," he said.

That was great if she ever had to play an acoustic version of the song in the future, but it didn't help her now. She did recognize that Max was generous to offer the help, however, so she smiled her thanks.

"Sam says you're to sit in on the interview," Butch told her when he came hurrying back.

So she didn't get to participate in the part she enjoyed—the music—but was forced to endure the part she hated—the scrutinizing questions. Wasn't that just wonderful? She perched herself on the last stool and watched as the microphone that had been arranged at crotch level to pick up the sound of her guitar was moved in front of Max. She was happy for him, glad that he got to pick up his favorite instrument and play for his fans. He deserved that. He needed that. But it wasn't exactly good news for her.

Still, Reagan refused to sulk. She closed her eyes and took several deep breaths, recalling how it had felt to be onstage at Madison fucking Square Garden the night before, playing before thousands of amped-up fans who had cheered for her as much as anyone in the band. But was that true? Wouldn't they have cheered even louder if Max had played for them?

Reagan sat up straighter as they went on the air and the disk jockey spoke into his microphone.

"I'm Jack Bryant and we have Exodus End in the studio with us today, with the added treat of Maximillian Richardson playing guitar for the first time since his botched carpel tunnel surgery earlier this year. You are suing the hell out of that doctor, aren't you?"

"My lawyer is on it," Max said with a bitter smile.

"That hack owes restitution to every last one of your fans," Jack said. "When do you think you'll get back to playing regularly?"

"Soon," Max said.

"He can play acoustic," Steve said. "I guess we could do all our shows that way."

"Or not," Dare said, his nose crinkled in displeasure.

"Give him more time to heal," Logan said. "We've got Reagan until then." He reached over and slapped her on the back, nearly unseating her from her stool.

Reagan smiled at him, glad he'd remembered she existed.

"Will you have more corrective surgery?" Jack asked Max. "With a better doctor?"

Max pressed his left hand into his chest, shielding it with his right. "I'd rather not go under the knife again if I can avoid it."

"Understandable. Hey, isn't your father a famous surgeon, Dare?" Jack asked.

"Yeah," Dare said with a chuckle. "He could give Max an awesome boob job."

"I'd pay to see that," Steve said.

"I'd pay *not* to see that," Jack said. "So what are you going to play for us today?"

"Bite," Max said.

The four members of the band exchanged some sort of subliminal signal and began to play. Steve was going at a wood block as if he had a full set of drums at his disposal. The sounds coming from the three guitars lined up beside her brought goose bumps to Reagan's skin. And while they delighted her ears with a sound so pure and perfect that she held her breath, she couldn't take her eyes off Max. The care he showed his instrument—the love—was apparent in every strum. It was as if he'd just been reunited with the love of his life and they were making love for the first time in ages. His voice was as rich and deep as ever, and it was obvious that he was an exceptional singer, but he didn't love singing with the same intensity he loved to play. Anyone with eyes could see that.

Reagan would never replace Max in Exodus End. She didn't want to. Not after seeing—*feeling*—how much Max had lost when he'd given up his guitar. His image blurred out of focus as her eyes filled with tears. She didn't belong there. Max belonged. She would never be a true part of this greatness. It wasn't hers to own.

"Amazing," Jack said as the final notes of the song faded to silence. "Is that a tear in your eye, Reagan?"

She pressed the back of her hand against one leaky eye. "Yeah. What can I say? I was moved."

Reagan continued to feel like a fifth wheel for the entire segment. Everyone else was having a great time, and she laughed when someone made a joke or offered a witty comment when called upon, but she never felt a part of what was going on around her. She felt more like an observer than a true participant, so it was a relief when Baroquen entered the studio and took over for the last ten minutes of the segment. She didn't stick around to hear the newcomers, but instead headed to the ladies room. She couldn't get her phone out of her pocket fast enough.

She dialed Ethan and sucked in a shaky breath when he answered. "You did great," he said. "Did you even make it out of the booth before you called me?"

"You were listening?"

"Of course I was."

"Ethan, I feel so . . . lost? Alone? I don't know. I feel . . . off."

"Where's Trey? Isn't he there with you?"

"I'm in the ladies room." Why had she gone there to call Ethan instead of seeking out Trey? Trey was always super supportive and would be more than happy to give her more advice than she needed. But she didn't want advice just then. She just wanted someone to listen, and Ethan was the best listener she'd ever met. Mostly because he was unlikely to share what he was thinking.

"I didn't play once during that entire segment," Reagan said. "No one even told me we were playing the songs acoustic until a guitar was shoved into my hand."

"Someone screwed that up," he said.

"But that's not why I feel this way. Not really. I feel this way because I know I'm not a part of this, Ethan. I'll never be a part of it."

"So you find something else that you can be a part of."

"Like what?" Her own attempts at forming bands had been laughable at best and total disasters at their worst.

"I don't know. Maybe Trey has some suggestions."

"I'm asking you."

"I'll think on it," he said. "Stop being so restless and live in the moment."

Reagan grinned through her tears. "You're starting to sound a lot like Trey."

"Can't be helped. He's pretty amazing."

"He is."

"Tell him hello for me. I'll see you both tomorrow night."

"Can't wait."

Trey was waiting for her in the hallway when she came out of the restroom. "You always go to him first," he said. Yet he didn't look angry or upset.

"How did you know?"

"He sent me a text." Trey lifted his phone. "And a dick pic."

Reagan pouted. "He didn't send me—" Her phone buzzed in her hand as Ethan's dick pic landed on her phone.

"I really miss him," Trey said as they compared pictures and discovered they weren't identical.

"You miss him or his dick?" Reagan asked.

"Him," Trey said. "But I wouldn't tell him to keep this to himself." Trey ran a finger down the length of Ethan's cock on his screen.

"I got another text too," Trey said with a huge grin and flicked to a different picture. "From Brian."

Expecting to get an eyeful of Brian's dick for some reason, it took Reagan a moment to absorb what she was seeing. It was a screenshot of the current top album sales on iTunes. Sitting securely in the number one spot was Sinners' latest release.

"Oh my God! You're number one," she said, linking both arms around Trey and jumping up and down. "I'm so excited for you guys!"

Dare came up beside them and took the phone out of Trey's hand. "Is that the current metal chart on iTunes?"

"That's the overall music chart." Trey pecked Reagan on the lips several times. "Every genre."

Dare pulled the screen to his face for a closer look. "Are you fucking serious?"

"Oh yeah, we rock." Trey shifted Reagan to his side, never allowing her to slip from his embrace, and exchanged a knuckle bump with Dare.

"That you do, little brother."

"In the car!" Butch yelled down the corridor. "We have to get to Atlanta sometime today."

CHAPTER 26

Overwhelmed with pride, Reagan squeezed Trey's hand and leaned into his arm. He should be with his band celebrating the smashing success of their new album, but she was glad he was with her and grateful to have good news to dwell upon for a change. *Good* news? Hell, this news was monumental. Metal albums rarely reached the top of a general music sales chart. Even the members of Exodus End were chattering excitedly about Sinners' well-deserved accomplishment as they took a limo to the city's outskirts to rendezvous with the bus. By the time everyone had shoved their belongings in the storage compartment and boarded, Steve was already in the back lounge. Nothing unusual about that, but when he called for Reagan and Toni to join him, Reagan's suspicions rose.

"They're both taken," Logan pointed out. "No threesome for you, Aimes."

"I don't know," Reagan said. "I only had one partner in bed this morning. Maybe I'd feel more at ease if I did partake in this threesome of Steve's. What do you say, Toni?"

"Sounds interesting," she said. Logan gaped at her, but instead of prolonging his torture, she caved immediately. "Just teasing."

"I know you're teasing," he said, though his facial expression made Reagan believe otherwise. "But why do you always have to tease *me?*"

"Payback," Toni said. She entered the lounge and plopped down on the white sectional next to Steve. "What did you find out about Bianca and Susan?"

Reagan had completely forgotten that they'd asked Steve to figure out what was going on with his ex-wife, Bianca, and Tamara Brennan, who Toni still called Susan.

"I put Butch in charge of finding out more about this tabloid," Steve said, picking up a copy of the *American Inquirer* and shaking it at Butch, who'd entered the lounge behind Reagan. She had never seen Butch in the lounge, though he spent half his life on the bus. She'd suspected there was an invisible fence under the floor that shocked him if he tried to cross the threshold.

"You were supposed to find out," Reagan said to Steve. "Not put Butch on it."

"What's the point of having a lackey if you don't boss him around?"

"I heard that," Butch said, writing on his clipboard. "No supper for Steve," he said under his breath.

"So what did you find out, Butch?" Toni asked.

"Not much. *American Inquirer* has only been on stands for a few months, which I guess is good for us, because its circulation is relatively low for a tabloid."

"That is good news," Toni said, nodding eagerly at Butch and then again at Reagan. Reagan knew Toni felt responsible for the stories being published in the first place. She didn't want them circulating any more than Reagan did.

"With some digging, I found out *American Inquirer* is actually owned by a business conglomerate. Tradespar West." Butch lifted his eyebrows at Steve, who unexpectedly slammed his fist on the table.

"You've got to be shitting me," Steve said.

Butch shook his head. "I wish I were."

"Max!" Steve yelled. "Get your record-label-ass-kissing self in here."

"What's going on?" Reagan asked, her confused gaze darting from Steve to Butch to Toni. The two men were in various stages of outrage. Toni looked as lost as Reagan felt.

"Yeah, I don't get it," Toni said. "What's Tradespar West?"

Steve snorted. "They're a vast network of entrepreneurs who own all sorts of companies, most of them in the entertainment industry. Movie studios, a publisher or two, agents, production companies, advertising giants, a modeling agency, I guess a tabloid now, and most importantly, our record label. Max!" he called again.

"Do you have to be so noisy?" Max asked, massaging one temple with his fingertips.

"You know that tabloid that published all those bullshit stories about us last week?" Steve asked.

"And this week," Reagan said, eyeing the latest copy, which was demanding she read it, even though she knew it would upset her.

"Not really," Max said.

"Guess who owns them?" Steve asked.

"You?"

"Tradespar West."

Max crossed his arms and shrugged. "So?"

"*So?*" Steve shot to his feet, crushing a page of the tabloid in his fist and thrusting it in Max's direction. "Don't you see what this is?"

Max's uninterested gaze shifted to the crumpled paper. "A page from a tabloid."

"A publicity stunt. I bet you every article in these pages is about stars connected with Tradespar in some way."

"*Every* star is connected to Tradespar in some way," Max said. "Directly or indirectly."

"But if that's true, then why have they been so focused on Exodus End?" Toni asked.

"Because," Steve said, "our record sales have leveled off over the years, and they're looking for ways to increase sales."

"And making our temporary rhythm guitarist out to be a whore sells albums," Max said. "Is that what you think?"

Reagan forced herself not to cringe at the word *temporary*, especially since the man she was replacing was the one who'd said it. Was he ready to start playing guitar again? She noticed he wasn't wearing his wrist brace, and her heart plummeted. Was her moment in the spotlight about to end? Because even though she hated the publicity, she was in no way prepared to give up the stage.

"There's something suspicious about all this," Steve said. "Don't you think?"

"I think you're paranoid," Max said.

"Reagan saw Bianca at Phil's visitation," Steve said.

When Max looked at Reagan, she nodded.

"That's strange," Max said, "but I'm not sure it's suspicious."

"She was acting like a reporter," Reagan told him, "but she snuck inside the mausoleum. She left as soon as Steve and the rest of you guys arrived."

Toni spoke up. "And her sister, Susan—"

"Tamara," Steve corrected.

"Her sister *Tamara* is the one who stole my data. She'd been working for my mom for a couple of months before I was given this job. She was actually hired to write the interactive biography, but I talked my mom into letting me take her place."

"Okay, so a couple of women from Steve's past are on a mission to destroy the band and they focus on her." Max flipped a hand in Reagan's direction. "Why Reagan?"

"Maybe they want me to leave," Reagan said. Was that it? Was that why they'd completely trashed her reputation? So she'd step aside?

"Doesn't matter what they want," Steve said. "You're under contract for a year. You can't go anywhere."

A muscle in Max's jaw flexed. "What if I'm ready to play again before her time is up?"

Reagan's stomach churned, and she stared down at her hands. They looked so small and incapable. So unlike Max's.

"The contract says she plays, the contract says she stays. Sam will never let us breach that contract. You know he won't."

Max nodded slightly. "So what do you want me to do about this tabloid situation?"

"Ask Sam what he's up to," Steve said. "Ten bucks says he's behind this entire thing."

"I'll ask him," Max said. "Not sure why you think he'll admit to anything."

"Because he likes you," Steve said. "He thinks the rest of us are a bunch of idiots, but you're his best pal. He trusts you."

"What are you guys talking about back here?" Logan asked from the doorway.

"Steve's continued search for a reason to cut loose from our record label," Max said. He brushed past Logan to leave the room.

"We don't need a reason!" Steve called after him. "But we have millions of them," he said under his breath.

The bus rumbled as they headed south. Reagan already had a hard time figuring out her place in the band, but if Max wanted her gone, she didn't have a place at all.

"I think I should talk to Max," she said. Everything going on outside the band was enough to drive her insane; she wasn't sure she could stand causing tension within it as well. She loved these guys. Loved their music. Had been a devoted fan since she'd first heard them on the radio. She refused to be their downfall, either internally or externally. If she had to give them up to save them, she'd make that sacrifice. But first she needed to know what was going on inside Max's head. She was no stranger to dealing with emotionally closed off men—Ethan and her father both kept their feelings securely locked inside. But she managed to reach them on occasion. And though she wasn't sure if she'd ever be on speaking terms with her father again, she knew he cared. Knew even though he rarely showed it.

Dare and Trey were sitting toward the front of the bus, laughing.

"Mom said the only way she'll forgive you is if you have the wedding at her house," Dare said.

"She's already forgiven me. I talked to her last night after she talked to you. Reagan and I are getting married in Vegas."

"Just like Brian," Dare said. "How original."

Reagan tugged her attention from the happiness near the front of the bus and settled it on Max, who was sitting at the dining table staring at his hands.

"Can I join you?" Reagan asked.

He started and glanced up, his eyes clouded with worry. "Join me for what? I'm just sitting here."

"I would have said, 'we need to talk,' but I didn't want to scare you." Those four little words struck fear into the hearts of most men.

"I don't scare easily," he said, but he slid closer to the wall, as if distance from her was a suitable shield.

"Good to know," she said, sitting across the booth from him.

She could hear Dare and Trey discussing Sinners' new album and would definitely rather be a part of that conversation than the one she was about to have.

"How's your wrist?" Reagan asked. "I noticed you aren't wearing your brace."

Max flexed his hand. "Healing," he said.

"Enough to play?"

"Soon," he said.

How soon? She licked her lips and rubbed her engagement ring, looking for the strength to ask questions she didn't really want answered. "If you're ready to—"

"I'm sorry," he said, reaching across the table and squeezing her hand. "I didn't realize . . ."

"Why are you sorry?" What didn't he realize?

"Right before the tour started, I told Sam I wanted to get back to playing as soon as I could, that having you here as my crutch on the tour would slow down my recovery. A year is a long time to rely on someone to do your job."

It didn't feel very long to her.

"Sam said he'd take care of it. That's all he said. *I'll take care of it.* I thought he'd renegotiate your contract for a shorter duration or . . ." He shook his head. "I don't know what I thought. I didn't much care what he did as long as you were out of the way when I was ready to play again."

Reagan was so stunned she didn't know what to say. She'd thought Max had supported the arrangement. She'd had no idea that she was stepping on his toes. She'd been so focused on herself and how she was adapting to being a member of the band and how the world was out to get her that she'd never considered how Max felt when he watched her stand in his spotlight and assume part of his identity. To a musician, an instrument was part of who they were. Playing was an extension of the music inside their heart, their mind, their soul. She knew that as well as anyone.

No wonder the guy was always so subdued.

"I didn't know he'd try anything in his power to get you to break the contract," Max said.

"What?" Reagan asked, her head snapping up. "*Me* break the contract? Why would I break it?" Especially if it was the only thing keeping her there.

"You don't see what Sam's doing," Max asked, "using that contract as a weapon against you? Making you change your look, forcing you to do things onstage you're not comfortable doing, using you as the cornerstone of a slur campaign. Every time you say you *don't* feel comfortable doing something, that's where he shifts his focus. How miserable can he make you before you give up?"

She'd never thought of it that way, but Sam did go out of his way to make her hate that contract. And whenever she baulked at his suggestions, he was the first to point out that it was in that odious piece of paper she'd signed without even reading and she *had* to comply.

"When that didn't make you leave, I guess he sought a different source of intimidation—that damned tabloid—to make you hate this life, fame, being in the spotlight."

"He wants me to leave that badly?"

Max shook his head. "Actually, he thinks you're fabulous. He's only trying to make me happy. I'm his only shot at getting the band to stay with our current record label, so he's dedicated to keeping me on his side. But seeing you like this, seeing what they've done to you, how they've hurt you . . ." He shook his head. "It has to stop. You've been through enough."

She wouldn't argue with him on that, but the fact that Max didn't want her to be a part of Exodus End hurt far more than he could know. Still, it *was* his band, his life, his music, his fans, and his career that she was encroaching upon. She was outsider. And she'd always be an outsider.

"If you wanted me to leave, all you had to do was say so," she said.

"I don't want you to leave."

"But you said—"

"I didn't know you then, Reagan. I didn't realize how forcing my hand would affect you or everyone around you. I'm going to tell Sam to call off his dogs."

"I think it's too late," she said. "Trey asked me to marry him because of this mess!"

"That isn't why I asked you," Trey said, sliding into the booth beside her and holding her trembling hand.

Dare stood next to Trey and shook his head at Max. "That was a pretty shitty thing to do to her."

They'd been eavesdropping? Not that she was surprised. It was entirely too easy to do in such close quarters.

"I didn't even realize Sam was doing that to you until just now. I wish I had figured out that he was involved days ago," Max said.

"Days ago? Don't you mean *weeks* ago?" Reagan asked. Sam had been making her life hell from the beginning.

"He took it too far when he involved the press. I didn't realize he was responsible until Steve mentioned Tradespar West."

"How are they involved?" Dare asked.

"They own the tabloid."

Reagan turned her head to watch Dare's profile. She couldn't tell if he was mad or concerned about the connection. He didn't seem surprised, though.

"Could it be a coincidence?" Dare asked.

Max shook his head. "Doubtful. Just like it's not a coincidence that the head editor of the *American Inquirer* is Bianca."

Dare gaped at him. So it *was* possible to shock Dare Mills.

Dare eventually collected himself to speak. "I know you don't want to hear that Steve is right—"

"Then don't say it. I'll talk to Sam when we get to Atlanta. I think he's trying to get Baroquen to do a surprise opening number."

"Oh, Steve is going to love that," Reagan said. She knew how pissed he'd been when Sam had told him his buddy Zach's band was being replaced on the European leg of the tour. Hell, at this rate, Reagan might be replaced by then. Or merely discarded.

"Steve doesn't know what's best for the band," Max said. "He only knows what's best for himself."

"Am *I* what's best for the band?" Reagan asked.

"For now," Max said. He slid out of the booth and walked to the lounge at the back of the bus.

For now. As those two words sank in, Reagan straightened. This situation wasn't going to continue for the rest of her life. She wasn't going to play rhythm guitar for Exodus End forever. She wasn't always going to be the focus of their fan's adulation and criticism. She wouldn't stand in the spotlight next to these wonderfully talented megastars for all eternity. She got all that. For the first time she truly understood what that meant. What she didn't get was why she felt so relieved at the realization. This situation was temporary. Her shitty contract—temporary. Her sudden drop into infamy— also temporary. She could survive the negative publicity. It too would end. Shit. This opportunity was already getting away from her. She needed to take advantage of her good fortune and stop moping around feeling sorry for herself. She'd never been that kind of woman before. How had fame changed her so much in such a short space of time?

"What the fuck is wrong with me?"

"You look perfect from where I'm sitting," Trey said.

She cupped his face between her hands and kissed him because he was a total sweetheart. "I'm such an idiot. I've been going about this all wrong."

"What?"

"I've been trying so hard to fit in when what I should have been doing was trying to stand out."

"Finally she takes my advice." Dare shook his head and rolled his eyes at her.

"You didn't . . ." Her face went slack as she recalled snippets of advice and encouragement that Dare had offered her from day one. He *had* encouraged her to be herself all along. "Know it all."

"He is a smug bastard, isn't he?" Trey got a slap across the back of his neck for his barb.

Dare took Max's vacated seat across from them. "This isn't my first rodeo, kid."

"You ride bulls now?" Trey asked.

"Nope. I just take them by the horns and wrestle them to the ground."

"I always thought you were more of a go-with-the-flow kind of guy," Reagan said.

"Usually." Dare nodded agreeably. "But if I see something I want, I refuse to back down."

"Smug and stubborn," Trey said.

"Tenacious," Dare corrected.

"Same difference," Trey said.

"Not really," Reagan said. "Stubbornness is annoying, but tenacity is admirable."

"And it is my goal in life to be admired by Reagan," Dare said, his smile brightening his entire face.

Sometimes Reagan could overlook how damned gorgeous the man was and think of him platonically, but when he smiled like that, she couldn't help but feel giddy.

"Hey," Trey said, poking his brother's hand. "No flirting."

"I'm not flirting," Dare said. "The woman is going to be my sister by marriage in a couple weeks."

"I always wanted a hunky older brother," she said with a grin.

"No flirting!" Trey insisted.

Reagan's future was racing toward her at light speed. What if she took a wrong turn and spun completely out of control?

"I can't believe you're so selfish," Steve said, stomping out of the lounge. "Everything is all about Max. Just because you're our vocalist doesn't make you our god."

"Just because you're our drummer doesn't mean you have to bang everything that will let you," Logan called after him.

"Not the time for lame jokes, Justa Bassist," Steve snarled. He stomped around a bit and then yanked a bottle of fire whiskey from a cabinet.

"A little early to be drowning your demons, isn't it?" Dare asked.

"Fuck off," Steve spat. He took his bottle to his bunk and jerked the curtain closed.

Max exited the lounge with Butch trailing him. "I told you I didn't know Sam would take it that far," Max said to Steve's curtain.

"You always blow everything out of proportion."

"And you are always forgiven for every shit thing you do to people."

Max glanced at Dare, and Reagan wondered if he was thinking about how he'd gotten the woman Dare loved pregnant all those years ago. Or were there other things he'd done that Dare had forgiven? Even though Reagan had temporarily taken over part of Max's position in the band, she felt she knew him the least of Exodus End's members.

"I'm going to make this right," Max said.

"How?" Steve asked. "What's done is done. You fucked up, but as usual someone else suffers the consequences." The whiskey bottle glugged behind the closed curtain.

"I guess I'm not as perfect as you are."

"Or as gay," Logan said from the doorway of the lounge.

"Logan, don't make me get up and beat your ass," Steve threatened.

"Hey, I didn't even know you *liked* me liked me until I read that tabloid article."

"If that tabloid has a low circulation," Butch said, staring down at his clipboard as if it had the answer to all life's questions, "how come every concert-goer in both Albuquerque and Phoenix had a copy?"

Dare turned in his seat to look at Butch. "How did you get a copy? It's not like you go out and buy little-known tabloids on a regular basis."

"A member of the crew gave it to me," Butch said. "T-bone or Big Mike or maybe it was Little Mike." Butch shrugged and shook his head. "I don't remember."

"How did they get it?" Dare asked.

"I don't know. You'll have to ask them."

"That is weird," Reagan said. She wasn't sure why she hadn't questioned the spread of that story earlier. No one had bothered them much in New York, not even the press. She'd assumed it was because New Yorkers had more important worries than her over-used cooch, but maybe they just didn't know about it. Her father had known, though. And he never read tabloids.

She pulled her phone out of her pocket, unblocked her dad's number, and chanced sending him a text. She was still too chicken shit to talk to him, and she knew he hated text messaging, but maybe he'd answer this one.

How did you get a copy of that tabloid?

She didn't expect him to answer at all, so was surprised when her phone dinged with a response almost immediately.

You sent me a copy in the mail.

Why in the fuck would she send him a copy?

Are you sure?

It had your return address on it.

Where was it postmarked?

His answer didn't come for a long tense moment.

"Who are you texting?" Trey asked close to her ear. "Ethan?"

"My dad. He says I sent him a copy of the tabloid in the mail."

"Why the fuck would you send him a copy?" Trey asked.

"Exactly."

Her phone dinged with her father's reply. *Postmarked in Seattle. Are you going to talk to me now? You won't answer my calls.*

Technically, she'd blocked his calls.

You don't want to talk, Dad. You want to yell. I'm upset enough about this without you raking me over the coals.

Someone needs to keep you in check. You're completely out of control.

Bye.

She didn't read his response. Whatever he had to say was something she didn't want to hear. "It was postmarked in Seattle."

"Isn't that where Toni is from?" Dare asked.

A huge knot of rage formed in the pit of Reagan's belly. Had Toni proved her a sucker? Was she actually responsible for all this mess and hiding behind a web of lies about Susan/Tamara?

"Toni was on tour with us then," Dare said. "She couldn't have mailed it from Seattle."

"She went home for a couple of days," Reagan reminded him. "She could have mailed it to him then. Toni!" she called, sliding out of the booth and heading for the lounge. She found Toni making out with Logan on the sectional at the back of the bus. Reagan didn't bother to wait for them to finish before she asked, "Did you mail a copy of that fucking tabloid to my father?"

Toni pulled her mouth away from Logan's. Her lips were swollen, her eyes glazed, and her cheeks flushed. "What? How can you even ask me that?"

"I guess it could have been Logan. He also went to Seattle." Reagan crossed her arms over her chest and leaned back against whoever had come to stand behind her. She'd assumed it was Trey, but when her support took a step back, she glanced over her shoulder to find she'd been pressing her ass into Max's hip. She was surprised he was the one who'd followed her.

"Paranoid much?" Logan asked. "Of course neither of us would mail a tabloid to your father. I didn't even know you had a father."

"He lives in Arkansas," Toni supplied. "A band teacher at a high school."

"Knowing that would have made it easy for you to track him down and mail him a copy," Reagan said, but she already felt she had the wrong culprit. Toni would look guilty if she'd done something wrong. The woman didn't know how to hide her emotions.

"I wouldn't do that," Toni said. "It had to be Susan."

"Tamara," Logan corrected.

Toni scowled at him. "Well, whatever she calls herself, she lives in Seattle. Or she did. I'm not sure where she is now."

"I bet Steve could track her down," Logan said. "Through Bianca."

"Probably easier to go directly through Sam," Max said.

"Sam?" Logan scrunched his brow. "How is Bianca connected to Sam?"

"I have no fucking clue," Max said. "But I intend to find out."

CHAPTER 27

TREY TOOK a deep breath and puffed out his cheeks. For all his insistence that Ethan and Reagan be open about their relationship, he'd never actually met the parent of a lover before. What if Mrs. Mendez hated him? Would that plant another seed of doubt in Ethan's subconscious, because the guy already had a full garden of doubt growing there. He didn't need another weed to sprout.

Reagan squeezed his hand. "Rosa is a total sweetheart," she said. "She'll love you."

"She loves *you*," Trey said. "I'm probably not the kind of partner she wanted for her son."

"I think you're wrong," Reagan said. "She wants Ethan to be happy, and you make him happy."

"*We* make him happy." He squeezed her hand and lifted it to his lips, kissing her knuckle just above the rock he'd put on her finger only days before.

Reagan smiled and leaned against his arm. "We."

Ethan was easy enough to spot as he stepped off the escalator. Not only was he several inches taller than most of the people milling about baggage claim, he was also the most gorgeous man in the vicinity—all dark and feral. A young woman tripped over her own rolling suitcase as she gawked at him.

The short woman beside him had to be his mother. There was definitely a resemblance through the eyes and nose, but it was the way she corralled her hulk of a son like a toddler in an unfamiliar place that made Trey chuckle under his breath.

Reagan stood on tiptoe and waved until she caught Ethan's attention. Trey tongued the hoop in his lip, wondering if he should have removed some of his jewelry before they'd arrived. He had left his tongue piercing out. At least he wouldn't sound like he had a speech impediment, even if he did look like every mother's nightmare.

"Your hand is all sweaty," Reagan said, tugging her hand free of his and wiping it on her jeans.

"Sorry."

"Reagan!" Rosa shouted her welcome and wrapped Reagan in a tight hug. After a long squeeze, she held Reagan at arm's length and shook her head. "Why do you never visit me? I must feed you. You're all flesh and bones."

"Skin and bones," Ethan corrected.

"I'll visit soon," Reagan promised. "After the tour is over."

"This is Trey," Ethan said, adding under his breath, "Please remember what I warned you about on the plane."

What he'd warned her about? What was that supposed to mean?

Rosa beamed a friendly smile at him, her dark eyes scanning his face and settling briefly on the piercings in his brow and lip, and on the multiple piercings in each of his ears. She took a step toward him, both arms raised as if to hug him, but then she glanced at Ethan, dropped one arm and merely shook Trey's hand. "Nice to meet you. Congratulations on your engagement to my Reagan." She cringed as she said it, as if someone were twisting a knife in her side.

"The pleasure is mine," Trey said, trying to win her over with his best smile, but she turned away.

"Where is luggage?" She turned toward the nearest carousel.

Trey attempted to catch Ethan's eye. He knew he couldn't throw himself into his arms and kiss him until he was giddy and breathless, but he would at least like to lose himself in Ethan's gaze and know that he was still loved. But apparently there wasn't time for either him or Reagan. Ethan kept them both at an impersonal distance as luggage was collected and stowed in the trunk of a taxi. Rosa sat in the front seat with the driver, asking him questions about the sites they saw as they drove into Atlanta. In the back seat, Reagan sat between Trey and Ethan, holding Trey's hand openly on her lap and taking Ethan's more discreetly between her leg and his.

"We've missed you," she whispered to Ethan while their driver was occupied with his very inquisitive copilot. That part of Atlanta wasn't exactly known for world-renowned sites, but Mrs. Mendez seemed to think she was touring Rome.

"It's all I can do to keep myself from dragging you both to the floor for a proper reunion," Ethan said, the low timber of his voice playing havoc with Trey's senses. And though his body was very much ready to cooperate with that plan, his heart and his head were not so amenable.

"Are you sure about that?" Trey said, releasing Reagan's hand and leaning against the taxi door so that their legs weren't touching.

"I'm sure."

"We haven't seen you in days," Trey said, "and I didn't get so much as a high five in the airport."

"If I touch you, I won't be able to hide how I feel," Ethan said.

"I don't want you to fucking hide it," Trey grumbled.

"You're the one who publicly proposed to Reagan. Even if I'm ready to let the world know how I feel about you, I can't now, can I? You're engaged."

"I had to give the press something big to get them to agree not to post those pictures of Reagan naked in the hotel lobby," Trey snapped.

"That's why you proposed?" Reagan asked.

"No," Trey said. "That's why I made sure every reporter in New York was in attendance."

"Oh, look," Rosa said loudly in the front seat. "That's an interesting building."

"It's a McDonald's, Mamá," Ethan said.

"We have no McDonald's like that in my neighborhood."

Ethan's expression softened, and he reached over the seat to squeeze his mother's shoulder. "How far to the hotel?" he asked the driver.

"Just a few more minutes," the man said, taking his eyes off the road long enough to glance in the rearview mirror at his back-seat passengers.

"Did you get a room for Mamá?" Ethan asked.

Reagan giggled. "She has to share with Butch."

"Who is Butch?" Rosa asked.

"My boss," Ethan said.

"I thought Reagan was boss."

Ethan rubbed the back of his neck. "Uh, Reagan is my employer. Butch is my boss. And there is no way I'd ever let you share a room with him."

Trey was trying very hard to stay mad at Ethan for his lack of greeting in the airport, but he'd missed him so much that he allowed himself to grin at the fierce protectiveness Ethan showed for those he loved.

Rosa turned and smiled at Reagan, a spark of mischief in her dark eyes. "This Butch"—which sounded more like *Booch* when she said it—"is he handsome?"

"Uh, he's okay. If you like walruses." Reagan choked on a laugh.

"I like man with meat on bones."

"I didn't mean . . ." Reagan glanced at Ethan, her brows drawn together, before turning her attention back to Rosa. "Butch is physically fit. Very muscular. Not fat. He just has a rather prominent mustache."

Rosa smiled and turned to face the windshield, her hands clasped together demurely in her lap. "I like man with texture around lips. Very nice for kissing."

Trey's eyes widened and then focused on Ethan. He snorted on a laugh at Ethan's shell-shocked expression.

"Mamá, I thought you were waiting for Papá to come to his senses," Ethan said.

She shrugged. "Yes, well, I won't wait forever. Maybe I give that cheater his extra dessert."

"His *just* deserts." Ethan corrected her as if it were an automatic reflex.

"I'm sure Butch would love to spend time with you," Trey said, mostly because he couldn't resist teasing Ethan. "I don't think he's dated much since his divorce."

"Butch is divorced?" Reagan asked, and Trey nodded, wondering how she could be around the man every day and not know that he was divorced.

"He's married to his job," Ethan grumbled.

"I like a man who has a job," Rosa said quietly.

Ethan groaned and covered his face with both hands. Trey's earlier anger was completely gone now. Not much got under Ethan's skin, but apparently the thought of his mother dating did.

When they reached the hotel, Ethan and Trey went after the luggage while Reagan escorted Rosa into the lobby, their arms locked at the elbow and their heads close together as they whispered about some conspiracy.

"So," Trey said to Ethan. "How do I win her over? She doesn't seem to like me much."

"She's not supposed to like you publicly," Ethan said. "You are marrying the woman she thought would be her beloved daughter-in-law."

Ethan slung a bag over one shoulder and pulled out the handle of a blue-and-white-polka-dot rolling suitcase.

"I should have asked you if you were okay with it before—"

Ethan shook his head, his eyes resting on someone standing behind Trey. "Not the time or the place," he said, walking away.

Trey sighed, lifted two heavy duffle bags—had Ethan brought some weights?—and followed Ethan, his gaze riveted to the wide cut of Ethan's shoulders that tapered into a set of narrow hips and a nicely rounded ass. Had Trey actually made their situation worse by trying to make it better? Maybe after the wedding, public interest would wane, but then if Reagan was caught "cheating" with Ethan after she was married, it would be considered adultery, not just labeled promiscuous behavior. Why did this have to be so damned complicated? Was it anyone's business who Reagan took to her bed? Trey knew it wasn't anyone's goddamned business who he took to his. He didn't care who knew he was in love with and had sex with a woman *and* a man. But Reagan cared. She was letting the world hold her to a double standard, and so was Ethan for that matter. Now Trey was afraid that he was contributing to their hesitance rather than abating it.

On the elevator, Reagan used her key card to access the secure level of the hotel.

"Where's all the security?" Ethan asked. "Have they been slacking off in my absence?"

"The guys had an event downtown that I talked myself out of," Reagan said. "Are you in a hurry to introduce your mama to Butch?" Reagan raised her eyebrows with the question.

"No."

Rosa laughed. "I can handle myself, mijo."

"Meehyo?" Trey said aloud, before realizing she was speaking Spanish. He'd taken a few semesters in high school, but was far from fluent.

"Son," Ethan translated.

"You also mijo," Rosa said with a smile as she patted Trey's shoulder. "My son."

Trey bit his lip, which was inexplicably trembling.

Ethan squeezed Rosa's shoulder. "Just a few more minutes," he said to her.

She sighed and nodded.

A few more minutes until what? Reagan handed Rosa a set of key cards. "We're staying right across the hall."

Good plan, Trey thought. It would be less likely for Rosa to hear squeaking mattresses, heads pounding against headboards, and copious amounts of moaning coming from her son's room if she stayed across the hall rather than next door. Though if she happened to share a wall with Steve, no telling what she'd hear.

Rosa opened her door with her key card and they all followed her inside. Ethan set her luggage near a closet and took his bags from Trey. Jeez, he'd assumed the duffle bags belonged to Ethan. How long was Rosa planning on staying, a year?

"Okay now?" Rosa asked, lifting her eyebrows at Ethan.

"Okay now," he said.

Trey grunted as he was hugged with enough force to drive all the wind from his lungs. It took a moment for him to return Rosa's enthusiastic embrace as the tighter she hugged him, the more his heart swelled in his chest. Perhaps her acceptance meant more to him than he'd realized. All the important people in Trey's life accepted who he was. And that was vital to his well-being. He could only imagine what it felt like to have a parent or a sibling not love you unconditionally. He was glad—for Ethan's sake—that he had such a mother. He didn't think Reagan was so lucky with her father's affection, but they wouldn't know if they didn't give the man a chance to prove himself.

Trey was pretty sure Ethan was a tad misty eyed as he watched his mother offer her sincere blessing. Rosa patted Trey forcefully on the back and then drew away. "Tell me all about you," she said, taking Trey's hand and leading him to the sofa. He obeyed without question. He was sure Rosa was used to getting her way. A woman didn't survive raising seven sons if she didn't have a solid backbone.

"*All* about me?" If he did that, he was sure she'd revoke her blessing and lock her son away.

"Yes, everything. Ethan, Reagan, sit," she said, patting the seat beside her.

Ethan sat and drew Reagan onto his lap. She relaxed against him, and he buried his face in her neck, inhaling what Trey knew to be her comforting yet exciting scent. He wished he could join their quiet reunion, but he had Ethan's mom to win over.

"I was born in Southern California," Trey began. "My father is Plastic Surgeon to the Stars, my mother is a folk artist who believes the world is her canvas, and my older brother is one of the most famous guitarists in the world. It's a wonder I don't have an inferiority complex."

"Ethan tells me you are famous guitarist also," Rosa said. "Like Reagan."

"Maybe like Reagan," Trey said, "but not like Dare."

"We're not even close to Dare's level of fame," Reagan said. "Thank God," she whispered under her breath.

"What else?" Rosa asked, leaning toward him eagerly. He supposed what was ordinary to him was exotic and exciting to some people. For the most part, he led a charmed life, and he didn't apologize for his good fortune.

With little encouragement, Trey told Rosa all about himself. He did leave out the X-rated stuff, so his life story didn't really take all that long to tell.

CHAPTER
28

E THAN BREATHED a sigh of relief when his mother decided she was tired and wanted to rest in her hotel room until dinner time. As much as he adored the woman and was happy to watch her affection for Trey grow by the minute, he very much wanted to be alone with his lovers. Well, as alone as three people could be together.

"I'm a little jealous," Reagan said as they crossed the hallway to their suite.

"Of what?" Trey asked, sliding his key into the lock.

"She barely spoke to me the entire time. You're her new favorite."

"She just wanted to know more about me," Trey said. "I'm sure her fascination is temporary."

"Like mine's been?" Reagan squeaked when Trey poked her in the ribs before following her into the room.

"You're her only daughter," Ethan reminded her as he stuck the Do Not Disturb sign in the key slot and closed the door. "She has to put up with *eight* sons now. You'll be back on top before—"

His words were silenced by Trey's unexpected kiss. "Missed you," Trey murmured against his lips.

The man had a way of getting Ethan worked up instantly.

"Jeez, Trey," Reagan teased, pulling the heavy duffle bag from Ethan's hand and dropping it on the floor with a loud huff. "You could at least let him get into the room before you start throwing yourself at him."

Now that Ethan's hands were empty, he filled them with Trey's ass, pulling his groin against his, breath catching when he felt how hard Trey was for him.

"You did miss me," Ethan said against Trey's lips.

"All of you," Trey said, fumbling with Ethan's fly. "Not just your cock."

Ethan groaned when Trey's hand slid into his pants and gently stroked him, massaging his cockhead with his thumb.

"But I need fucked, E. Been needing it for days."

"It's true," Reagan said, slipping her shirt off over her head and tossing it aside. "I tried to satisfy him." She lifted her palms and shrugged.

Ethan wrapped his hand around Trey's throat, and Trey groaned. Ethan knew what Trey craved—to be utterly dominated and fucked into submission—but Ethan didn't want Reagan to be hurt because of those needs. Trey could have them fulfilled without making her feel insecure in her position. "Did you make Reagan feel like she's not enough for you again?"

"If I did, I didn't mean to," Trey said, turning his head to look at Reagan. "Did I hurt your feelings?"

"Does it hurt your feelings that I don't feel completely satisfied unless both of your cocks are inside me?"

Trey shook his head, and Ethan relaxed his hand, kissing the red marks his fingers had left behind. Even though Trey liked him to be rough at times, Ethan didn't want to leave bruises. The man was precious to him.

"Well, there you go," Reagan said. "When you're not here, Ethan, we both feel like something is missing. So don't leave us again."

Ethan smiled. How wonderful was it to feel wanted? Loved? Needed? Pretty fucking spectacular.

"I'm glad he went," Trey said.

Ethan winced at the sudden pang in his chest. Trey was glad they'd been apart? How could he say that? It had been the longest four days of Ethan's life.

"I know that much of the guilt and uncertainty weighing you down is gone," Trey said, staring into his eyes. "Now you can completely put your head and your heart into our time together. It won't be just about our bodies."

"It was never just about our bodies." Ethan scowled. "Okay, at first it was just about our bodies, but my heart has been in it for a while now."

"As much of it as you were willing to give," Trey said. "Now you can give me your all."

That sounded decidedly terrifying.

"The way you've always given your all to Reagan."

"You two are making me cry," Reagan said, pressing the back of her wrist to one eye.

"I'd rather make you moan," Trey said, reaching out to pull her into their embrace.

Ethan kissed the tears off her cheek. "Why are you crying?"

"Because I'm happy," she whispered. "Couldn't be any happier."

"Give us an hour," Ethan murmured in her ear, "and we'll see if that still holds true."

Reagan giggled as Ethan attempted to pick up one perfect lover in each arm and carry them to bed. He managed to get their toes off the ground—sort of—and take a rushed step. "I think I need to work out more," he said as they stumbled toward the bed.

"Maybe if you weren't encumbered by the pants around your knees," Trey said, tugging at his pants leg with his toes.

"And this shirt is definitely holding you back," Reagan said, lifting the hem and sliding her hand up his belly.

"I do feel stronger when I'm naked," Ethan said with a laugh. He completely understood why Reagan had been shedding happy tears. Their reunion was emotional bliss. The physical bliss to come—and they would all be coming shortly—was just a bonus.

The pair made short work of his clothes and the strength in his legs as they knelt at his feet and delighted his cock with their mouths—two sets of lips, two tongues, two breaths. Together they kissed and licked, suckled and blew his overly excited flesh until he had to stop them. His body was accustomed to multiple sexual encounters a day, so going almost a week without had him ready to explode all over their faces. As they remained kneeling at his feet but kissing each other instead of performing amazing magic on his cock, Ethan couldn't stop the involuntary rocking of his hips.

Trey's eyes lifted to meet his, and he grinned that heart-stealing impish grin against Reagan's lips just before grabbing Ethan's ass and urging him forward. Ethan's heart stuttered over several beats and then raced as they let him in. He thrust gently into their combined mouths, groaning at the feel of their caressing tongues as they kissed each other around him.

Ethan's belly tightened as he fought release. He wished he could go on gently fucking their kiss, but the urge to pound himself into receptive flesh completely overwhelmed him, unleashing the sexual beast that both of his lovers appreciated—only not when he was in their mouths.

He reached for Reagan, hauling her to her feet and pulling her toward the bed. He heard Trey's sigh of disappointment. "I can't fuck you both at the same time," Ethan said as he wrestled with Reagan's remaining clothes and prayed that she was hot and wet. "So you're just going to have to fuck me this time, Trey."

"Yesss," he heard Trey say from the floor behind him.

After tipping a now naked Reagan onto the edge of the bed, he spread her legs wide and knelt between them. He devoured her pussy—sucking and licking and tonguing her center—until she'd gone from delightfully damp to dripping wet. She begged him to take her, so he did, mindful to enter her with ever deepening thrusts until his balls rested against her. When he ground into her, he was rewarded with her breathless moan of satisfaction.

Trey kissed his shoulder tenderly, and Ethan held his breath as lubed fingers slid against his ass.

"Relax," Trey murmured.

Ethan released his breath in a harsh gasp and concentrated on relaxing even while every instinct was telling him to mercilessly pound the pussy he was buried within. Ethan lowered himself over Reagan's body, her hot belly and breasts burning into his skin. He pressed his face into her throat and spread his legs to ease Trey's penetration. Heat flooded his body as his ass was filled slowly—oh God, slowly, too fucking slowly. The uncomfortable pressure was soon chased away by blinding pleasure. Ethan moaned and then sucked a breath through his teeth as Trey grasped his hip and directed his motions. He let Trey have complete control of his pleasure as he slowly pulled out of Reagan's body and Trey pulled out of his. In the final inch of withdrawal, Trey's hand pushed at Ethan's hip, directing him slowly back inside the haven before him and popped free of Ethan's clenching ass. Ethan groaned, wanting Trey inside him, but Trey merely pressed his cockhead against his opening, not breaching him again until Ethan was buried completely inside Reagan once more.

"God, yes," he groaned as Trey entered him again.

Ethan wasn't sure how long the relentless pleasure continued. The care Trey showed at pleasuring him tugged at Ethan's heart while Reagan's pussy tugged at his balls. He was caught between the perfect rhythm of his two beloved musicians, and as their tempo increased, so did his pleasure and excitement until he was coming without knowing the exact instant his peak had been reached. His ass tightened around Trey's cock, and Trey began to thrust faster as he sought his own release. Ethan reached between Reagan's legs and frantically rubbed her clit until her back arched and her pussy tightened around Ethan's spent cock. Trey and Reagan cried out in unison as they climaxed together. Ethan groaned in relief—it would have been terribly greedy of him to take all the pleasure for himself—and then collapsed against Reagan, snuggling into her neck and inhaling the sweet vanilla fragrance of her skin mixed with the sharper scents of sweat and sex. Trey relaxed against his back, and Ethan shifted onto his elbows, so he and Trey didn't completely crush Reagan, though she wrapped her arms around him to pull him closer. She opened her eyes and smiled up at Ethan.

"I love you," she said. After a long moment when her smile widened even more, she looked behind Ethan's shoulders. "And you," she said. "I love you."

Ethan could see his face and Trey's reflected in her lovely blue eyes, and he knew without a doubt that she did love them both and that they were blessed to share her devotion.

Here, wrapped in a cocoon of love and affection, mutual attraction and sexual gratification, it was easy to forget that much of the outside world was against their extraordinary love.

With shaky arms, Trey pushed off Ethan's back and disappeared into the bathroom. Ethan tried to melt into Reagan's limp body so he didn't have to move. Not yet. He'd missed them both terribly and wasn't ready to return to being a separate person.

"How did your brothers take the news?" Reagan asked, her hands gently massaging his back.

He snorted softly. "Juan mostly wanted to know how we have sex."

"Tell him very well, thank you." Reagan kissed his neck.

"And Carlos refuses to speak to me."

Her gentle kisses stopped as she shifted her head to stare up at him. "I'm sorry. I know you're close."

Ethan shrugged. He figured Carlos would get over it or he wouldn't. His negative opinions about Ethan's lifestyle wouldn't change who Ethan was. "It doesn't matter."

"Of course it matters." She touched his face, tracing its

contours with her fingertips. "I wish I'd been there to offer my support."

"You were there," he said. He caught her hand, bringing her palm to his lips. "You're always with me."

The mattress sagged beside them as Trey returned and cuddled against Reagan's side. When he smiled his typical impish grin at Ethan, Ethan couldn't resist shifting enough to kiss him. These two were both so precious to him. Both of them. Precious. He hoped they never again spent time apart.

"What did I miss?" Trey asked.

"Reagan's guilt trip," Ethan teased. He pulled out to lay on his side next to her.

"I do feel guilty," she said. "You're both so good to me, and I've been so focused on my little problems lately—"

"Reagan, they aren't little problems," Ethan said, slipping an arm around her waist. Finding Trey's arm already there, he settled his hand on Trey's elbow so they could hold her together.

"Your problems aren't little either," she said. "Coming out to your family couldn't have been easy, and I wasn't there for you. I kinda just fluffed it off. But you're always there for me. Trey is always there for me. Whenever I need you, no matter what the problem, you never let me falter. I haven't thanked either of you for being so wonderful. I've been taking your love and support for granted, and I'm sorry I didn't recognize what I've been doing."

Ethan lifted his head and met Trey's eyes. They exchange a look of incredulity. Did Reagan really feel like she was taking advantage of their love? He probably shouldn't speak for them both, but in this case he knew they were on the same page.

"You don't have to thank us or apologize for needing us, silly," Ethan said. "You should take our love and support for granted, because we love and support you. Always."

"Always," Trey echoed with a nod.

"I know that when I need your support," Ethan said, "I can count on it and on you, just as you can count on me."

"And me," Trey said.

Reagan placed a hand on Trey's head and stroked back the silky black strands to reveal a slender scar that curved over his ear. Ethan hated that scar, not because it disfigured an otherwise perfect head, but because it reminded him that Trey had been hurt. Long before he'd met Trey, Trey had almost died. Some homophobic asshole had hit him in the head with a baseball bat. Ethan didn't like to think of

Trey in pain and mortal danger any more than he liked to think of something harming Reagan. He agonized over the thought of either of them being anything but gloriously happy.

"Promise you'll lean on me sometimes," Reagan said. "Don't treat me like I'm fragile. I can support you both."

"You do," Ethan insisted.

Her muscles relaxed and her fingers went still on the scar she was absently stroking.

"Do you feel better now that you got that nonsense off your chest?" Trey asked.

"Nonsense?"

"Like either of us would complain about you relying on us when you need to." Trey snorted and got a poke in the ribs for his taunt.

"H-hey!" she sputtered. "That was really bothering me."

"Noted," Trey said. "Can we go back to worshiping you now?" Trey scooted up so he could look down into her grinning face.

"Well, I suppose," she said, rolling her eyes at Trey and making Ethan laugh.

He remembered once thinking these two would be the death of him, but he knew better now. They were the life in him.

E THAN WAS INTENTIONALLY AVOIDING Butch. Not because he was afraid of his boss's wrath for his unexpected leave of absence in the middle of the tour, but because he had his mother in tow and she was determined to meet the mysterious mustached man. Not happening. No way. Not on his watch.

"It's very busy and loud here," Mamá yelled over the backstage din. "How do you stand this noise every day?"

"I live for our days off," he said. "Though watching them onstage makes all this chaos worth it."

Ethan didn't need to explain to his mother who *they* were, but he did have to watch how much interest he showed them in public. Trey and Reagan were engaged now and if anyone thought Ethan was coming between the two happy lovebirds, he'd be the villain. He didn't want to be the villain. He wanted the loves of his life to be happy. He'd do anything to ensure their joy.

"Good, you're back," Steve said as he approached them unexpectedly behind the stage.

Ethan was pretty sure Steve had never said more than two words to him the entire time he'd been in Exodus End's employ, so he was more than a little wary of his sudden eagerness to see him.

Mamá stared at Steve with wide eyes. Maybe it was because he was so tall or so shirtless or had gorgeous long brown hair or could wear a pair of white leather pants without looking like a tool, but Ethan figured it was because he looked like he should be modeling underwear on a catwalk in New York.

"Can I help you?" Ethan asked, instinctively shifting his mamá's short body behind him.

"You used to be a pig, right?"

Ethan raised his eyebrows. Sure, people slurred law officers behind their backs, but it was rather unsettling to have it done to his face. Even if he wasn't technically on the force any longer.

"I was a police officer, yes."

"Detective?" Steve leaned closer eagerly.

He would have loved to have been a detective, but after he'd tried to prove his mariachi-band-playing brother was a hardened gang member, he doubted he possessed the right instincts. "Beat cop."

"You took that a bit too literally, am I right?" Steve laughed.

Ethan forced a terse smile. Yes, he'd beat up a couple of perpetrators while he'd been on the force, but that wasn't why he'd been a beat cop. "I was a patrolman. Why do you ask?"

"Sam denies his involvement, but I know he's behind everything. I know it. And I need someone to prove it. I figured you'd be a good candidate since he ruined Reagan's reputation, but I'll just hire someone. A PI or something. Sorry to bother you." He turned to go, but Ethan caught his arm.

"No idea what you're talking about," Ethan said. "But if it involves protecting Reagan, I'm your guy."

With Mamá as a witness, Steve filled Ethan in on a few goings-on that had happened in his absence—and which Reagan had kept to herself. The band thought Sam was responsible for starting the tabloid rumors, that he was somehow connected to the *American Inquirer* and its head editor, who just happened to be Steve's ex-wife. That was a bit too coincidental for Ethan's tastes. However, when Max had confronted Sam about his involvement that morning, Sam had denied everything.

"He wasn't even ruffled by our accusations," Steve said. "That made Max think he was innocent, but it made me think that Sam was expecting our confrontation."

"So what do you want me to do?"

"Find Bianca and figure out how she's involved."

"She's your ex-wife," Ethan pointed out. Why didn't he just call her and ask?

"Which is exactly why she won't tell me shit." Mamá cleared her throat at his foul language, and Steve flushed. "Pardon, ma'am."

"But you think she'll talk to me?"

"She might if she thinks you're a cop and she's under investigation."

"So you want me to impersonate an officer of the law, interrogate a potentially innocent woman, and report my findings back to her estranged husband?"

Steve nodded. "Yes."

"And you don't see a problem with this plan?" Ethan asked, not sure if he should be amused or exasperated.

"I'll pay you."

Ethan crossed his arms at his chest. "It's not the money. It's the law-breaking part I have issue with."

"Well . . . maybe you could get a private investigator license, and then it wouldn't be an issue."

"Well, maybe I'll look into that," Ethan snapped.

"Yes," Mamá said, nodding.

Steve waved Ethan away as if he were an annoying fly and stalked off.

"I think he's mad," Mamá said.

"He's just used to getting his way. Spoiled-rockstar syndrome."

"You're not going to help Reagan?"

He hadn't said that. He'd just said he had issue with breaking the law. He didn't have a problem looking someone up and asking them a few questions. He didn't have to pretend to be a cop to do that. He also didn't have any authority to persuade them to answer, so anything he was told would have to be offered voluntarily.

"I'll try," he said.

"Good," Mamá said. "And maybe get Magnum P.I. license while you at it?"

Ethan snorted and shook his head. *Thanks, Steve, for putting that idea into her stubborn head.* "I'll think about it."

Max had called for a rehearsal that afternoon because he wanted to add the acoustic version of "Bite" to the set list so he could play guitar onstage. He was so excited about playing—and

Max rarely got excited about anything when he wasn't performing— that no one had had the heart to tell him no. If Reagan was glum to be shifted aside, she didn't show it. She joined Ethan and Rosa in the wings to watch.

"I like this better," Mamá said. "Is not so loud. Except those drums." She winced and covered her ears with both hands.

Apparently Steve's idea of acoustic meant to dominate the song with impromptu drum solos, and no amount of arguing would convince him to switch to a single wooden block for the piece.

"He very stubborn," Mamá said. "Did you tell Reagan what he asks of you?"

Reagan turned her questioning blue eyes on him. He hadn't thought informing her about his non-plan was important since he didn't know how much information he'd get out of this Bianca woman.

"He wanted me to do a little detective work on the connection between the tabloid and their manager. I had to tell him I wasn't in the position to do so. From a legal standpoint."

"Don't you think he make a good Magnum P.I.?" Mama asked.

"Just PI, Mamá, no Magnum," Ethan said, trying not to show his amusement. "Magnum was the name of Tom Selleck's character on the show." In the 80s, his entire family had religiously watched *Magnum P.I.*, *Hill Street Blues*, *Miami Vice*, *Remington Steele*, *Cagney and Lacey* and any other crime drama of the day. Maybe that was why he'd wanted to become a police officer. He'd been an impressionable youth, and his mother had always been enamored with members of law enforcement. She still held them in high regard.

"He would be good at it," Reagan said.

Ethan shook his head. Evidence contradicted their claim. "Like I was good at figuring out who was threatening you at the beginning of the tour? Like I was good at finding evidence to associate my brother with a gang?"

"I tell Carlos not to wear that yellow bandana." Mamá crossed her arms. "I tell him this *many* times."

"You're too hard on yourself," Reagan said. "You'd be good at anything you set your mind to."

She stood on tiptoe to offer him a kiss of encouragement, but he stepped back before someone saw her kissing a man who was *not* her very public fiancé. Reagan scowled and turned her attention back to the stage. When the drum-heavy acoustic version of "Bite" came to an end—and Ethan had to admit it sounded fantastic—Mamá clapped enthusiastically, drawing a smile from a nearby member of the crew. Reagan tilted her head and squinted at the three guitarists onstage.

"I wonder if they'd listen to a suggestion," she said.

"What kind of suggestion?" Mamá asked.

"A musical one." Reagan shrugged and headed for the stage. Ethan couldn't repress the pride swelling in his chest as Reagan went to voice her opinion. She might not see it, but he recognized how far she'd come in the weeks she'd toured with the band. They all stopped what they were doing to listen to her. Unfortunately, Ethan couldn't eavesdrop over the din of the backstage noise behind him.

Mamá squinted at the musicians as if that would hone her hearing. "What she asking them?"

"No idea," Ethan said, but her bandmates were nodding and she was smiling, so she must be getting the results she wanted.

When she returned, Reagan rocked up and down on her toes and after emitting a little squeal of excitement gave Ethan's hand a quick squeeze before dropping it. "They said yes!"

"To what?"

"Cello."

Ethan blinked at her. "Cello? In a metal song?"

"An *acoustic* metal song," she said. "The guys want to hear how it sounds before they allow me to play it live, but they were open to my suggestion."

"They will love it," Mamá said, giving Reagan the encouraging hug Ethan longed to give her. "You have so much talent on cello."

Reagan's smile faltered. "Now I just have to go to my dad's house tomorrow and beg him to let me have my grandmother's instrument. She *did* leave it to me when she passed away."

Ethan frowned. As much as he'd like Reagan to make peace with her father, showing up at his house and demanding a cherished family heirloom seemed like a terrible idea. "Are you sure about this?"

Reagan shrugged one shoulder, but her pretty brow was creased with worry. "Maybe he won't be home. I know where he hides the key."

"You could just buy a new cello at a music store," Ethan suggested.

Reagan shook her head. "It won't sound as good as hers. And it *is* my cello, even if Dad insists I leave it with him. She gave it to me so it would be played, not hidden away."

"Your grandma be proud for you to play her cello for everyone," Mamá said.

Reagan gave her another tight squeeze. Ethan didn't mind sharing his mother with Reagan in the least. He loved that the two had forged such a strong bond. That bond was the reason it had been impossible for him to tell his mother he'd blown it with Reagan and that she had dumped his sorry, undeserving ass.

"There's my beautiful fiancée," Trey said, drawing Reagan into his arms for a kiss and a loving embrace.

Ethan's stomach knotted with longing. Not for sex; he never felt lacking in that department. But their easy and expected public displays of affection? He was completely left out in the cold in that regard. He didn't even *like* to be affectionate in public, so he wasn't sure why being excluded ate him alive. Mamá seemed to recognize his need for a hug and gave him a squeeze.

"This is hard on you," she whispered. "I hope it is worth it."

"It is."

She leaned away and reached up to run a hand over the back of his head and gently squeezed the nape of his neck. Her eyes were sparkling with unshed tears, so he had to look away. His gaze landed on Reagan and Trey, whose foreheads were pressed together as they talked music. Another time he felt like the third wheel.

"I'll go with you," Trey said. "We can announce our engagement. Maybe that will win your dad's favor."

Reagan snorted and then busted out laughing. "Oh yes, babe, you're his dream son-in-law." She ran a finger along the hoops in one ear and another down the colorful tattoo sleeve that completely decorated one arm. What Ethan wouldn't give to be able to touch him like that right now.

"I clean up pretty good," Trey teased as he kissed her nose.

"Do you want me to go along?" Ethan asked, steeling himself for rejection.

"Of course," Reagan said. "I might need a bodyguard."

"Are you going to tell him the truth, then?" Trey said, hope dancing in his gorgeous green eyes.

"*Fuck* that!" Reagan said. She quickly slapped a hand over her mouth. "Sorry, Mrs. Mendez," she mumbled from beneath her hand.

"S'okay," Mamá said, flicking her hand at their surroundings. "Lots of fucks I hear around this place."

Butch appeared unexpectedly at Ethan's side. "We need you

outside," he said. "There's a situation."

Reagan grabbed Butch by the arm before he could get away. "Butch, I'd like to introduce you to Rosa. She's my guest, so I want you to treat her extra special."

The man stared down at Ethan's mother for a long moment. He then took her hand and kissed her knuckles without breaking eye contact. Mamá giggled and said, "Your mustache, it tickles."

Nope, no way, not happening. Ethan grabbed Butch's shirt at the shoulder and spun him around. "What kind of a situation?"

"We caught people distributing free copies of *American Inquirer* to the fans waiting outside. A *lot* of free copies."

Ethan focused on Reagan. All the color had faded from her cheeks, and the smile had vanished from her lips. How could they do this to her again? Just now she'd just been so happy. So alive. So wonderfully *Reagan*. At the mention of that damned tabloid, she'd crumbled in defeat. He detected even fear in her. Ethan wouldn't tolerate this bullshit extinguishing his little spitfire.

"Are you fucking kidding me?" Ethan stormed off, seeking the source of Reagan's continued turmoil. This was bullying. And the only way to stop a bully was to confront a bully. He wouldn't rest until someone's throat was in his fist and he was glaring hatefully into their cowardly eyes. Unfortunately, he didn't know who that throat and those eyes belonged to just yet. But he would find out one way or another.

He found several members of the security team behind the building discussing the situation. Several bundles of printed papers were stacked at their feet.

"Did you see who was passing them out?"

"Some kids," Big Mike said. "Said some guy gave them twenty bucks each to hand them out to the crowd."

"And the guy?" Ethan said.

"He was wearing a blue sweatshirt and jeans. That's all any of them could tell us."

"I'd like to talk to them."

"They left."

"Hey!" someone yelled across the parking lot. "That's the asshole that Reagan is cheating with."

Ethan stiffened and turned his attention to the group of tough-looking biker women who were pouring over the pages of a copy of the *American Inquirer* and pointing at his picture and then at him.

"That *is* him!"

"Leave them alone, you giant asshole. Trey is in love with her! They're getting married!"

"Maybe you should go back inside," Butch suggested. "We know what to look for at the next venue. If this happens again, we'll be ready next time."

Ethan rubbed his forehead. Every instinct told him to circle the building and look for suspicious characters in blue sweatshirts handing out twenties to kids, but he was pretty sure he'd be lynched if he tried. Trey was the kind of guy women wanted to defend, and Ethan was the kind of guy they liked to tear apart. He was smart enough to know when his patrol experience would prove useless. Whoever was behind this—assuming the guy paying off kids was directly involved—was most likely long gone. Ethan knew what he needed to do to catch him in the act. He had to arrive at the next venue ahead of the buses and stake out the place until someone arrived with a delivery of tabloids. If he caught them distributing, he could get to the bottom of this shit.

However, he did have a few extras crowding his schedule the next day. Keeping his mother entertained and out of Butch's sight was minor compared to the potential backlash from Reagan arriving on her father's doorstep. In the past, he would have done what he thought was most important—and that was always catching the bad guy—but he was a changed man. He was one hundred percent devoted to Reagan and Trey, and he wanted their opinions. He couldn't guarantee that he'd follow their suggestions on how to proceed, but he did want to hear what they had to say.

It took him a while to hunt them down backstage. They were no longer in the wings where he'd left them, and ever-enthusiastic Toni Nichols was giving Mamá the gold-ticket tour of the place. Better her than Butch, he thought as he asked them if they knew where he could find Reagan.

"She was crying," Mamá said, glancing worriedly toward a set of double doors. "She didn't want anyone to think they've defeated her, so she went with Trey to calm down."

"They're so mean to her," Toni said. "And I'm sick of it. I should have thrown that Susan imposter out of a window when I had the chance."

"I'm not so sure she's the one that needs tossing out of a window," Ethan said.

"Well, I'm sure she does," Toni said, a defiant fist planted on each hip. "I can toss more than one jerk out of a window, you know."

Ethan was almost successful at not laughing at the image of this sweet, nerdy, completely endearing woman tossing jerks out windows.

Toni blinked at him behind the lenses of her large round glasses. "Are you laughing at me?"

Ethan shook his head. "I'm just glad you're on my team." He winked at her and then turned to his mamá. "Will you be okay here if I leave you for a few minutes?"

"I'll be fine. Go love Reagan." She waved him away. "She needs you more than I do."

"She should be in her dressing room," Toni said.

Ethan headed in that direction, hoping he'd misunderstood his mother asking Toni about Butch as he hurried away. After locating the correct room, Ethan knocked on the door and waited for a response.

"Who is it?" Reagan called.

"Your concerned bodyguard," he responded.

She opened the door, showing reddened eyes and anger-flushed cheeks. He loved that Reagan was emotional—her deep emotions made her a passionate woman, and from the start it had been her passion that had drawn him to her—but the amount of stress she was under concerned him. The warring emotions she experienced had to be bad for her. Part of him wished Exodus End would just fire her so she could find a moment of peace. Another part of him was too proud of her to seriously consider that wish.

"You okay?" he asked, knowing damned well she wasn't. Not really.

"Come in," she said. "What did you find out?"

He checked down the hallway to make sure no one was watching him enter her dressing room; they simply didn't need another story about their tawdry affair splashed all over the tabloids and the Internet. Thank God Trey had thus far managed to keep her from reading about herself online. The vast majority of the paparazzi who'd been following them were publishing their stories online. While he'd still been in Texas, Juan had showed him hundreds of online articles he'd wished he'd never seen. And the viral memes were even crueler than the pseudo-journalism stories.

As soon as the door was closed behind him, Reagan pressed up against his chest, and he wrapped his arms around her. He was surprised to find her alone. "Where's Trey?"

"Having a word with his brother."

"About?"

"Hell if I know. How many copies were distributed?"

"I'm not sure exactly, but there were several bundles that weren't handed out. The crew got them in time."

"Did you figure out who is behind this disaster?"

"Not yet, but I know a way I can find out. Would you be terribly upset if I left early for Little Rock in the morning and staked out the arena for suspicious characters?"

"We're going to my father's in the morning. Butch already got us a car to use."

"You're right, that's more important. I'll try to catch them next week in Grand Rapids or Minneapolis."

"Another tabloid will be out by then," she said, closing her eyes. When she opened them again, she smiled. "Even though he's never met you in person, we already know my father hates you; let's see how Trey holds up against him. I'd rather you try to catch the bad guy for me."

He hoped the relief he felt didn't register on his face. If she needed more support as she confronted her father, he wanted to be there for her. Truthfully, he didn't think he'd be able to hold his temper in check if her dad started belittling her. And as good as it would feel to tell the asshole off, his temper wouldn't make anything easier for Reagan. She loved her father. He was the only family she had. And Ethan knew that deep down she didn't want to be estranged from him. She just wanted him to love her and accept her, even the parts of her life he didn't agree with. If the one person on the planet who should love and accept her without conditions could do that for her, Ethan was sure she could do that for herself. It pissed him off that such a self-serving piece of shit still held that much power over her, but he understood. His own mother's influence would likely always motivate him.

"Are you sure you don't want me there?" he said. "I know how much he upsets you."

"I'm sure." She kissed him and rested her forehead against his shoulder. "I know you're dying to do some detective work. You're going to look into that private investigator license, right?"

He chuckled. "I think you've been spending too much time with my mother."

"Not nearly enough," she said. "Maybe we should go find her before she seduces Butch."

Ethan stiffened and glanced at the door. "That's a great idea."

"Aww, Butch would make a great stepdaddy." She laughed as Ethan jerked open the door and pulled her into the hall.

Not happening. Nope. Not on his watch.

CHAPTER 29

REAGAN GAPED at Trey and then snapped her mouth shut so hard her teeth rattled. He wasn't kidding when he said he cleaned up well. The green-and-black-checked dress shirt fit his trim upper body like a second skin, covering tattoos she thought were sexy as fuck but knew her father wouldn't appreciate. A snug-fitting pair of black pants would have made him look like he was off for a day at a respectable office if not for the Doc Martens he wore with them. He'd taken out the jewelry from his various piercings and wore his hair slicked back so it didn't cover one beguiling green eye. He pulled off the clean-cut look almost as well as he did the bad-boy look.

"Too much?" he asked, lifting his toes off the floor as he looked down.

Reagan shook her head. "You look great."

Trey slid both hands down his sides and into his pockets, jingling keys and change with nervously twitching hands.

"You ready?" she asked, finding his nervousness endearing. The man was a rock star, yet the thought of meeting her father had him jumpier that a cat on speed.

"I guess." He blew out a long breath before scratching at one clean-shaven cheek. "How did Ethan get out of this again?"

"He's on a secret mission," Reagan said, though Trey knew exactly what Ethan was doing that morning. She only hoped his stakeout produced results. "Besides, Dad might think something's odd about me introducing him to my new fiancé with my supposed ex-boyfriend in tow, don't you think?"

"Depends on if you're going to tell him the full truth or not."

"I'm not." She'd already decided that.

Trey held a hand out to her and she took it, noting that both of their palms were sweaty. "Then let's go," he said.

They headed out of Little Rock to Reagan's hometown of Benton, about thirty minutes southwest of the city. She gave Trey directions to the modest brick split-level that she'd lived in most of her childhood. The neighborhood was family friendly and less than a mile from the high school, so it had been an ideal place for her and her father. She was surprised that driving down the familiar streets warmed her heart and brought back sweet childhood memories she didn't often dwell upon. She hadn't thought she'd miss the place at all, but she'd been mistaken. Her teen years had been the backdrop for a bitter battle between father and daughter, but before she'd found a will of her own, they'd been happy. She couldn't deny that. It was midweek near the end of May, so Reagan wasn't sure if her father would be home or at work. She was oddly glad to see his car parked in the short driveway.

"I guess he's home," Trey observed.

"Guess so," Reagan said, unfastening her seat belt.

"I was expecting something more Addams Family—gnarly trees in the front yard and a thundercloud forever overhead." He leaned forward to peer up at the cloudless blue sky through the windshield.

Reagan slapped his thigh and laughed. "Perhaps I gave you the wrong impression of my childhood. It wasn't all bad. I wasn't locked in a tower and fed nothing but bread crusts and water."

"That's a relief," he said before exiting the car. Remembering his manners, he hurried to her side and opened the door for her. "Maybe we should have rehearsed what to say."

"I'll do the talking," she said. "You just back me up. But don't do an Ethan and immediately pick a fight with him. My dad treats me like a naughty little girl."

Trey's impish smile made an appearance. "You are naughty and little, but you're no girl."

"Not that kind of naughty." She pinched his ass. "Dad expects me to be a certain way, but I'm not the person he thinks I should be. That pisses him off."

"Hey, he's the one who raised you."

"*Not* to be like my mother. At least he tried to. Guess I got some bad genes in the mix." She winked at him to let him know she'd come to terms with all that long ago. It didn't mean she'd ever learned to like it.

"You never talk about your mother. I thought she'd passed away."

Reagan shrugged. "I don't think she has, but I wouldn't know unless someone told me. I haven't seen her since seventh grade."

While Trey puzzled out her dysfunctional family, Reagan went to the front door and found it locked. Rather than fish out her key, she rang the doorbell. Normally she'd let herself in, but she had Trey with her and she wasn't expected. She didn't want to give her dad a reason to start yelling at her the second she walked through the door.

A shadow appeared behind the frosted glass of the sidelight. A moment later the door opened and her father stood there, eyes wide. He had a few more wrinkles, his graying hair was a bit thinner on the top, and he'd lost at least ten pounds since she'd last seen him. Still, he looked pretty damned good.

"Surprise!" she said, throwing her arms around him and hugging him.

Dad barely lifted his arms before saying, "Is this the guy?"

She heard Trey's boot scrape against the cement step as he straightened.

"So you know?" Reagan asked, leaning away and putting on her I'm-the-happiest-woman-alive smile. "I'm getting married!"

"How could I not know?" Dad asked, his tone weary. "It's all everyone at work is talking about—the staff, the administration, the students. I had to take a day off just to get away from all the prattling."

"We're playing a concert in Little Rock tonight, so I thought I should bring him by to introduce you." She glanced at Trey, who was about five shades paler than usual—so, basically, transparent. "This is Trey Mills. My father Gary."

"Nice to meet you, sir," Trey said, wiping his hand on his slacks and extending it toward her father.

"You aren't fooling anyone," Dad said. "I know who you are. What you are. You're a *rock star*." He said it as if speaking the foulest pair of words in the entire English language. "A dirty, drugging, over-sexed, amoral, piece of debaucherous trash."

"You got that right," Trey said. Reagan was pretty sure she'd never loved him more.

"Dad," Reagan said, "don't be a jerk. You don't even know

him."

"I know all I need to know." He turned his back and shuffled into the house, but to Reagan's surprise, he didn't slam the door in their faces.

"Have I ever mentioned that my mom ran off to follow a rock band on tour and never came back?" Reagan whispered to Trey.

"Uh, no. You failed to mention that critical detail."

"My bad." She took Trey's hand and stepped over the threshold, leading him into the house. She noticed the new floors immediately. A warm brown wide-planked wood had been laid to replace the worn beige carpet. "The floors look great, Dad."

"Had them done before last Christmas," he said. "Not that you'd know that."

She'd spent Christmas with Ethan's family because holidays with them were actually enjoyable. That fact didn't make her feel any less guilty. "I'll spend this Christmas with you. Me and Trey. I promise."

"Or you can come out to California and spend Christmas with us," Trey suggested. "Get away from the cold. My parents have an awesome pool."

"Of course they do," Dad said as he disappeared into the small kitchen off the living room. "So when is the baby due?"

Trey's brow crumpled, and he looked at Reagan. "What's he talking about?"

"I'm not pregnant, Dad," she said when they'd entered the kitchen and found him filling a teakettle at the sink.

"Then why are you in such a rush to get married?"

"Maybe because I love him. Maybe because everyone loves him. You might even love him if you'd give him a chance."

"I doubt it." He set the tea kettle on the stove and turned the burner on.

"We hope you'll come to the wedding," Trey said. "Two Saturdays after next. In Las Vegas."

"Of course it is."

"Dad, please. Can't you be happy for me for once?"

He stared at her for a long moment, and she was sure he was going to at least smile, but he turned to the refrigerator and pulled out a carton of eggs instead. Trey reached for her hand and she took his gratefully, squeezing his fingers as if she'd never let him go. And frankly, she wouldn't. No amount of disapproval from her father could change how she felt about him. How she felt about Ethan.

She was glad she hadn't forced him to come along. At least one of them could escape this feeling of condemnation.

"We'll book a flight for you and a hotel room," Trey said. "You just have to show up."

"I might be busy that weekend," he said, taking a bowl from a cabinet and cracking two eggs into it.

They weren't invited to share his breakfast; it was his way of telling them they shouldn't dally. What had happened to her once close relationship with her father? Had she irrevocably destroyed it by leaving? She sighed wearily and pressed her fingertips to her eyebrow. She didn't want to argue about her decision to become an adult against his wishes. Not when there was a more important issue to argue about.

"I guess we'll leave you to your breakfast then," she said. "Trey has some hard drugs to do, and I simply *must* suck a few strange dicks before lunch."

Trey winced at her provocation, but she couldn't stop herself.

"Leaving so soon?" Dad didn't seem to care one way or another.

"Yep. And I'll be taking Grandma's cello with me." She headed toward the den where she'd spent countless hours rehearsing and not only because her father had insisted upon it, but because she'd loved playing.

Dad cut through the back of the kitchen and headed her off in the hallway, slamming the door to the den and standing solidly in front of it. "You can't take it," he said, his blue eyes blazing behind his square-framed glasses.

"It's mine. She left it to me."

"It's not in there. I sold it."

Reagan gaped at him, mouth opening and closing in stunned disbelief.

"He's lying," Trey said, standing behind Reagan and taking one of her shoulders in each hand.

"Are you accusing me of lying in my own house?" Dad bellowed.

"I am," Trey said. "There's something you should probably know about me. I give zero fucks what you think of me. I'm here for Reagan and only Reagan. And she does care what you think of her."

"Good," Dad said.

"It isn't good, it's awful. Have you tried to quash her spirit her entire life or just since she started thinking for herself?"

"I don't—"

"You have!" Trey yelled, throwing out a hand for emphasis. "Maybe if instead of trying to find faults in your daughter you could focus on everything amazing about her—her talent, her passion, her sense of humor, her capacity to love and to forgive. She'd even forgive *you* if you gave her the opportunity. Maybe you should take credit for raising her to be perfect, but maybe you can't. Maybe she's perfect despite you."

Dad stared at him as if he couldn't believe that someone was dumb enough to think she was perfect—which she admittedly wasn't—but it sure felt amazing that anyone, much less Trey muthafucking Mills, thought she was.

When Reagan realized her father was never going to change his mind about her, her shoulders crumpled and she turned to face Trey. "Let's go. There's nothing here for me." Not her cherished cello. Certainly not her father's love.

A latch behind her clicked and then hinges creaked as the door to the den slowly swung open. When she turned, her father was staring at the new hardwood floor in the hallway. The den still had the original worn beige carpet. In fact, as she stepped over the threshold and glanced around, she found everything in the room was exactly as it had been when she'd left years ago. The only thing missing was not her grandmother's cello, which stood slightly dusty in its stand where she'd left it, but the stool she'd spent hour upon hour perched upon as she played. She didn't understand the significance of its absence.

"You didn't sell it," she said quietly.

"I could never. It's yours. Take it."

She opened the closet and retrieved the worn case—also right where she'd left it.

"Reagan?"

She glanced up at her father, confused by the tremor in his voice.

"Will you play it for me one last time before you go?"

A simple request, but an oddly weighty one. She wouldn't refuse him, though. As much as she wished she could deny his demands, she still wanted his approval, no matter how temporary.

"My stool is missing."

"I took it to school."

She smiled. "Budget cuts again?"

He shook his head. "I keep trying to find a student to fill it, but no matter how many try, none are ever talented enough to outshine its original owner."

Reagan dropped her chin to hide the tears suddenly swimming in her eyes. She wasn't upset that he was trying to find her replacement. She was touched that he missed her enough to try. She hadn't realized Trey had left the room until he returned with a chair from the kitchen table. Kneeling on the floor, she polished the smooth wooden surface of her cello ritualistically. Removing her bow from its case, she tightened the screw to stretch the bow hair to proper firmness. A quick rub of her thumb over the bow had her reaching for a cake of rosin. She'd missed this, she thought as she tuned the strings. On tour, a guitar tech handed her a perfectly tuned guitar and pointed her toward the stage. That little perk didn't give her the same feeling of personal connection to her instrument that she felt when she prepared the cello herself.

She settled into the chair and lifted her bow, gliding it across the four strings, her ear listening for even slight discrepancies from perfect tone.

"She has a great ear," her father said.

Trey's ornery grin told her that his mind had gone to the gutter—as usual—but he didn't comment.

Reagan took a deep breath and started to play. What began as a perfectly orchestrated rendition of Bach's Prelude to Cello Suite No. 1 in G soon morphed into the classical-inspired metal riff that she couldn't get out of her head, the one she'd tried to perfect countless times on the electric guitar even though it had never felt right. It felt right now. The notes consumed her, tugging at the part of her soul intrinsically bound with music and sound. She relished the feel of the strings beneath her fingertips, the shivers of delight and excitement dancing along her spinal cord, and the familiar jerky motion of her right shoulder and elbow as her bow played across the strings. When the last note faded, she dropped her bow and sucked in a deep breath.

"What was that?" her father asked.

"That was amazing!" Trey said, clapping. "That's what that was."

"Something I've been trying to compose on guitar."

"Too many strings," her father said, shaking his head.

She laughed and nodded. "Too many strings. Maybe I should switch to electric bass."

"Please tell me you're joking," Trey said.

"Joking," Reagan said, sliding her hand over the body of her cello, the familiar curve and hard smooth surface like a cherished lover beneath her touch.

"How could you give it up, Reagan?" Dad asked. "Don't you see that you were born to play cello? Your grandmother saw it in the two-year-old who tirelessly watched her play. I saw it in you every time you touched bow to string. I *still* see it in you." He shook both fists. "My God, did you hear what you just played?"

"I gave it up because you made me hate it, Dad. The constant pushing, your insistence that it was the only thing good about me, that it was the only thing I should focus on. There's more to me than this instrument, Dad. That's what you've never been able to see."

She looked to Trey for his support, but he was staring uncomfortably at his boots. Or maybe that smirk on his face was pride. He probably thought she never stood up for herself to her dad, but she had. Or she'd tried to. She'd wanted her father to understand she had broader dreams than the ones he though were appropriate for her, but when he'd obstinately refused to let her find the path she wanted to take, she'd felt she had no choice but to leave. And she didn't regret that decision for a second. She only regretted that it had destroyed any admiration he'd once had for her.

He didn't say anything, probably because he knew she was right. "Your mother called a few days ago," he said quietly.

It took her a second to recover from the surprise before she said, "What did she want from you this time?"

He shook his head. "Nothing. This time she wanted something from you. I didn't give her your number. Should I have given it to her? I tried calling to ask you, but by then you'd stopped taking my calls."

"I shouldn't have blocked you," she said. "I just couldn't stand one more person thinking I am what I was portrayed as in that fucking tabloid."

"I burned it," Dad said, the first smile of the visit gracing his lips. "And then yesterday I got another one in the mail. At least I think that's what was in the envelope. I didn't bother to open it."

She had to hug him for that. After setting her cello in its stand, she approached him, watching him for signs of rejection. He didn't turn away when she lifted her arms in his direction or when she crushed him in a fierce embrace. They hadn't touched since she'd arrived, and the little wounded sound he made in the back of his throat as he squeezed her uncomfortably tight unleashed her tears—damn the hardened old bastard for making her cry.

"Was it sent from Seattle again?" Trey asked, shattering the rare tender moment with her father.

"I didn't check," Dad said. "It's in the trash can in the garage if you want to dig it out."

Reagan chuckled when Trey said, "On it," and left in search of a clue.

"Should I have given your mother your number?" Dad asked.

"What did she want?"

"What do you think she wanted?"

Reagan hoped she was wrong when she guessed, "A backstage pass to an Exodus End show?"

"You guessed it."

Reagan closed her eyes and released a heavy sigh. "Give me her number. I'll think about calling her. I'm not sure I want her back in my life. She's only good at one thing."

Leaving. Reagan didn't have to say it. Her father knew it as well as she did.

"Maybe she's ready to settle down," he said, his gaze shifting to the floor. "It was good to hear her voice."

Reagan shook her head and pressed a hand to his scruff-roughened cheek. "Stop waiting for her, Dad. She'll never come back to us. Not for keeps." He was a brilliant man. Surely he should have figured that out after two decades of being strung along by the woman. Reagan had given up on her long, long ago.

"She's a free spirit," he said, his laugh bitter. "I tried to squash that out of you, and you left anyway."

"I'm right here, Dad. And if you'd stop trying to rule my life, I'd be here a lot more often. I miss you. Every day I miss you."

"I miss you too, tiger, but you know I can't sit on my hands and keep my mouth shut when I know you're throwing your talent away on mindless rock music." He visibly shuddered at the horror of it all.

Reagan laughed. "You're about seventy years too late, maestro. Like it or not, rock 'n' roll is here to stay."

"So you didn't come to get your cello because you've had a change of heart?" He lifted his brows, his eyes imploring her to tell him what he wanted to hear. That look was uncomfortably familiar to her.

She pressed her lips together. "Actually, I hope to play some classically inspired metal music on it for about thirty thousand people tonight. Assuming I can convince four infamous, career-driven metal heads that it's a good idea."

"It's a great idea," Trey said, holding up a slightly stained envelope. It still had a few coffee grounds stuck to the surface. "Mailed from Seattle three days ago."

"Before the newest edition was published?" Reagan pulled the envelope out of Trey's hand and examined it. No return address. Her father's address had been handwritten. The postmark was the only clue to its origins.

"I'm guessing that rag is printed in Seattle," Trey said. "Or maybe that's not a copy of the new issue."

"I'm going to open it and find out," she said, tearing at the seal.

All three of them flinched at the headline accusing her of cheating with Ethan while Trey attended a funeral. Someone had circled the picture of her and Ethan climbing the stairs to their apartment in black marker and had written, *What kind of slut did you raise, Mr. Elliot?* beneath it.

Dad snatched the paper out of Reagan's hand, nudged Trey aside, and stormed out of the room. By the time Reagan caught up to him, he'd already lit the gas stove and was about to touch the paper to the blue flame.

"Wait!" she said, pulling the paper from his grip before he burned the evidence. "There might be more clues."

"Clues?" he said.

"Someone is out to get me. I want to know who it is so I can put a stop to this bullshit."

"Hopefully Ethan has already caught the jerk," Trey said.

"You know Ethan?" Dad asked, pinning Trey with a heavy stare.

Reagan cringed, hoping that Trey didn't spill the truth and destroy the rare ceasefire between her and her father.

"Yeah, I love the guy," Trey said, and Reagan's stomach plummeted. "He's one of my best friends."

"Never met a man who could be best friends with his woman's ex," Dad said, watching Trey closely.

"I'm a little unusual," Trey claimed, his face brightening with a smile.

Reagan laughed. "A little?" When she leaned over to kiss his cheek, Dad stiffened. "You're one in trillion, babe."

She took the tabloid to the counter and spread it out, searching through every page for anything out of the ordinary. She had to chuckle at the devil horns someone had drawn on her pictures. She didn't know who she'd managed to piss off, but their animosity was so over the top it was almost humorous. Almost. Another message had been written across the back of another page, again in black marker. *Don't you think it's time you reeled in your little girl, Pops?*

"Pops?" She looked at her father, who was scowling. "Who would call you Pops?"

"Someone with a death wish," Dad said, and Trey laughed.

"Good one, Mr. Elliot."

"You can call him Gary," Reagan said. "You'll be his son in about two weeks."

Dad groaned. "Maybe you'll change your mind by then."

"Don't bet on it."

While Dad glowered, she and Trey went through the tabloid a second time. She couldn't explain why, but being proactive gave her the detachment she needed to think objectively about the situation. She was certain that eventually she wouldn't have to get mad or hurt. She could get even.

Her phone rang and seeing it was Dare, and assuming he was looking for his brother, she answered, "He's with me."

"He's always with you," Dare said, "but that's not why I'm calling. You're late for rehearsal."

The rehearsal she'd arranged. "Sorry. I got held up at my dad's. I'll be there soon with my cello and your brother in tow."

"Just so you know," Dare said. "Sam insists on having a say in this decision."

"Sam?" Dear lord, man, loosen the leash.

"Yeah, it's in—"

"The contract," she finished for him. "See you in about forty-five minutes." Assuming there was no traffic, that should give them time to get back to the arena. She ended the call and turned to Trey. "We have to go now. I'm late for rehearsal."

She went back to the den for her cello and carefully but hurriedly packed it into its well-worn case. She twisted the screw to loosen the bow hairs before packing the bow in a separate case. When she lugged the instrument to the kitchen, she was surprised to find her dad laughing at something Trey had said. So it was official: Trey Mills could steal any heart he desired. Even the heavily guarded one that beat within her father's chest.

"Since you have the day off, Gary," Trey said, "maybe you'd

like to see your daughter rehearse. I won't go so far as to presume you want to watch her rock the faces off thirty thousand fans tonight, but if you want to—"

"I have some yardwork I should catch up on," Dad said, glancing out the window at the now-overcast sky.

Should? Did that mean . . . "Please come," Reagan said, plucking at his sleeve. "It would mean a lot to me."

"I guess I should watch while I have the chance. I sure won't be following you all over the country like some star-struck groupie."

No, that would have been the type of thing her mother would have done.

Reagan was pretty sure she was dreaming when Trey backed the rental car out of the driveway, and her father pulled out behind them in his SUV.

"Are you magic?" she asked Trey as she turned to make sure that her father was indeed following them to the arena.

"Maybe a little." He lifted her hand to his lips and kissed her knuckles. He then dialed Ethan through the car's Bluetooth system.

"Hey," Trey said when Ethan answered. "Thought we should warn you that Reagan's dad is coming to the arena with us. Figured we should come up with our game plan. I vote that Reagan tells him she's only marrying me because she can't legally marry both of us; what's your vote?"

Reagan's head swiveled in Trey's direction, and she forgot how to breathe for a second. "You will *not* be telling him that!"

"Why not? It's true," Trey said.

There he went with wanting to tell everyone—even her staunchly conservative father—the truth. How dare he?

"I'll stay out of your way," Ethan said. "Mr. Elliot and I don't get along."

"You've never even met him," Reagan said.

"I've argued with him on the phone more than once."

"He's a toasted marshmallow," Trey claimed. "Crusty on the outside, warm and gooey on the inside."

"You must have caught him on a good day," Ethan said.

"Speaking of catching someone, did you catch anyone distributing tabloids around the stadium?" Reagan asked.

Ethan sighed. "No. Maybe they know we're onto them."

"How would they know that?" Reagan asked.

"Hold on . . ." Ethan carried out the final word for several beats. "Guess he didn't learn his lesson the last time. Next time you see me, you might be bailing me out of jail."

"What?" Reagan asked. "Ethan? What do you mean?"

He didn't answer, but the car's robotic feminine voice replied, "The call has ended." A beep followed.

"What the hell is he talking about?" Reagan asked Trey, as if he shared a psychic link with Ethan.

"How am I supposed to know? Sounded like he's about to get violent with someone."

CHAPTER 30

B Y THE TIME TREY PULLED UP to the arena, the violence had ended. And Ethan had gone a lot easier on the punk than Trey would have. The lanky rocker with black and burgundy bangs held a baggie of ice pressed against one eye, but he didn't seem to be bleeding anywhere.

"I didn't do anything," Pyre insisted from his seat on the curb. Ethan, Butch, and half the security team had him surrounded.

"You!" Reagan bellowed as she leapt from the rental car.

Ethan managed to capture her around the waist before the sole of her boot connected with Pyre's thin face.

"I didn't do anything!" he whined.

"Then tell us why you're here," Butch said tersely.

"I told you; I just came to see the show. You can't hold me prisoner. You're not cops. I'm not trespassing or loitering."

Butch looked at Reagan, shook his head, and lifted his gaze to Ethan standing behind her. "We're going to have to let him go."

"Search his car," Reagan shouted, struggling to free herself from Ethan's cross-body hold.

"You can't," Pyre said. "In fact, I should press charges against your *boyfriend* for hitting me in the eye."

"Why are you really here?" Trey asked, crossing his arms over his chest. "You should know better than to come within a thousand yards of Reagan after what you tried to do to her last month. You should be in jail. How did you manage to skate out of that unscathed?"

Pyre lowered his gaze. "Can I go now?"

"Answer my question," Trey said, squatting down at Pyre's level. He hated the guy, but doubted he'd get a word out of him in this intimidating situation. Half a dozen hard-muscled security guards, any one of whom could have used their hands as lethal weapons, had the fallen guitarist completely surrounded.

"I know the right people," he said, flipping over the bag of ice and pressing it to his eye again.

"Which people?"

"None of your business."

"I'm making it my business."

Ethan crouched beside Trey, apparently deciding intimidation wasn't going to get answers from the guy. Trey glanced over his shoulder to see why Reagan wasn't kung-fu-fighting Pyre's face and found her animatedly telling her father all about the horrors she'd experienced at Pyre's hand.

"Just tell us who you're working with," Ethan said, his tone no longer threatening. Pyre flinched away from him regardless. "Is her name Bianca, by chance?"

Pyre's pasty face went an additional shade whiter. "How do you know Bianca?"

Trey's heart thudded. Were they about to finally figure out what was really going on?

"We know she's the head editor of the *American Inquirer*," Ethan said, "a tabloid owned by the same corporation that owns Exodus End's record label. We know she's Steve Aimes's ex-wife and that she's bitter about their divorce and would love to get back at him for the pain and embarrassment he caused her."

"We know you're in love with her," Trey said, taking a stab at their connection.

Pyre snorted and shook his head. "Hardly." Pyre glanced up, the eye not obscured by an ice pack wide in his ashen face. "I don't know who you're talking about."

Ethan sighed and grabbed Pyre by the shirt, standing to his full height and dragging Pyre up with him until the tall skinny guy was on his tiptoes. "Guess I'm going to have to beat it out of him."

The baggie of melting ice dropped from Pyre's hand, and his eyes searched the crowd for assistance. He must have spotted an ally because he began to wave both arms wildly. "Uncle Sam, a little help here?"

Ethan chuckled. "Do you really think the government is going to save you?"

"Uncle Sam!" Pyre yelled. "Help me. He's going to kill me this time."

Confused, Trey turned toward the building and saw Exodus End's manager staring at them like a vocalist who'd forgotten the lyrics to all his songs.

"You're his *uncle*?" Reagan bellowed.

"What's going on?" Gary asked, his hand resting on his daughter's shoulder.

Ethan lowered Pyre's feet to the ground, but didn't release the front of his shirt. Trey supposed Pyre's connection to Sam explained why a band as mediocre as Hell's Crypt had started the tour as an opening act. It also explained why Sam had insisted Reagan not press charges against Pyre to avoid a scandal. It didn't explain what Pyre was doing in Little Rock or tell them if he was connected to the tabloid distribution. Trey was pretty sure Pyre did know Bianca. Or someone named Bianca. He scowled. Best to leave the detective work to Ethan, he decided.

"Why are you here, Peter?" Sam Baily said, sauntering over to the group, obviously over his initial shock of being outed as the dickhead's uncle.

"I just came to watch a show," Pyre said, sticking to his original story.

Sam sighed. "I can't help you anymore. Sorry." He turned to walk away, but Reagan stepped into his path.

"I demand that you explain everything right now!"

If Sam had been slightly more flammable, the look Reagan gave him would have instantly ignited him into an inferno.

"I'd rather not," Sam said. "It's not a very exciting story."

"Don't leave me here with these people." Pyre was whining.

"Shut up," Trey said, "before Ethan shuts you up." Having a big strong boyfriend was beneficial for more than one reason.

"If Trey wants me to resort to violence on his behalf, you must be exceptionally irritating," Ethan said.

Pyre cringed. He did shut up, however.

Sam sighed, his gaze focused on Reagan. "What do you want to know?"

"Are you his uncle?" She pointed at Pyre.

"Yes, an unfortunate fact. My sister asked me to help him see his dreams become a reality. The unfortunate part is that he's not as talented as you are."

Reagan tried not look proud at Sam's admission, but Trey caught her little grin of self-satisfaction.

"I slipped his demo tape into the finalists for the contest. Fuck, I invented that contest so he could work with the guys. Thought maybe they'd pull him out of mediocrity. But you won the contest, Reagan, so he insisted his stupid band join Exodus End on tour."

Sam rolled his eyes, and Trey found himself liking the dude for the first time since he'd met him.

"I convinced the label to add Hell's Crypt to the ticket as the first opening act, the one that plays so early in the evening that most of the fans aren't even in the parking lot yet."

"Uncle Sam," Pyre said, his tone pleading.

"Shut up, Peter. I've saved your ass one too many times."

"I didn't do anything," Pyre insisted.

Sam charged forward, fury radiating from every inch of his body. Ethan released Pyre's shirt and stepped back.

"You didn't stalk Reagan backstage?" Sam shouted in Pyre's face. "You didn't try to scare her into quitting the tour? And when that didn't work you didn't drug her? Try to kidnap her? Practically strangle her to death?"

"I should have won that contest," he said. "If I'd played for them—"

"You still wouldn't have beat her! She could outplay you in her sleep. Go home back to your mama, boy. I'm not going to stick my neck out for you again."

"Just one more thing," Ethan said. "How is he connected to Bianca?"

Sam blinked, and the fury drained from his face as quickly as it had built there. "Bianca? Steve's ex-wife?"

Trey and Ethan nodded in unison.

"This again?" Sam shook his head. "I already told the guys that she and I are not connected in any way. I didn't sic the tabloids on Reagan. You can blame your sweet little Toni and her money-hungry mother for that entire ordeal." He strode off without another word.

Trey noted that somewhere in the confusion, Pyre had slipped away.

Reagan crossed her arms over her chest and watched Sam enter the arena through a back door. "Why do I get the feeling he's still hiding something?"

"Who is that man?" Gary asked.

"Band manager," Reagan said. "He's been a pain in my ass since the beginning of this tour, and I recently learned that it was Max who originally put him up to it."

"Who is Max?" Gary asked.

Reagan linked her arm through her father's. "I should probably introduce you to my band. Trey?" she called over her shoulder. "Could you grab my cello? I'm late for rehearsal."

"Sure," he said, too happy that she was getting along with her father to complain about being her errand boy. They had roadies for a reason. Ethan followed Trey to the rental car, leaning close to him as he opened the trunk.

"I know that guy and Sam are somehow related to the tabloid."

"Probably," Trey said with a shrug. "But we're fighting this a different way now. Remember?"

"The wedding thing?"

Trey nodded. "And now the cello thing." Trey lifted the instrument from the confines of the trunk, careful not to bump it.

"The cello thing?"

"Have you seen her play this thing?" Trey asked.

"She played for me and my mom in a music store once."

"And did you weep at the beauty of it?"

Ethan laughed. "No, but Mamá did."

"It's hard to deny her talent when she plays guitar, but there's no denying it when she plays the cello. Now I just have to make sure the boneheads in her band let her play it tonight."

"Why?"

"Because I know people." Trey grinned. There was more than one benefit to having a little black book the size of an encyclopedia. "And I can get them here to listen to her play. And if they hear her play . . ." He shrugged. The possibilities were endless.

"Are you friends with everyone?"

"Not everyone," Trey said, walking perhaps a little too close to the man beside him. He couldn't help it, though. Ethan had an undeniable force that drew Trey like hippies to a music festival at a marijuana farm.

"How did you get along with Mr. Elliot?" Ethan asked as he held the door open for Trey and they entered the darkened interior of a corridor. The air-conditioned breeze ruffled Trey's already misbehaving hair.

"You mean Gary?"

"He lets you call him Gary?" Ethan asked, shaking his head incredulously. "Well, I guess that answers that question."

"Oh, he hated me at first," Trey said.

"For what? Five minutes?"

Trey grinned. "About that long. Are you jealous?"

"Glad." Ethan leaned closer as if to kiss Trey's forehead, but decided against it and smiled at him instead.

Someday, Trey promised himself, Ethan would kiss him in public. Not today, obviously. But someday.

Reagan was in the middle of introducing her father to her bandmates when Trey and Ethan arrived with her cello.

"Trey's your brother?" Gary asked Dare, as if it were the most astonishing news he'd ever heard.

"Last time I checked," Dare said, releasing Gary's hand after a firm shake.

Reagan took the cello case from Trey and kissed him. She exchanged a loving look with Ethan, but it had to be killing them both that they couldn't greet each other properly. While she was setting up, Ethan leaned in close to Trey.

"So what did she tell her father about me?" Ethan asked.

"Nothing," Trey said. "And don't push her yet. They sort of made up, but their relationship is still rocky."

"I wasn't going to push her. I just wanted to know how careful I need to be."

It chewed at Trey's insides to advise Ethan not to openly display his affection, but what choice did he have? He was so looking forward to the couple of weeks they'd have together between the U.S. leg and the European leg of the tour.

"So guitar . . ." Gary said as he came to stand next to Trey. Ethan immediately took two side steps to put appropriate bro-space between himself and Trey. "Is that your only musical background?"

"Yep," Trey said, realizing Gary was trying to find common ground with him. Music was probably the only interest they shared a love for. Well, that and his daughter. "I started with folk music."

Gary crossed his arms, his gaze trained on Reagan, who had taken a seat with her instrument and was adjusting a microphone in front of the strings. "Interesting." He didn't sound interested in the least.

"My friend Eric plays every instrument known to man," Trey said.

"I'm sure you're exaggerating," Gary said.

"Not really. I'll introduce you to him. He has an unusual fondness for music teachers. He's convinced one saved his life."

"So does this Eric person play in an orchestra?"

"Naw, he's my band's drummer."

Ethan snorted and covered up a laugh with a cough as Trey went from golden boy to enemy with that omission.

Gary crossed his arms over his chest and said, "I see," in a clipped tone.

Ethan smiled as his mother joined them.

"Someone told me Reagan will play cello for us," Rosa said, giving her son a huge hug and then embracing Trey as well. "So exciting."

If Gary thought it odd that she hugged his daughter's fiancé and the man she was supposedly cheating on him with, he didn't indicate so.

"Uh, Mamá, this is Reagan's father, Gary Elliot," Ethan said. "Mr. Elliot, this is my mother, Rosa Mendez."

Gary nodded at her. "Mrs. Mendez."

"You can call me Rosa," she said with a welcoming smile.

"Nice to meet you, Rosa. Reagan is quite fond of you."

He didn't seem too happy about it. Perhaps because Reagan blew him off last Christmas to spend the holiday with Rosa's family. Or maybe it had more to do with his apparent dislike of Ethan. He hadn't looked directly at him since he'd arrived.

"I adore her. And I adore her cello." Rosa sighed like a teenager in love.

Her reaction drew a very small smile from Gary.

"How was your breakfast?" Ethan asked. "With Butch."

"Very nice. He makes me laugh."

Further details of her date were forgotten as Exodus End finally started playing the acoustic version of "Bite" onstage. Reagan's accompanying cello was so haunting, it made the skin the length of Trey's spine tingle. The fairly simple riff that Max played was echoed with an extra triplet by Reagan on cello. When the band reached the solo, she really cut loose, adding her special blend of classically inspired metal music to the familiar string of notes. Dare stopped playing midsolo to gawk at her. A measure later, the rest of the band was staring. When Reagan recognized she was the only one still playing, she stopped and lowered her bow, looking at each of her bandmates in turn.

"Too much?" she asked. "Sorry. I'll tone it down a bit."

"No," Dare said immediately. "You keep doing what you're doing. I didn't mean to stop playing. I just wasn't expecting . . ."

"She plays so beautifully," Rosa said, dabbing at one eye with her sleeve.

"And she gave it up to play rock music," Gary said.

As they replayed the solo, it was obvious to Trey that she hadn't given up anything. She'd found a place where her two loves could converge. About halfway through the dueling solos—on cello and acoustic guitar—Sam strode across the stage. When Reagan noticed him standing over her, she stopped playing again and stilled her strings with one hand.

"Why do you bother with guitar when you play cello like that?" he asked.

"Precisely!" Gary said, throwing his hands into the air.

Well, that was *exactly* what Reagan needed—Sam and Gary ganging up on her.

"I can play both," Reagan said, straightening her shoulders. "And well."

"*Well?*" Sam shook his head. "You're a goddamned prodigy, kid. When you're finished with this little stint with Exodus End, I can make you a star with that sound. It's like nothing I've ever heard before."

"Actually, there's already a metal band that has cellos. Three of them." Reagan drew her bow across her strings as if to punctuate her claim.

"But they don't have accompanying guitars. And they aren't a beautiful woman. And they sound orchestral. You sound *metal*. How do you do that?"

"Sam," Steve called from behind his drums. "Get off the stage. She doesn't want what you're offering. Trust me."

Reagan shrugged and while Trey couldn't know what she was thinking, he was sure she didn't want Sam directing her career. Sam probably could make her a star, but she'd be miserable. She was a free spirit, and Sam was a dictator.

"So I'm assuming you're going to let her play this with us tonight," Max said.

"Of course. Keep practicing. I have some phone calls to make."

"What I wouldn't give to hear that man's phone calls," Ethan said under his breath.

"Play more!" Rosa called to Reagan, who smiled and waved at her.

Trey was so enraptured by the new sound Reagan was creating with the most famous metal band in existence—he might be a bit partial—that he didn't know Ethan had vanished until the band decided to take a break. All five of the band members were talking at once as they shared ideas on ways they could incorporate the unique cello sound into other songs.

"The fans won't like their favorites altered," Max was saying, "but we have some lesser-known songs we can add to the encore."

"Please say you mean 'Under the Bridge,' " Reagan said, her hands clasped at her chest. "I love that song. I know it was never a hit, but it's my absolute favorite. And it would serve acoustic well. Or maybe Dare and Logan could play electric and Max could play acoustic."

"I think I can handle that riff on electric," Max said. "You can take the fast parts on cello."

Reagan beamed and nearly flattened him with a tackle hug. Max chuckled and squeezed her almost as hard as she squeezed him.

While the band hashed out how they'd play the song—they'd never played it live before—Trey leaned toward Rosa. "Where did Ethan go?"

Rosa turned to the space where he'd been standing a few minutes earlier and then shook her head. "I don't know. Maybe the bathroom?"

Maybe. Or maybe he was figuring out what Sam was up to.

CHAPTER 31

E THAN STAYED a dozen steps behind Sam as he trailed him through the backstage area. It kept him out of Sam's sight, but at the same time it made it difficult to hear everything the man said into his phone. Not too difficult, though, since Sam's voice carried rather well through the echoing concrete labyrinth behind the backstage area.

"The idiot got himself caught," Sam was saying into his phone. "I told you to keep him away. He's easily recognizable. And now they know we're related."

Sam had to be talking about his ridiculous nephew, but who was he talking to? Sam stopped at a hallway intersection and looked both directions. Ethan shifted into a shadowed doorway just in case Sam happened to glance behind himself. Sam turned to the right, and after a moment, Ethan started after him again.

". . . every media outlet in the area," Sam was saying when Ethan was within earshot again. This corridor was empty and had tile floors, so he had to tread lightly. "We don't have time to pull much together here, so work on national media attention for the Grand Rapids show."

Ethan stopped moving when Sam paused to listen. He'd surely hear footsteps following him when his voice wasn't booming. Luckily for Ethan, the man was a loud talker and a terrible listener.

"Yes, I know that's the same day the next paper comes out," Sam responded. "But now I think there's a better way to get rid of her."

It took every shred of Ethan's self-restraint not to confront Sam right there. He *was* trying to get rid of Reagan and he *was* associated with the tabloid in some way. Sneaky lying bastard.

Sam turned unexpectedly and reached for a doorknob. Catching Ethan out of the corner of his eye, he spun in his direction. "What are you doing here?"

"Looking for the bathroom," Ethan said. "This place is a maze."

Sam squinted at him. "Were you following me?"

"Were you talking about Reagan just now?" Hell, Ethan was already caught. He might as well get some answers. "If you want her to go, just tell her. You don't have to hurt her to get her to leave."

"Why would I want her to go?" Sam smiled. "Record sales are finally on the rise."

"That's probably because the band is touring and promoting themselves into an early grave right now."

Sam opened the door. "Those efforts are local. Big impact on a few people. In this day and age, you have to think globally."

Before Ethan could ask him what the hell he meant, Sam entered the room and closed the door behind him. Ethan rushed forward and pounded on the door. "I'm not finished talking to you."

"I'm finished talking to you. Go guard Reagan or do something equally useless."

Ethan tried the knob, but the door was locked. He supposed he could camp out across the threshold and wait for Sam to emerge. Or maybe he should share what little he'd learned with Trey and Reagan.

But when he made his way backstage, he didn't have the heart to lessen their joy. Everyone was certain they were on to something big with Reagan's cello-playing, and Ethan was sure Sam would figure out a way to twist that into some promotional endeavor. And maybe that was okay. At least this had something to do with music rather than Reagan's personal life. He didn't think she'd mind being famous for being talented.

"Where did you disappear to?" Trey asked.

"I followed Sam. Overheard him talking on the phone. We can expect another tabloid to be released next Monday."

"It will be all about our engagement," Trey said, patting Ethan on the chest.

Ethan wasn't so sure.

By the time the concert started that night, Exodus End had

rehearsed the two new additions to their set list half a dozen times. The acoustic version of "Bite" and the slightly altered metal version of "Under the Bridge," accompanied by Reagan on cello, had everyone pumped for the show. The bands, the crew, security, and hell, even the food stand workers were talking about it. Mad Dog, the head sound guy, was so ecstatic to have a new sound to fiddle with that he was humming show tunes—mostly "One" from *A Chorus Line*—under his breath. Reagan had finally found her own place in the band. Not just as a replacement for Max, but her *own* place. Ethan didn't stop smiling until a horde of media vultures showed up right before they were set to hit the stage.

Ethan wasn't sure what Sam had arranged, but not only was the press box overflowing with reporters, there were also dozens of them in the wings, on the floor between the crowd-control barrier fence and the stage, and milling around the backstage area. They kept asking each other and anyone who looked like they might have a little inside information what was happening, but no one knew a thing, and anyone who knew wasn't about to share their information with the press.

Ethan expected Reagan to look positively green with nerves, but there was an unexpected air of confidence about her as she was asked, cajoled, and downright harassed about the surprise "big event" the members of the press were there to cover. Ethan guessed she wasn't worried that she'd fuck up. She'd played in so many cello competitions, the pressure didn't rattle her at all.

As usual, the band entered the stage from beneath the floor, rising up from the depths in a mood-enhancing show of lights and fog, thudding drums, heavy bass, and wailing guitars. As a member of the security team, Ethan was on high alert. There were more people backstage and around the front of the stage than usual. Even if the press wasn't a physical threat to the band, someone who might be could blend in with that crowd. He also kept an eye on his vertically challenged mom, who was doing her best to see through the crush of bodies around her. Even if she'd worn a size 18 shoe, standing on tiptoe wouldn't have elevated her high enough above the crowd.

"I can put you on my shoulders," Ethan teased.

Mamá covered her chest with one hand. "No. It's okay. I'll just listen."

When the opening song came to an end, Max spoke to the crowd.

"Good evening, Little Rock! How are you feeling tonight?" The audience cheered on cue. Max extended an arm toward Reagan to draw the crowd's attention to her. "Our talented lady on guitar hails from just outside Little Rock, so this is her home turf."

"It's good to be home!" Reagan said into a microphone, waving at the crowd with both arms and adding an excited series of hops that made Ethan hungry for some alone time with her.

The crowd went insane over seeing one of their own on stage.

"I promise she has a surprise for you a little later, but for now we're going to 'Bite' you with the original."

As the band performed, most of the members of the press were talking about the surprise they'd been promised. Ethan wanted to punch them all in the throat so they'd have no choice but to shut the fuck up. Trey found him in the wings trying to glare a hole into the forehead of a particularly noisy reporter.

"How was Reagan before she went onstage?" Trey asked, standing on tiptoe to get a glimpse of the stage over the sea of heads.

"She seemed fine to me. Better than fine. Like she was in her element."

"There were so many reporters around her, I couldn't wish her luck," Trey said. He waved at someone, and Ethan recognized Mr. Elliot at the stage margin. Either he didn't see Trey's greeting or he was ignoring him. Mr. Elliot had his complete attention focused on Reagan and was scowling at either her suggestive attire or the fact that she was rocking out on electric guitar. Maybe both made him cranky. Trey lowered his waving arm and wrapped it around Ethan's mom, who'd given up on being able to see long ago.

"Are you enjoying yourself?" Trey asked her.

"It's loud!" she yelled. "You play loud too. But good job."

Trey chuckled and squeezed her. "That's the same thing my mom says when she comes to a show."

While the band performed their usual plugged-in version of "Bite," Reagan, Max, Dare, and Logan had to perform near the front of the stage while avoiding the gaping holes in the floor. Out of sight beneath the stage, the stage crew was scrambling to set up their acoustic equipment on the platforms on which they usually made only their initial stage entrances.

After the song ended, the band dashed for the stage wings. Technicians plowed their way through the throng of onlookers to collect instruments while the security team cleared the steps and a path for the musicians to make their way beneath the stage for a second entrance. Ethan smiled when Reagan gave her father a hasty hug as she passed. He, Trey, and Mamá were too far away for her to see, but she did seem to be looking for familiar faces in the throng of strangers.

The audience began to speak in hushed whispers, and then there was a collective gasp as all the lights went out and the stadium was bathed in absolute darkness. From a security standpoint, complete darkness was a nightmare, but its effect on building excitement was unmatched. The mechanism beneath the stage groaned as two guitars began to play the much slowed intro to the acoustic version of the song. Max and Dare—seated on stools—slowly rose out of the floor together, playing a series of chords in harmony. Steve's drums and Logan's bass soon joined to fill in the undertones, and then the haunting but rapid notes of a cello filled the stadium, increasing the tempo of the song to its usual furious pace. They carried the intro for several measures longer than usual, and the crowd went wild as Reagan was propelled from the stage floor, bowing her cello as though she was at war with it. Camera flashes were going off everywhere, and there was no stopping the reporters from crowding onto the sides of the stage. At least no one rushed the performers. Ethan wasn't against tackling someone to keep the band safe, but he'd much rather allow himself to be carried away by the song. Toward the end, Max's voice faded first, followed by the drums and bass, and then the guitars, until Reagan was playing alone. She slowed the repetitive riff. Slower. Slower. Slower still. Until the song faded into oblivion on one final haunting note.

Reagan lifted her bow overhead, and the audience erupted into explosive applause. She looked so happy in that moment that Ethan's heart constricted. This was what he'd wanted for her all along—pride in her talent, a place to shine, acceptance of deserved accolades, and overwhelming joy in her music.

He and Trey exchanged proud smiles. The urge to draw him close overwhelmed Ethan to the point that he had to shove his hands deep into his pockets.

"Ah!" Mamá said, tears sparkling in her eyes. "Our Reagan, she is a keeper."

Ethan laughed. "We definitely won't let her get away."

THE SURPRISE PERFORMANCE MADE Reagan an overnight sensation. Fans weren't the only ones who'd gone nuts over the two new songs in the set list. "Under the Bridge"—a song previously overlooked by all but the biggest Exodus End fans reached the number one spot on iTunes in under twelve hours. Reagan's unique style of playing had been featured on TMZ, and was the buzz on every radio station in the nation. The press had even interviewed her father about her classical music background. Fan-recorded cellphone videos were getting millions of hits on YouTube. The only person who seemed happier than Reagan about all the recognition was Sam. Ethan was starting to think he'd been wrong to assume Sam was purposely trying to hurt Reagan. It seemed she really was just a publicity stunt to him and that nothing he did was personal. He'd put her through scandals for attention and now that her reputation was recovering, he was putting her talent in the spotlight, again for attention. Apparently Sam didn't care if she was attracting negative publicity or positive publicity, not when people were noticing. Even those who had scarcely noticed Exodus End were enamored. And with recognition came a tide of creepy guys Ethan was forced to keep at bay. Trey wasn't the only man who'd proposed to Reagan in the last couple of days. More than a few fans had declared undying love outside the arena after the concert, and when the band had toasted Reagan at an impromptu after-concert bar hop, a couple of locals had tried to approach her, stars in their eyes.

Mamá had insisted she was fine with Butch dropping her off at the airport that morning, though Ethan wasn't fine with it. He'd wanted to say goodbye to her, sure, but he also didn't want *Butch* saying goodbye to her. They'd hit it off a little too well for his tastes. But Reagan was in need of her bodyguard today, so he couldn't shirk his duties. He'd already escorted two overzealous fans from the hotel restaurant during breakfast, and he was sure several of the dudes with press passes had stolen them from real reporters they'd rendered unconscious in the men's restroom.

He, Trey, and Reagan had had damned little time alone together since he'd returned from San Antonio, and the press, seduced not only by Reagan's talent but also by her recent engagement, wouldn't leave her alone. Ethan tried not to be jealous of all the affection she shared with Trey without any concern over who was watching, but he couldn't help but feel completely left out. Again. At least the bus was leaving soon. Maybe they could catch a moment's peace when they pulled out of Little Rock and headed for the upper Midwest. There were only three more shows on this leg of the tour. Surely he could retain his sanity for that long.

Ethan kept a sharp eye out for potential threats while Trey and Reagan said goodbye to her dad as they waited for the valet to bring his SUV forward. Mr. Elliot seemed completely accepting of his daughter's engagement to Trey—which was good. He also seemed to like Trey—which was baffling. He claimed to hate rock music and electric guitars and rock stars with loose morals; Trey was the embodiment of all those things. Perhaps Ethan had misjudged Mr. Elliot's ability to look past what he considered flaws to see the true person within. Ethan shook his head and caught movement out of the corner of his eye. Some teenaged boy was trying to catch a selfie of himself with Reagan in the background. He stumbled off the curb and almost fell on his ass.

"If you wait until she's not busy, you can ask her to take a picture with you," Ethan said.

The kid jumped as if he'd been caught committing a felony. "Seriously?"

"Seriously."

"So you, like, know her? Personally, I mean."

Ethan smiled at the awe in the kid's expression and nodded.

"Is she as cool in person as she is onstage?"

"Even cooler," Ethan assured him.

"I almost left after Sinners last night. Not a real fan of Exodus End. My *dad* listens to them."

The horror! Ethan thought wryly.

"They were pretty good, I guess." The kid shrugged as if he were talking about some unknown opening band. "But Reagan makes them cool, so I'm glad I stayed until the end."

It was one kid's opinion, and Ethan hated to even think it, but maybe Sam was right. Maybe Exodus End did need an image change to help them appeal to the younger generation. But then, maybe they didn't want to appeal to that generation. That generation tended to steal music online instead of paying for it, and if the band catered too much to kids, they might alienate the fans they already had. Ethan was glad he didn't have to concern himself with such a conundrum.

Reagan waved at her father as he pulled away and then gave Trey a tight hug and a tender kiss. "That went so much better than I thought it would."

"So you're ready to tell him everything?" Trey asked, his gaze lifting to meet Ethan's.

"Not yet. But I think soon. Maybe."

Ethan knew she needed more time, and maybe if the negative press stayed at bay for more than a day, she could handle telling her father that there was more to her relationship with Trey than she'd led him to believe. A whole extra person more.

"Is she not busy?" asked the teenaged boy beside Ethan.

He'd already forgotten he was there.

"Reagan?" Ethan tapped her on the shoulder, and she turned, dazzling him with a brilliant smile.

"Do we have time to go back to the room before the bus leaves?" she asked, the suggestion in her blue eyes making his pant legs shorten.

"Maybe," he said, now wishing he'd told her young fanboy to get lost. "Do you have a few minutes for a fan?"

Her gaze shifted to the kid beside him wearing an official Reagan Elliot T-shirt, and she smiled. "Of course."

"I just want a picture," he gushed.

When she wrapped an arm around his shoulders to get in the frame, he began to tremble uncontrollably. She threw up a set of rock horns on one hand and he snapped a selfie, cringing when he looked at it. "It's all blurry."

"I got it," Ethan said, taking the phone and adjusting it until the pair came into view.

"And, uh, could Trey—" The kid motioned to the other famous guitarist just hanging around a hotel breezeway.

Trey grinned and squeezed into the shot. Ethan feared the kid was going to have a stroke while sandwiched between the two talented musicians. Reagan kissed the kid's cheek, and Trey manhandled Reagan's boob in their next shot. Ethan laughed as they turned the opportunity into a hilarious photo shoot—the three of them playing air guitar, peeking over each other's heads like a makeshift totem pole, displaying silly duck faces, and checking their invisible watches as if waiting for an important event. Ethan wasn't sure how many pictures he'd taken, when Butch appeared at his side.

"Your mother is a delight," he said. "She made her flight without a problem."

Ethan handed the phone back to the kid and avoided looking at Butch. "Should we head for the bus?" he called to Reagan and Trey, who gave the excited kid a parting hug before starting toward the bus parked around the corner.

The fan immediately began flipping through the photos on his phone. Ethan was sure they'd be all over social media within ten seconds. And he was sure that would be good for Reagan's image. It often took a lot of positivity to overshadow even a little negativity, but her taking the time to be silly with a young fan was a start.

Ethan trailed behind Trey and Reagan with Butch at his side. Ethan liked Butch. Admired him, even. Butch was a great guy. But any man who even thought of making a move on his mother was at the top of his shit list.

"Do you think she'll be in Vegas for Reagan's wedding?" Butch asked. If he was trying to be nonchalant about his interest, he was failing.

"Probably," Ethan said.

"Do you think Reagan will invite me to the ceremony?" he asked loudly.

"Of course you're invited!" Reagan called over her shoulder. She stopped so she could loop her arm through Butch's and walk beside him. "So did you kiss her goodbye?"

Butch chuckled. "No. I chickened out."

"She likes mustaches," Reagan said, grinning at Ethan's discomfort. "She said so herself."

"I'll keep that in mind," Butch said, the corner of his thick mustache twitching with the hint of a smile.

Ethan didn't bother suppressing his snarl.

CHAPTER
32

S ITTING on the sectional in the back lounge of the tour bus, Reagan looked over the contract carefully, but it might as well have been written in Sanskrit.

"Don't sign it," Steve said, shaking his head.

"If she doesn't sign, we can't release the single," Max said. "She has to sign it."

She didn't *have* to sign anything, but she wanted to. She wanted something she was a part of to help the band. Sam had approached them about doing a live recording of "Under the Bridge" on their final U.S. tour stop in Atlantic City. Since Reagan was prominently featured in the live version, she either had to give up her rights (not happening), strike a deal (a scary proposition), or refuse to let them release the single with her cello accompaniment. Apparently whoever had written that shitty contract she'd signed when she'd won the contest hadn't thought to include a provision about having the right to release live-recorded music with her playing cello. She mentally stuck her tongue out at the person responsible for her original contract.

"At least have a lawyer check it over," Dare advised.

"Just let me pull one out of my pocket here," Reagan said, sliding her hand into the back pocket of her jeans. "Damn, I guess he escaped."

"The show is tonight," Max said. "If we want to get on top of this, we have to do it before the window of opportunity disappears."

"All you care about is money," Steve said.

Max shook his head. Everyone but Steve seemed to recognize what truly drove Max, and it wasn't cash. Max was afraid to fail, afraid to fall into obscurity after they'd risen to the top. And Reagan would love to help keep that from ever happening.

"I want to sign it," Reagan said. "I think having my name featured as part of an Exodus End release would be phenomenal. I'm just sure there's something in here that will bite me in the ass." She squinted at something called a non-compete clause. She was pretty sure it was a bad thing. Did it mean she'd never be able to release another song featuring her on cello or just not with another band? And what happened if she later started her own band and wanted to include some cello pieces—would that go against the contract? Or did the contract end when her contract for this tour ended? "What I wouldn't give to have a lawyer right now."

"We have a lawyer on tour," Trey said. He was reclining on the sofa, sucking a cherry lollipop and staring up at the lounge ceiling.

"Who?"

"Jessica Chase."

Sed's fiancé was indeed a lawyer, but not the kind Reagan needed. "She's not a contract lawyer, is she?"

"She plans to focus on sexual harassment lawsuits," Trey said, "but she understands legalese. Wouldn't hurt to ask her opinion."

Reagan and Trey found Jessica in the RV where most of the Sinners girlfriends and wives lived while they followed the tour. She was bouncing baby Malcolm in one arm and scowling at a seating chart in her opposite hand. Malcolm cooed and reached out for Trey as soon as he came into view.

While Trey entertained Malcolm, who giggled nonstop at his godfather's silly faces, Jessica read through the contract. "That non-compete clause has to go."

"How should they reword it?" Reagan asked, peering over the top of the page.

"Not reword it, take it out entirely."

"I don't think they'll agree to that," Reagan said.

"You have something they want, something they can't get from anyone else. Tell them it goes or you aren't signing."

Jessica didn't have any idea how hard the ball was that these people played with. "But—"

"No but. Those are your terms. And while you're at it, try to get this royalty percentage bumped up. Start at thirty percent. See how they like that." Jessica grinned at her.

"Thirty percent? That says three."

"Which is ridiculous. Tell them you'll take your exciting new cello music elsewhere. And also have them put in a termination of rights clause. You don't want these people to own the rights to your part of that song forever, do you?"

Reagan leaned forward as if a change in position would help her arrive at the correct answer. "No?"

"Hell no. They make their money off your hard work. In exchange, they connect you with an audience. To be honest, you're bringing the audience to them. You should get a much larger cut of the profits."

"Oh. I guess that makes sense."

"I know it's hard for you creative types to see beyond delivering your work to the fans, but this business will eat you alive if you let it. Don't let it, Reagan. If they don't jump on the contract changes you want, don't cave. Stand your ground. Make them feel like you don't need them. That you'd be better off without them."

"You sound like Steve," Reagan said, surprised that a woman as smart as Jessica would share an opinion with a hot-headed anarchist like Steve Aimes.

"Well, then, maybe you should listen to him."

"He'd have everyone completely abandon the establishment."

Jessica shrugged. "If the establishment no longer works, why keep it?"

Jessica wrote down the terms Reagan should fight for in the contract negotiations. "Uh . . ." Reagan swallowed the queasiness in her belly. "Maybe you should do this for me."

"I don't have the right license, or I would," Jessica said. "If you want, I can call some friends who do this sort of work."

"Can they negotiate this today?"

Jessica's eyes widened. "Today?"

Reagan nodded. "They want to record at tonight's show."

"They could record it and not release until the contract is signed."

"Don't give them any wiggle room, Reagan," Trey said. He immediately bent over to blow a raspberry on Malcom's stomach. "They give you what you want or you tell them to shove their contract up their executive asses."

"You can do this," Jessica said, patting her back. "But leave shoving contracts up their executive asses out of the negotiations."

Reagan chuckled, and after thanking Jessica for her expertise, she returned to her band to discuss her plans. Trey managed to sneak the baby out of the RV and onto Exodus End's bus, much to Dare's delight. One of those two Mills brothers needed a baby of his own, and since she would be the one that would have to make one with Trey, Reagan volunteered Dare for fatherhood.

When she told the guys her plans to negotiate the contract, they were supportive, but when she sought Sam to relay her demands to the higher-ups, she went alone.

She found Sam in the room he'd commandeered for his office inside the arena. She waited for him to finish his phone call before sliding the contract across the folding table that served as his desk. "I won't sign this unless the no-compete clause is removed, a termination of rights clause is added, and my royalty share is raised to . . . twenty-five percent." She knew she wouldn't get even that much and asking for thirty percent seemed insulting as there were four other band members who should also get their fair share of the royalties.

Sam slid the contract back toward her. "No."

"No?"

"You're wasting your time, mine, and theirs if you honestly think they'll agree to any of those terms."

"Oh," Reagan said flatly. "Well, in that case . . ." She lifted her gaze to Sam's and could tell he thought she would back down and just sign the damned thing. "No deal."

She didn't bother taking the contract with her. She had no plans of signing it. Before she could open the door, Sam said, "Sit down. Let's hash this out."

"I'm not signing . . ."

"The guys say they want this. Sit."

She sat. "The guys say they want it?"

"Max said they did."

"Is Max the only one you speak to?"

"Typically. He understands why the record label required I be the band's manager. I get shit done."

"You definitely tried to ruin me as quickly as possible," Reagan said. She pursed her lips into a sour scowl.

"I didn't try to ruin you," Sam said. He was busy scratching notes in a margin of the contract and didn't look at her as he spoke. "I merely used what you gave me. Be glad I haven't let her publish the entire truth."

"Who?"

"My little mole." He laughed.

"Bianca?"

"Why is everyone so fixated on Bianca?" Sam turned the page and circled a paragraph, marked out a couple of lines, and then wrote more notes in the margin.

"Her sister then?" Susan? No that was what Toni knew her as. "Tamara?"

Sam either hadn't heard her or was purposely ignoring her question. "I'll try for twenty-five percent split equally among the five of you, and we'll limit the no-compete clause to the next year and offer them first right of refusal in its place. I know they won't limit their rights to the live version of the song. They already own the rights to the studio version."

"I didn't come here to compromise."

Sam sighed and scratched through some handwritten notes. "The first right of refusal could actually play in your favor," he said, "but I'll take it out. You have no idea what's best for you."

She couldn't help but be ticked off by his condescension. Or the fact that she always felt like he was threatening her to keep her in line.

"Are you working in the best interest of Exodus End or yourself?" Reagan asked.

"Neither. So are you ready to go forward with this agreement?"

"The record label?"

"I can't get the ball rolling on this until you assure me you'll sign if—and that's a big if—they'll agree to these changes."

"Will you stop talking over me? I want to know who you're working for."

"Tradespar West. Just as Exodus End does. Just as you do."

"What about your nephew? Does he work for them too?"

Sam's fingers gripped his pen so tightly, it almost snapped in half. "Poor judgement on my part. I always did have a soft spot for my little sister. It seems she can talk me into anything."

Well, that would be one person on the planet. "So is Bianca your sister?"

Sam lifted an eyebrow at her, his expression asking if she'd been dropped on her head as an infant one too many times. "If Bianca was my sister, don't you think Steve would know that?"

Reagan nibbled on her lip. "So you don't know how Bianca wound up being the editor of the *American Inquirer*, how her sister ended up working for Toni's mom so she could snoop on the band, or if your nephew is distributing tabloid papers before the shows to spread my so-called notoriety?"

"I didn't say that," he said, pointing at her with his pen. "Sign here."

"You haven't even talked to anyone about the changes yet," she said, crossing her arms. "I'm not signing anything."

"It's all for the good of the band, Reagan. You have to trust me on this."

"I wouldn't trust you if you paid me."

"I do pay you."

"The band pays me."

"And who pays the band?"

"The record label."

"And who owns the record label?"

She felt like she was on some stupid game show, but she answered. "Tradespar West."

"Exactly."

She was missing something here. One very important piece of the puzzle. Someone had to make decisions for the corporation. "Who's the CEO of Tradespar West?"

"You're looking at him."

Reagan's head tipped forward as if the idea were too large for her brain to support. "What?"

"When I say you're not going to get a better deal than what's already in this contract, you can bank on that."

"Do the guys know you're in charge?" Is that why Steve was so insistent that they drop their label?

"I'm not in charge," he said. "The board of directors is in charge."

"And how often do they vote against your wishes?"

"Just once," he said. "When I wanted to break your contract and replace you with Peter. They were too afraid of the legal ramifications. So we thought we'd try other means to get you to leave, but now I'm glad you stuck to your guns. You're solid gold, sweetheart. Sign the contract."

She wouldn't sign that contract for anything now. Even if it promised her *all* of the profits, had every clause written to favor her best interests, and offered her a million-dollar advance, she still would have turned it down.

"You can use that for toilet paper." She slid out of her chair.

"So you won't be playing cello onstage anymore?" he said to

her back.

Her heart panged in protest. She loved that she'd found her niche and feared that if she stopped now, her moment in the spotlight would fade into oblivion and her music would never again see the light of day. Still, that was a risk she had to take. "Not if it benefits *you* in any way."

"It benefits us all, Miss Elliot. But it mostly benefits Exodus End. If they don't get their record sales out of the sewer, it's only a matter of time before they fall. Is that what you want for them?"

Of course she didn't want that for them, but she was having a hard time buying that their sales were that bad. She saw the crowds at their sold-out shows. A band couldn't have that many devoted fans and fall. It just didn't add up.

"They'll be fine without me," she said, and as much as it pained her to admit that, she knew it was true.

"Ah, well, it's your career. If you want to throw it away, that's your decision. If you see Max, can you send him in to talk to me?"

"Sure."

She was lying. Something told her that she should keep Max as far away from this man as possible. Max believed Sam's rhetoric, but would he still believe it once she told them that Mr. Samuel Baily wasn't only their manager, he was also CEO of Tradespar West? It mattered less to her now that Sam and his multiple companies were out to get her and more that he could take down Exodus End. Or try to. But why would he do that? She was still puzzling over those questions when she returned to the tour bus. The only two present were Trey and Dare, still fawning over Malcolm. If they didn't knock it off, her ovaries were going to decide a baby was exactly what she needed in her life.

"How did the negotiations go?" Trey asked.

"Not well," she said. "Dare, did you know Sam is the CEO of Tradespar West?"

He blinked at her and then chuckled. "Is that what he told you?"

"Yes. He's behind everything. The contest, Pyre getting off so easy after trying to kill me, the interactive biography, and the tabloid stuff. Everything."

"I highly doubt that, Reagan. He's just our band manager. When would he have time to run a conglomerate?"

"He isn't around much really," Reagan said, feeling stupider by the second.

"He was probably just trying to manipulate you into signing the contract," Dare said.

What Dare said made much more sense than Sam's claims, but she still wanted to believe that he was behind it all. Maybe Ethan could do some digging and find out if Sam really was in charge of Tradespar West. When she had concrete evidence, she'd warn the rest of the guys. Until then, she'd keep this to herself. "You won't tell anyone that I fell for Sam's teasing, will you?" she asked Dare.

"Of course not. He is the king of bullshitting. The man should have been a politician."

That was a scary idea. It was bad enough that he managed a chart-topping band and even more unsettling that he might run a conglomerate of entertainment businesses that could make or break any career. More than likely she'd pissed him off today. And that likely meant that he'd be after her again.

She wondered what other artillery he had in his arsenal of destruction.

CHAPTER 33

I T WAS so wonderful to have time off, and even though Reagan had waited anxiously for Sam's ax to fall, they'd ended the tour on a high note. Several tabloids had picked up on *American Inquirer*'s claims of her cheating on her soon-to-be-husband with her ex-boyfriend, but better-known magazines were reporting on the upcoming wedding instead. They still hadn't caught the lowlife who'd distributed copies outside the arenas, but she was growing a thicker skin now. The mean things some people said to her didn't affect her nearly as much as they had in the beginning. Or perhaps she was just getting better at hiding her feelings.

She, Ethan, and Trey were spending a relaxing afternoon poolside at the Mills estate when an unexpected visitor showed up. Well, she and Trey were relaxing poolside. Ethan was swimming laps as if he planned to race Michael Phelps in the near future.

"Do you ever answer your phone?" Sed asked Trey as he sat on the edge of the lounge chair beside Trey's.

"Not when I'm on vacation. I figured you'd be dealing with last-minute wedding arrangements until Saturday," Trey said.

"That's why I'm here. I need to ask you a favor."

"What is it?" Trey sat up, eager to do Sed's bidding. Reagan smiled and turned the page in the biography about Janice Joplin she was reading. Trey was like a faithful puppy whenever Sed was around. Whatever favor Sed asked, Trey would oblige.

"The band that was supposed to play at our reception backed out. They all got food poisoning or herpes or something."

"Me and the guys can stand in," Trey said. "Eric can sing and—"

"I don't want you guys to worry about entertaining other guests. I was hoping you could ask your brother to convince Exodus End to play."

"You want Exodus End to play at your reception?" Reagan asked.

"I've called all over town and every band for hire is already booked. So I started calling my friends, and they're all out on tour this summer. Literally everyone is touring. There's no one else who can do it."

"I'll do it," Reagan said.

Sed bit his lip. "You're in the wedding party."

"So just the guys then?" Reagan said, not feeling insulted, exactly, but definitely recognizing that she'd never be considered a true part of Exodus End.

"Not that I wouldn't want you to play. It's just that Jessica—"

"Would kill him," Trey supplied. Sed nodded.

"This wedding has to be perfect, or I'm afraid she's going to lose her mind. She has every detail involving her wedding party planned out and if I mess it up—"

"She'll kill him," Trey repeated, and Sed nodded again.

"Sounds fun," Reagan said. Reagan hadn't even started planning her wedding to Trey yet. She didn't even have a dress picked out.

"So do you think you can talk Dare into it?" Sed asked Trey.

"Dare? No problem," Trey said. "It will be more of a challenge to get the rest of the guys onboard. They'll have to rehearse. On their precious days off."

"If they're just playing their regular set list, they won't have to rehearse," Reagan said, setting her book down. She was getting absolutely no reading done. "I think they know all their songs by heart."

"They can't play their songs. They'll have to play stuff people can dance to. And our song. And all the other songs that Jessica picked out months ago. Fuck. Maybe I should hire a DJ and forget live music." Sed sighed and raked his hands through his short hair.

"Let me figure it out for you," Trey said. "I'll try to get a live band—Exodus End or some other band—but if I can't get one onboard, I'll find a perfect substitute. Let me worry about this. You worry about Jessica making it through the wedding without needing a straitjacket."

"You'd do that for me?" Sed asked.

"Of course."

"You're the best." Sed handed him a piece of paper. "Here's the song list."

"Hey, Sed," Ethan said, reaching for a towel to dry the water coursing from his hard, tanned body. Reagan was pretty sure he was dripping cold water all over her legs on purpose, but it felt too refreshing to complain. "What are you doing here? Trying to escape those last-minute wedding preparations?"

"Shit, that reminds me," he said. "I have a favor to ask you too."

"Me?" Ethan said, pausing with the towel pressed against his neck.

"Jessica has been tearing her hair out trying to figure out how to include you in the wedding. She feels awful that Trey and Reagan are paired up in the wedding party and you don't have a role."

"She doesn't have to include me."

Sed made a motion of part nod, part head-shake. "Just go with it, please."

Reagan was suddenly overjoyed that her wedding would be an impromptu affair. It was mostly for show anyway. And that show was going to be on the lackluster side.

Ethan nodded. "Okay. How can I help you?"

"Could you usher for us? Please? One of my cousins refuses to do it and of course, that's somehow my fault."

"No problem," Ethan said.

"Are you sure you even want this big fancy wedding of yours?" Trey asked with a laugh. "Both you and Jessica are completely stressed out."

Sed blew out a breath. "This will all be over in a few days, and then we can get to the good part. The honeymoon." He grinned and looked almost himself for the first time since he'd arrived.

"That *is* the best part. Where are we going on our honeymoon?" Trey asked, reaching over to take Reagan's hand and grabbing Ethan's as well.

"Europe," Ethan said. "When we go back on tour."

"I was thinking we should rent a private island for a week," Trey said. "No one for miles but the three of us."

"Yes, let's do that," Reagan said. Then they could love each other with their guards completely down. It sounded like nirvana to her.

Sed stood and leaned over to bro-hug Trey and then shake hands with Ethan. "Thanks for helping out, guys. I have to go find a pair of appropriate socks somewhere. Whatever that means." He waved at Reagan and hurried off to complete the next task on his list.

"Do you think we should do some planning for our wedding?" Trey asked Reagan.

"Don't wanna," she said.

"Me neither," Trey said with a laugh. "Guess I'd better call Dare."

"You'll probably have to bring out the puppy-dog eyes for this one," Reagan said. "Better invite him over."

By the time Dare arrived, they were sitting around an outdoor table and eating the delicious salad and sandwiches Gwen had prepared. She was running down a short guest list for Reagan and Trey's wedding, as only a few family members and close friends were attending. The bulk of the invitations were going out to the media.

Ethan hadn't said a word the entire meal. He'd become broodier than ever when his attempts to discover if Sam Baily was indeed the CEO of Tradespar West had been met with several layers of creative—and convoluted— business structure. The CEO was named as the business alias of a limited liability company that was in turn owned by another LLC partnered with a corporation in Switzerland. Reagan had begged Ethan to join them today for some playtime when he'd wanted to stay home and dig for more information. At least that was why she thought he was gloomy. Maybe he was upset about her marrying Trey.

"So who should I pick to be my best man?" Trey asked as soon as Dare had stuffed half a sandwich in his face.

"I'll do it," Dare said midchew. Somehow the man managed to look cool even when he was talking with his mouth full. "But only if you grovel."

"I have someone else in mind." Trey turned to Ethan. "Would you be willing to stand beside me as I marry the woman you love?"

Gwen sucked in a startled breath, but Reagan smiled. Trey had Ethan pinned with one of his sappy can't-live-without-you looks, and Reagan knew Ethan wouldn't refuse when lost in those eyes.

"Are you sure you want that?" Ethan asked. "It might make things a little awkward."

Having your boyfriend as your best man while you married his and your girlfriend was awkward? Why would Ethan think that? Reagan snorted at her thoughts. It would be totally awkward but also perfect.

"You could be my maid of honor instead," Reagan said.

"Or," Dare said, "he can wear one of those half-tuxedo, half-ball-gown costumes and be both."

"I think I'll stick to pants," Ethan said.

"So that's a yes?" Trey asked.

"No," Ethan said flatly before breaking into a smile. "That's an *of course*."

Trey leaned in to capture Ethan's mouth in a loving kiss. Reagan expected Ethan to pull away—both Gwen and Dare were present and Ethan never kissed Trey in front of anyone besides Reagan—but Ethan pulled him closer and deepened the kiss.

Gwen squeezed Reagan's hand. "Do you have a dress picked out?"

"Dress?" Reagan said flatly. "I don't have to wear a dress, do I?"

"I'll call my friend Sandra. She has a wedding boutique on Rodeo Drive. It usually takes weeks to get an appointment for a wedding consultation with her, but I'm sure she'll make room for us."

"Rodeo Drive?" Reagan squeaked, surprised Gwen rubbed elbows with the rich and crusty. The woman was such a free spirit and earthy, not at all the type of woman Reagan imagined frequenting Rodeo Drive.

"If you'd rather shop a thrift store for a secondhand dress—"

"We'll try the Rodeo Drive thing first," Reagan said. Hey, this would be the only wedding she ever had to half the men she loved, so she might as well get the dress. There wasn't time to plan anything truly special.

"I'll give Sandra a call. Trey?"

He was still making out with Ethan, so he didn't respond.

"Trey!" Dare said, slapping him hard on the back. "Quit swapping spit at the lunch table."

Trey drew away from Ethan—all glassy eyed with desire—and scowled at his brother. "What?"

"You and Ethan need to get fitted for tuxes," Gwen said. "Today. Have them send the measurements to some tuxedo rental place in Vegas so they'll have them ready when you arrive."

"Can't I just wear the same tux I'm wearing to Sed's wedding on Saturday?"

Gwen sighed. "If that's really what you want to do. Ethan, what do you think is best?"

Ethan flushed and stammered, "I-I don't have a tux yet. Sed just asked me to usher. Do ushers wear tuxes?"

"Depends on the wedding. You'll have to call Sed and ask."

"Shit, that reminds me why I made Dare come over," Trey said, turning to his brother.

"It wasn't because you wanted to show me how enthusiastically you make out with Ethan in your mother's presence?" Dare paused with a potato chip halfway to his mouth when Trey turned on the puppy-dog eyes. "Whatever crazy favor you're about to ask me for, my answer is no."

Trey added his big-brother-I-need-you pout to his expression. "How do you know I'm going to ask you for something?"

Dare turned his head to one side and closed his eyes. "Not falling for it."

"Fine," Trey said. "I'll just ask someone who cares."

Dare groaned and squeezed his eyes more tightly closed. "What is it?"

"Sed's reception band had to—"

"I'll do it," Dare said. "Put away the kryptonite."

Reagan pressed her lips together so she didn't bust out laughing. So Dare *was* aware that his baby brother's wishes were his greatest weakness.

"So you think you can get the guys to agree to play?" Trey asked, nonchalantly unwrapping a cherry sucker and popping it into his mouth.

"What guys?" Dare asked, his brow crumpled in confusion.

"Your band. You can't play a gig without them."

"What gig? We're on break."

"Sed's reception band backed out and they need a replacement. I promised him Exodus End would do it."

"You did what?"

"You know Sed saved my life. I owe him so much." Trey had put "the face" away, but he'd found a bit more Dare kryptonite in his bag of tricks.

"I'll ask them," Dare promised, laughing when Trey launched himself into his lap and sent his chair tipping backward, sprawling them both across the pool-side patio.

"You're the bestest big brother in the world," Trey said with the over-acted earnestness of a fifties' sitcom's adorable youngest son.

Ethan laughed. Reagan and Gwen exchanged eye rolls.

"Are you coming to Sed's bachelor party Thursday night?" Trey asked Dare.

"Are *you* going to be there?" Dare asked, sounding annoyed.

"Of course."

"Wouldn't miss it." Dare shoved Trey onto the patio so he could recover some of his dignity.

Trey hopped to his feet and handed Dare the piece of paper with all the songs Jessica had chosen. "These are the songs you all will be playing at the reception."

Dare's scowl deepened and deepened further as his eyes scanned the page. "You're fucking kidding, right? Exodus End doesn't play 'My Girl' or 'Cherish' or 'Can't Help Falling in Love' or *any* of the songs on this list except 'Freebird.' "

"You do on Saturday," Trey said, slapping his brother on the chest and turning him toward the door. "You'd better take beer when you break the news to the guys. They are going to *kill* you."

Reagan was dying to see the rest of Exodus End's reaction to the news, but she had a date with her future mother-in-law.

Trey slipped his arms around Ethan's neck and leaned over the back of his chair. "Ethan, will you help me set up for the bachelor party while Reagan pretends to be all girly with Mom?"

"She's a lovely woman. She's going to make a spectacular bride," Gwen said and patted Reagan's hand. "She doesn't have to pretend."

Buying a wedding dress was a once-in-a-lifetime experience that Reagan should be sharing with her own mother, but she'd rather be with Gwen. Reagan didn't even *like* her own mother, and Gwen was absolutely amazing, the kind of mother she'd have chosen if newborns actually got to pick the one they wanted.

"That's a fact no one can deny," Ethan said, his heavy gaze making Reagan flush.

"Time is getting away from us," Gwen said. "I'll call Sandra." She took several dishes with her as she went into the house to call her bridal-boutique-owning friend.

"Your mom is great," Reagan told Trey. "As is yours," she added, turning to Ethan as she thought of how sweet Rosa had always been to her.

"Have you called *your* mom?" Trey asked.

He knew damned well she hadn't, though she did still have her number tucked inside her purse in case she was stricken with a sudden case of insanity and felt the urge to talk to the home-wrecker.

"Nope. So what are you guys doing for Sed's bachelor party?" Yes, she was definitely changing the subject.

"Oh, just the usual stripper orgy," Trey said, nibbling Ethan's ear.

Trey was being even more affectionate toward Ethan than usual. Reagan wondered if it had something to do with their upcoming wedding.

"Male or female strippers?" she asked, picking pieces of tangerine out of her salad and popping them into her mouth one at a time.

Ethan laughed. "We do have a bit of a conundrum in that regard, don't we?"

"Not as far as I'm concerned," Trey said. "We'll get both. The more strippers the merrier."

Gwen dashed out of the house. "She can get us in right now if we hurry." She grabbed Reagan's wrist to tug her out of her chair, and Reagan grabbed the remains of her delicious sandwich to stuff in her face as she jogged after her.

"Trey, clean up the table," Gwen said as she pulled Reagan through a door and into the garage.

"Mom, that's why you have a maid."

"That's why I have a son," she said as she closed the door with a grin.

As soon as they'd left the driveway with Gwen in the driver's seat and Reagan still trying to finish her sandwich, Gwen turned to her and smiled. "Now we can really talk."

They hadn't been *really* talking before?

"Woman to woman."

Oh.

"So how are your parents dealing with this sudden decision to get married?"

"Uh, well, my mother doesn't know. And Dad knows only about Trey."

"He doesn't know about Ethan?"

"Nooooo," Reagan stretched out the final vowel until she had to draw a breath.

"This must be rough on him."

"My dad?"

"Well, probably," Gwen said, coming to a stop at a crossroad. There was no oncoming traffic, but she didn't pull out. "But I meant Ethan. He's being so strong for the both of you, but it has to hurt to be the one left out."

"He's not really being left out," Reagan said. "He knows this wedding is just for show. Mostly to get the press off my back."

"So you don't really want to marry my son?" Gwen asked.

"Of course I do. I just . . . I wish it was possible to marry both of them."

Gwen released a heavy sigh. "In a perfect world, you could."

They parked outside a store that made Reagan incredibly self-conscious about her old cargo shorts, black tank top, and worn black boots. She had a sudden panic attack that this would be like the scene in *Pretty Woman* where the boutique sales team refused to serve what they considered a lowly piece of filth and sent her packing.

But once inside, she found her fears were unfounded.

Dressed in a smart pink suit with diamonds sparkling on her fingers, around her throat and wrists, and on the lobes of both ears, Sandra was about Gwen's age and obviously adored her eccentric friend. The thin, elegant woman was more than gracious when she shook Reagan's hand loosely and waved at her assistant to offer her a glass of champagne and decadent-looking chocolates.

"Thanks so much for working us in," Gwen said, giving the sparrow-like Sandra a hearty hug. "I know your schedule is booked over a month in advance."

"Anything for you, Gwen," Sandra said. "This will be a delight. She's absolutely stunning."

Reagan snorted—certain the woman said that to every bride-to-be—and then covered her nose and mouth with one hand. "Sorry," she mumbled. She did have manners somewhere. She just had to remember where she'd left them.

"So what are you looking for, dear?" Sandra pressed her fingertips together in front of her chest, as if she were praying extra hard, and pinned Reagan with a pair of hazel eyes. "Something trendy or traditional? Sexy or elegant? Full-skirt or mermaid?"

"I have no idea," Reagan admitted.

The assistant was circling Reagan, eyeing every inch of her body until Reagan shivered involuntarily. The woman locked gazes with Sandra, and they said in unison, "The backless Sophia Tolli."

While the assistant dashed to a rack, Reagan was ushered into a dressing room. A moment later a gown was hung on a hook beside her, and Reagan gaped at it. The bodice was covered with feminine embellishments. The skirt, made of plain white satin, was long and full at the bottom, yet fitted around the hips.

"Not sure this will fit," Reagan said. "I have a big . . ." She almost said ass, but caught herself. "Rear end."

"And a beautiful back," the assistant said. "It will fit. And show off your curves."

"My small boobs?"

"Trust us. We've fitted thousands of brides in all shapes and sizes. This will look fabulous on you. Especially with that long neck of yours. Ah!" she said, as if enraptured by the length of Reagan's neck.

So Reagan allowed the assistant to help her put on the dress—which she wouldn't have chosen in a million years if left to her own devices—and then stared unblinking at the stranger in the mirror.

It was perfect.

The assistant opened the dressing room door and said, "Gwen?"

Reagan stepped out of the dressing room feeling beautiful and self-conscious at the same time. Afraid to touch the gown, she didn't know what to do with her hands, so just waved them up and down at her sides.

Gwen turned from her conversation with Sandra and pressed a trembling hand over her chest. "Oh my. Yes, sweetheart, we have a winner."

"Show her the back," the assistant said, taking Reagan's hand and leading her to a low pedestal surrounded by mirrors.

The back of the gown was scandalously low cut. She could see the top of her panties peeking up above the lace border just above the upper curve of her ass. Seeing the problem, the assistant—even though they weren't on a first-name basis—reached under the wide satin skirt and tugged Reagan's panties out of view.

"Wow," Gwen said. "What I wouldn't give to have the back to pull that off."

"You and me both," Sandra agreed. "And that neck that goes on for miles? She'll stop his heart, Gwen. Are you sure you want to risk your son's life?"

Sandra winked at Reagan, who flushed. She knew it was the woman's job to sell dresses, but she made Reagan feel good about herself. She couldn't remember another woman ever making her feel good about her body. Men who wanted to bed her, sure, but never another woman. She wondered if that was something most mothers did for their daughters. Hers had never been there to give her that needed level of confidence, so she didn't know.

"Do you want to try a few others?" Gwen asked.

Reagan shook her head, spinning slightly on the pedestal to make the skirt twirl.

"We'll take it," Gwen told her. "We need it by next Friday. Can you get the alterations done by then?"

"It doesn't need many," Sandra said. "I'm sure we can get them done if you're willing to take this one off the rack instead of ordering one."

"Is that okay with you Reagan?" Gwen asked.

"Yes." Hell, she wanted to wear the thing out of the shop.

Gwen was trying to talk Reagan into a pair of pretty white heels when Reagan's phone rang. Not sure how she'd ever convince the woman that she would be wearing her boots under her spectacular gown, Reagan gladly answered Dare's call.

"Hey, kiddo," Dare said. "I hope you aren't busy."

"Just picking out my wedding dress. Nothing important," she teased.

"We're going to need you to play guitar at Sed's reception. Max overdid it already and had to put his brace on again. Not every song. A lot of them need only one guitar, so I can handle all of those. But some songs need two guitarists."

She hated to agree without consulting Jessica. She knew the woman had every second of her special day planned to the minute, but she was sure Jessica would rather her reception songs sound good than have one of her forty-five-thousand bridesmaids sitting at the right table the entire time. And the guys *needed* her. She loved that they hadn't hesitated to ask for her help.

"Are you rehearsing at your house?" she asked.

"Yeah. All the guys are here already. And believe it or not, they're having a blast turning all these mushy love songs into metal masterpieces."

She believed it. She wasn't sure Jessica wanted all those mushy love songs to *be* metal masterpieces, however, but Reagan couldn't wait to hear what the guys were doing with the songs.

"Let me finish up here, and then I'll be over."

"Did you get a dress?" he asked.

"Yep. One I probably can't afford. But I figured what the hell, I'll just charge it to Dare's credit card." She couldn't resist teasing him.

"You do that, little sis. We'll see you when you get here."

"See you."

"And, Reagan?"

"Yeah?"

"Don't let Mom stop at any flea markets or junk yards. If you do, you'll never escape her shopping frenzy."

Reagan chuckled, figuring that the media for Gwen's artwork had to come from such places. "Thanks for the tip."

"I've been in your shoes more than I care to admit," Dare said.

Reagan glanced down at the white heels pinching the hell out of her toes. "I'd like to see that," she said, knowing he couldn't know she was teasing him again. "See you soon."

Gwen seemed disappointed that they couldn't spend the rest of the day finding treasures at flea markets, but she was gracious enough to take Reagan to Dare's house. On the drive over, Gwen shared stories about a mischievous young Trey and the older brother who thought his mission in life was to keep the little cuss out of trouble.

"Do you have any siblings?" Gwen asked.

"Nope. It was just me and my dad."

"You must have been lonely."

Reagan shrugged. "A little. But I'm making up for it now."

Gwen laughed. "Good for you. I know Trey has never been happier. I'm so glad he finally found what he needs in a relationship."

Reagan squeezed Gwen's arm. "He's so lucky to have a mother like you. I can't even tell my dad the truth, much less expect his blessing."

"He might surprise you," Gwen said, turning into Dare's drive and pushing the intercom button outside the massive gate.

"Is that you, Gwennie?" Reagan recognized the voice of Dare's butler, Harold.

"The one and only. I'm dropping off Reagan. Can you open the gate?"

"Only if you promise to give me one of your fantastic hugs when you get up here."

Gwen laughed. "You're the devil, Harry."

"Still waiting for you to divorce that rich plastic surgeon of yours."

"For you? Not a chance."

The gate rattled open, and Gwen drove up the long curving drive, coming to a halt beneath the portico of the sprawling colonial-style mansion.

As down to earth as Dare was, the man wasn't shy about flaunting his wealth. Or maybe he was just accustomed to luxury. He hadn't exactly been raised poor.

Harold let Reagan into the house and told her they were waiting for her in the music studio. He was too busy flirting with Gwen to give her more direction. Racking her memory of the day she'd met Exodus End and Trey—what a fun time that had been!—and jammed with the guys in Dare's studio, she headed down what she thought was the correct hall off the main foyer. She knew she was in the right wing by the décor. Music paraphernalia graced the entire length of the hallway. By the time she passed the glass wall that showed off the spectacular swimming pool and hot tub, bringing back steamy memories of her first "date" with Trey—lord, she'd been impulsive that day—she could hear the very heavy strains of an altered "Twist and Shout" coming from an open door at the end of the hall.

Reagan stood in the doorway and did the twist while she waited for the song to conclude. Everyone was smiling—even Max, who seemed to smile less and less frequently these days.

When the final note on Dare's guitar died away, she hopped up and down and clapped enthusiastically. "That was awesome. Love it!"

Steve's bass drum thudded as he shifted on his stool to lean across his drums. "If the whole drop-the-label-and-go-indie thing doesn't work out for us, we can do metal weddings for a living."

Max rolled his eyes and shook his head. If he didn't already know that Steve would *never* drop the subject, he wasn't paying attention.

"You can read music, right?" Dare asked.

"Of course. I played in orchestra for almost fifteen years."

"Right. Duh." He scooped a stack of sheet music and books of musical scores from a table and dropped them into her outstretched arms. "Can you go through this and find all the songs Jessica wants played? I think we're still missing a few."

"Aww, you guys are so sweet to do this for her," she said in a teasing tone, but it was true. What they were doing was incredibly sweet of them all. She was sure they had better things to do on their two weeks off.

"It's fun," Logan said.

"Is Toni here?"

He shook his head. "She's at my place working on that book. If it hadn't brought us together, I'd hate the damned thing. All she wants to do is work, work, work."

"And have sex," Steve said.

"Well, that too." Logan grinned, his entire face lighting up in a way that drew Reagan's appreciative attention. She couldn't help it; the man had a great smile.

The band spent the entire afternoon working through the wedding songs. They rearranged the order of the songs a bit so that the ones that required a second guitar were at the end. That way Reagan could do her bridesmaid duty for as long as possible. Reagan gave Jessica a call to make sure she was okay with that decision.

"Hey, Jess, how are you doing? Are you all ready for Saturday?"

"No," she said, her voice cracking.

"What's wrong? Is there anything I can do?"

"The caterer can't get enough oysters for the oyster bar. Some contamination issue or something."

Not a crisis in Reagan's mind. She was not a fan of oysters.

"My dress didn't come in yet. They assure me it will be here on time, but I won't believe that until I have it in my hands."

"If they said it would be on time, I'm sure it will."

"Some of our favors have Sed's name misspelled. It's three letters—how do you fuck that up?"

"People will probably get a kick out of it."

"They'll probably be wondering who *Ted* is and why I married him instead of Sed. And now the reception band has canceled on us. Sed's been running around all day trying to find a replacement."

"We've got that one covered. Actually, that's why I called."

"You found someone? Oh, thank God." Jessica released a deep breath.

"Exodus End is going to cover your song list." And by cover, she meant make every last song sound metal.

"Are you serious?" She laughed. "I can't wait to hear Max sing like Celine Dion."

Reagan snorted. Oh, he sang "My Heart Will Go On" wonderfully, but he didn't sound anything like the famous mezzo-soprano.

"They need me to play a few songs with them."

"Oh, no," Jessica said. "You aren't dropping out as a

bridesmaid, are you?"

Reagan guessed Jessica had heard so much bad news that she'd come to expect it.

"No, of course not. I can't wait to help you celebrate your big day. We want to rearrange the order of some of the songs so I can sit with the bridal party at the beginning of the reception and play with the guys for the later part."

Jessica sniffed. "You'd do that for me?"

"Don't cry. It's not that big a deal. We just wanted to make sure that it was okay to play the songs out of order."

"The first one has to be our song, but you can rearrange the others. That's fine."

"Great. I'll tell the guys. And, Jessica?"

"Yeah?"

"Sed wouldn't care if you married him in your underwear, oysters are gross, and I'm sure Ted is a lovely guy. Everything is going to be fine. You'll see."

"Thanks, Reagan. And tell the guys I owe them one."

Reagan turned to her bandmates. "She says she owes you all blow jobs," she said loud enough for Jessica to hear.

They all hooted and hollered their approval. Jessica just laughed. "You're so bad."

And it felt good to cut loose. Reagan hadn't realized how hard she'd been trying to be good for the press. She was going to enjoy every second of her time *out* of the limelight.

CHAPTER 34

TREY SHUFFLED forward and dropped his load of heavy boxes on Brian's kitchen table with a thud.

"Do you think you have enough beer?" Ethan asked, eyeing the stack of 24-packs.

"That's just the domestic stuff," Trey said, returning to his car for the brown bottles and the green bottles and some clear bottles too. Ethan helped him shove the cans and bottles into the tubs they'd filled earlier with ice.

"Did you get all the snacks?" Ethan asked.

"Yep. In the front seat. Couldn't fit them in the trunk."

They made a single trip to the car, overloading their arms and hands with sacks of junk food so they wouldn't have to go out more than once.

"I can smell those fajitas," Trey said, inhaling deeply as they entered the kitchen. His man could cook some damned fine Mexican food, and it hadn't been all that hard to convince him to give up his entire morning to cook.

Large metal trays lined the kitchen counter, and Ethan pointed to each in turn. "There's also tacos, enchiladas, quesadillas, toppings for loaded nachos, and I tried to make tamales, but that was a complete failure. Too bad Mamá isn't here."

Trey laughed and kissed his beard-stubbled chin. "Do you really want your mother at a rock star's bachelor party?"

"No way in hell," Ethan said, rubbing the back of his neck and grinning sheepishly. "But I do want some of her tamales."

"Maybe we'll go visit her before we head to Europe. I still haven't met your forty-five brothers."

"Six brothers," Ethan said, his smile fading. "And some of them are more close-minded than others. So maybe it's best if you don't meet them."

Trey knew he could win over anyone he tried to charm, but he wouldn't push the issue. He wanted Ethan to be relaxed and have a good time tonight. He was sure Ethan needed to unwind as much as he did, and bringing up topics that bothered Ethan would eat at him all night. Trey was quite familiar with his broody moods by now.

Sed came downstairs barefoot, wearing shorts and a T-shirt, his short hair still wet from a shower. "Dear lord, something smells good."

"My man can cook," Trey said, turning to the counter and lifting the foil off one of the pans.

"And my man can buy beer and junk food," Ethan said.

Sed laughed. "He is good at that."

"When is everyone supposed to get here?" Trey asked, glancing at the clock above the oven door. "I can't be expected to wait when I'm starving." He selected a strip of seasoned beef and stuck it in his mouth. The kick of cilantro and lime on his tongue made him moan in bliss.

Sed shook his head. "You have no self-control, Trey Mills."

"Where's the fun in that?"

Sed nodded in Ethan's direction. "Thanks for cooking, man. Appreciate it."

Ethan nodded, the hint of a smile on his lips. "No problem. I actually enjoy it."

"Not as much as I do," Trey said, sampling a strip of green pepper from the fajita tray and then an onion. And another strip of beef. Might as well grab one of those homemade tortillas while he was at it. Was that sour cream next to the guacamole? And Ethan's homemade pico de gallo? Oh lord.

The doorbell rang, and Sed went to let the guests into Brian's house. Sed's apartment was actually better equipped to sponsor a bachelor party, but the ladies were having their own gathering at Sed's place tonight, so Brian had volunteered to host. He'd taken Malcolm to his parents' house to babysit quite a while ago. It was their first time being responsible for their tiny grandson on their own, so Brian was probably showing them instructional videos and adding thick padding to all the walls and the floor or some such shit.

"I've got the strippers," Eric said, pushing half a dozen blow-up dolls into the house one after another. Trey could only imagine what he'd looked like driving down the interstate with a convertible full of blow-up dolls. Eric, followed by Jace carrying what appeared to be a bowling ball on a chain, carried the final sex doll indoors between his palms. It was shaped like a sheep. "This one is for little man." Eric squashed the balloon sheep into Jace's crotch. "Aw, the Love Ewe loves you already, Tripod."

Jace stuffed the Love Ewe under one arm. He was so used to Eric giving him shit that it no longer bothered him.

"I've got the movies," Brian said, rushing into the house and kicking a defenseless blonde blow-up doll out of his path.

"Porn!" Eric shouted, grabbing a sack out of Brian's hands. "What do we have here?" He pulled out a DVD case and scowled. "*Finding Nemo?*"

Brian's face fell. "Shit, did I grab the wrong sack?" He yanked the bag away from Eric and pulled out a copy of *Toy Story* and not the dirty one. "Then what did I leave with my parents?"

Trey snorted at his horrified expression and took another bite of the fajita he'd accidentally assembled.

"I'll be back." Brian rushed out of the house with his sack of children's flicks. Seconds later tires squealed as he peeled out of the driveway.

More of Sed's friends showed up and descended on the spread of Mexican food like a pack of starving hyenas.

"And you were worried about leftovers," Trey said to Ethan as he scraped the last bit of nacho cheese out of a crockpot and plopped it on his plate of loaded nachos.

Since Brian had yet to return with their traditional bachelor-party entertainment, Sed switched on a baseball game on the big-screen TV and they all crowded into the family room with their paper plates of food and their beer and their willingness to get loud and obnoxious. Jace sipped wine straight from a bottle, listening to Eric prattle with his mouth full. Sed was entirely absorbed in the baseball game, as were most of the other guys. A few guests were tucked into corners in smaller groups, shooting the shit with friends they hadn't seen in a while. Trey sat on the sofa as close to Ethan as humanly possible, surprised that he didn't squirm to put space between them with all the dude-type witnesses in the room. Ethan helped himself to Trey's enormous plate of nachos and sort of paid attention to the game.

Brian returned near the bottom of the fifth inning, looking relieved that everyone wasn't sitting around staring at a blank, porn-less TV screen. "My dad refused to let me have my videos back unless I brought him along. I hope that's okay."

"I can only stand about ten minutes of a crying baby," said Malcom—the man that the perfect, should-never-be-crying-for-ten-minutes-in-the-first-place baby was named after—as he entered the room behind Brian.

A hush fell over the group and everyone stared. Malcolm O'Neil was a living rock legend, one of the greatest guitarists who ever lived. And people revered him. Not Trey, of course. He couldn't stand the guy, the most arrogant, self-serving prick he'd ever met. But most people thought Malcolm O'Neil was a god. Even his son—Brian "Master" Sinclair—was a nobody compared to his father.

"Wait," Ethan said. "Malcolm O'Neil is Brian's father? Are you fucking shitting me?"

Wonderful. Even Ethan was impressed.

Brian and his dad went into the kitchen, everyone in the room rubbernecking to watch the great Malcom O'Neil pass by, and then when he was out of sight, they returned to watching their ballgame or bullshitting or stuffing their faces. All Trey could wonder was how Brian felt about having his father at what was supposed to be a fun and relaxing evening. Brian's greatest ambition had always been to make the man proud of him, so when his dad was around, he became this scarcely recognizable, boot-licking, nervous imbecile.

Brian returned to the room with a plate containing a broken taco, cheese-less nachos, the bottom half of an enchilada, and four bottles of Corona. His eyes met Trey's, and with a look of relief he approached the sofa, squeezing himself into the small space between Trey and the sofa arm. Even though Ethan shifted over to give them a bit more room, Trey was squashed between them like an uncomfortable passenger on an overcrowded subway.

"Couldn't tell him no?" Trey asked.

Brian glanced over his shoulder at his father, who'd been drawn into a group of his worshippers near the kitchen doorway. "What do you think?"

Brian set his plate on the sofa arm and twisted the top off his first beer. He downed the entire thing before opening a second.

"We agreed not to get too drunk tonight," Trey reminded Brian. "We have a lot of shit to do tomorrow to help Sed get ready for the rehearsal dinner."

"I can hold my liquor."

Trey snorted. "Sure."

"Who wants to play sex-doll poker?" Eric called over the crowd.

Trey had no idea what that entailed, but it sounded like more fun than watching Brian get wasted because his dad was a tool. Trey enjoyed a good baseball game, but this one featured two teams he didn't care enough about to hate and was a total snorefest of strikeouts.

"I'm in," Trey said, wriggling out from between Brian and Ethan. He smiled down at Ethan and asked, "Do you wanna play, E?"

"Does it involve public indecency with a plastic woman?" Ethan asked, his dark eyes fixed on Trey's.

"Probably."

"All right, then," he said, rising to his feet.

Trey caught Brian's expression as he shuffled between him and the coffee table. He didn't seem too happy about being deserted. "You can play too," Trey offered.

"Maybe later," Brian said as he tossed back the remains of his second beer and opened his third.

Eric had coerced Jace into playing, so with Trey and Ethan, Trey's guitar technician, Jake, and one of Sed's cousins, who introduced himself as Ben, they had six players either self-confident enough or foolish enough to sign up for Eric's crazy game.

"We need one more," Eric said. "Where's the groom?"

Sed was cajoled into joining with insults about his manhood. He took their taunting good-naturedly, in a surprisingly good mood now that he wasn't running all over town making last-minute wedding preparations. Once he was seated, Eric kept Sed's attention while Jace snuck around his other side and clamped a heavy black manacle around his ankle. The ball attached to the other end of the chain barely moved when Sed jerked his foot in surprise.

"What the fuck is this?"

"Ball and chain!" the guys chanted. "Ball and chain!"

"Take it off, Jace," Sed demanded.

Jace grinned. "Sorry, Sed. I don't have the key."

"Who has it?" Sed made a grab for Eric, but was hindered by the ball on his leg enough to allow his drummer to avoid Sed's grasp.

"Aggie has it," Jace said, calmly taking the vacant seat across from Trey.

Sed sagged back in his chair. "And how do I get it from her?"

"Dungeon or patience," Jace said.

Apparently Sed chose patience.

Eric made sure each player had a blow-up doll on his lap. Jace was stuck with the Love Ewe—naturally. Every time Trey glanced across the table at Jace with that blow-up sheep sitting on his lap, he couldn't help but laugh. It was even funnier than watching Sed drag that heavy ball around with him when he got up to grab another beer.

"So how does this work?" Ben asked, his arm hooked casually around his doll's waist.

"Low hand each round has to demonstrate proper lovemaking techniques with his doll. It's educational and fun," Eric said. "And maybe a little messy."

Sed gave Eric a stern look. "*Pretend* to demonstrate proper lovemaking techniques."

"Fine," Eric said, rolling his eyes at Sed as if he were the most boring man who had ever lived. "We'll just *pretend*. But the winners get to choose the sex act the loser has to demonstrate."

Trey lost the first hand, and the guys really took it easy on him. His sex doll—who he'd affectionately named Kiki—had to give him a blow job. He was fully clothed as he pretended to ram his cock into the very unsexy hole that served as her O-shaped mouth, but as the guys cheered her on, he got into it. He grabbed her by the ears as he bounced his crotch into her unnaturally peach face and then flipped her upside down, her oddly pointy legs sticking straight up in the air, and then he spun her around and around in circles—feet up, then down, and then up again as he twirled her body like a fan.

"The propeller technique," he said, still spinning the doll in circles. "Yes, Kiki, just like that. Suck and spin. Suck and spin."

The guys around the table were laughing so hard, Trey thought they might pass out, so he clutched the back of Kiki's head and pretended to blow the biggest load of his life into her mouth before returning to his seat. He propped Kiki back on his knee and then dabbed at the corner of her mouth with his fingers. "You let a little get away from you there," he said. "And after telling me you swallowed."

After a second round of laughter died down, Jace dealt the next hand.

Ethan leaned in and whispered, "I think we might have to try that out for real sometime."

Just the mental image of Ethan spinning around him had Trey gasping for air as he laughed.

Guys were now cramming into the room to watch the game. Jace lost the second hand and had to demonstrate doggie style on his Love Ewe. Eric made sheep baa-ing noises the entire time. Jace lost the next hand as well. Missionary with a sheep looked dangerous—what with the flailing hooves. When Jace lost his third hand in a row, he started to get suspicious, but he cow-girled the hell out of that poor sheep. Trey could honestly say that Jace pretending to get it on with a blow-up sheep while Eric made very inappropriate baa-ing noises was the funniest thing he'd ever seen. Even funnier than imagining Ethan as his dick propeller.

"Jeez, Jace, you suck at poker," Jake said. "But you do know how to fuck a sheep properly."

Jace stole the blow-up doll off Jake's lap and forced him to take the sheep. Jace seemed prepared to show that he could do a fake woman as well as he could bone a plastic sheep, but Sed lost the next hand. He was all sorts of serious as he pretended to get it on with his blow-up doll on the surface of the table. Trey didn't know whether to laugh or get turned on by the deep, rhythmic thrusts of Sed's hips.

"This brings back memories," Eric said, watching Sed's demonstration like a State Fair judge.

"You are taking this way too serious, Sed," Jace said, blowing out an uncomfortable breath.

"I can go all night," Sed told him.

"I'm sure you can," Jace said. "Trey, hurry up and deal."

"We'll finish this later, babe," Sed told his plastic partner before he pulled her off the table.

Trey attempted to stack the deck so Ethan would lose. He so wanted to see how Ethan would handle his demonstration. Unfortunately, Trey stacked it wrong—he'd never learned to cheat properly—and all the shitty cards he'd meant for Ethan ended up in his own hand. When Trey's seven high lost to Ben's king high— yeah, his hand sucked *that* bad—Eric immediately called for Trey to demonstrate a threesome.

So maybe he'd get Ethan out of his chair in another way.

"Not sure if I'm talented enough to demonstrate a threesome," Trey said with a crooked grin.

"Threesome, threesome, threesome!" chanted the guys

watching the game.

Ben tried to hand off his blow-up doll for Trey's threesome, but Trey just laughed. "Wrong kind of threesome, bro."

Ben scrunched his brows over a pair of blue eyes so similar to Sed's, the two men could have been brothers. "Huh?"

Trey rose from his chair, pressing Kiki's back close against his front with one hand gripping her unlifelike boob. Were there really guys out there who could get off with one of these things? "I'll do it, but I need some help."

Ethan's eyes widened when Trey took his wrist and attempted to pull him to his feet.

"I'll help," Brian said in a deep, slurred voice. "Just like old times."

Trey turned and lifted an eyebrow at Brian. Yes, they'd participated in multiple threesomes in the past. Come to think of it, Trey had once fucked Brian's wife in the ass, not long before she'd finally agreed to marry Brian. Trey had even stolen a kiss from the sensual guitarist that day—as it had been Brian who Trey had really wanted. Had always wanted. In Trey's mind, Myrna had simply been the glue between them, the puzzle piece that allowed Trey to be as close to Brian as he'd allow.

Trey glanced down at Ethan, who had slumped into his chair as if relieved.

There wasn't any danger in Trey demonstrating with Brian. Trey didn't have an uncontrollable, insatiable need to touch him anymore. He was surprised that Ethan wasn't more jealous, however.

"Kiki really likes anal," Trey said, grinning at the crowd, "So I'll get her worked up."

Trey wasn't quite as serious as Sed had been, but he didn't spin her around like a propeller this time as he bounced the doll's unlifelike rear hole on his crotch.

"Slow it down a little," Brian said, shifting to stand in front of Kiki.

"You don't actually *touch* each other, do you?" Ben asked way loud.

"Just a little," Brian said, his hand splaying over Trey's back.

Brian's intense brown eyes held Trey's gaze as they moved together in a familiar rhythm with nothing but a blow-up doll between them.

Why is he staring at me like that?

Brian had never held Trey's gaze when they'd shared the company of a woman. If he had, Trey would have been enraptured. But his feelings had changed. Now he just felt uncomfortable. What was Brian's deal? When Brian was drunk, he was always super horny and had incredibly poor judgement, but he'd never once looked at Trey the way he was looking at him now.

"They get the idea," Trey said, stepping back and releasing his hold on Kiki.

Unsteady on his feet, Brian crashed hip first into the table, and Trey had to grab him to keep him upright.

"I think someone needs to sleep this off," Trey said. "How many beers have you had?"

"All of them." Brian closed one eye and tossed a hand out for emphasis, which made him career into the table again. "And I washed them down with some whiskey."

Something was eating at him deeply. Brian never got that sauced unless he had a problem he didn't want to deal with.

Brian stumbled backward, almost sitting on Sed's lap, before he found his feet again. He then swallowed hard, his face going instantly white.

"Are you going to throw up?" Trey asked.

Brian shook his head, blinked hard as if overcome with dizziness, turned another shade paler, and then nodded. He rushed toward the half bathroom off the living room. Trey darted after him in case he needed help.

"Hey," Eric called after them. "It's my job to hold Sinclair's hair when he pukes."

And he was definitely puking. At least he'd made it to the toilet.

Ethan came to stand next to Trey outside the mostly closed bathroom door. "Need some help?"

"Once he's done puking his guts out, I'm going to put him in bed. Let him sleep this off." And find out what was eating at him.

Ethan showed none of the jealousy he usually did when it came to Brian. Maybe he'd finally figured out that Trey was over him.

"Let me know if you change your mind," Ethan said. He glanced over his shoulder before he leaned in and offered Trey a deep, searching kiss. Passion surged between them, and by the time they pulled apart, Trey was breathless with excitement. Catching movement over Ethan's shoulder, he shifted his gaze and focused on Brian, who was standing in the doorway with an odd expression on his face.

"I feel better now," Brian murmured. "But I should probably go home."

"You are home," Trey said with a chuckle.

Brian glanced around at his opulent new home. "Oh, yeah."

"I'll help you to bed."

"You sure your boyfriend will be okay with that?"

Trey shrugged. "Why wouldn't he be?"

After a brief, soul-searching look into Trey's eyes, Brian turned away, flushed the toilet, and then rinsed out his mouth and washed his hands in the pedestal sink. He leaned heavily on Trey as they went upstairs to the master bedroom. After insisting that he had to brush his teeth, Brian let Trey tip him onto the king-size bed in the center of his enormous room.

Trey pulled off Brian's boots and tossed them into the walk-in closet before helping him out of his jeans.

"You don't look at me that way anymore," Brian said.

"What way?" Trey asked, pulling back the covers.

"The way you look at him."

"I love him," Trey said, tucking a sheet around Brian's shoulders.

"And you don't love me anymore," he whispered.

Trey brushed a long lock of Brian's hair from his face. "Of course I do. Just not in the same inappropriate way I once did."

Brian shook his head and then closed his eyes. "It was never inappropriate. I was out of line for never acknowledging it. Not even to myself."

"Yeah, well, that's in the past. Don't let it eat at you."

"I miss you, Trey. For as long as I can remember, you were always there, always taking care of me."

"And who is taking care of you now?"

"You. In Myrna's absence."

"You're happy with her, aren't you? And with baby Malcolm?"

"Absolutely."

Trey grinned at him and shook his head. "So what's with the jealousy, Bri? Is that what this is? Are you jealous of Ethan? Of Reagan?"

"Why didn't you ask me to be your best man?"

"Uh." Trey's heart sank low in his chest.

"I've been your best friend for fifteen years, and—"

Trey covered Brian's mouth with his fingertips. "I should be marrying him, Brian. Not just Reagan, but Ethan too. Asking him to stand beside me as my best man was the only way I could think to involve him. And that's nowhere near enough to show how important he is to me. To both me and Reagan. Not even close. I actually wish you *were* my best man instead of Ethan." Trey straightened, drawing his fingers from Brian's lips. "I wish you could stand beside me as I married them both, but the world just doesn't work that way."

"You want to *marry* the guy?" Brian asked.

Trey smiled. "With all my heart."

"Then why did you ask Reagan to marry you?"

"Because I want to marry her."

"I don't understand how you can love two totally different people at the same time enough to marry them both. The sex? Yeah, I get that. I know from experience that it's awesome. But the commitment? I can't wrap my head around it no matter how hard I try."

"Which is why you and I never would have worked out. And I'm okay with that."

Brian stared deeply into Trey's eyes for a long moment and then nodded. "Me too."

"Good," Trey said. "Now the next time something is bothering you that much, try talking it out *before* you reach for the booze."

"I probably won't remember any of this tomorrow."

"I won't let you forget," Trey said. He crossed to the door, but paused with his hand on the light switch. "Hey, Brian?"

"Yeah," he murmured, his eyes already closed.

"Will you be my *second* best man at my wedding to Reagan next Saturday?"

"I thought you'd never ask."

CHAPTER
35

E THAN WAS on hold. Again. Every time he called *American Inquirer*'s main office in Seattle and tried to reach Bianca Aimes-Brennan, he was put on hold and left on hold until his patience wore thin and he hung up. Maybe someone else would have more luck reaching the woman. While he sat listening to the elevator rendition of "Wouldn't It Be Nice," he clicked his pen in agitation. He'd wanted to give Reagan the answers she sought as a wedding gift, but he was starting to think that he'd never get through to the head editor of *American Inquirer*. Maybe he could reach her sister, Susan Brennan, or rather, Tamara.

He hung up the landline and reached for his cellphone, dialing the *American Inquirer* office again, this time from a different number.

"You've reached the main offices of *American Inquirer*. Our office hours are eight a.m. until six p.m.—"

With a frustrated groan he hung up on the recording.

Standing behind Ethan's chair, Trey leaned against his back and kissed his ear. Trey's arms tightened around his chest, and Ethan lifted a hand to press Trey's hands against his thudding heart.

"Find out anything?" Trey asked.

"No," he said. "It's as if they're intentionally avoiding my calls."

"I'm sure they are. Why do you care so much anyway? You can't stop them from printing their stories. Unless they publish blatant slander, they're protected by the first amendment."

"I don't really care." Well, he sort of did. Unsolved mysteries drove him crazy. "I'm trying to figure this out for Reagan." He peeked behind Trey and found him unaccompanied. "Where is she?"

"Still in bed," Trey said.

The night before, they'd stayed at Sed and Jessica's reception until it had completely ended—long after the newlyweds had left for their honeymoon. Reagan and the guys of Exodus End had kept the party rolling far past the allotted end time. She'd been exhausted when he'd carried her into the house and tucked her into bed hours past midnight.

Ethan had kept to himself most of the evening. Even though some of the guests knew that he, Trey, and Reagan were a thing, most of them only knew about the Trey and Reagan side of the triangle. He'd worn his professional bodyguard look as he'd watched the two of them interact, hoping no one could tell how much he wished he could be a part of their good time.

"Now that Sed's big day is over, I suppose I should concentrate on mine," Trey said, scooting into the chair across from Ethan. "I know we still need to get rings. What else is there left to do?"

Reagan had her dress, and they had their tuxes on order. The all-inclusive wedding and hotel package was already booked in Vegas. Reagan had sat them down for about an hour to pick from the available colors and ceremonies and music-type stuff. Ethan shrugged. "Can't think of anything."

"How did Jessica spend six months planning a wedding?" Trey said. "It boggles the mind."

"Did you get the cake?"

"Included in the Vegas deal."

Ethan nodded, remembering that it was one of the options they'd had to decide on with their package. "License?" he asked.

"Included."

"Transportation to the chapel?"

"We'll have the car since we're driving there from Los Angeles."

"Bachelor party?" Ethan said.

"Sed's was enough for me, thanks. I guess we just have the rings to worry about, then," Trey said. "Should we go with six or just three?"

Ethan cocked his head at Trey. "You just need two."

"You don't really think I'm letting you out in public looking the way you do without a ring on your finger."

Ethan's heart overflowed with love, and he produced a short

laugh. "Well, seeing as I'm not getting married . . ."

"You don't want to wear a ring to symbolize our commitment to each other?"

"I wouldn't be against it, but I don't see why it's necessary."

"Because I want everyone to know you're taken," Trey said.

"And you always get what you want," Ethan said, his heart warmed by Trey's insistence that he be included in the exchange of rings, even if Ethan put his on with no witnesses and without the privileges—and ramifications—of a legal marriage.

"Always. So do we get six rings or three?"

"Why would we need six? Are we adding several more people I don't know about? Keeping up with you and Reagan is enough of a challenge without adding three more to our mix."

Trey rolled his eyes. "I mean one ring from me to you and a second from Reagan to you. And one from you to me and second from Reagan—"

"Oh," Ethan said, feeling like a total moron. Each of them would wear a ring from the other two. Duh. "That would be best, I think."

"I think so too. Let's go wake up Reagan and remind her how thoughtful we are."

"How thoughtful *you* are," Ethan said, taking Trey's hand and linking their fingers. After watching Trey erect that huge bro box to thwart Brian's advances at Sed's bachelor party, Ethan felt closer to Trey than ever and trusted him to never betray him. Maybe Ethan was finally comfortable enough to show his affection for Trey in front of others. The guy did turn him into a warm puddle of lovesick goo.

CHAPTER
36

STILL MOSTLY ASLEEP, TREY NUZZLED his face into the warm neck before him, inhaling the familiar scent of his lover. His cock twitched with sudden interest, and his hand slid slowly up a silky-smooth belly until he found the small pert breast he sought. He gently stroked the attentive tip until it pebbled. He dropped a soft kiss on Reagan's bare shoulder, hoping she was up for a bit of loving on their wedding morning. He was craving pussy and already imagining sinking into the slick warmth between her thighs. Unfortunately, she hadn't stirred yet. He knew why she was still unconscious. They had rolled into bed rather late. Or was four a.m. considered early? He was already up regardless. His cock had always been an early riser.

A hard chest pressed up against Trey's back, and a strong hand, slightly larger than his own, covered the back of his hand and pressed his palm more firmly into Reagan's breast, forcing Trey's gently coaxing touch into a deep and sensual massage. Ethan was always so rough and impatient, just how Trey liked him. Trey smiled in perfect contentment and melted into the hard body behind him. The rigid cock prodding him in the ass now had Trey's attention. Ethan was also an early riser.

"Good morning," his deep voice murmured in his ear.

Trey shuddered in anticipation. On second thought, maybe he was craving cock this morning. And if luck was on his side, he'd have both before he got out of bed.

That afternoon Trey would legally wed the woman before him,

and afterward, in a private exchange of rings, he'd emotionally marry the man at his back. In this knowledge, Trey experienced a contentment he'd never known possible. Their relationship was far from ordinary, but it worked for all of them. He didn't even care that the world might never know how committed they were to each other. He knew it and they knew it and that was the most important element.

"Reagan?" Ethan lifted his head over Trey to whisper in Reagan's ear. "You want in on this?"

"Sleeping," she murmured.

Ethan's hand moved from holding Trey's against Reagan's breast to slip between Trey's belly and her back. He tugged Trey more securely against his chest and nestled his hard, hot dick against Trey's ass before sliding his hand down. Down. Trey's belly quivered with anticipation. Ethan knew exactly how to get him off, and he didn't waste any time in getting down to business. Ethan encircled Trey's cock in a loose fist and stroked his length, prodding Reagan in the hip with each tug.

"Reagan," he whispered loudly. "Trey thinks you need to wake up and ride his cock."

"Sleeping!" she insisted. She launched a spare pillow into Ethan's face.

Trey chuckled. "Looks like it's just me and you this morning." He glanced over his shoulder at the gorgeous man massaging his cockhead in a most delightful way. If Ethan kept touching him like that, Trey would lose himself to bliss far too soon.

"She'll wake up if we rock the bed hard enough," Ethan said, a devilish gleam in his dark eyes.

Ethan released Trey's cock, and Trey rolled over in his arms to face him. There'd been a time when he'd thought there would ever be only one man he could love. He now knew just how wrong he'd been about that. He stared into Ethan's brown eyes, stroking the rough stubble on his strong jaw. Ethan smiled, his expression softening.

"If you keep looking at me like that," Ethan said gruffly, "I might have to go easy on you instead of fucking you until you scream my name."

Trey leaned in to kiss him, idly wondering if Reagan would treat either of them differently once she married him that afternoon. He didn't have any boundaries when it came to his pair of soulmates; he loved both of them with all his heart. There was no need to find balance when you gave everything you were—inside and out—to the people you loved. Ethan was getting better at it every day, but Trey knew he still struggled to figure out where he fit. Maybe Reagan had agreed to marry the wrong man. Maybe she should marry Ethan instead, because Ethan seemed to need the reassurance of forever more than he did. Trey was secure enough in his position in their relationship to step aside. The only problem was that he and Reagan were both in the public eye, so if Trey suddenly disappeared and she married Ethan, there'd be a huge scandal. Not that they hadn't lived through more than one of those already.

"What are you thinking about?" Ethan said.

Trey must really be unresponsive if Ethan was asking him that.

"About the wedding," Trey said. "Maybe Reagan should marry you instead of me."

"Actually, she should marry both of us," Ethan said, "but that's never going to happen. People just don't get us."

"As long as we get each other, that doesn't matter to me. Does it matter to you?"

Ethan shook his head. "But I think it matters to her."

Trey turned his head to look at Reagan. His heart warmed at the sight of her sleeping unaware of the concern her two lovers had over her continued happiness. Two fingers pressed against his jaw, and Trey turned to meet Ethan's eyes again. "Just don't forget about me when the two of you are legal," he said. "Promise."

"The two of us getting married won't change the way either of us feels about you. But if our getting married upsets you, hurts you, we should call it off. It's just a piece of paper, Ethan. What we have together means far more to me than propriety, legality, or what anyone in the world thinks."

Ethan shook his head. "I want the press off her back. And we both know this is the only way that's ever going to happen, her marrying you in front of dozens of witnesses. Maybe they'll finally leave her in peace."

Ethan was letting Reagan marry Trey because he loved her, and knowing how important her peace of mind was to Ethan made Trey love the man even more. Trey kissed him gently, but as was always the case between the two of them, the physical expression of their love soon became wildly heated and all either of them could concentrate on. Ethan's deep, seeking kisses soon had Trey out of his head with lust. Trey rolled Ethan onto his back and stretched out an arm to collect the large barbell stud from the nightstand. He could feel Ethan's belly quiver beneath his as he inserted the stud into his tongue.

Trey flicked the metal ball against his teeth and grinned at Ethan crookedly. "You're trembling, E," he said. "Do you think you're about to get your cock sucked or something?"

"Reagan is still sleeping," Ethan reminded him.

"That's her loss." Trey kissed his way down Ethan's muscular chest, being sure to remind him that he had his tongue piercing in by flicking one small nipple repeatedly.

Ethan's belly tightened beneath Trey's lips when he continued kissing toward his target. When he reached it, he licked Ethan's cock from base to tip and then set to driving his lover mad by flicking his tongue and barbell against the sensitive rim of Ethan's cockhead, round and round until the first bead of Ethan's pre-cum glistened against his skin. Trey gently inserted the ball at the tip of his tongue into the small hole at the tip of Ethan's cock.

"Don't," Ethan gasped brokenly, but as Trey carefully drew the smooth ball of metal in and out of the tiny opening, Ethan's big muscular body began to tremble uncontrollably. "Stop," he said through a harsh breath.

Well, okay. If he didn't like it, Trey wouldn't force the issue. He lifted his head, and Ethan groaned.

"Don't stop."

Trey grinned crookedly. Ah, he'd misunderstood. Trey took his time pleasing his lover, doing things to Ethan's sensitive head that he enjoyed himself.

Ethan usually had Trey by the back of the head by this point and would be thrusting into his mouth, but this morning he was stroking Trey's hair and watching him through heavy eyelids. Trey took Ethan's uncharacteristic tenderness as a challenge. He sucked him into his mouth, writhing his pierced tongue against the ridge on the underside of Ethan's cock as he bobbed his head rapidly. When he lifted his head to take a deep breath, Ethan grabbed him by both arms and tossed him onto his back on the mattress beside him.

"Enough," Ethan said in that deep sensual voice that made Trey's balls tighten and his ass quiver with anticipation. He knew he was about to get fucked and fucked hard. God, yes.

Ethan covered Trey's body and kissed him while he fumbled with the side-table drawer. Trey gasped in delight when a moment later a thick finger slick with lube pressed inside him. Trey tried to roll onto his stomach, preferring to be held face down when Ethan fucked him ruthlessly, but Ethan pressed one hand into his chest to keep him lying on his back.

"Slow down," Ethan murmured as he leaned over to kiss him.

His kiss was demanding but tender, and when he entered Trey's receptive body, there was none of the usual urgency. Ethan filled him completely, fully, and then lifted his head to stare down at him. "I do love you, you know," he said.

"I know."

"No matter what happens today, I'll always love you."

Trey blinked at the sudden emotion stinging his eyes. The words almost sounded like a goodbye. "Ethan?"

"Shh. Just let me love you."

Ethan trailed kisses over Trey's jaw and throat, thrusting his hips gently. Trey moaned when Ethan's hand circled his cock and stroked it in time with his slow, deep thrusts.

After a few moments, Ethan shifted to his knees and sat back on his heels. Trey lifted his hips to keep him inside, and Ethan stuffed a pillow under his lower back. Trey watched Ethan worship his cock, first with slow strokes of his fingers and then with his mouth when he rounded his back to kiss and suckle Trey's cockhead. The whole time, Ethan possessed his ass with those slow, deep strokes that drove Trey insane with need and pleasure.

"Now that is a beautiful sight to wake up to," Reagan said from the far side of the bed. "I never knew you were so flexible, Ethan."

Ethan's hot breath stirred over Trey's saliva-damp cockhead as he laughed. "Kirk has been working with me on that, actually. I'm sure he never imagined how I'd use those yoga poses he insisted on teaching me."

"God, he's driving me insane," Trey said breathlessly. Ethan could only suck him when Trey's hips were raised so far off his thick cock that he almost—but not quite—fell free of him. Trey's body couldn't decide if it liked to be sucked or fucked better, and Ethan alternating between the two forms of exquisite pleasure had him out of his mind.

"Do you have your tongue piercing in?" Reagan asked, sitting up on the bed beside him.

"Yeah. You said— You said— F-f-fuck, E, I can't, I just can't. You said you wanted to sleep." Trey finally managed to complete a thought. His eyelids fluttered as Ethan completely shattered his concentration by licking and sucking at the very tip of his throbbing cock again before angling his hips to drive himself deep. *So deep. Yes, fuck my ass. Fuck it hard. Oh God. Don't stop sucking. Yes, like that. Oh please.*

Ethan's thrusts were growing in strength and frequency, which Trey relished, but at the same time, he didn't want those strong lips to ever stop teasing his tip.

"I did?" Reagan said. "I was obviously still delirious from last night. I'm awake now."

"Then g-get over here," Trey said.

She hesitated for only a second before hurrying to straddle Trey's face. She clung to the headboard, her back arched as Trey did his best to lick her clit with the ball in his tongue the way he knew she liked it. When Ethan's hands began to stroke his length, Trey lost all ability to think.

Reagan shifted her hips so she could look down at him. "I'm late to the party. You're way past foreplay, aren't you?" She grinned at him and tapped his nose with her index finger.

His only response was his eyes rolling back as Ethan shifted his angle of penetration and found his sweet spot. "Oh God, E. Right there. Yes."

"Don't make him come yet. I want him too."

Trey whimpered when Ethan gave the tip of his cock one final lick and then straightened his back. He gripped Trey by the hips and thrust into him hard several times, the harshness of his strokes giving Trey just enough control to hold back his impending orgasm.

Reagan turned to face Ethan, holding on to his broad shoulders and straddling Trey's hips. Ethan grabbed Trey's cock and rubbed him against her wet pussy until Trey couldn't take anymore.

"Please," he groaned. "Oh God. I need her. I need you both."

His cock entered her hot, wet center, sending pleasure down his length, into his balls, into his ass, until his entire body was consumed. Reagan began to rise and fall over him, matching Ethan's strokes with a rhythm they'd perfected. Trey clung to the sheets, so possessed by his pleasure that he could do nothing but moan in rapture. Through cracked eyelids he watched his lovers embrace each other as they made love to him. Ethan's hands stroked Reagan's back, her breasts, and her glorious ass as she rode him. She slid her hands up the back of Ethan's neck and drew his mouth to hers, kissing him deeply. She moaned against his lips, and Ethan's answering growl made gooseflesh rise on Trey's skin. Reagan took Trey faster, taking him higher. Trey tried to hold back, but the pleasure was too intense.

"Reagan." He gasped a warning. "Reagan, hurry!"

Ethan reached between their joined bodies to stroke her clit. Her moans became frantic as she rode Trey faster and faster. Ethan drove into Trey's ass with the same relentless pace, matching her speed. Fucking Trey harder. Harder. Sweat pooled on his belly, trickled down the side of his face. His toes curled under.

Oh God. Don't come yet. Not yet.

He bit his lip and held on.

Wait for her. Wait.

Her moans of increasing intensity were making it impossible to ignore the feel of her soft flesh sliding up and down his length.

Finally Reagan cried out, and her pussy clenched hard around Trey's cock as she let go. He shattered into a million pieces of bliss as he immediately followed her over the edge. Trey's ass clenched in hard spasms around Ethan's driving cock as he erupted inside Reagan with a loud cry, his cum jetting into her body in vigorous spurts. Ethan soon followed him, his fingers digging into Trey's ass as he buried himself to the hilt and cried out against Reagan's shoulder. She wrapped her arms around Ethan as his cock pulsed violently in Trey's ass and he filled him with his fluids.

Trey went limp, so completely spent that his muscles forgot how to contract. Reagan climbed from his lap to lie beside him. She traced lazy circles on his sweat-soaked belly, drawing quivers of overstimulation from his exhausted flesh. Ethan carefully tugged the pillow from beneath Trey's back and slowly pulled out. Trey sucked a ragged breath through trembling lips as Ethan gently wiped his tender ass clean with a towel.

Reagan's hand slid across Trey's stomach, and she turned on her side to cuddle against him.

"I love you," she whispered.

He tried to move his arm to embrace her, but he was still incapable of motion.

She lifted her head. "And you, Ethan. I love you."

"We love you too," Ethan said. "I'm sure Trey would echo my sentiment if we hadn't just fucked him into a coma."

That was exactly how Trey felt. Like he'd been fucked into a coma of unparalleled bliss.

Trey tried to form words, but they came out as a murmured chain of nonsensical syllables.

Reagan chuckled and snuggled closer.

Ethan made a trip to the bathroom but was soon back in bed

with them, pressed against Trey's opposite side. His two lovers held hands with each other on his belly, making him smile. The sex they shared was unmatched in its intensity and pleasure, but what really made Trey feel complete was the love and respect they had for each other. Trey's impending and perfectly legal marriage to Reagan was just an illusion to hide the far more beautiful relationship going on behind closed doors. He had no doubt that the love he felt for these two people was stronger than any negativity others might throw their way. Fuck the haters. If they had an issue with his feelings for these two very different people, that was their problem, not his. He'd always been a lover. Loving had always been one of the biggest parts of who he was, and now he was twice the lover. He finally felt whole and refused to change for anyone. Nobody could ever take who he was away from him.

Trey relaxed with contentment as he drifted off.

CHAPTER 37

R EAGAN PLUCKED at the white fabric of her wedding gown's satin skirt. *White?* Ha! *Wedding?* Gulp!

"Are you really going to wear combat boots with your wedding dress?" Toni asked her as she fastened a set of pearls around Reagan's neck.

Reagan checked her reflection in the mirror and didn't recognize herself. Her hair was arranged in short, silky curls around the glittering tiara of a veil. Her makeup was heavy but tasteful and made her look far more elegant than she felt. And she was wearing pearls, for fuck's sake. *Pearls!* The only thing on her body that felt remotely normal was the combat boots hidden beneath the yards and yards off satin.

"Yep," Reagan said, surprised such an ordinary word could come out of the mouth of the regal-looking woman in the mirror.

"Are you nervous?" Toni said, tugging at a bit of fabric here, a length of tulle there.

Reagan blew out her cheeks. "I'm not sure. I feel like I'm going to throw up—does that mean I'm nervous?" Or did it mean she was scared? Or maybe that her breakfast sausage had been spoiled. It wasn't like she'd actually tasted it as she'd forced herself to eat it.

A quiet knock sounded on the door, and Reagan jumped. Her father poked his head inside, his eyes misting over at his first glimpse of the bride.

"It's time," he said, a breathless hitch in his voice.

Time? Already? Reagan took a deep breath and then another

and reminded herself that the ceremony was primarily for show. She wasn't giving up Ethan just because she was marrying Trey. In her heart, she was already married to them both. This wedding was just for legalities and public perception and . . . She swallowed the tight, queasy feeling rising up her throat.

"They've started. Are you ready?" Dad asked, holding out a hand in her direction.

She took it, crinkled her nose when she realized how damp her palm was, released his hold to wipe her hand on her pristine gown, and then took his hand again.

"You look beautiful, tiger," Dad said as he led her to the hall.

"Thanks." She patted the lapel of his gray tuxedo. "Looking pretty dapper there yourself, Daddy-O."

Reagan caught a flash of a red skirt belonging to one of her wedding attendants before the double doors leading to the chapel closed. She tried to breathe through her anxiety as they waited for the wedding march to begin and the chapel doors to open.

The muffled wedding processional music ended inside the chapel, and the familiar strains of the wedding march swelled on a pipe organ. Or at least the recording of one did. Reagan closed her eyes—this was it—gave herself a mental shake—this was it—and took the first step at her father's side. Oh God, this was it.

The chapel was packed—with reporters. Reagan forced her attention off the cameras and to the men she loved. Trey smiled at her in encouragement. Her heart fluttered at how handsome he looked. How familiar and loving. She could do this. Her gaze shifted to Ethan, standing beside Trey as his best man, except it wasn't Ethan. It was Brian. She closed her eyes and opened them again, hoping to rid herself of the hallucination, but the image didn't waver. The man standing beside Trey wasn't Ethan. Brian and Dare were there with Trey, as expected, but no Ethan.

No Ethan.

Her gaze shifted to her side of the pulpit. Her friends who'd come all the way from California—Jamie and Summer—as well as Brian's wife, Myrna, stood on her side as they'd been told. Still no Ethan. She scanned the front rows, checking familiar faces, but none belonged to the one she most needed to see.

She was suddenly standing before Trey and her father was giving her away and all she could think was *Where is he?* He promised he'd be there.

"It's okay," Trey said, offering her a supportive smile. "Don't forget to breathe."

"Where's Ethan?" she whispered.

"He went to get the rings."

"The rings?" They'd been in such a rush to get to the chapel after spending the morning recovering from their lovemaking that they must have forgotten the rings.

Trey nodded, blinking rapidly. "He never came back."

They stared at each other for a long moment. The clergyman was prattling on in the background, but Reagan didn't hear any of it. Not really.

Ethan wasn't there.

That could only mean one thing.

He wasn't okay with this. He'd never been okay with this. She was marrying one man she loved at the expense of the other.

"I can't do this," she said, not sure she'd actually spoken aloud until a single tear slipped down Trey's cheek and he closed his eyes.

His hands tightened on hers, but she managed to pull them free.

"I love you, Trey," she said, touching his warm cheek. She half expected him to flinch away from her, but he leaned into her palm instead. "Do you believe me?"

He nodded slightly. And one of them was trembling.

"I'm sorry. I can't marry you. Not like this." She turned, searching for an escape route. The double doors at the back of the chapel beckoned. She scarcely noticed the camera flashes as she gathered her obnoxious skirt in both hands and fled.

CHAPTER 38

O F ALL THE WORST possible fucking days to witness an accident, Ethan thought as he pressed down on the motorcyclist's heavily bleeding thigh with both hands.

"Did someone call an ambulance?" he yelled at the crowd of onlookers who'd gathered but didn't seem too keen on getting involved.

"It's on the way," someone called.

"Am I going to lose my leg?" asked the man bleeding all over Ethan. "I can't lose my leg." He tried to sit up, but Ethan leaned an elbow against his hip, cringing when blood spurted from between his fingers. "I can't lose my leg! *I can't lose my leg!*" Each time he said it he became more frantic. More panicked. Louder.

"You're not going to lose your leg," Ethan said evenly. He was more worried that the man would lose his life if they didn't get the bleeding stopped. "Stay calm. Help is on the way." Ethan needed to get a tourniquet around the top of the man's thigh; the pressure of his hands wasn't enough to stop the bleeding.

Ethan looked around the wreckage for something he could use. The SUV barely had a scratch on it. The motorcycle beneath its front wheels was unrecognizable. "Does anyone have a rope or something I can use as a tourniquet?"

The people around him murmured among themselves as if he was speaking a foreign language.

"A belt? Or a tie?" Wait, he had a tie. For once. Trying to keep as much pressure on the femoral artery as possible with one hand, he loosened the knot at his neck with the other. "Can someone give me a hand?" Jesus. You'd think these people hadn't ever been at an accident scene before. A wail of sirens sounded in the distance. Never a cop around when you needed one, he thought wryly. Just an ex-cop.

Ethan worked the length of black satin beneath the leg he was pushing into the asphalt. There was no way he could do this all on his own. It was a man in blue—and gray—that finally lent him the hand he needed. He and the state patrolman worked to tighten the tie around the victim's thigh even though the man was screaming in pain. The ambulance arrived a few minutes later and the paramedics took over. Ethan climbed to his feet and looked down at the blood-stained condition of his suit.

"Off-duty cop?" asked the officer who'd helped him tie the tourniquet.

It pained him to admit it, but he said, "I'm no longer on the force."

"That's a shame. You probably saved that guy's life today."

Ethan sure hoped so.

"Are you late for your own wedding?" The officer nodded toward his now macabre formal attire.

Ethan groaned. "Not my wedding, no." He couldn't very well show up at Trey and Reagan's wedding covered in blood. He had to hurry if he was going to get cleaned up in time to make it to the ceremony.

He gave the officer his identification and contact information—in case they needed a witness later—rinsed his sticky hands with a bottle of water and climbed into his car. The officers on the scene stopped traffic so he could get turned around and avoid the motorcycle wreckage and be on his way. He could still hear the sickening crunch of the wreck. The SUV had changed lanes right in front of him. Unfortunately, the motorcyclist had already been in that lane.

Ethan cringed when he noted the time. The ceremony would be starting in less than ten minutes. He wouldn't have time to wash up, change clothes, and get to the chapel. He didn't want to miss the ceremony, but more importantly, the rings were in his pocket. He tried calling Reagan, calling Trey, calling anyone who might have a phone at the chapel, but no one answered. He had several anxious messages from Trey asking where he was, if he was okay, telling him he understood if he was upset, but would he please call him anyway.

Ethan bit his lip. They probably thought he was absent because he didn't want them to be united as man and wife, but he wasn't worried about that. They could be legally married. He believed in his heart that the three of them would always be together. None of them was truly whole without the other two—they'd proved that. A piece of paper didn't matter to him, *Reagan* mattered to him. *Trey* mattered to him. And he no longer cared who knew it.

He parked behind the chapel, stripped off his ruined suit jacket and the red shirt beneath. He opened the trunk of his car—glad his overnight bag was still inside—and tried to find something appropriate to wear. He settled on a black T-shirt. There were spots of blood on his pants as well, but as the loud strains of the wedding march echoed from the chapel, he decided he didn't have time to change those too. He hurried around to the door they'd told him to enter at the quick rehearsal the night before and let himself inside. Someone he didn't recognize stopped him before he burst through the side door into the chapel.

"You have blood all over your face."

"I'm late. Let me in. I'm the best man. I have the rings."

The wedding march ended, and he could hear a loud muffled voice, but he couldn't make out the words.

"There's a bathroom right there." The usher, or whoever the guy was, pointed at a slightly open door. "Go wash up. You can't go in there looking like that."

Hey, he'd changed out of his blood-soaked clothes, what more did they want from him? With a resigned sigh, Ethan hurried into the small bathroom and gasped when he caught his reflection in the mirror. Yeah, showing up to a wedding with streaks of blood and sweat and dirt down his face probably wasn't the best idea. He hurriedly scrubbed his hands and face with liquid soap and dried off as best he could with brown paper towels. He at least wanted to watch them say their vows to each other—he couldn't miss that. And they'd need the rings for that, wouldn't they? He had to get out there now.

The usher let him through this time, and Ethan eased the door open, not wanting to disturb the ceremony. He wasn't sure what he was looking at. Trey was standing at the altar alone, staring up the aisle, ashen-faced and trembling. At first Ethan thought he was waiting for Reagan to make her way down the aisle to him, but the bridal party was rushing up the aisle, as were several of the guests and Reagan's father.

Ethan dashed to Trey's side and collected his quaking body in his arms.

"Ethan," Trey murmured, clinging to his shirt as his legs went out on him.

Ethan pulled Trey against him, cradling the back of his head as Trey buried his face in his neck.

"What's going on?" Ethan asked, staring at the chaos at the end of the chapel where everyone was trying to filter outside at once.

"She's gone. She left. She doesn't want to marry me."

"What do you mean, she left?"

"She left." Trey sniffed and swallowed.

Ethan felt a hot wetness against his throat, and it took him a second to realize Trey was crying. Ethan's joy, the light in his soul, his every happiness, was bawling his eyes out.

"She'll come back," Ethan said, forcing Trey backward so he could see the truth in Ethan's eyes. "She'll come back."

She had to come back.

"She'll come back." Ethan cupped Trey's face between his palms and kissed him, pouring every tender emotion he'd tried to repress for this man into the meeting of their lips. He didn't care that the press had noticed them. Didn't care that the nosy motherfuckers were twittering about his shocking behavior or taking picture after picture. All Ethan cared about was that Trey knew his love was true and everlasting.

When they drew apart, Trey blinked up at him, his tears no longer flowing—thank God—but his lashes spiky and wet. "You kissed me," he whispered, the hint of a smile on his lips. "In public."

"You'd better get used to it," Ethan said. "I love you, Trey. Do you believe me?"

He expected Trey to brighten at his words, but instead he grimaced. "That's what she said right before she left me."

"Well, I'm not going anywhere without you," he said, taking Trey's hand and tugging him up the aisle. "Let's go get our woman."

Trey came to a sudden stop after only a few steps. "Is that blood, Ethan?"

"It's not mine," he said, heart galloping at all the attention they were getting. "I'll explain later." While he didn't care who knew that he was unapologetically in love with a man—*this* man—Ethan enjoyed being the focus of the press's attention even less than Reagan did.

Someone shoved a microphone in Trey's face. "Was your

engagement to Reagan just a cover-up for your homosexual relationship with Ethan Conner?"

Trey cringed. "No. I want to marry Reagan because I love her."

Ethan didn't want to deal with the bullshit right now. "Get out of our way!" he bellowed. And to his surprise, the crush of reporters moved aside to let them through.

By the time he got Trey outside, the entire wedding party and all the guests had dispersed. Not that he blamed them. They probably didn't want to answer awkward questions either. There was no sign of Reagan, only more reporters, who descended on them like vultures scenting the death of a forbidden love.

CHAPTER 39

REAGAN SUPPOSED IT WAS FITTING that her father had been the one to tuck her into a taxi and escort her to the airport. In her wedding dress, no less.

"You have a lot of explaining to do," Dad said the second the taxi door shut. "Why were you in such a rush to marry that young man? The truth."

Reagan groaned and curled into her knees as best she could in her constrictive attire. She didn't want to explain to her father. Not now. Not after she'd undoubtedly pulverized Trey's heart by leaving him at the altar. Not when she hadn't spoken to Ethan about why he'd suddenly decided not to support her marriage to Trey.

"Reagan?" He nudged her in the arm, and she scooted as far from him as possible. "Tiger," he said, with a bit less hostility, "talk to me."

When she continued to ignore him, Dad said, ""Pull over and stop the car," to the cab driver.

"You want to get out here?" the cabbie asked, obviously surprised that the side of an interstate seemed a good place to drop off a man in a tuxedo and his daughter in a wedding gown.

"I want to go home, back to Arkansas," Reagan said. To hide. She expected her father to think that was the best idea she'd ever had, but apparently not.

"Tell me the truth, Reagan. Why did you back out of your wedding? I thought you were in love with Trey."

"I am in love with Trey. It's just . . . It's . . . It's complicated, okay?" Too complicated to explain to a conservative-minded man like her father. "Just take me home. Please."

He stared into her eyes for a long moment as she wordlessly pleaded with him to do as she asked, just this once, without arguing with her, without making her feel shittier than she already felt. She dashed a tear away with the back of her hand, and Dad closed his eyes. When he opened them again, he leaned toward the driver. "We're going to the airport after all," he said. "Sorry for the confusion."

Thank God. Reagan leaned into him, unable to fight the tears any longer, and he wrapped a sturdy arm around her shoulders.

"Are you sure?" the driver said. "It ain't safe to pull off the side of the freeway like this. I won't do it again."

"I'm sure. I apologize for the trouble."

"Better be a big tip in this for me," the driver grumbled under his breath as he checked the lane for an opening in the traffic zooming by.

"You're not off the hook, Reagan," Dad said calmly. "You're still going to tell me everything that's going on."

She couldn't.

"I won't be angry with you when you explain."

"I'm not going to explain," Reagan said, shifting out of his hold. Why couldn't he just allow her to live her life? "It's none of your business."

"You're my only family, tiger. My flesh and blood. My progeny and my responsibility. It is my business. It—you—will always be my business."

"I don't . . . I don't want you to be disappointed in me." Disgusted by her? Both? She pressed a trembling hand to her forehead to try to settle the confused thoughts swirling through her brain.

"I could never be disappointed in you."

She dropped her hand and gaped at him. "How can you say that? My entire adult life is a disappointment to you."

"It's not." He shook his head. "I would have chosen a different path if I had your talent, but that doesn't mean I'm disappointed in the path you did choose. It's your life. I just want you to be happy."

She wasn't buying it. They'd been arguing for six *years* about how she was throwing her talent away on rock music. "You hate what I've become."

"I thought I did, but seeing you up on that stage in Little Rock,

I was proud. So proud."

He hadn't told her that. And she still wasn't sure she believed him. She wanted to. Knowing he was capable of being proud of her made her want to tell him about her love life even less than before, but also gave her hope that he could accept her.

"Does this have something to do with Ethan?" he asked

Reagan went completely still. Maybe if she played possum, he'd forget she was in the cab.

"You dated him before Trey, right? You still live with him now?"

Reagan nodded slightly.

"So you still have feelings for him?"

She nodded again—the small action terrifying.

"Is that why you left Trey at the altar?"

She had done that, hadn't she? Ugh, how terrible for Trey. How clichéd of her.

"You probably should have sorted out your feelings before you rushed into getting married. You're obviously confused."

But she wasn't.

"I understand my heart perfectly," she said. "I love Ethan. I've loved him for years. Romantically for a while and then when I found out he enjoys the company of men, I thought our relationship shifted to friendship. But it's more than that now. It's both."

"You're in love with a gay man?" Dad had that traumatized look he sported when anyone discussed something that went against his moral fiber.

She inhaled one very big breath and said, "I'm in love with two of them." Once she got started, she couldn't stop. She also couldn't look at her dad as she confessed her crimes against propriety.

"Well, that's not exactly correct. They aren't gay men. Ethan is bisexual. He likes both men and women, and he fought those urges the best he could, but he is who he is and he's finally accepted that. Trey . . ." Her heart twisted just thinking about him. He must be hurting terribly after the way she left him, humiliated him, in front of all those reporters. "Trey is the same, except he's not afraid to let his love show. When I started dating Trey, I thought he was straight, and he tried to be straight for me, but he couldn't deny who he was for long. It's just not in him. So I got this great idea of allowing my new bisexual boyfriend to satisfy his sexual needs with my gay—at least I thought Ethan was gay at the time—roommate, only my plan didn't go as planned. We all ended up together." She lifted her gaze to her father's stunned face. "In one relationship. Me and Ethan. Me and Trey. Ethan and Trey."

"You're shacking up with two men?"

Reagan groaned. "You make it sound so dirty." And it was pretty dirty, but in a very good way. It was also pure and beautiful in an even better way. "It's not just about having great sex all the time, Dad. We love each other."

A horn blared as the cab crossed into the next lane. The driver was busier watching his passengers in his rearview mirror than the traffic on either side of them.

Dad's face had gone red. Anger? Embarrassment? She couldn't tell which. "We're going back to Arkansas."

"Good."

"I should have never let you leave in the first place."

"You couldn't have stopped me. And you won't be able to stop me next week when I go back on tour."

"Do you actually think you're going to get back together with them?"

"If I can." She might have destroyed what they had. And that scared her so much, she couldn't dwell on that possibility. Not yet.

CHAPTER 40

S ITTING WITH HIS BARE FEET IN THE WATER, TREY STARED at the mosaics that his mother had tiled into the bottom and sides of the pool. He probably should have gone with Ethan to support him while he took his test—the first step in joining the Beverly Hills PD—but Ethan had dropped Trey off at his parents' house saying it would make him nervous if he stayed and that Trey could support him from afar. Trey always sat by the pool when he was depressed. And because they hadn't seen or heard from Reagan since she'd fled the chapel in Vegas two days before, he was at an all-time low.

A shadow crossed behind him, and a foot nudged him hard between the shoulders, sending him flopping face first into the water. Trey bobbed to the surface, sputtering. He slicked his bangs out of his eyes and glared up at his brother's grinning face.

"Get out of your funk, little brother. We have things to do today."

"I'm not doing anything with you, assface."

"Mom is throwing a party this evening, and she doesn't need you glooming up the place with your moodiness."

"I'm not moody," Trey said. "I'm heartbroken."

"I don't know why. Your secret love affair with Ethan is all anyone is talking about right now."

"Of course it is," Trey muttered, pushing himself out of the pool with both arms. "They think Reagan left me at the altar because she couldn't stand hiding my *secret* homosexuality."

"You can't blame Reagan for not wanting to marry you—you're a wreck. You've always been a wreck and you'll always be a wreck."

"Thanks for cheering me up, bro." Trey scowled and shoved Dare in the arm with one dripping hand.

"You're welcome. Now dry off and get dressed. We're in a hurry."

"To do what?" Trey asked, reaching for a towel.

"To straighten out the wreck that is Trey Mills."

"I'm not going to a psychiatrist."

Dare laughed. "There are better ways to patch you up. Get dressed."

By the time he was sitting in the passenger seat of Dare's car, he was more curious than annoyed. "Where are we going?"

"You'll see."

Dare drove toward the coast and encouraged Trey to talk. Talk about Ethan and Reagan and if he really wanted to patch up their relationship. So it turned out he was having a psychiatric session after all. His shrink's couch just happened to be the leather seat of a cherry-red Corvette.

"So if you could have anything you want, you'd want to marry *both* of them?" Dare asked, waving at several gorgeous blondes in the convertible next to them at a red light.

"It can't happen," Trey said. "The law says—"

"Fuck the law."

Apparently Dare was feeling uncommonly rebellious that afternoon. When the light turned green, the powerful muscle car's tires squealed as he punched the accelerator and shot off, leaving the giggling women in the dust.

"I sometimes wonder if it would be better . . ." Trey glanced out the window at the palm tree trunks flashing by. "If I can't have them both, maybe I'd be better off with neither of them."

"That's the worst idea you've ever had," Dare said. "We'll fix this." He nudged Trey with his elbow. "Do you believe me?"

Trey wished people would stop asking him that question. "How?"

"By taking you three idiots out of the equation."

"Huh?"

Dare chuckled. "Hold on."

He downshifted and took a corner so fast, Trey was sure they'd banked on two wheels. Dare insisted that his various cars needed their exercise—as if they were racehorses rather than machines—and he was definitely running this one through its paces. When they returned to their parents' house, the entire driveway was full of cars. Trey cringed, not wanting to rub elbows with a bunch of his father's associates—mostly doctor friends and their significant others. Then his eyes zeroed in on a familiar pink Thunderbird. It was unquestionably Myrna's car. A green vintage Corvette convertible belonging to Eric Sticks, the Harley that Jace rode, and Sed's Mercedes were all parked in the drive as well. Why would his bandmates be there?

"Dare," Trey said, turning to his smugly grinning brother. "What's going on?"

Dare didn't answer, just shut off the car and climbed out of the driver's seat.

Heart thudding in his chest, Trey eased the car door open and followed.

CHAPTER
41

E THAN WAS LAUGHING with a couple of fellow job candidates when someone knocked on the glass of the waiting room's interior windows. The smile dropped off his face when he recognized his mother. He leaned forward so fast, his crossed ankles slipped from the edge of the coffee table and his shoes landed on the floor with a hard thud. What the hell was she doing in California? And at the police station?

He darted to his feet and hurried out into the corridor.

"Are you done soon?" she asked, fanning her flushed cheeks. "I was waiting for you by your car, but you never came out. I think this takes way too long. Maybe he died or something."

"What are you doing here, Mamá?" he asked, his heart thudding with panic. "What happened?"

"Nothing bad. We'll fix this for you. You'll see."

"Fix what?" And who was *we*?

Her little smile told him she had a secret she planned to keep. "So how did the test go?"

"I think it went okay." Actually, he was pretty sure that even though he hadn't had time to study, he had aced it, and he knew he'd pass the physical portion scheduled for the next morning. He was more worried about the interview, if he even managed to get one. He was lucky they let him take the test with such little notice. But he had an unexpected champion by the name of Butch Carter. Until yesterday, Butch had failed to mention that his brother was chief of police in Beverley Hills or that he was capable of pulling a few string to get Ethan a chance to apply. No guarantees—and Ethan was fine with that—but an opportunity to return to the career that he preferred.

Ethan's mother searched his eyes. "If you get the job, will you not go to Europe with Reagan?"

"Mamá, I don't know where she is, if she's even going to Europe."

"You must not have looked very hard for her."

"You know where she is?"

Mamá nodded and started toward the door, gripping her purse tightly in both hands.

"Is she outside?" Ethan tilted his body to look through the glass exterior door and into the parking lot.

"No. I will take you to her."

His mother wasn't the only one who'd been waiting in the parking lot. His brothers were out there as well. All of them. No, on second glance, the one he was closest to in age and friendship—the one he *had* been closest to—was missing.

"There he is," Juan called, waving. "My brother who is famous for kissing dudes."

"Shut up," Ethan said, shoving Juan's shoulder once he was within reach. Last night he'd talked to all of his brothers on the phone—with the exception of Carlos, who refused to speak to him—and none of them had been overly upset by the truth he'd shared. Or surprised. Juan wasn't one to keep a secret, so they'd had plenty of warning before being confronted with scandalous pictures of their oldest brother enjoying the company—and tasty lips—of a man. So while Ethan wasn't surprised they weren't threatening to beat the gay out of him with ball bats, he was astonished to see them. No one had mentioned coming out for a visit. Had he forgotten his own birthday in the confusion?

"What are you all doing here?" he asked.

Surely, he didn't need five assistants to talk to Reagan. He preferred their reunion to be a bit more private.

"Eh, Carlos didn't come," Mamá said, waving a dismissive hand. "Too busy playing his music at some wedding."

"You should let him play at your grand opening, Mamá," Juan said, hugging and tickling her at the same time until she slapped at him with her purse to get him to stop.

"What grand opening?" Ethan asked. Jeez. No one ever kept him in the loop about anything. He had talked to these closed-lipped

OLIVIA CUNNING

idiots yesterday, for fuck's sake.

"Mamá is starting her own restaurant. Without Papá and his little chica."

"Can you afford to do that?" Ethan asked, his practical side winning over his pride in her decision.

"I must do this. My kitchen is much too small."

"She's been selling boxed lunches out of her house for the past week," Miguel said. "Word is already out that she's cooking again, and everyone wants her food."

"Papá tried opening a place with his waitress chica," Juan said, "but no one goes there. No one." He laughed and drummed on Miguel with both palms.

"He gets what he deserves," Mamá said, her eyes narrowed.

Ethan gave her a hearty squeeze and kissed the top of her head. "I'm proud of you. You'll do great."

"You should thank Butch. He says I must try working from home first and if I succeed, then I should open my own restaurant. He says I can do it. And I know I can."

Ethan cringed. Ugh, no, not Butch. He already owed Butch one for the job lead and another for the good reference. And now he owed him for helping Mamá see her worth. Owing that man was sure to bite him in the ass someday. But Ethan was glad Butch had given his mamá the confidence to move forward. Ethan still hadn't told off his stepfather, but maybe her success was the best revenge.

"We're going to be late," Pedro said. "Isn't traffic in Los Angeles always really bad?"

"Pedro!" Ethan said, hugging brother number four. "I haven't seen you in a year. How's school?"

And by school, he meant graduate school. Pedro was working on a master's degree in chemical engineering.

"Busy," he said, "but I wanted to come and support you."

"Support me? In what? Aren't we going to see Reagan?"

"Duh," Juan said, and rolled his eyes.

"Shush!" Mamá said, waving six of her seven sons toward Ethan's car.

"Shotgun," Arturo shouted.

"Mamá gets shotgun," Raùl said. "You get the trunk."

"Someone is going to have to ride in the trunk," Ethan said, wondering how they thought five grown men could fit into the back seat of his car.

Pedro pointed at the black suitcase sitting behind Ethan's

sedan. The enormous piece of luggage alone would take up the entire trunk. "You need a bigger vehicle," Pedro complained as Miguel and Juan climbed into the back seat.

"How did you get here in the first place?" Ethan asked.

"Bus ," Mamá said. "From airport."

"And how did you know where to find me?"

"Butch."

Naturally. Ethan was going to have to have a heart-to-heart with that man. His mother was still a married woman, and Butch was embedding himself into her personal affairs much too quickly. *Affairs?* Ugh. Why did he have to think *that* word?

"We wanted to see you as much as possible," she added.

Arturo shook his head. "We told her we should just go to—"

"Shush!" Mamá said while Arturo opened her door for her.

"To the *place*," Arturo continued. "But she wanted to arrive with all of us at your side."

"To show your support," Ethan guessed.

"Exactly."

"For *what?*" Ethan asked, still completely confused about why they were all there.

"Get in the car, Ethan," Mamá said from the passenger seat.

Pedro shoved the single large suitcase into the trunk and then piled in on top of his four brothers crammed into the back seat. It was a good thing they were on the small side, but they definitely didn't have enough seat belts.

"If we get pulled over, I'm screwed," Ethan said under his breath, smiling to see almost all of his brothers squashed into his car. He was suddenly reminded of trips they'd taken as a family in their beat-up minivan. They'd never made it out of Texas, but there'd been plenty to keep them occupied in the Lone Star State. The youngest, Juan, was eighteen now and had graduated high school, so Ethan guessed they really were all grown men even if he'd always see them as his obnoxious—and dear to him—little brothers.

"Keep your head down, Arturo," Juan said, shoving the back of Arturo's head to force his face into Raul's thigh. "Or we'll get pulled over."

"Can't. Breathe." Arturo slapped the window as he sought oxygen.

"Where are we going?" Ethan asked as he started the car and shifted into reverse.

"Gwen's house."

"Gwen? Trey's mom?" But his mother had spoken to Gwen for less than two minutes after Reagan had fled the wedding in Vegas. And they were suddenly besties and planning family get-togethers?

"Yes. The address is—" Mamá pulled a piece of paper out of her purse. "Seven oh—"

"I know the address. I thought we were going to find Reagan."

Mamá smiled and squeezed his knee. "We are."

Ethan shook his head and pulled into the flow of traffic. None of this made any sense.

CHAPTER 42

REAGAN PULLED her gaze from the scenic palm trees outside her car window and glared at her father. The man was driving her nuts. "No one is going to *destroy* grandma's cello," she insisted for the fifth time.

"You left the man at the altar, tiger," Dad said. "He's bound to want to hurt you as much as you hurt him. He knows how much that cello means to you."

"Which is why he would never, ever damage it."

Her life had become one disaster after another since she'd walked out of her own wedding. And she knew she deserved the bad karma that had descended upon her. When she'd arrived at the airport two days ago—her only thought to escape back home to Little Rock—all the flights were full until the following day, so they'd gotten temporary lodging near the airport to wait for their flight. She'd left her purse, her phone, her identification, her money, her credit cards—everything—at the chapel when she'd rushed off, so she had no way to call and her fucking dad wouldn't allow her to talk to anyone, somehow thinking isolation was the best policy until she got her shit together. Which maybe it was, but now she was regretting telling him anything—everything—because once again he was determined to rule her life.

She was pretty sure all those phone calls Dad had been getting and not answering were actually Ethan and Trey trying to reach her. Reagan wasn't sure if she was ready to talk to either of them—she couldn't think up a big enough apology for what she'd done—but being in contact with them should be her decision, not her father's. The only call he'd actually answered had been from her mother. Reagan didn't have to hear his soft-spoken greeting of *Robin* to know it was her. She simply had to witness the doe-eyed look on her father's face to figure out who he was talking to. Reagan had been so disgusted by his stupidity—how could he even speak to that home-wrecking bitch?—that she'd gone for a walk to try to sort through the disaster she'd made of her life. When she'd returned, he'd been on the phone with the local police, certain she'd been kidnapped by crackheads.

Yesterday, happy to put the day from hell behind her at last, they'd headed to the airport for their flight to Little Rock. Turns out, security wouldn't let her on a plane without identification—*duh*— and she wasn't sure who had her purse, so they'd searched Vegas for signs of familiar faces for an entire day. No luck. Then Dad had the brilliant idea of renting a car and driving to Los Angeles to track people down. Which Reagan needed to do. After sleeping on it, there was no longer any doubt that she needed to apologize to Trey and she needed to hear an explanation from Ethan and she needed to explain why she'd run off. She felt horrendous for hurting Trey. For hurting them all. She'd seen the news stories about what the press thought was going on between the three of them. Saw images of Ethan kissing Trey at the front of the very chapel where she was to have married Trey. She still didn't know why Ethan had decided to show his face *after* she'd fled. She was so confused about how to fix the giant mess she'd made that she couldn't think straight. She couldn't eat. She couldn't sleep. She knew she had fucked things up in a big way, but she couldn't come up with any way to make them right. There was no way Trey would ever forgive her for humiliating him in front of God and everyone. As the news stories said, maybe the two gay lovers were better off without her in the picture.

And now Dad was on this never-ending loop about getting her cello back. Not find her purse, her phone, her life. Nope, he was worried about the damned cello. Being trapped in a car with him for six hours as they drove from Las Vegas to Los Angeles had been an exercise in pure torture. The man drove so slowly, she was pretty sure a turtle could run laps around the rental car.

"Take the next exit," she said when they finally got to the familiar area near her apartment.

"I know where to go," he said, zooming—or rather idling— past the exit.

"Dad, you missed it." She wanted to get home. She prayed that one of the guys was there, because her house keys had also been in her purse. Running off with nothing but the wedding gown on her back had gone much worse than she could have ever anticipated. Hell, her dad had bought her an "I love Las Vegas" T-shirt and a pair of pajama shorts in the airport gift shop so she'd have something to wear other than the cumbersome white satin dress that had once symbolized her commitment to Trey but now only reminded her that she was a truly awful coward. If she'd been brave enough to reveal the truth from the beginning, instead of trying to live a lie, she could be sorting things out with the men she loved instead of floundering here alone. Well, as alone as she could be with her father breathing down her neck.

"Where are we going?" she asked when he took an exit a few miles down the road.

"To get back what belongs to you," he said.

Reagan crossed her arms and shook her head. "And you know where to find it?"

"I know exactly where it is."

"How?"

"A little bird told me."

Reagan looked out the window to take her mind off strangling her father and was surprised to find they were in the hedge-and-wall-lined residential streets of Beverly Hills. The man was hopelessly lost—obviously—but she knew he was too damned stubborn to admit it. He was following directions on his cellphone, so she suspected he had googled addresses of the stars like some ridiculous tourist. Gah! He drove her crazy.

When they turned onto a familiar street, her heart skipped a beat. Maybe her dad knew more than she realized.

"Is Trey at his parents' house?" She sat up straighter in her seat as Dad pulled into an overcrowded driveway. One of the cars belonged to Ethan. The others belonged to . . . she didn't care. She was unfastening her seat belt before the car had come to a complete stop. Dad caught her arm before she darted out of the car.

"Don't forget your wedding dress," he said. "It's in the trunk."

"What?"

"Can you just listen to your old man without arguing for once in your adult life?"

"I need to talk to Ethan and Trey."

"Get the damned dress, Reagan."

She'd never heard her father swear. Not ever. And he only called her Reagan when she was about to get scolded, so she had no choice but to grab the huge black trash bag that her wadded-up dress had been shoved into.

Dad linked his arm through hers and made her walk up the driveway when every instinct told her to run. Not *away from* this time. But toward.

Dad rang the doorbell.

"Dad, tell me why we're here. Why do I need my wedding gown?"

"You can't get married without a wedding gown, tiger." He stroked her hair as he used to do when she was a little girl, and planted a wet kiss on her forehead.

"I told you I can't marry Trey when I love Ethan as much."

The door opened, and Gwen's face brightened with a wide smile. She was wearing a free-flowing pink dress and had matching flowers woven into a braid that coiled at the back of her head. "There you are. I was going to be upset if you broke my son's heart twice in one week."

"Is Trey here?" Reagan stood on tiptoe to peer into the house. The entire foyer was filled with familiar faces.

"He is."

"And Ethan?"

"Naturally."

"Can I see them?"

"Everyone knows it's bad luck for a bride to see her grooms before the ceremony."

"Grooms?" Was she hearing things?

"Reagan!" Toni called as she separated herself from the crowd. "I have your purse. You left it at the chapel Saturday."

"Thank you," Reagan said, opening her purse and pulling out her phone. The battery was dead. Damn, she couldn't call Trey or Ethan and ask them what the fuck was going on. She needed to see them immediately.

"Where's your dress?" Toni asked.

Reagan shoved the trash bag into Toni's arms and brushed past Gwen to enter the house. "Trey?" she called over the din of multiple conversations. "Ethan?"

"You'll see them soon," Gwen said, slipping an arm around her waist and corralling her to a guest room off to one side of the foyer.

"Why won't anyone tell me what's going on?" she shouted.

"Your father didn't tell you why you're here?" Gwen asked, pulling Reagan's crumpled gown from the trash bag and laying it across the bed.

Reagan's eyes filled with tears. No, he hadn't told her, but she'd figured it out. "I'm sorry, Mrs. Mills, but I can't marry your son. Not at the expense of Ethan's feelings."

"But you'd agree to marry them both, wouldn't you?" Gwen asked. "And for them to marry each other?"

Reagan blinked at her. It was a lovely idea, but the government *still* had a say in who could marry who, even if gay marriage was legal in many states. "I would jump at the opportunity. But there's a law—"

"Fuck the law," Dare said from the doorway. "Is she about ready? The grooms are getting antsy."

"Get out!" Toni said, throwing a pillow at Dare's face. "She could have been naked in here."

"But isn't," he said, his gaze meeting Reagan's. "Could you hurry things along, sis? You know I can't stand it when my brother is upset. If you don't get moving, I'm going to strip you naked and stuff you into that dress myself."

"Darren Edward Lunar Mills! You behave yourself," Gwen said.

"I must be in trouble," Dare said, winking at Reagan. "She used *both* my middle names."

Reagan was in a trance—thoughts racing, palms sweating, ears ringing—as Toni and Gwen helped her put on her worse-for-wear wedding gown. "We can't get married," she muttered. "It's not legal."

Gwen forced Reagan to sit on the edge of the bed and squatted down so that they were eye to eye. "Does it matter that it's not legal? Really? Or is it more important that the people close to you are allowed to acknowledge the love you share with Trey and with Ethan and that they have for each other? Don't you want to openly celebrate all that love with us today?"

Reagan took a deep breath and let it out slowly.

Gwen squeezed her hand. "If you'd rather call it a commitment ceremony or a love fest, that's fine. But Rosa has her heart set on a wedding."

"Rosa's here?"

"Everyone is here. So do you want to make this thing with my son and Ethan legit? At least in the eyes of everyone who matters?"

Reagan stared fixedly at the closed door above Gwen's head. "Why bother asking a question you already know the answer to?"

Gwen stroked a lock of hair behind Reagan's ear. "Because I want you to admit that I'm brilliant for throwing this thing together in two days."

Reagan laughed. "Are you the one who convinced my father it was a good idea?"

"Not directly, no. But I did get that ball rolling."

She scooted off the bed and hugged Gwen, feeling blessed to have this woman in her life. Between Rosa and Gwen, she was no longer without a mother. She had two of them.

"Should we do something with your hair?" Toni asked, examining Reagan's bed-head as if it was a puzzle worth solving.

"I don't want to keep my soon-to-be-husbands waiting another second," Reagan said. She rushed to the door, tossed it open, and stopped in her tracks in front of the woman blocking her way. It was like looking in the mirror—if a mirror was capable of aging her twenty-five years. "Mom?" she croaked.

"Someone told me my very own daughter was marrying a rock star. I couldn't miss that, now could I?"

Reagan was too happy to be angry at her mother for showing up whenever she felt like it and too used to being deserted by the woman to have any hope that she'd stick around for long. She gave her a quick hug and said, "We'll catch up later." Much later.

Reagan hurried through the now-empty foyer and followed voices to the back of the house. Everyone had congregated poolside. Dad held a hand out to her when she reached the open French doors near the kitchen.

"Mom's here," she whispered a warning to him, knowing how the woman rattled him.

"Whose bright idea do you think it was to bring you here?" he asked.

Her mother had convinced Dad that this was a good idea? But how had Mom even known about it? The tramp didn't deserve to be a part of Reagan's special day. She hadn't earned it.

Reagan took a deep breath and let her anger toward her mother go. She didn't care how any of this had come about. She was here, about to wed the men of her dreams. They hadn't rehearsed the ceremony or even discussed it, and it didn't matter. None of the steps that got her here mattered at the moment. Only the outcome mattered. She just wanted to see Ethan and Trey and assure them that she loved them with everything she had in her. They could sort out the details and any hurts or hard feelings later. Now she just wanted everyone they cared about to witness with their own eyes how powerful their love was. How pure and perfect. Unusual, perhaps, but she wouldn't have settled for an ordinary love. Not when she knew what was right for her. This was right. Their being together had always felt right in her heart, but now she finally *knew* it in her head. And to hell with anyone who didn't agree.

Gwen rushed past with her husband in tow and disappeared into the crowd. She must have told their guests that Reagan was now present, because a hush fell over the crowd and everyone turned to stare at her. Instead of the nerves she'd felt when standing before many of the same people at an impersonal chapel in Las Vegas, she was overjoyed to see everyone.

"What are we supposed to do now?" she asked her dad as the chorus of "Let's Get It On" by Marvin Gaye began to play from the backyard's sound system.

"Darren!" The hissed name came from Gwen.

"My bad," Dare said. "That's for after the ceremony."

The crowd erupted in delighted laughter.

"We can start the wedding night early," Trey called from somewhere across the yard.

Her dad's hand securely in hers, Reagan rushed toward Trey's voice. There were no practiced steps to a wedding march, just a mad dash across colorful mosaic tiles to a different Marvin Gaye song—"How Sweet It Is." Reagan would have to remember to ask Dare about his Marvin Gaye fanboy crush later. When she finally made her way through the crowd and the two men of her dreams came into view, she stopped, the rush of emotions overwhelming. She blinked back tears of joy.

Trey and Ethan stood beneath a fabulous mixed-media sculpture made of pieces of musical instruments. They were holding hands before a welcoming face she recognized—Rebekah Stick's father. In this impulsive crowd, it was handy to have a minister on speed dial.

Rosa stood to Ethan's left, Gwen and George to Trey's right. Reagan's dad squeezed her hand and then released it so she could take the final few steps to Ethan and Trey's outstretched hands. She meant to take their hands like a sane person, but instead she crashed into the space between them, wrapping her arms around them both.

"I'm so sorry I left you at the altar in Vegas," she said against

Trey's neck and pressed her lips against the pulse thrumming in his throat.

"It's all right," he said, brushing a kiss against her hair. "I knew we were a package deal from the start."

She tilted her head back to stare into Trey's eyes, so grateful to see sincerity in their depths and no animosity. Not even hurt, just a happiness reflecting her own. She shifted her attention to Ethan and cupped his face in her palm, searching his eyes for traces of doubt. She found none of that either. Just more happiness.

"You weren't there beside him when I came down the aisle, Ethan," she said, hoping it didn't sound like an accusation. She wasn't blaming him for her mistake. She just didn't understand why he hadn't been there.

"It wasn't because I didn't want to be."

"So you weren't against me marrying Trey?"

"I'm only against it if I'm not included," Ethan said.

And he hadn't been included. But he was this time. This time was the way it should be.

"I'm against that as well," she said.

"He got held up saving some guy's life," Trey said, the adoring gaze he leveled at Ethan making Reagan's belly flutter. Seeing their love for each other was as big a thrill as experiencing it for herself. Well, almost.

Reagan laughed. "Of course that's what you were doing. I'm a complete idiot. I'm sorry I doubted you."

"Should I begin?" Reverend Blake asked.

Reagan shifted away, took Trey's and Ethan's free hands in hers, and smiled at Reverend Blake expectantly. "I'm ready," she whispered, her heart so full, she could scarcely breathe.

"Dearly beloved," Reverend Blake said, shifting his attention to the crowd behind them. "That's all of you folks."

Their enthusiastic claps and cheers made Reagan turn to grin at them.

"We are gathered here today to witness a most unusual union between three people."

"I still can't figure out how that works," whispered Ethan's youngest brother, Juan. Rosa slapped at him before pressing the back of her hand to one teary eye.

Reverend Blake continued. "Love is a gift from God—one that should not be ignored or mistrusted or taken lightly but embraced and cherished. Treasured. And if that love is shared by a man and a woman, a man and a man, or a man and a woman and another man, who are we to question the gift given to them? Love is love. It is eternal. It is a blessing. Love is not always easy or as we expect it to be, but it is worth the struggle. Love is always worth a fight. Just because it's a challenge doesn't mean it's wrong. Take the love given to you and don't let it fade. Keep it strong and alive. Nurture it as if it were the most precious commodity in existence. Because it is."

Reagan couldn't believe those words were coming out of the mouth of a religious leader. In her experience, religious types were the first to pass judgement on alternative lifestyles. Well, second after her father. But Dad was standing beside her now because he loved her. That too was a gift, and she should appreciate it more.

"Now for the sticky part," Reverend Blake said, causing several guests to laugh. "Do you Reagan take this man Trey and this man Ethan to be your unlawfully wedded husbands in the sight of God and your family by blood and the friends who are the family of your heart?"

She looked at Trey and smiled before saying, "I do." She shifted her gaze to Ethan, smiled again, and repeated, "I do."

"Do you, Trey, take this woman, Reagan, and this man, Ethan, to be your unlawfully wedded wife and husband—did I say that right?—in the sight of God, your family and friends, and no members of the press?"

Trey laughed and said his heartfelt *I do* to Reagan and then to Ethan.

"One more," Reverend Blake said, turning to Ethan, who looked a little pale behind his bronze skin. "Don't worry, I didn't forget you. Do you, Ethan, take this man, Trey, and this woman, Reagan, to be your unlawfully wedded husband and wife in front of all witnesses here today—in body and in spirit?" Reverend Blake glanced up at the heavens.

Ethan nodded at Trey and forcefully said, "I do." And then he met Reagan's eyes and said, "I do."

"The rings," Reverend Blake said. "All six of them."

"Six?" Reagan gaped at the rings tied to a bright pillow with ribbons in the colors of the rainbow.

"Two each," Ethan said. He surprised her by reaching for one ring out of a pair of small golden bands. It seemed any reservations he'd previously held had completely vanished.

Ethan took her left hand in his and slipped the band over the knuckle of her ring finger. "Reagan," he said, "I've already loved you through thick and thin, for better and worse, for poor and less poor, but still not rich, and I vow to continue to do the same for the rest of my life. This ring symbolizes my promise to love you and protect you always. I've got you, sweetheart. I won't ever let you fall or turn my back on you. I'll always be your shield from the storm. You are my partner for life."

While she sniffled over his words, Ethan slid one of the medium-size rings onto Trey's left ring finger. "Trey, I'm not sure I knew how to love someone properly until I found you. The idea of giving my full heart to anyone terrified me. You showed me how to give my love to two people and feel stronger for my weakness. This ring symbolizes my promise to love you and protect you always. I will never again hide how much you mean to me, because I couldn't if I tried. You opened my eyes as well as my heart, and I'm a better man for knowing you. You are my partner for life."

"Mijo," Rosa whispered through her tears. She blew her nose on the tissue Gwen handed to her.

Trey reached for one of the largest rings on the pillow and slipped it onto Ethan's finger. He then took Reagan's second ring and put it in place against the one Ethan had already given her. Trey shifted Reagan's left hand over Ethan's and held them together in a firm grip as he searched Reagan's eyes and then Ethan's and then Reagan's again.

"I'm so fucking happy right now, I don't know where to begin," he said. He smiled, not his usual ornery grin, but one that lit up his entire face.

"That's why I went first," Ethan said with a deep chuckle.

"I never in my life thought I could have everything I wanted, everything I needed. I was prepared to give up something vital to me in order to love the only way I know how to love—with all my heart. Yet somewhere along the way I realized I can't truly love if I deny what I need to feel complete. The strange thing is, you both make me feel complete, not just when you're together, but as individuals as well. It's synergistic. Two halves made me whole, and with us three united as one, I'm overflowing with love and friendship and companionship. What we have is complicated, and that's precisely what makes it perfect. I love you both." He lifted their hands to his lips, kissing Reagan's knuckles as well as Ethan's. "Separately as individuals, together as a couple, the three of us united. You belong to each other and to me, and I belong to you. I have a big crazy mess of feelings inside me when it comes to the two of you, and I can't imagine anything making me happier. So . . . with these rings I promise to do everything in my power to make you both as overjoyed to spend your lives with me as I feel at the opportunity to spend my life with both of you."

Gwen clapped excitedly.

"That's an easy promise to keep, Trey Mills," Reagan said, since she couldn't imagine anything could put a damper on the happiness she felt at the prospect of spending her life with Trey and Ethan.

"What can I say?" he said with a shrug. "I'm an easy-going guy."

Reagan looked down at the pillow and at the two rings waiting for her. She didn't know how she should approach this—she hadn't had time to think about vows. She hadn't even known she was going to be reciting vows today. Should she pledge to each of them separately as Ethan had or pledge to them as a unit as Trey had? What would mean more to them? She couldn't say. She loved them individually as well as loving them as a unit.

Fingers trembling, she lifted one ring in each hand and slid them into place above the bands they'd exchanged with each other. How did one put to words such overwhelming feelings?

"I think that before I tell you how much you mean to me and how devoted I am to both of you, I need to apologize. To everyone."

Trey scowled. "You don't have to apologize for anything."

"But I do. I let fear hold me back. I was more worried about what people thought of me and what people might think of us than I was about being a good partner, and I'm sorry. It won't happen again. And so . . . With these rings I promise to ignore the haters, love you both without regard to what any outsider thinks, says or does, and be the woman you deserve—the best I can be."

Trey glanced at Ethan. "She can be better than she already is?"

"Not in my eyes."

Trey's gaze rested on hers again. "Just be you, baby."

"A stronger me." She knew she could do better.

"You have enough pressure on you as it is. You don't have to prove anything to the world or to us."

"Are you arguing with me about my vows, Trey Mills?" she asked, shaking her head as she grinned at the two of them. They were both absolutely wonderful. No matter how often she fucked up, they were right there being supportive, forgiving, accepting.

"Just love us forever," Trey said. "That's the only promise we want from you."

As if she could deny either of them that. "I promise to love us forever."

EPILOGUE

O N THE WAY TO THE AIRSTRIP, REAGAN CALLED her dad
to tell him goodbye. She wasn't sure how reliable her
phone service would be in Europe, so she might not
connect with him for a while. Which reminded her—she was going
to Europe! She'd have celebrated her sudden excitement by running
around in circles and dancing the cabbage patch, but she was sort of
strapped down in the passenger seat of Trey's car.

"I thought you'd be gone by now," Dad said when he
answered. "Thanks for remembering to call." His voice was low.
Sad. She was pretty sure she knew why, but she asked anyway.

"Did you hook up with Mom after my union ceremony?"

"We had a nice time." His tone was defensive. He obviously
was no longer having a nice time.

Reagan clenched her hand into a fist. Why did Gwen have to
invite her mother to the happiest day of her life? Just because Reagan
had had a piece of paper in her purse with the woman's number on
it didn't mean she wanted to be in contact with the home-wrecker.
Of course, if Gwen hadn't called her mother, Dad might have never
agreed to unite his only daughter with two men, but Reagan just
couldn't forgive that woman for the damage she'd done to her
childhood and to her dad's entire existence.

"I'm sure you had a great time. Until she left you *again*. Dad,
when are you going to learn?"

"Never. The heart wants what the heart wants."

Reagan couldn't deny that truth. She just hated that her mother hurt him so deeply and that he kept going back for more. But he was right; the heart wanted what the heart wanted. And as her gaze settled on Trey beside her and then on Ethan in the back seat, she knew her heart had exactly what it wanted.

"Have a safe trip, tiger," Dad said. "Call when you can."

"I will. Be sure to eat regular meals, Dad. I worry."

"I don't want you to worry about your old man," he said. "I want you to take the world by storm. People across the globe will be completely blown away by my amazing daughter, Reagan Elliot. Mills? Conner? What are you going by these days?"

She laughed. "Just Reagan."

"I love you. Don't let all those men push you around."

"I won't. You raised a tiger, remember? Rawr!" She curled her fingers into a claw and swiped at the dashboard.

"I remember. Bye now"—he sniffled almost imperceptibly— "my little tiger."

She hung up, wishing he was there so she could hug him before embarking on her next journey.

Trey squeezed her knee. "I'm glad you and your dad are getting along. Family is important."

She smiled and ran a finger over the phone in her hand. "Especially when it's always been just the two of you."

"I have a few extra brothers you can borrow at any time," Ethan said, reaching over the seat and patting her shoulder.

"You'd just force me to take Juan." The ornery little cuss. She couldn't deny that she adored him despite his tendency to say whatever was on his mind. Or maybe she liked him because of that.

"Mamá would let you have Carlos too," Ethan said with a laugh.

"She seemed to enjoy his trumpet playing after our union ceremony." And Ethan had nearly crushed him to death with a hug when he'd discovered Carlos had come to show his support despite his obvious and continued discomfort with his Ethan's lifestyle.

"Well, you can't let him know that," Ethan said. "That's her little secret."

"I bet you twenty bucks that he ends up playing at the grand opening of her new restaurant, just like Juan suggested," Reagan said.

"I'll take that bet," Ethan said.

Reagan figured she'd soon be twenty bucks richer. Rosa was proud of her sons, all seven of them. She was particularly proud of the one who'd put his BHPD application on hold for three months so he could be at Reagan's side for the duration of Exodus End's world tour.

Trey turned into Dare's drive, and after being let through the massive wrought-iron gate, drove around to the back of the extensive property where Exodus End's private jet was kept. The last time Reagan had been on the sleek plane parked on Dare's airstrip, she'd joined the mile-high club with Trey. Maybe she'd renew her membership with Ethan today. She couldn't imagine all three of them fitting into the small bathroom near the back of the plane, but she was willing to give it a go if they were up for it. They'd had to put their honeymoon on hold until the tour was over, so they'd yet to have their sexual fill of each other. Not that she imagined they ever would.

After stowing her own luggage beneath the jet, Reagan left Trey and Ethan with the rocker-styled copilot to figure out where their bags would fit. She climbed the steep steps, smiling at the lovely pilot who greeted her from the cockpit.

As Reagan slid past Steve with her carry-on bag, he said, "Free at last." He crossed his ankles and stretched his arms to the ceiling before folding them behind his head.

"Which woman are you escaping this time?" Reagan teased as she plopped down on the sofa behind him.

"No woman. The band took a vote last night—after this tour we are ditching the record label."

"Max agreed to that?"

She glanced around the small luxurious jet and saw that while Dare and Logan had already settled into their seats, there was no sign of Max.

"He was outvoted. Dare finally came over to our side."

"Numbers don't lie," Dare said.

"But Sam Baily does," Logan said.

"Did you get the results of the audit already?" Even as she'd been concentrating on her romantic life—and mess—while they'd been on break, the band had focused on finding out just how deep Sam Baily's hands were shoved into their pockets.

"Preliminary ones," Steve said. "Enough to convince Max that he. Was. Wrong."

"Don't be a dick," Dare said. "There's no reason to rub it in his face."

Reagan was curious to know what that audit had revealed, but knew they couldn't disclose the information due to a clause in their contract. It was no wonder Steve had always fought to free them from that paper shackle; it completely ruled their lives. How would the band change after they found a new path, one that didn't involve Sam Baily?

Reagan didn't have a vote on any of the band's deeper issues—she was still an outsider and okay with that fact—but she felt bad for Max. He wanted to hold on to their roots so tightly that he was afraid to leave the ground, even when the soil where they'd planted those roots was corrupt and toxic.

"Max is coming with us, isn't he?" Reagan asked.

"Of course," Steve said. "He's a little put off now, but once he sees how far we can go on our own, he'll get over it."

There was also the chance that without a huge publicity machine behind them, they'd fall into obscurity.

"Can I sit by you?" Toni asked, nodding at the empty space beside her that Reagan had reserved for Trey or Ethan. The long sofa did have four seat belts, so there was plenty of room for her.

"Um, sure," Reagan said. "I figured you'd want to sit by Logan. It's a long flight."

"He said he wants to take a nap."

"It's your fault I'm so tired," Logan called out, as usual completely focused on whatever Toni happened to be doing. He slapped Steve's thigh. "She kept me up half the night teaching her about butt plugs."

"For you or for her?" Steve asked, peering around his seat at Toni, whose face was cherry red.

"Both."

"No wonder you want to sit by me," Reagan said. "Your boyfriend has a big mouth."

Toni sank onto the sofa next to Reagan. "He has a wonderful mouth." She pulled a notebook out of her bag. "I thought we could work on my article to pass the time."

Reagan's stomach twisted into knots. She was allowing Toni to write this article for Trey and Ethan's sake, she reminded herself. She wanted people to know the truth about their relationship. There would be backlash—of that she had no doubt—but she could get through anything with Trey and Ethan by her side. As if they knew she was thinking of them, the pair boarded the plane, Max behind them.

"That's everyone, Jordan," Max said to the pilot as the copilot brought up the rear and secured the hatch.

"Ah, good," she said, her crisp British accent carrying through the interior of the small jet. "My schedule is only partially shot to bloody hell then."

Max took the front-most captain seat next to Dare, while Trey and Ethan settled on the sofa beyond Toni.

"The rest of my band has to take a commercial flight," Trey said with a snigger.

"With those Baroquen harlots we met in New York," Steve said. "After this tour we can pick whoever *we* want to open for us."

"Let it rest," Max said quietly.

Reagan was surprised when Steve did exactly that. She guessed he figured he'd won a battle he'd been fighting for years. Best to take Dare's advice and not rub it in.

The takeoff went smoothly, but before they'd even leveled off, Toni flipped open her notebook and held her pen poised above a blank page. "So," she said, "how should we begin?"

Reagan looked over Toni's shoulder at the two men discussing which type of dog made the best pet—Trey was partial to golden retrievers, and Ethan loved a well-trained German shepherd. Both stopped talking to look at her, as if sensing she needed them. She did. She always would. She smiled and shifted her gaze to Toni.

She knew exactly how to start the article that would let the world know she was blessed beyond comprehension.

"Loving two men is a lot easier than you'd imagine."

AUTHOR'S NOTE

I thought I should start this note by explaining why it took six extra months to write *Outsider*. One of those months was spent sitting at my mother's hospital bedside while she was in a coma, hooked to a ventilator—when I say she nearly died, I'm downplaying all she went through in January. I would not give up on her, and I was at that hospital every day to make sure the doctors and nurses didn't give up on her either. The next two months I spent assisting my mom with her recovery after open-heart surgery and her weakness from being comatose for so long. Soon after she was *mostly* on her feet again, they found a spot of cancer in her lung. It was caught early by some blessed health care worker who took a closer look at the X-ray of Mom's new heart valve. So Mom's next medical adventure was radiation therapy treatments. We're still waiting to find out if her cancer is in remission. We're hopeful. What else can we be? I'm not a skilled enough author to convey the relief I feel that I get to be with my mom—my best friend and greatest champion—a little longer. Because even if she lives to be a hundred and twenty, it won't be enough time with her.

During those four months of hell and happiness (She survived. That's the happiness part.), I didn't write a word. I couldn't. And when I did start writing again, I spent two additional months trying to remember how to lose myself in a sexy, fantasy rock-and-roll world when reality had become much too vivid for this prefers-to-live-in-her-head author. But I'm back on track now and ecstatic to have finished this book.

Outsider started as one of the wedding stories in *Sinners at the Altar*. If you're interested in the original, which would have been called *Choose Your Illusion*, it's now chapter thirty-six of *Outsider*. When I started writing *Choose Your Illusion*, I found myself explaining a whole lot of backstory to get the reader up to speed on what happed to get our happy threesome to the point of settling for a man-and-wife marriage, and I thought, jeez, there's so much backstory here, I could write an entire book about it. So I did.

As always, it takes more than an author to publish a book. I'd like to thank my editor, Beth Hill, who never complains about taking all those commas I stick in the wrong places and putting them in the spots they belong. She's a rock star. I'd also like to thank my beta reader and dear friend, Cyndi McGowen. She's also a rock star. I'd use other verbiage, but to me "rock star" is the best compliment I can give a person. Special thanks to advice-giving rock stars Evelin Rodriguez and Jerry Maese for their assistance with Spanish and also helping to make Ethan's wonderful Mexican-American family more realistic. Thanks to my close, personal rock stars Sean Davis and Sommer Darnell at Vulpine Press for all their hard work and putting up with my mood swings. Thanks to Charity Hendry, design rock star, for another fantastic cover. And thanks to my Mom for still being strong when she was at her physical weakest. She's the greatest rock star I know.

More Sole Regret stories are heading your way soon, as well as Sed and Jessica's honeymoon story, *Lost in Paradise*. Next up in the Exodus End series is drummer Steve Aimes' story. Can he make a Baroquen woman whole again or will he just piss her off?

ABOUT THE AUTHOR

Combining her love for romantic fiction and rock 'n roll, Olivia Cunning writes erotic romance centered around rock musicians. Raised on hard rock music from the cradle, she attended her first Styx concert at age six and fell instantly in love with live music. She's been known to travel over a thousand miles just to see a favorite band in concert. As a teen, she discovered her second love, romantic fiction—first, voraciously reading steamy romance novels and then penning her own. Growing up as the daughter of a career soldier, she's lived all over the United States and overseas. She currently lives in Illinois. To learn more about Olivia and her books, please visit www.oliviacunning.com.

COMING SOON

He's used to having any woman he desires...
Exodus End's party-boy drummer Steve Aimes doesn't apologize for being a rock star. He owns the lifestyle and the hearts of thousands of women eager to cater to his every whim.

And then he meets Roux...
Steve resents the distractingly gorgeous keyboardist and her band for invading Exodus End's tour. He can't figure out why the strong-willed Roux refuses to jump into his bed. The faster she does, the sooner he can get her out of his head and move on.

She's not to be taken lightly...
Roux Williams hasn't had an easy life, but her band, Baroquen, finally got its big break. They're touring Europe with mega superstars Exodus End and are determined to take the world by storm with their musical talent. After living through a nightmare, success and happiness are finally within Roux's grasp.

And then she meets Steve...
Has a more irritatingly sexy man ever existed? All he cares about is having a good time and getting in her pants. But as she gets to know him—the real Steve behind the rock star façade—her defenses start to crumble and her trust builds. So when her world shatters again, she can only conclude that any contentment she'd found was...

STAGED

Book 3 of the Exodus End World Tour series
Coming in 2017

INSIDER
EXODUS END WORLD TOUR #1

Toni wants to be an insider.
Logan just wants inside her.

She's finally ready to rock...
Toni Nichols set aside her dreams to raise her little sister, but now she's reaching for the stars as the creator of a revolutionary interactive biography about Exodus End. She's on tour with the rock band to immerse herself in their world, but how will she ever gain the trust of four veteran superstars who've been burned by the media before? Nobody said this was going to be easy. Then again, good things can come in hard packages.

He's always ready to roll...
Adrenaline junkie Logan Schmidt lives for the rush of playing his bass guitar before thousands of screaming fans. When he's not performing onstage or in the bedroom, he's looking for his next thrill in extreme sports. So why does a sweet, innocent journalist get his heart pumping and capture his full attention? Is Toni the real deal or just digging up dirt on his band? Logan's eager to rock Toni's world and roll her in the sack, but when she starts to get too close to his heart, she takes her insider look to a place he may never be willing to go.